Wicked Writings
Volume I: A Horrifying Horror Anthology

EDITED BY MEAGAN J. MEEHAN

WWW.STITCHEDSMILEPUBLICATIONS.COM

ISBN: 978-1-945263-18-7

Ordering Information:

Quantity sales. Special discounts are available on quantity purchases by corporations, associations, and others. For details, contact the publisher at the e-mail address above.

Orders by U.S. trade bookstores and wholesalers visit Lightning Source or Ingram Spark

Printed in the United States of America

Curator s Note

This book is a compilation of stories from three horror-genre-themed writing classes which I designed and taught between March of 2018 and March of 2019. These pages contain over two dozen incredibly unique tales told from various settings, time frames, and character perspectives. I was absolutely amazed by the talent uncovered via the online class and it is truly an honor to have the opportunity to publish the work of these talented authors via this collection.

Sincerely,
Meagan J. Meehan

Special Thanks

I would like to extend special thanks to *Chilling Tales for Dark Nights*, who helped me organize the class, my parents Mary and Michael who are constant pillars of love and support, and to each and every one of my students. This book was originally intended to be published in 2019 but was delayed for over a year due to unforeseen events. Yet every one of the authors remained professional and understanding. I extend my deepest gratitude towards them and sincere thanks for making this class such an utter success and a delight to host. I hope to run many more in the future and meet new and talented writers. And, finally, to Lisa Vasquez and the entire staff of *Stitched Smile*. Thank you so much for making the dream of publication a reality for so many writers!

Contents

Foreword from Author AJ Horvath

Biography: AJ Horvath is an aspiring horror writer, dabbling in ink and madness. She resides in Michigan with her wife and daughter. With a love of all-things-horror and Halloween, she spends her time checking out new books, movies, and attractions along that same vein.

Author's Note: This story is based on the ritual performed in Tana Toraja, a remote part of Indonesia. Their use of tree graves and their belief that nature will absorb those lost young souls is beautiful.

The Nature of Things by AJ Horvath

Pushing her dark bangs back off of her forehead, Maria sighed as she stepped back to view her work. The block of wood seemed to mock her as she took in the progress of the last few hours. It was uninspired, blocky, and lifeless. With her art installation only a couple months away she really needed to get back on track; however, her art was not the first thing on her mind.

Maria and her husband, Nathaniel, had been trying for the past year to get pregnant. They already had the beautiful house, well-paying jobs, nice cars, and the ability to vacation anywhere their hearts desired; yet Maria was still not satisfied without a child to call her own. The past year had been filled with doctors' visits, various uncomfortable treatments, and utter despair as the doctors determined that they would not be able to be pregnant. Nathaniel had held her as she cried herself to sleep for months on end. A child was the one thing she wanted most and yet she could not have it.

Nathaniel's stern voice broke the trance and she emerged from her workshop to see her husband red-faced and swearing at a large man in blue coveralls.

"What the fuck is this shit? My wife needs quality wood for her installation and you dumbasses bring this?" he spat unaware of his wife who had settled next to him.

"What's going on?" Maria asked as she gave the delivery man a sympathetic smile.

"This jackoff brought your wood delivery but take a look at this awful thing! It is scarred and gnarled! It's complete trash."

As Nathaniel ranted, Maria eyed the large log. It was indeed gnarled and mottled with strange bumps as if the bark had been growing over itself. She brought her hand up to the log and instantly felt a tingling sensation on her fingertips. She stared at the log as if in a trance and was only brought back by her husband's continued verbal lashing of the poor delivery driver.

"This is perfect," Maria said, staring at her now silent and befuddled husband. "I can use this for the installation. It is exactly what I need."

She read the nametag on the delivery man's shirt before speaking again, "Brian, please bring the log back to my workshop over there. Nathaniel, I think we are all set love, you can go back to your office if you would like," she added, dismissing him.

"Okay, if that's what you want," Nathaniel said somewhat confused. He turned his attention to Brian, "Your supervisor will hear about this." He walked away; the gravel of the path crunched under his feet. "Don't forget to take your blood pressure meds Nathaniel, seems like you have had quite the rush this morning!" Maria called to his shrinking form.

Maria turned and smiled at Brian who was readying the log for the workshop.

"Don't worry about him," Maria assured, "He's a bit of a hothead but I'll put a good word in for you."

The man smiled and went about getting the log into Maria's workshop.

* * * * *

Nathaniel sat heavily into his high-backed office chair. He hated when Maria did that, when she would go over his head and make him seem like an ass.

Never mind though, he thought, *with a new piece of lumber, she will be too busy to bother me about babies and adoption.*

He dug into his pocket and pulled out his phone, and dialed.

"Hey baby," he crooned, "what are you doing tonight? The missus will be busy working on her weird art and I am oh so lonely."

He smiled as he received the exact answer he was looking for. He eagerly grabbed his briefcase--more out of habit than actual need--and walked briskly to the workshop. Peeking his head in the door, he watched as Maria surveyed her newest log. He had no idea why she wanted that gnarly, diseased looking tree, but if it kept her occupied, he wasn't going to complain.

"Hey babe," he called out and Maria's head swung over to meet his gaze. "I got to go into the office," Nathaniel explained, gesturing to his briefcase. "I'll probably end up staying in town tonight, it might be a late one."

Maria nodded and turned back to the log, "See you then," she said dismissively. He shrugged and made a quick dash for his car and was off to the city.

Maria had a ritual with her carvings. She sat with the piece and waited for it to speak to her. She placed her head against the rough bark, the electric tingling returned and she absentmindedly smiled. She wondered where the trunk had come from as she had never received something in such rough shape before. Most likely it was a logging company error but she could not resist the pull this log had on her soul. She knew it was destined to be something magnificent, maybe even something that would change her life.

That night, Maria fell into a deep sleep. She had gotten used to Nathaniel's constant late meetings and although it was hard at first to sleep without him, it was now second nature.

She found herself in a lush jungle. The surrounding foliage was a mix of vibrant greens, strange bird calls echoed through the trees, and there was a sweet smell in the air that she couldn't quite place. She began to walk slowly, making her way towards a towering tree in the distance. A laugh echoed through the air and she stopped cold. Between her

16

and the tree stood a child…at least that is what Maria *thought* it was. Her heartbeat quickened and the child smiled.

She awoke suddenly, the image of the child's smile still burned in her mind. She wiped her hand across her brow which had become slick with a film of cold sweat. She quickly grabbed her robe and slipped into her slippers as she made her way hurriedly to the door. Inspiration had struck her and, when that happened, not even a hurricane could stop her.

* * * * *

Nathaniel came home to an empty house. He tossed his briefcase onto the leather couch and called out to Maria. His voice echoed through the large house and he knew just where to look for her. He made his way back to her shop, slapping at the bugs that swarmed around his head. He hated living outside the city but Maria had insisted it would help them reduce stress and allow them to finally get pregnant. He relented and now he was condemned to sit out here getting eaten alive by mosquitos in Bumblefuck, New York.

He knocked on the heavy door that lead to Maria's studio and waited for a response. He heard hushed voices through the thick door and jealousy began to flow through is veins.

"Maria?" he called loudly, turning the knob and letting himself in.

The whispers stopped abruptly. Maria sat next to a partially constructed statue.

"Hey, sweetheart," she said, coming over to give him a quick peck on the cheek. "Glad you made it back but, I am very busy. I have to get this done. I know exactly what this log is going to be!"

She sounded giddy and pressed his arm slightly in an attempt to push him out the door.

"Oh, okay, well just let me know if you need anything," Nathaniel stammered to the now closed door.

Irritation flared in the back of his mind, but he calmed himself with the thought of his prior night's adventure. Samantha was truly a talented woman and with Maria so engrossed in her work, maybe he could have some more fun under the radar. . .

* * * * *

In the beginning her enthusiasm for her work had been charming, not to mention the large paycheck her talent brought in. Nathaniel had been a nobody in the art world before her and when he noticed her at a party that he had snuck into, he knew he had found his cash cow. He wined and dined her and found that while she was not the woman of his dreams, she could certainly make his dreams come true financially. With her connections, he was able to build his clientele and make a name for himself in the local art scene.

His forays on the side had started slowly. A girl after a party one night, then two, then it was almost every night a week he would find someone new claiming that he was working late nights in the city or even using his high blood pressure as a way to find additional time to be with one of his myriads of women. Maria never seemed too upset and he thought he had it all until she had brought up the idea of having a child. Nathaniel never wanted a child although he did tell Maria he wanted a whole bunch when they first started talking--but that was all part of the game to win her heart, her money, and a way into the art world. He didn't want to share his money with her let alone a snot nosed little brat. Pushing the disgusting thought out of his mind he laid down on the large bed hoping to stave off a migraine that he knew was forming from the stiff pain in his neck.

* * * * *

Shadows swirled around him and a dense fog was clinging to the leaves and trees around him. Nathaniel had no idea where he was but the odd sounds, plant life, and sticky temperature made him think of the jungle. Another dark shadow swooped past him causing him to stumble back. "Hey," he called out, hesitating before chasing after whatever had just came by him. He ran for a few moments and then stopped in his tracks. A large tree stood before him, its sides covered with large holes that were covered in wigs and vines. He couldn't quite tell but they seemed like small doors. He took a few tentative steps forward to the tree and stopped cold as a small hand crept around the tree trunk. Its skin was pale and mottled with blackened decay. He stood in horror as the rest of the figure appeared.

It was, or Nathaniel thought, it could possibly be a child, but it was hard to tell from the sagging flesh and bones that were before him. He tripped and fell backward pain shooting up his back as scrambled on his hands looking to see what he just tripped over. A small, lump of flesh began crawling towards him. He swallowed back vomit as he realized it was the remains of a young infant. When he looked up from the monstrosity before him several more young faces had encircled him on the wet, jungle floor.

* * * * *

Maria's brow furrowed as she continued to shave away layers of the wood to form the appropriate shapes and details that the log needed to convey. She threw down her tools in frustration, something wasn't right! She just couldn't get the details down pat; everything was fuzzy and out of focus.

She took a step back and knew that she was on the right track, maybe a nice bath would help ease her muscles

19

and clear her mind. She placed her hand firmly on the wood, feeling a connection with it and what it would become. Her heart raced as a large electric pulse pushed up her arm. She smiled and slowly made her way out of the workshop. Inside, she tiptoed past Nathaniel's open office door not wanting to alert him to her presence. She wanted to be left alone to soak in the tub and let inspiration take over her mind.

The hot water felt amazing on her skin and she could feel the muscles in her back and arms relax as she submerged herself in the tub. She closed her eyes and within minutes she was back in the jungle.

She walked confidently towards the tree again, this time the child was not there. Disappointment filled her as she got closer to the tree.

Where did the little one go?

She looked around the wide tree trunk but saw nothing but the same green foliage that surrounded the entire area. Then laughter echoed behind her. She turned and was face to face with the small child from her previous dream. The small girl's eyes were bright and her smile wide as they looked up at Maria. A rustling in the brush brought her attention up to the edge of the clearing. In the trees and bushes stood more small children, their eyes wide and wary. The little girl in front of Maria signaled for her to kneel and she did slowly, her knee sunk into the soft soil. The child took her face into their small hands and slowly pressed our foreheads together.

Maria awoke with a splash. The bath water was now cold and she rushed to grab her towel and dry off. Moving into the bedroom, she put on a thick sweater to ward off the chill that had crept into her body and sat on the edge of the bed. The images had run so quickly when her forehead had touched the young girl's.

She walked quietly to Nathaniel's office and found it was empty. She tiptoed to the living room and found him passed out on the couch, a half empty bottle of bourbon sitting on the coffee table. Making her way back to his office she rifled through his files until she found what she had been looking for--the proof the dream-child said would be there. She gathered the items up in her arms and nearly ran to her workshop.

* * * * *

Tears and wood shavings mingled together on her cheeks as she worked tirelessly on the carving before her. She didn't even stop when she pricked her finger on a sharp tool she was using to detail the piece; her blood mingled with the wood dust and ran freely down her arm.

Eventually, she stepped back. She had no idea how long she had been working on the piece…but it was done! It was finally complete, every detail meticulously displayed in the wood before her. Exhaustion pulled at her small frame and her eyes became heavy.

Maria barely made it to the couch which she kept in her studio for situations such as this. As soon as her eyes were closed, she was greeted to the warm sun on her skin and the tinkling of laughter.

* * * * *

Nathaniel awoke bleary-eyed, his neck was stiff and his head was pounding. He was shaken and needed to get that horrible dream out of his mind. He rubbed his neck as he walked slowly toward the bathroom, ready to take a shower hoping the hot water would help. He expected to see Maria's sleeping form on the bed but she was not there. Sweeping the room, he spotted that the alarm clock next to the bed read 4:30 am.

That's odd.

Maria was never one to get up early, it usually took Nathaniel's constant nagging to get her up before 8am. He dressed quickly, throwing on a plain white t-shirt and grey sweats, he saved the Armani for the city. He called out Maria's name and it echoed back to him through the large house. Then he slipped on shoes and made the short walk to her workspace. The gravel crunched eerily under his feet and echoed into the woods causing goosebumps to erupt on his skin. Rubbing his arms, he twisted the knob and let himself into the workspace.

The studio was dark except for the glow of a ring of candles set at the foot of a shrouded mass. The vision before him left him feeling a bit spooked but he made his way towards the veiled figure. He gently tugged off the canvas fabric, being extremely careful to avoid the flames, and found himself faced with a beautiful rendition of a young child.

Every detail was meticulously carved, its features bright and exuberant. It reached up as if searching for the hand of a parent and its eyes seemed to see into Nathaniel's soul. He jumped in surprise as Maria spoke from behind him.

"Ah, I see you have found my newest creation," she exclaimed, a smile wide on her face. "Isn't she beautiful? You see, this is what I envisioned our daughter might look like," she added and a glint of hatred flashed in her eyes.

"Oh, Maria dear, I know how much you want a child, but you know what the doctor's said. It just isn't possible," Nathaniel stated trying to sound sincere.

"They conveniently left out the detail that you had taken care of that yourself," she said matter-of-factly.

Fear flickered in Nathaniel's eyes. *How does she know that?*

"What are you talking about, dear?" he asked, his voice betraying him a bit.

"Cut the bullshit Nate. I know your secrets. I know about the doctors and your secret trip for a vasectomy! Patient privacy is a great thing for scumbags like you, but the truth always comes out in time. I also know about your little escapades with all those other women in the city! Just do yourself a favor and stop lying. While you are at it, get the fuck out of my life," she spat, fury burned in her eyes.

"Maria, I don't know what you're talking about! Why are you making these horrible allegations?"

"The children told me," she said, gesturing to the carving with a longing, loving, stare.

Nathaniel laughed. "The children? Do you hear yourself? I'm going to call Dr. Renaldi and see about getting you admitted to St. Augustine's. All this pressure for your installation has caused you to slip from reality!" Nathaniel fumbled to retrieve his phone from his pocket.

"I thought you might try and pull something like that," Maria snapped. "You see, I knew you wouldn't believe me so I did some real fact-finding. I have all the paperwork here as well as some of the screenshots of your chats with the various women you have been fucking on the side. I would leave now and never come back if I were you. I don't ever want to see your disgusting face again!"

Nathaniel's face burned with both shame and anger, but mostly anger.

Who the hell was she to threaten him, to tell him to leave?

He grabbed a tool from the nearest table to him and took three quick steps toward his wife. The sharp tool glinted in the candlelight as he raised it, poised to strike. Suddenly, there was movement to his right; he turned quickly and saw a shadow dart to the back corner. Then more little footsteps scurried, echoing all around him. He heard the giggling as he spun at each little sound.

Maria turned to face him, saw the sharpened tool in his hand, and realized just what he was about to do. "They told me you would do this too, but I just couldn't believe them! You are at their mercy now," she declared through tears.

The small shadows swirled around Nathaniel forming into faceless children as their small decaying hands grasped at his body. His eyes grew wide with fright; then his right hand grasped his left arm and chest tightly. In moments, his body fell to the floor and ceased moving. The tiny frolicking shadows slowed and, one-by-one they entered the sculpture, causing the wood to crack and split as if it was dry as kindling. As the last shadow entered, the soft dark flesh was revealed.

Maria took the small extended hand in her own. Tears of joy filled her eyes as she felt the warmth of her daughter's hand in hers.

Foreword from Author Alex J. Samuel

Biography: Alex J. Samuel was born in a small town in Ontario, Canada, where his passion for scary stories began at campfires during summer camp where the counsellors told them every night. Alex consistently practiced telling stories when he was younger, but it wasn't until he moved to Manitoba (where he attended high school) that he started writing short stories after being encouraged by his English teacher to do so. He wrote many short stories and his teacher was very impressed with the plots, structures, and twist endings of most of his stories. Eventually, Alex started entering them into contests where he won prizes and/or made it to the shortlist of applicants. His inspirations come from authors like Stephen King, the original *Twilight Zone* TV show, and video games that he plays whenever he has time. Alex is also inspired by the memory of horror films that he and his sister watched together when they were young. However, the majority of the stories come from Alex's dreams and nightmares, including the occasional daydream when he's awake.

Author's Note: The inspiration for *The Red Light* came from my neighbor. My friends and I would occasionally walk to the park at night and see an intense emitting red light coming from his front doorway; it just looked so strange and bizarre. They also wouldn't usually be home, but the light was always on. Eventually, I came up with a short story that all started with the main character seeing the light and the rest, as they say, is history. I want to dedicate this short story to my friend and colleague Stephen since he helped motivate me to write it and reviewed it a few times when I was having difficulty picking an ending from the multiple endings I wrote. I wouldn't have been able to write it without him. Thank you, Stephen. The inspiration for *False*

Awakenings came from a friend and former co-worker of mine named Sandra, who is also an aspiring writer. It's actually based on true events that both her and her mother struggle with which is false awakenings. I got so much insight from her and the stories she told about what has happened to both her and her mother throughout their lives (and even today). Hence, I would like to dedicate this short story to her. I wouldn't have been able to write it without her. Thank you, Sandra. I hope for us to work on other stories together in the future.

The Red Light by Alex J. Samuel

I roll over on my side… can't sleep… it was muffled, but I swear I heard a scream or something from next door. Maybe it was just my imagination, but I should probably go check it out. I grab my phone from my nightstand, ugh, it's only 2 AM. Slowly rolling out of bed I turn on the light, throw on a sweater, jeans, and some shoes. I leave my room and turn on some more lights as I head through the kitchen out the front door. I continue walking outside until I'm off my driveway onto the road towards my neighbor's house. I see a strange dark light coming from the front door, but I'm pretty sure they've always had that same light since I moved into my house last summer. I swear they leave it on all day and all night.

I pull out a cigarette and decide to have a quick smoke before I go in to try to go back to sleep. Standing in front of my neighbor's house, I can see a part of their backyard from the side. They have one of those outdoor string lights with multiple lightbulbs hanging off of it. My eyes linger down from the light, and I see a dark figure behind it, it looks like it might be a person on all fours or crouched. I squint my eyes and remain still. Whatever it is, it's not moving, but it's definitely looking my way. I hear a noise from the house next to theirs, so I turn to take a quick look, there's nothing. I look back, and the figure I saw is gone. Maybe I'm just seeing things like when I'm in bed looking around my room and sometimes the darkness forms into a figure…just my mind playing tricks, I guess.

I decide to walk further down the road while smoking, hopefully getting some fresh air during a light stroll will help me sleep. As I'm walking, I notice the street lights seem different; like a darkish brown, it's sort of what I see when I try to perceive the color red, maybe they finally replaced the bulbs since most of them were burnt out.

I eventually reach the old research center. They were trying to develop new forms of electricity for the community, but unfortunately, they ran out of money and couldn't pay their bills. They had to close down a few months ago which is too bad, there were talks that they were on to something. Strange, there are lights on inside. Maybe they got more funding.

An ambulance speeds around the corner past me with its sirens on. I jump; I think that's my cue to walk back home.

As I walk back onto my driveway, I take another look at the neighbor's house. The light is still on at the front, everything seems quiet as usual, perhaps even more so. Not paying attention I walk into my car setting off the alarm, I fall down.

"Jesus Christ!"

I fiddle around in my right jean pocket. I'm almost certain I left my keys in this pair of jeans. Ah got it. I take out my keys and turn off my car alarm, I bet I woke up the whole neighborhood. I get back up, brush the grass off myself and open the front door. As I walk into the kitchen, I pause and look around, I know I left the lights on but they also seem different like the street lights; again, a darkish brown.

I pull out some peanut butter and throw some bread in the toaster. Peanut butter and toast with a little bit of milk usually does help me fall asleep. I grab a glass, open the fridge, and pour some milk. I grab a butter knife and wait on the toast. I stare mindlessly at the toaster while waiting and take a sip of my milk but then I heard a noise.

PAT PAT PAT PAT PAT

I quickly turn around and start choking on my milk. There's someone or something in my living room just outside the kitchen. I try not to make a noise but I'm going to cough from the milk soon. It's looking around when I finally cough. It quickly turns to me in the kitchen and starts rushing towards me. I try to make a break for my room, but it tackles me to the ground.

"Hey what are you doing?!" I see that it's my neighbor. "What the fuck?! Get off of me!"

He's not joking around, I can tell he wants to hurt me, maybe even kill me. He's using so much force, if I don't do something soon, he's going to overpower me. I grab his left arm with mine and try to push him off with my right. He lifts his right hand, makes a fist, and hits my right arm in the middle. I scream in pain; I think he broke it. He starts digging his nails into my chest and scratching my head. I can't defend myself with only one hand. I look around and see a knife to my left; I dropped it when he tackled me. I try to reach out to grab it but he's got me pinned down and his aggression is overwhelming. I don't know what to do but the pain is becoming unbearable. All of a sudden, the toaster makes a noise and launches my toast which distracts him. This is my chance; I quickly grab the knife and jab it into his face as hard as I can. He falls on top of me, I slide away from him and try to catch my breath.

"Holy shit! I killed him!"

I grab my phone out of my pocket and dial 9-1-1.

"Hello, 9-1-1. What's your emergency?"

"Hello, my neighbor tried to kill me, I think I killed him, I need…"

I start to fade; I think it's from the pain. My vision starts to get blurry, and I can't understand what the 9-1-1 operator is saying. Everything goes black.
*****

I open my eyes; I'm in a hospital bed. I look down at my arm; it's in a cast. There's a man in the bed next to me.

"Hey, kid. You awake?"

"Yes…"

"Alright, alright, good. You need to get out of here."

I try to move around a little, "What? Why?"

"Haven't you noticed anything strange happening?"

"My…my neighbor tried to kill me."

"Yeah, okay. I had something similar happen to me. I was working at the DyTech Industries research center in the south end and…"

"The old research center?"

"Yes, that's the one, now let me finish. My colleagues and I were testing a new type of energy source. Some of our scientists discovered a stone that was emitting some form of energy in this old abandoned town not far from here. At least they *thought* it was abandoned. While they were extracting it, they found that locals were worshipping it. They were warned not to take it, but they did anyway."

"Why? What are they using it for?" (Make sure to always add quotes when they are speaking!)

"To make a long story short, I was part of the team that did the testing and converted the stone's energy into electricity. We decided to test it at midnight, but something went horribly wrong. I noticed the light produced from the electricity was unusual and my co-worker started to act strange. He attacked me, and he was going to kill me like your neighbor, during the struggle, I had used my pen to pierce through his eye. If I hadn't, I'd probably be dead."

I look away at the window.

"You don't believe me."

"I don't know what to believe."

"Well, how do you explain your neighbor trying to kill you then? Hmm…"

"I don't know; maybe he was on some bad drugs or something."

"Okay and what about it happening to me too?"

I stay silent.

"That's what I thought."

"So, what exactly do you think is causing people to go crazy?"

"I think it's the light that's causing it. The electricity from the stone is somehow affecting people through the light and power it's creating."

"Okay so let's say this is true. What do you want from me?"

"I need you to take my I.D. badge and turn off the machine at the research center."

"Why can't you do it?"

The old man lowers his blanket showing multiple wounds that look like he was stabbed numerous times.

"He used his nails. No way I can make it there without recovering from this, plus they got me on a bunch of morphine, I don't know if I can even walk straight."

I get out of bed; I'm still in quite a bit of pain.

"Okay, I'll go."

"Great kid, grab my I.D. and get out of here. The machine is scheduled to transition all regions of the community to the new electricity."

"So that means…"

"Yup, soon everyone will be affected."

"I grabbed his I.D. and turn to the door but then turn back at the old man.

"Wait, why aren't we affected by the light?"

"I have a theory. Are you color blind?"

"Red-green, why?"

"Ah yes, I am as well. If my theory is correct, that means that we probably can't fully perceive the light the stone is producing well enough for it to affect us in the same way."

"I see."

As I start to walk towards the door to the main hallway the old man grabs me.

"However, I believe the light still affects us. I've been…seeing and hearing things that I know aren't there. Like hallucinations. I'll be honest, I'm not even certain that you are actually here."

He let go of me and I continued to the door to the hall and open it, "Alright, thanks for the warning and good luck to you, old man."

34

"You as well."

As I walk through the hall to the elevator, I notice how empty it seems, but it's probably still early in the morning.

I make it to the elevator and click the button to go down to the main floor. I hear the elevator slowly coming up to me, but then the power goes out. It comes back on right away, and I notice something, the light is a darkish brown.

"Oh no."

I hear noise from behind me; I slowly turn. A bunch of the patient rooms down the hall open up. I see a little girl with what looks like a broken leg walking out of one of the rooms, the bone is sticking out and moving as she walks. Another person is slowly crawling out of a different room; he must be paralyzed from the waist down. One more leaves her room, bleeding from her neck, it's dripping onto the hallway floor. I'm so scared. I can't move. I can't make a noise and let them hear me. The elevator reaches my floor.

BING!

"Oh shit."

Everyone looks at me, I run inside the elevator and press the button to the main floor. They all run and crawl unbelievably fast at me. I'm not going to make it.

I hear the old man yell: "Come and get me! I'm in here you bastards!"

They all descend upon his room, as the elevator doors close, I hear his blood-curdling scream…I reach the main floor.

BING!

I slowly walk out of the elevator. No one seems to be in the main lobby. I make my way outside and see an abandoned ambulance; I enter the driver's seat; the keys are in the ignition. I turn it on and make my way to the old research center.

As I drive through the community, I see that all of the houses and buildings along the way have the same light. I hope I'm not too late.

I pull up in front of the research center and put the ambulance in park. I notice that there's a hearse here. It wasn't here when I previously arrived during my walk earlier. I get out and make my way to the entrance.

The main doors are locked, I look over and see there's an I.D. scanner. I scan the old man's I.D. and the doors unlock. I open the door and go inside.

There are papers and files all over the place. I go up to the front desk and look for any information to found out where the machine might be in the building. I find a memo from a Dr. Klassen:

Meet me in the basement tonight to test the machine. I know it's going to work. I can feel it. Ever since we've been working on this project, testing the stone they brought in, I think it's been trying to communicate with me. I feel its energy and power whenever I get close to it. Have you been feeling the same thing? Sometimes I see and hear things when I'm around it, but that might be from all the overtime they have us working.

Alright, the basement must be where it is. I take the stairs down to the basement. I see the machine and start heading towards it. There's a man there facing it.

"Well hello there."

"Hello. What are you doing here?"

"My name is Dr. Klassen and I'm a scientist that works here. The real question is, what are you doing here?"

"Don't you know what's happening, what the light that stone is producing is doing to people?! I'm here to stop the chaos and turn the machine off."

"Turn off? Why would you want to do that?"

The doctor turns around, he looks pale, and his one eye is damaged. I freeze.

"Because people are getting killed!"

"Yes, but what's life without death."

He smirks at me.

"The light the stone produced after our tests were successful, they changed me. I lost control and attacked a colleague, he stabbed me in the eye with a pen. I was dead, you see, or at least they *thought* I was dead. I woke up in the morgue, no vision in my left eye but I felt different, stronger, and I didn't lose control of myself when I saw the light again, though I have this incredible urge to kill. Something strange also were that those affected by the light wouldn't hurt me, they listened to me. Perhaps, it's because I can only see the light with one eye and some parts of my brain were damaged or maybe it affects people differently but I think the stone chose me to be its messiah, it brought me back for a reason maybe it's trying to bond with me somehow."

The doctor pulls out a syringe.

"I had been wondering though, I helped make the stone's energy into electricity, but what would happen if I created a concentrated part of the stone into a liquid and injected it into my bloodstream. The light changed me, so I'm sure this would to."

"Are you crazy?! Don't do it!"

The doctor jams the syringe into his leg and then throws it away after its contents are emptied into his body. He starts screaming in pain and laughing at the same time. He drops on the ground and holds himself up with his hands. I see his bones moving around in his body, skin ripping, eyes bleeding, as he starts vomiting blood and growing in size.

"YOU SEE, I'VE BECOME A GOD! WORSHIP ME, AND I MIGHT LET YOU LIVE!"

"Oh fuck."

I run to the control room and close the door. He starts hitting the glass window by the control panel. I find the master power to the machine, grab the handle, and pull it down turning it off. The lights go out with it.

"NO!"

He continues to try to break the glass; It's not going to last much longer. I walk into the corner and hope it's a quick death…No, I'm not going to die, not after everything that's happened! I look around the room, there's an airduct (one word) that I can crawl in. I kick the air duct cover a few times as hard as I can and then rip it off and climb in. I hear the glass break behind me as I crawl as fast as I can forward, then it gets quiet, I'm safe for now…but how am I going to get out of here alive?

I reach another air duct cover, what looks like an office is on the other side. I break the cover as quietly as I can and crawl out.

The lights go back on; that thing must've turned the machine back on. As I'm about to leave the office I see a picture, it's the old man from the hospital. I hear a voice behind me.

"Hey, kid."

I turn around. "Old man?"

"Well, it's Dr. Batic, but I guess we didn't really have time for introductions, did we? Though you could've had the decency to read my name on my I.D. before you used it."

"How are you alive? I'm pretty sure I heard you die."

"Ah but, alas, I'm here."

"How did you get here?"

"Well, I don't really know. Maybe something distracted the patients from killing me, and I ran off with some painkillers to be able to meet you here."

The old man seemed different and was acting strange.

"Okay well, I'm assuming that Dr. Klassen is your co-worker and the one you stabbed in the eye. He just finished turning into a monster from injecting himself with liquid made from the stone and is currently trying to kill me and I'm sure anyone in general that gets in his way. Also, the machine is back on."

"That all?"

"Are you trying to be funny? What are we going to do?"

"Hmm, okay I have an idea. We could try to lure him into the incinerator."

"Alright, where is it?"

"In the basement, across from the control room."

"I have to go back to the basement?"

"I'm afraid so."

I sigh. "Okay. How do I activate it?"

"There's a big red button on the outside, once he gets in just hit it and the doors will close locking him inside to burn."

I notice a small AM/FM radio alarm clock on the desk where the old man is standing and pick it up. Maybe I can use this to get him inside.

I quietly walk outside of the office and make my way back down to the basement. I start to feel goosebumps and an unnerving sensation that I can't shake as I arrive, but there's no one down here, and I can't hear anything. I slowly crouch and move towards the incinerator until I hear a crunching noise. It's him, he's trying to eat pieces of the stone! I continue to move towards the incinerator while he's occupied. I go inside and place the AM/FM radio alarm clock down after setting it to go off in three minutes. Slowly, I make my way out and hide behind a concrete pillar. I count the seconds, one seventy-five, one seventy-six, one seventy-seven, one seventy-eight, one seventy-nine, one-eighty. The radio goes off, he immediately jumps up and runs into the incinerator to attack the radio, I ran and hit the button.

"Try to come back from this!"

He turns and sees me but it's too late to make it through the door, he starts hitting the door as it almost closes, then I hear him hitting everything else inside, a weird noise starts coming from the room.

"Kid it's going to explode!"

I start running towards the control room, but it explodes forcing me to slam against the wall. It takes a lot of effort for me to open my eyes and for a moment I can't move. I keep trying and eventually I'm able to move my only working arm and try to lift myself up, but I drop back down after lifting myself about halfway.

"You know what you have to do."

I look over, and it's the old man.

"What?"

He points at the syringe next to me, there's still a bit of liquid in it.

"No, I can do it myself, and I don't want to turn into a monster like Dr. Klassen."

"Puff, he wasn't worthy, he was no god, just an animal. I thought he might have been worthy but I was wrong."

I try again and barely manage to get myself up.

"What are you talking about?"

He doesn't answer me. I limp to the control room and reach for the handle to turn off the machine.

The old man screams at me. "NO!"

I stop. "What's wrong with you?"

I grab the handle, and then the old man grabs my throat and lifts me up slightly.

"Ah! Stop it!"

"I can't let you stop the machine."

His grip gets tighter, and his hand must be on fire or something because it's burning my throat. I start to scream in agony.

I'm still holding the handle, and with my last bit of strength I pull it down turning the machine off. I drop back down to the ground; the old man is nowhere to be found. I look over at my broken arm, it's smoldering, I quickly put it out with my burnt shirt. Was I grabbing myself? It felt so real. Are these the hallucinations the old man was talking about? I look over at the stone, I know objects like rocks can't express emotion, but I see and feel like the stone is angry somehow, I feel like it's calling for me to get close. I shake it off but as I continue to look at the stone I suddenly black out.

* * * * *

I wake up. I'm in bed, I think I'm at the hospital again. I look at my arm and freak out, it's gone and sewed up just below the shoulder. As I try to get out of the bed, I realize I'm strapped in this time. The lights in the room change color.

"Tsk, tsk, tsk, Thomas."

It's the old man. How does he know my name?

"You've been a bad boy, Thomas."

"What's happening? How are you here?"

"What? You didn't think this guy and his team were the only people trying to decipher the stone and all its secrets, did you? Well, I guess the stone is sort of me."

"What are you are?!" (This makes no sense, did you mean *"What are you?"*)

"Basically, I'm the consciousness of the stone represented by a person you know, or should I say knew. I'm trying to get in to you but you seem to be quite the challenge. I bet it's because of the whole red-green color blindness thing you got going on but I get in eventually, I always do. Just takes time."

I try even harder to get out of the straps. The old man creeps towards me and slowly leans into my ear and whispers: "Another thing I should mention…this isn't a hospital."

My eyes widen, and I continue to try to get out of the straps almost flipping the bed. All of a sudden, a man and woman both in lab coats wearing some type of sunglasses come in and grab my bed rolling me out of the room. I see a new bigger machine attached to the stone and several people working around it as they take me somewhere.

They bring me to another room and lock my bed in place before leaving. There's a fat bold man sitting in a chair in front of me.

"Good morning, Thomas. I've been told you've been through quite a lot."

"What do you want."

"I just want some answers. That's all. You're the only one alive from when we arrived at the research center. My first question is, why doesn't the light affect you? We monitored you in the other room there and switched the city power to the stone's temporarily. It didn't seem like anything changed in you, though you did talk to yourself and mumble."

"Why should I answer you?"

"I'm not your enemy Thomas. We fixed up your arm and treated you here at our facility. It would be rude not to answer me, but of course, if you don't, I'm sure I can find a way to make you talk."

The fat bold man opens up a bag with different types of knives and sharp objects. I swallow hard.

"Alright, okay, I think it's because I'm red-green color blind and I can't fully perceive the red light the stone is producing."

"Hmm, interesting."

The man and woman in lab coats from before barge in. The woman starts talking.

"Mr. Sherburne, we're ready to try the next test."

"Excellent, bring him downstairs to the machine."

I angrily look at him.

"What?! Why?"

"We have more tests for you Thomas."

They grab my bed and roll me down. Half a dozen people are surrounding me.

"Okay, test number two. Ready?"

Another person by the machine answered.

"Yes, everyone put on your glasses."

All of the people put on these weird looking glasses and look at me.

"Three, two, one!"

The person next to the machine pulls a lever and the light in the room changes, and it seems so much more intense, I can feel it on my skin which I wasn't able to before.

"Hello again, Thomas, did you miss me?"

It's the old man again.

"Leave me alone!"

Mr. Sherburne gets close to me.

"What's wrong, what did you see?"

The old man walks up to the bed in front of my feet.

"Do you feel that Thomas? It shouldn't take much longer now."

I point in front of my feet.

"You don't see him."

Mr. Sherburne turns and hits one of the people's glasses off. Everyone freezes.

"Shawn, are you okay?"

The guy falls to his knees and coughs up some blood.

The old man looks at him and then back at me.

"Well, he was easy to get inside of."

The guy slowly gets back up and looks at Mr. Sherburne.

"Shawn..."

The guy quickly rushes at Mr. Sherburne and starts tearing at his chest. He screams in agony.

I try to get out of the straps, but they're too strong.

The old man walks closer to me.

"Just let me in. I can make you one of my crusaders, not a mindless creature like this one."

I keep struggling to get out. "HELP! HELP!"

The old man looks disappointed.

"Come on, it's probably going to happen soon anyway. The people here strengthened the light. I know you can feel it going inside your skin."

One of the people that surrounded me earlier quickly undoes the strap on my left arm and runs off. I then undo the strap around my cast and jump off the bed running towards what I think is the exit, but the old man is blocking it.

"Sorry, Thomas, but it's too late. You're mine now."

He reaches out with his hand and pokes me. I fall to my knees and cough up some blood. Suddenly…I have the urge to kill everyone in this place

False Awakenings by Alex J. Samuel

The clock radio reads 3:15 am. I am semi-conscious to the fact that although it is the middle of the night, my body feels twitchy and electric. I try to close my eyes and go back to sleep, but it's no use. As soon as the thoughts start swirling in my head, I know morning has come for me. I slowly sit up and crawl out of bed. I notice that my husband is already gone. There's an imprint of where he had lain on the bed; he must have left for work early this morning. I walk to each of my children's rooms to wake them up, but they're gone as well.

I head into the bathroom and start my shower. The hot water is flowing strong and steam has already started filling the small room. I am almost completely undressed when I catch a glimpse of myself in the now foggy mirror. I turn around to face it directly and frantically start wiping the steam off, causing moist wet streaks to run down the mirror, distorting the image in front of me. I am looking at myself, but it's not me at all. My mother has been dead for ten years now, taken too soon by a ravenous cancer that deprived her body of any muscle or fat, yet I am looking at her now. My cheeks are sunken and dark circles cradle my eyes.

I make my way downstairs to the kitchen and start the coffee. Everything is quiet; all I can hear is the coffee dripping. I decide to walk back upstairs to get dressed while I wait. After a while, I head back downstairs, throw on my coat, grab my coffee and keys, and head out the front door.

BEEP BEEP BEEP

My alarm shrieks. I wake up again; I was dreaming….Am I still dreaming? My husband is lying next to me. I remember the test to make sure I'm awake. On my nightstand I leave my pack of cigarettes, there should be three left in the package. I turn over in bed and count them out, one…two…three. I should be awake. I get out of bed and check on both of my children again, they're both in their beds. I walk back to the bathroom in my room, it's closed. I never close the door. I start trying to open the door but it's locked. What's going on? Who's in there?

"Hello, open the door!"

I lean my ear against the door. I think for a moment, was there a lighter on my pack of cigarettes? I look at the nightstand, it's not there. I must be dreaming again. The sunlight from my room window recedes and it starts to become too dark for me to see. I try to turn on the lights, but they don't work. I start to panic and wish I'd wake up soon. I sink into the floor and try to scream, but only a quiet whimper comes out. I feel paralyzed; I struggle to move my body. I hear a distant voice and I strain to reach its sound.

"Sandra! Sandra! Sandra!"

I wake up to my husband shaking me.

"Are you alright? You must have been having a nightmare."

I look over at my nightstand, my pack of smokes is open showing three cigarettes and my lighter is on top.

"Yes, I'm fine, thank you. I better get ready for work."

I am finally ready to leave for work and leave through the front door. Thankfully, I don't wake up in my bed again. I drive to work and sit at my desk.

My office is quiet. The sound of the clock ticking is all I can hear for the most part. Occasionally, I overhear a conversation between co-workers or a phone call follow-up with a client's inquiry. My monitor is starting to wear out my eyes and the clock feels like it is getting louder. *Tick tick tick tick.* Suddenly, it's quiet. I look over the wall of my cubicle, everyone is gone. The clock reads noon, and I guess everyone has left for lunch. I turn back to my monitor to log in to my computer.

"ERROR. Wrong log in"

I enter my password again.

"ERROR. Wrong log in"

My head starts buzzing. I am trying to concentrate on remembering the login information that I have been using for over five years…did I change it? All of a sudden, I can't remember it at all. Trying not to panic, I decide to get up and go get something to eat and maybe clear my head a bit.

As I stand waiting for the elevator, the buzzing in my head is getting louder. The down button blazes bright red and I start to feel the ground shifting under my feet. The DING of the elevator arriving startles me, but the door doesn't open. I hear the DING again. This time it is louder and more deafening. DING. The walls start spinning around me and I feel like I am going to pass out. I hear my name being called from a distance…

I wake up with a start and realize I am still at my desk. My back is aching from slouching over, and a small puddle of drool has started pooling. I look up to see my manager standing over me, looking very unimpressed. I was dreaming again...it felt so real.

"Sandra your completed work items are pretty low and you're falling asleep at your desk, I think you should go home for the day." His tone is serious.

"I'm sorry sir I guess I'm just really tired and worn out. I'll see you tomorrow."

"I hope you're more productive or we might have a problem here."

"Yes, don't worry I'll be better tomorrow."

I quickly gather my things and head out of the office. I go to the elevator, and press the down button. As I'm waiting, I reflect on how real my dream was, I notice there's a scratch above the down arrow on the elevator button, I recall it was there in my dream as well.

DING.

I jump up, frightened by the loud noise from the elevator. I walk closer to the door but the elevator still hasn't opened, AM I DREAMING AGAIN? I start breathing heavily, trying to catch my breath and calm down. The door finally opens. I head inside and take it down to the main floor.

As I'm driving home, I notice a sleep clinic. I pull into their parking in front of the building and walk inside. A young woman greets me from the reception desk,

"Hello, how are you doing today?" A cheery blonde looks up from her computer.

"Hi, I'm wondering if I can schedule an appointment."

She checks her monitor, keying in a few characters, "Yes of course, we actually have an opening in about 20 minutes. Is that okay with you?"

"Yes, that's fine, thank you."

"And may I ask what your appointment is for?"

"I'm having some problems when I fall asleep, I'd like to have a quick check up and consultation."

"Alright, just take a seat and the doctor will grab you when he's ready."

I sit down and watch the television in the waiting room. The screen is displaying multiple sleep disorders and their symptoms. They describe sleep apnea, I don't think I have that, I'm sure my husband would've noticed. Insomnia was next but I'm not having trouble falling asleep. Then hypersomnia, maybe I have it; did fall asleep at work. The doctor appears in the doorway. I notice that he is tall and handsome.

"Sandra, I'm ready to see you now. Would you kindly follow me?"

I follow him to a room behind the reception desk. He sits at a cluttered desk and summons me to sit down. As he clears away some space and pulls out an old tattered notebook, and begins looking for a blank page. When he is ready, he speaks.

"Hello Sandra, my name is Doctor Reed. I heard that you are having problems with your sleep. Would you be able to explain this in further details for me?"

I begin listing my symptoms. I describe the feeling of being awake when I am still asleep. I continue with the vivid feeling of paralysis that sometimes grips me during the episodes. I also tell him about the incident at work and how I'm worried that it might be jeopardizing my job. After some thought, he starts to explain.

"Well it seems you may be experiencing false awakenings which are vivid and convincing dreams about awakening from sleep. In some cases, a person can also fall asleep but the brain will act as though they were still awake. You won't know that you're actually dreaming until you wake up."

I am beginning to feel some relief at the prospect that I had been experiencing something that could actually be explained. He continues.

"There are two types. Type 1 is when the dreamer believes they wake up but they do not necessarily wake up in realistic surroundings, like their bedroom, and will either actually wake up in their bed or fall asleep in their dream and wake up later. This is the most common type. Type 2 is when a person appears to wake up in their natural surroundings but slowly starts to notice persons, places, sounds, objects, and feelings that seem to be different or strange in some way. This is the least common type. Pre-lucid dreaming and sleep paralysis may occur with both types. As well, there could be more than one false awakening in a single dream. That being said, you seem to be experiencing symptoms from both types."

Trying to absorb all the information, I ask anxiously, "Well, what can I do about it?"

"Unfortunately, there isn't too much we can do other than monitor your sleep. I'm going to prescribe you some sleeping pills. These will help you fall into a deep sleep and should minimize dreaming altogether. I also want you to wear this device on your head before you fall asleep and return after thirty days so I can go through the data and understand your brain waves and sleep patterns in more detail."

He hands me a metal contraption, which looks like a headband. Its blinking red lights remind me of something out of a science fiction movie.

Driving home, I feel better than I have in weeks. Finally, someone is actually validating my situation. Maybe, I wasn't going crazy after all.

* * * * *

The next couple weeks are pure bliss. Every night I take the pill the doctor prescribed, I sleep through the night, dream-free. The sleep pattern device takes a little getting used to, but once I fall asleep, I don't notice it all. When my alarm goes off, it is actually morning and I even noticed that my performance at work was improving.

I have just completed my daily quota at work, as I am writing a note on a client's file, I notice a new email. I click on the email, there's no sender. no message, and no attachment. I open my web browser to submit a ticket to investigate the email, maybe someone was trying to mess with our system with a virus or something. As I fill out the form it requires me to attach the email I received, I look back at my mailbox. The email is gone. I shrug it off and clean up my desk a bit. I restart my computer and head home for the day.

After I get home, I hang up my keys on the wall by the front door and start walking into the living room. As I am walking, I hear my keys fall on the ground, I look over to the front door and don't see them on the wall or on the ground by the wall. I pause for a moment and look at the ground by my feet, the keys are there. Did I think I hung them up but actually keep them in my hand? I pick them up off the ground and walk back to the front door and hang them up on the wall. I guess I must be more tired than I think; maybe I should try to go to bed earlier tonight after dinner.

That evening, I fall asleep on the couch after supper. My husband is at his weekly poker game, and the kids are playing quietly in their rooms. I wake up to the sound of the key in the front door. Groggily, I begin to open my eyes and am surprised to see my husband already in the house, sitting across from me in his favorite armchair. He begins to tell me about his night, but I find I can't keep my eyes open. His voice fades away as I fall back to sleep.

I wake up again and I sit up quickly. My husband is no longer there, sitting in his armchair is my mother. She looks so young and vibrant, just like she did before she got sick. I know in my mind that I must be having a dream, but I don't want to resist it this time. I have wanted to talk to her so many times since she died, and this was my chance. We chat casually about the kids and my life. For the first time in a long time, I am aware that I was dreaming, but don't feel the familiar fear that usually accompanies the realization. I start to feel drowsy again, but will myself to stay awake for a few more moments with her. Eventually, the fatigue is too overwhelming, and I am asleep again.

When I wake up again, I am still on the couch. My neck feels crimped, like I've been sleeping on it the wrong way. I sit up and start to stretch my arms into the air. I stop short as I notice that there is someone new visiting me now. A man that I have never seen before sits perched, like a bird on the edge of the chair. I am struck silent as I watch his head bob up and down and though his mouth is moving, I can't hear anything he is saying. He is starting to freak me out now and I begin thrashing around on the couch, I will myself to wake up.

I may really be awake this time. I realize that I had fallen asleep without taking my pill. I am sure this is the reason for the bizarre dream. I will need to discuss this with Doctor Reed.

* * * * *

The next morning, I head to the sleep clinic. While waiting in Dr. Reed's office, I contemplate the past couple weeks. I am feeling more rested and the bad dreams seem to be getting less frequent. I hope he has some good news for me. He enters the office and greets me,

"Hello Sandra, how has your sleeping been since the last time we spoke?"

"It's been amazing! I've been sleeping great and performing better at work. I do miss dreaming as often as I was but it's worth the trade-off to prevent all the false awakenings I was having."

"That's good to hear, I assume you brought back the device."

I pull it from my purse. "Here you go."

"Thank you. We're just going to review your brain waves and sleeping patterns. I'll get back to you when it's complete but from what you told me there shouldn't be any irregularities." He takes the device and places it on his desk.

"Alright well, thanks again Doctor Reed. I really appreciate it."

"No problem, it's what I'm here for and I'm glad I could help."

I head out the door.

* * * * *

As the door closes behind Sandra, I begin closing the clinic for the night. I walk up to the front and lean on the reception desk.

"Alright Katie, you're free to go home for tonight. See you bright and early tomorrow morning."

54

"Thanks Doctor Reed. Have a good night."

I follow her to the front door and lock it behind her. I walk back to my office and I am about to turn off the lights, I notice I left the device Sandra gave back to me on my desk. I look at my watch. It's not that late, I guess I could take a few minutes and look it over. I'll have less to do tomorrow.

I sit down at my desk and plug the device into my computer. It is going to take several minutes to load everything up. I lean back in my chair and yawn. I need to get a faster computer. I start to play with my wedding ring and then grab Sandra's file from my desk drawer; it's in a black folder. I use those folders for some of my clients who have less common sleep issues.

The file finishes downloading.

Alright then, let's take a look...Everything seems to be fine for the first few days...Whoa. What's going on? Every night her brain waves are spiking slowly, last night was the worst. I've never seen anything like this. And her sleep patterns...they're all over the place! Her body must have slowly become immune to the medication! Maybe even made the false awakenings more intense! I have to call and warn her. I look at her file and see if she left a phone number.

"Hello?" a young boy answers.

"Hello, yes it's Doctor Reed. I need to speak with Sandra please."

"Oh, umm my mom's not here right now."

"Okay well I need you to please tell her to call me back right away. It's very important."

"Okay. I will. Bye."

I put down the phone and lean forward in my chair. I can't even imagine what's going to happen if she goes back to sleep.

* * * * *

55

I feel so happy as I drive home, for the first time in a long time…I feel like everything is okay. Doctor Reed made me feel so much better today. He seems confident that everything should be alright.

I pull into my driveway and walk inside.

My son is sitting in front of the television, playing some loud and violent video game. "Hey honey, how's it going? He barely looks up.

"Fine." He mutters.

"Anything happen while I was gone?"

"Hmm, I don't remember. No, I don't think so."

"Where's your sister?"

"She's doing homework in her room."

"That's good, do you have any homework?"

He glances up at me with a sly smile, "No…"

I put my hands on my waist, "Go do your homework!"

He sighs, "Okay..." His feet make a scampering noise on the carpet as he heads up to his room.

I walk into the kitchen and notice the dirty dishes piled in the sink. There is a faint smell of something still lingering. I guess my husband made dinner tonight. I feel such relief as I'm feeling pretty tired tonight. I walk up the stairs to my bedroom and crawl into bed.

I wake up, it's still dark outside. I look at my alarm clock, its 2am. Something's wrong, I can't move...I struggle to look at my body, I try moving my legs, then my arms, then everything at once. I can't move any part of my body. I try not to panic. My eyes are scanning the room frantically; they freeze on the closet at the foot of my bed. There's a dark figure in there, a man, he's just watching me. He knows I see him. I start to feel goosebumps throughout my body, the sensation is overpowering. My body starts to feel warm and when I blink, the man is gone, I still can't move. I try looking around my bedroom; my husband is lying next to me. I try to speak but I can't move my mouth, so I start to just make any noise possible. He starts to move; he must hear me! He turns over to face me and I am horrified to see that it is not my husband at all, but the man from the closet! He puts his hand over my mouth and pushes my head aggressively into my pillow. I feel pain under his weight.

I wake up and proceed to slowly sit up in my bed; it must've been a nightmare. The clock reads 2:30am. I guess I can still get nightmares every now and then, even with the medication. I should tell Doctor Reed next time I see him. I lay my head back down and fall back asleep. After what seems like a deep and restful sleep, I wake up before my alarm goes off. The clock radio reads 5:45am. I grab my robe and head out into the hallway. The shower is already running. It roars behind me, the steam in the bathroom is getting thicker and denser. Breathing heavy now, I realize that I must be dreaming.

My heart is pounding as I go into my bedroom. There doesn't seem to be anyone in the bathroom. I look down to see the outline my husband's body under the covers. His breathing is slow and steady and for a moment, I can relax. But I know I can't be tricked into the normalcy and familiarity of the situation...something is not right. I just have to wait for what might happen next. I look at my nightstand, my cigarettes and lighter aren't there.

A scream from my daughters' room startles me. I turn and run to her. She is sitting up in her bed, terror in her eyes and I realize she must have been having a nightmare. Forgetting that I might not be awake, my maternal instincts kick in and I run to comfort her. I reach for her and pull her toward me. Next thing I know, I am in the middle of her room, holding her arm. Ligaments and muscle dangle from the lifeless limb. She does not react at all, just sits on the bed, smiling sweetly. My heart is racing and my breath is getting laboured as I realize that I am still sleeping and in the midst of a horrible dream…again.

I wake up, open my eyes and notice that I am not in my bedroom. I am alone in my bed and there is nothing but darkness surrounding me. I get out of bed and start to walk around. I can't see very far in front of me but I continue anyway. Eventually, I can see a canvas with a huge frame around it. As I move closer to it, I can start to make out an image on the canvas, it is me. I am watching myself sleep in bed in my bedroom from above. Slowly I lift my hand up, I am about to touch the image but then it changes. The canvas is completely dark, leaking smoke; I put my face through and pull the rest of my body in.

I am at a park in my neighbourhood, it is quite dark, and the street lights around the park cast enough light for me to only see dim images around me. I put my hand in my pocket and pull out my cigarettes and lighter. I realize that this must be a dream. I have a full pack of cigarettes to smoke during this beautiful night at the park. I put one of my cigarettes in my mouth and light it. I breathe in the smoke and exhale. I feel very relaxed and calm as I my eyes catch sight of one of the old trees in the centre of the park. Someone is walking behind me.

"Well hello there Sandra." I turn around to see Doctor Reed standing in one of the beams of light. He seems taller in the shadows of the park.

I smirk, "Hello Doctor."

"Can I bother you for a cigarette?"

"Sure."

I hand him a cigarette and light it for him. He inhales the smoke and slowly breathes it out.

"So, Sandra, do you think you're dreaming?"

I laugh. The sound of it breaks the silence in the serene park. "Of course! I am but I don't mind this one."

"How do you know what's real or not?" His question hangs in the air, before he continues, "What if this is something that's already happened but you're recalling it as

58

a memory? What if you're actually awake? I am not sure that you are able to distinguish the difference anymore."

I am quiet for a moment. When I finally decide how to answer, my voice is raised and it is apparent to me that I am getting really frustrated with him.

"What does it matter? I'm sure I'll have another false awakening or nightmare before I actually wake up. The technicalities surrounding your theories aren't too important to me, I'd just like to know for certain if I'm awake or not and be able to wake up when I want to."

"What if you never know for sure?"

The street lights all turn off, I can't see anything. The alarm shrieks.

BEEP BEEP BEEP

Foreword by Author Alicia Sarazin

Biography: Alicia is an aspiring writer and science communicator. She prefers writing horror and has a special interest in folklore, especially obscure folklore which she credits as being truly haunting sources of inspiration.

Pond Scum by Alicia Sarazin

Rain pounded against the roof of the car like a barrage of tiny fists, and another bright flash split the sky. Lori shrieked and huddled further into the mass of blankets in which she had cocooned herself in the back seat. The wild wind whipped and howled against the sides of the car, moaning like a vengeful spirit trying to get into their metal sanctuary. The girl's small frame shook beneath her fluffy barrier, and she continued to whimper.

"It's okay, kiddo. It's just a little storm," Jacob said from the front, not taking his eyes off the road. In this weather he couldn't risk getting distracted. The roads were muddy and visibility was low and he could not afford to lose the car too. He could barely hear his wife's soft snores from beside him over the deluge. He remained calm and stoic in the face of nature's wrath, as no obstacle was too great for a man running solely on caffeine and spite.

"It's scary, daddy," the small voice from the back whined, muffled by her blanket, wavering with innocent fear. "I want to go back home. We didn't have scary storms at home."

Jacob felt his ire rising against the back of his neck and in his face, but with a heavy sigh, he brought himself back down.

"I know you miss home, but we can't go back. We told you that. Now quiet down or you'll wake your mother," he replied sharply. Months of stress and sleepless nights had worn his patience thin, and he worked on controlling his breathing. There was a time and a place for this, and in the middle of a storm in the backwaters of god-knows-where was not it.

Although, he doubted Lori could actually wake April. Even with the thunder, lightning, wind, and the close encounter with some stupid deer in the road a few miles back, she was still snoozing away, her face pressed into her seatbelt. Jacob had to wonder what demon possessed his wife to allow her neck to bend at that angle.

Underneath her blanket bundle, Lori did her best to quiet down, as her father requested. She knew she had made him angry with her comment about home. She knew why they couldn't go back, and she knew talk of home made her father mad. She didn't like when he was mad. He always said really mean things and made her and mommy cry. He said he was sorry, but it always happened again. Lori curled into herself deeper and bit her tongue to supress a quiet sob. She would not bother her dad with the storm or home anymore. She would try not to, at least.

*****

The family continued on in relative silence, Lori drifting off as the lightning began to fade with the passing of the storm. Jacob did his best to stay alert, sipping from his Red Bull whenever he felt sleep begin to sink its teeth into his eyes.

As he finished off the last of the can with a large gulp, a mailbox came into view, and Jacob breathed a sigh of relief as he pulled onto the side road presumably leading to the home of April's great-aunt, Carla.

She was truly a godsend, having offered the family her home until they could piece their lives back together. April only vaguely remembered who she was when they received the call, as she had not seen Carla since she was a teenager. She had admitted that she felt ashamed at not having kept contact with such a kindly woman, especially after the death of her husband. She regretted not reaching out at the time and had vowed to make up for it during their stay.

Jacob snorted at the thought. As if they really had time for that. The way he saw it, if any second was not spent fixing their situation, it was as good as wasted. They didn't have time for idle chitchat.

A bump against a raised rock on the road jolted Jacob from his thoughts, and he quickly refocused on driving. He reached for his energy drink again, trying to take another sip, but only a dribble escaped from the empty tin. Jacob grunted in annoyance and crumpled the flimsy can in his fist, dropping it to the floor. He returned his hands to the steering wheel, although with a much tighter grip and a scowl upon his lips.

The moist dirt squelched under the tires of the car as they finally pulled into their destination. The old Victorian-style home loomed above him, darker than the dark night it stood against, with only the glow from the windows showing that it was inhabited.

Had they arrived during a sunny day, the house may not have been so foreboding. It may even be beautiful when one could see it in detail. But as it was currently presented, Jacob thought that it looked like a haunted house ride, especially with the lightning in the far distance behind it. All that was missing to complete the scene were a swarm of bats and an evil laugh sound effect.

It was probably for the best that Lori wasn't awake. She always spooked easily, and he really wasn't in the mood to deal with that.

"Hun, wake up," Jacob said as he prodded his sleeping wife, "we're here."

April stirred from her awkward position, a loud crack resounding from her bunched-up shoulder and neck. She stretched as much as possible in the confines of her seat, popping more joints, and rubbed her eyes groggily.

"It sounds like hell out there," she said hoarsely. April smacked her lips together, the taste of sleep upon her dry tongue. She reached into the compartment between the seats and grabbed a bottle of water. The arid feeling in her mouth faded with each gulp, and she turned to the back seat once she had her fill.

"How you doing back there, LoLo?"

Lori did not stir, her head hanging heavily forward as she breathed evenly in her sleep.

"Oh, that position can't be comfortable," April sighed. Jacob barked out a laugh.

"You should talk. You should have seen how your neck looked," he chuckled. "How it hasn't broken is beyond me".

The pair laughed softly as Jacob parked the car, trying to get as close to the door as possible, hoping to minimise the dampness they had to endure. Though the storm was not as violent as it had previously been, the slow rain still came down heavily in fat drops. They exchanged a determined glance as they flung the doors open and raced to the house, practically slamming their fists against the doorbell.

After a short time that felt like a soggy eternity, the lock on the door clanked open and the smiling, tired face of Auntie Carla appeared bathed in warm light.

"Oh my goodness, my girl," the elderly woman said as she held out her arms to April, "you have grown so beautiful and strong." She kissed April's cheeks, her bright lipstick rubbing off against the damp skin.

"You must be freezing! Come, grab your things quickly so we can warm you up. I will go make some tea."

Carla shuffled back into the house, leaving the door open. April and Jacob immediately began racing back to the car, flung open the trunk, and threw as many bags as they could inside the open doorway.

Lori stirred due to the noise and the bouncing of the car, only to be picked up by her father and hauled into the house before she could even process what was happening. The car was locked up, the door was closed, and the family took their time warming up with Carla in the living room for a chat.

Through half-conscious, Lori hand clung to her mother's sweater as they sat on the old loveseat. The house around her creaked and moaned, the branches of the ancient trees outside scraping against its panels and windowpanes. Her eyes darted around, bleary and heavy. Her gaze eventually landed on the old woman in the chair across from her. Her face was heavily wrinkled, and her hands were gnarled and warped. She appeared to be missing many teeth and her fingernails were long and cracked. Lori pushed her face into her mother's side and whined.

April and Jacob talked to Carla for a while, about their situation, their former jobs, what they needed to do to get back on their feet.

"Goodness, dear. That sounds awful. Makes me glad for my retirement," Carla said as she picked up her tea for another sip. "Your students must have been devastated".

"Nothing brings out the best in students like their teacher leaving", April said with a sheepish smile. "Really shines a fond light on all the spit balls and drawings of dicks on test papers."

Carla chuckled against her cup. "Sounds like a rowdy bunch you had."

"Yeah", April sighed wistfully, "but they made me proud, y'know?"

An irritating tapping caught April's attention and she turned to see Jacob rapping his nails against the cup in his hands, an almost pouty look upon his face, eyes narrowed and his lips downturned in a vague scowl. His leg shook up and down as he glared at nothing. Carla had noticed as well.

"Are you alright, dear?" Carla asked, clearly concerned, and Jacob visibly tensed.

"I'm fine. Just tired," Jacob said sharply. "I'm going to sleep. Thanks for the tea".

April lowered her gaze and supressed a sigh. This always happened when the topic of their jobs came up. As deep as Jacob's denial about the circumstances of his termination was, some part of him knew he would garner no sympathy by telling the story. His temper made holding his tongue a herculean task. But Jacob's comment must have reminded her brain of how exhausted she was, and April suddenly felt like she could barely keep her eyes open. She looked down at Lori, who was still pushed into her side, and saw that she had once again fallen asleep.

"He's right, it's late," April said as she turned back to Carla. "And Lori is already out cold".

The women said their goodnights as April gently shook Lori awake. As much as April did not want to disturb her slumber, she was getting too heavy to carry. They shambled out of the room and upstairs, zombie-like in their exhaustion. Lori flopped down on the bed presented to her, and barely registered the kiss goodnight as she drifted off and April left the room to go to her own bed.

*****

Lori awoke in an unfamiliar place, in the dark of the early morning. In her hazy state, she was not entirely aware of how she got there, but she was absolutely terrified. There was an eerie sound coming from outside, like the moaning of a woman. Fingers clawed at her window and the sides of the house, and the roof above her creaked with the footfalls of a terrible creature. Lori's eyes were wide as they tried to adjust to the dark, and she pulled her blankets over her head. She lay in confused terror as the noises around her continued.

There was suddenly a loud BANG, and Lori screamed as she scrambled out of the bed to the door. She flung it open to find herself in an unfamiliar hall, where she fell to her knees and began to cry loudly. From down the hall, she heard a door slam open followed by quick footsteps. She began to hysterically crawl backwards, away from the noise, and she shrieked as a pair of arms grabbed her.

"Lori! LoLo, what's wrong?!"

Lori began to sob as she realised, she was in the arms of her mother. She continued to cry as April picked the girl up and carried her to the room her parents were sleeping in. On the bed between her parents, she slept fitfully, kicking and stretching her body out, keeping her parents from resting.

Lori awoke to a bright room, the late morning sun shining through the open blinds. Her parents were gone, and she hauled herself out of the room in search of them.

She found them in the kitchen, and barely registered the dead look on their faces, as she was too occupied staring down Auntie Carla who sat in a chair at a small table drinking a cup of tea. Carla smiled at Lori, who turned away. Lori was certain the old woman was a witch.

The rest of the day was uneventful. Things were unpacked and put away, and Lori did her best to stay out of her parents' way. Consumed by boredom, she went to look around the outside of the home.

In the pale autumnal sun, Lori wandered out into the open area beyond the front garden. As the weather was much colder here than back in California, all the trees were either red and brown, or entirely bare. The wind whipped and whirled around them, chilling Lori to the bone even through her sweater. She shivered, not only from the bite of the wind, but from the unearthly whistle it made as it danced through the naked forest, the clattering of the branches mimicking Lori's own chattering teeth.

Standing just outside the perimeter of the house, Lori noticed something that very much piqued her curiosity. A lake. Well, more like a big pond. From where she stood, the water looked as black as pitch, and it was slightly choppy in the wind. She continued towards it, seeing a small dock that went out a bit on the open water. The tip of a sunken boat peeked out of the depths next to it, still tied to one of the rotted pegs on the walkway. The wood itself was old, splintered, and falling apart, and Lori knew better than to walk on it. The water was also kind of smelly, clearly stagnant, and green goo floated on the surface.

She walked down to an area that dipped closer to the water, a sort of rocky beach covered in water-worn pebbles. Looking around, Lori picked up a flat stone and weighed it in her hand. Satisfied with its dimensions, she tossed it out and it didn't skip as she had intended, instead just sinking as soon as it hit the water.

Lori stuck out her lip and pouted. She looked down to find another stone to skip. Her next attempt was more successful, skipping twice before sinking into the murky water. Lori fist pumped at her success, but picked up another to give it one more try. Picking up another flat stone, she moved back into position, her tongue sticking out of the side of her lips in concentration. She swung her arm and the stone sailed in a slight arc before skipping against the water two, four, six times.

Lori jumped and cheered. She had never skipped a stone so many times before. Pleased with her success, Lori turned to find something else to do, but as she turned away something caught her eye. A shape was floating towards her from the centre of the pond. It didn't look like a piece of wood, or some pond scum, and it looked fuzzy.

Lori's eyes widened in horror as the thing came into focus. It was the carcass of a rabbit. Its belly had been ripped open and its insides were missing, the cavity old and brown. Lori screamed as she scrambled back up the embankment and ran to the house, where April now stood by the door, having gone outside to keep an eye on the girl. Lori ran to her mother and buried her face in her stomach.

"Mom, something in the lake killed a bunny!" Lori yelled, although her voice was muffled by April's clothes.

Mild disgust rose in April's throat at the thought of a dead animal in the glorified puddle. As if it couldn't get more disgusting.

"Alright, LoLo", April bent down to her daughter's height. "Come back inside, and I'll go deal with the bunny. Okay?"

Lori nodded, and let April lead her into the house and put on a movie for her on the mother's iPad, before she ventured back to where Lori had been playing to find the dead thing. As she approached the lake, April's nose scrunched up at the smell. The water really did reek, but despite the smell, she could not find the rabbit. She figured that it must have sunk into the putrid depths. Shrugging, she made her way back into the house, and was relieved to see Lori was fully absorbed into *The Emperor's New Groove*.

* * * * *

The peace did not last, as another fit occurred on the second night. The noises of the old house put Lori on edge, especially after her encounter with the rabbit's corpse, and all it took was the bang of shudders, or perhaps the house creaking, or just something Lori had imagined. She slept between her parents again, keeping them awake with her awkward positions and movements.

Her parents did not complete anything the next day, as they were too tired due to the previous night. They spent their day staring blankly at the wall, too tired to be properly angry at Lori, who had opted to stay inside and watch a movie, although, she soon became curious about the lake again. What ate that rabbit? Was there a monster in the lake or in the woods surrounding it?

Lori slipped on her coat and boots and went back out to investigate the lake, shouting a quick explanation to her zombie-like parents, who merely groaned in acknowledgment.

69

As she cautiously made her way back to the water's edge, Lori felt trepidation rising in her chest. She'd seen dead animals before, as she'd witnessed the occasional piece of road kill and having buried her pet hamster last year, but something about this particular rabbit filled her with a fear she could not explain. Lori wrung her hands as her steps crackled on the rocky shore, but she relaxed slightly as she saw that there was no dead rabbit, releasing a breath she had not realised she was holding in. Her heart still racing, Lori turned her eyes out to the water. It was calm today, and putrid mist rose from its surface in the cold air. A sudden ripple caught Lori's attention and she focused her gaze on the other side of the lake. A large shape rested among the cattails on the opposite shore. It was mostly submerged, and only looked like a large lump. Lori's heart rate picked up as she took a small step back, the pebbles beneath her boot crackling together. The sound startled her into a panic, and she scrambled up the shore, not daring to look back at the shape.

Lori raced into the house and bounded up the stairs, all but throwing herself into her bed and pulling the covers over her head. The stench of the mud on her boots permeated the confined, plush space as Lori caught her breath, but she had to emerge seconds later due to the smell.

Now away from the lake, she rewound the events by the shore in her mind, trying to discern what the shape actually was. As she concentrated on the memory harder, the shape came into focus as though she had reached an epiphany, but something deep in her brain was quick to correct her. The shape had revealed itself.

With her newfound knowledge and her fascination overcoming her fear, along with the head-rush of the revelation, Lori left her bed, exited the room, and made her way to the shore once more.

* * * * *

70

On the third night of screaming and crying for her parents, Jacob had enough.

"You will stay in this room! We need to sleep, dammit, and so do you!" And with that, he slammed the door.

Lori curled up in a ball on the bed, her back against the wall as she wept quietly into her knees.

As time passed in her fearful solitude, Lori got up to turn on her light. In the glow from the lamp, her fear dwindled and exhaustion from so many sleepless nights took hold. Lori's stinging eyes began to feel heavy, and as she drifted off into a fitful slumber. She woke up many times, but her father's wrath and the light kept her in her bed. When the sun rose, Lori was exhausted, but she had made it through the night un-eaten by monsters.

As her parents were marginally better rested that morning since Lori didn't wake them up again, they began to search for work, and they threw themselves into their searches completely. In her solitude, Lori had to make her own entertainment. Auntie Carla did not have Wi-Fi, and usually watched boring talk shows and news instead of cartoons. Her mother and father did have hotspots for Internet, but Lori was not allowed to use it because they feared that she may use all the data, and they desperately needed it. The use of the iPad for movies had apparently been a one-time deal.

Her parents were gracious enough to bring a DVD player and a box of movies and hooked it up to a spare TV in from the attic. It was pretty old, probably from the 90's, and was clearly what Carla used before getting her slightly newer flat screen. Jacob made a fuss about how the clunky thing almost killed him on the way down the stairs and declared that Lori had better be grateful.

With the rig set up, Lori could occupy some of her time re-watching her favourite films. It entertained her

71

enough to keep her from pursuing her parents' attention. Aside from movies, Lori had really taken to wandering outside. After several weeks of routinely ambling around the rocky, damp, smelly shore, her parents finally took notice. April was relieved that Lori had found something to do while they were occupied, and Jacob was glad Lori was out of his hair. He was still pissed about how she had woken them up for three nights and containing the harsh words he had was no easy feat.

Lori's wanderings concentrated around the lake. If one were to watch her from a window, they would see her sitting on the shore, skipping rocks, collecting sticks, or just sitting there and staring out at the water.

Carla would eye Lori wearily, not wanting the child to fall in. As she was old and quite frail, it was unlikely she could pull Lori out on her own. She also remembered the incident with the rabbit. She was surprised an animal was near the lake so recently, for the carcase to be that fresh. Carla briefly mused at how long it must have been for an essentially mummified rabbit to be considered fresh. It wasn't the first time she had found an animal carcass around the property, but it had been a very long time ago.

The old woman leaned her hand into her palm and thought back to the days when she and her husband lived in the house together, and how the lake had been crystal clear. Back then, the surrounding woods teemed with wildlife, and it wasn't uncommon to see deer grazing around the house in the early hours of the morning. The change had happened soon after her husband passed away. The water of the lake became murky and began to smell. It was as though George's death had tainted the water.

Soon after, animal carcasses began to appear around the property, with snouts dipped into the water, as though they had died while drinking. The bodies always disappeared quickly, most likely dragged away by some predator, although she sometimes saw clumps of fur, small bones, and even antlers washing up on the shore. It had stopped a few months later, most likely because there were no more animals in the area. At least, there was no trace of any.

Snapping out of her memories, Carla sighed. She wanted to get to know Lori better, but the girl seemed to be avoiding her. Her parents hadn't bothered to properly introduce them, and given Lori's episodes in the night, it was clear that the child spooked easily. Although, it made her wonder why she would return to the lake.

The sun already hung low in the autumnal sky when Carla called out to Lori to come in for lunch. April was passed out upstairs, exhausted from another long drive to and from what was most likely another unsuccessful interview the previous day, and Carla figured she could use the opportunity to get closer to Lori.

The hunched shape did not react at first, but her head perked up after the second holler, and it came walking towards the house. The shape approached timidly, wringing its hands.

"Come along, dear", Carla made her voice as mellow as possible. "Come inside for some lunch with me, hm?"

Lori nodded and followed the elderly woman into the kitchen, where some sandwiches had been set out, along with a glass of juice. The sat in general silence, as Carla tried to make small talk, and Lori quietly answered her questions through her sandwich.

Eventually, they migrated to the living room, where Carla finally put on some cartoons, and Lori curled up in an armchair to her great aunt's side. Eventually, the elderly woman looked over and saw that Lori had fallen asleep in the chair. Seeing how peaceful she looked, Carla could not help but stroke the child's hair. She was a good kid, and it was a shame she had to deal with something like this at her age, just when girls were beginning to learn about themselves.

Carla remembered hearing about April and Jacob's situation when she was talking over the phone with her cousin, who had heard it from an old friend of April's father. When she had called initially, April had been very courteous and grateful for the call, but the way she slurred her words and forgot what they were talking about mid-sentence tipped Carla off to the fact that April was drunk, which was honestly understandable for the situation she was in. April had explained their woes, how Jacob had been fired from his job due to a *"petty disagreement"* with his manager, and April had been fired a few weeks earlier due to, as April put it, *"parents being overprotective and entitled about their children's classroom experience"* and *"they don't understand how stressful it is dealing with their shitty kids all day"*. Carla thought she had heard April take another gulp of whatever poison she had picked.

Carla had offered that April's family stay with her out of kindness and affection for them as family, however distant, but seeing how the couple barely handled the responsibility of a child and how hard it apparently was for either of them to find a job, she had to wonder if there was more to the story than she had been told.

Carla continued to run her rough hands through Lori's amber locks, lost in thought. Then she too dozed off. When she came to, Lori was no longer in the chair beside her. Pulling herself from her seat, Carla made her way to the window, and saw Lori once again out by the lake, skipping stones. The elderly woman hung her head as she walked back to her chair, feeling despondent. Who wouldn't, if they were rejected in favour of a stinking lake?

* * * * *

Sitting at the table, April and Jacob stared blankly into space as they absently lifted food to their faces.

74

April tried hard to pay attention to the words of her daughter. It must have been difficult for her to be alone all the time, and she was glad that Lori was warming to the creepy house up a bit. She really did want to appreciate the creativity and perseverance Lori was putting on display but driving back and forth from job interviews and events and conferences had drained her of any brain capacity beyond lifting the fork to her face.

Jacob could barely hear Lori over his own racing thoughts. He was exhausted but the stress was getting to him, and his daughter's constant rambling wasn't helping. Job interview after job interview yielded nothing. He was lucky if he got an interview at all. He didn't hear back from most of the places he sent his resume to. He thought back to his job in the bay area, and how easy it had been. The thought of it all made his blood boil, and his grip on the fork tightened.

"...and today, miss mermaid and I went looking for pretty stones on the shore!" Lori's voice drifted into her parents' ears.

"Miss Mermaid?" April said, tiredly lifting her gaze, her attention directed at her daughter briefly.

"Uh-huh. I met her in the lake a few days ago! She's really nice and really pretty," the child said giddily. "And she brings me flowers, and shells, and sings songs for me and..." Lori continued to chatter about her mermaid friend.

"That's nice..." April tapped out again, drinking the remainder of her wine in two large mouthfuls, too tired to focus on her daughter's account of her mythical friend. An imaginary friend was pretty common at Lori's age, and expected considering the circumstance. If either parent had the energy to be happy for Lori, they would have. Carla simply smiled fondly at them, as she listened to the young girl talk about her friend that lived in the lake.

"And what does this mermaid look like?" Carla asked, trying to encourage Lori's imagination, and perhaps create some sort of bond. Lori leaving her alone in the chair weighed on her mind, but she did her best to ignore it.

"She's super pretty but looks kind of weird. But she's a fish lady, so you would expect her to be weird," Lori stated, shovelling another bite of casserole into her face.

"Weird but pretty, you say?" Carla said in an amused tone.

"Uh-huh! Her skin is really pale and she has long black hair," Lori mimed long hair as she said this. "Her eyes are also totally black and kind of buggy."

"She sounds very strange," April piped in briefly. "Are you sure she's a mermaid?"

"Yep!" Lori chirped cheerfully. "She has a crown of white flowers and I think I saw a bit of her tail."

"Well, I'm glad you made a friend," Carla said, smiling. A vague grunt came from Jacob's direction, and silence fell over the table again, but Lori was obviously in higher spirits than she was before.

* * * * *

The next morning, Jacob left for yet another function. He basically had to drag himself out of the house. As he exited the domicile, he noticed a small shape by the lake in the morning mist. He approached it, wondering why Lori was out so early. As he drew closer, he could hear Lori talking to someone.

"Whatcha doing there, kiddo?"

Lori quickly spun around to face her father. From what he could see she was building a small structure out of the damp earth.

"Hi daddy! I was talking to Miss Mermaid," she said brightly. Ah yes, the mermaid.

"And what about the, uh, mud castle?" Jacob crouched down to be closer to Lori's level.

"That's just for fun", Lori stated.

Jacob glanced at his watch and got back up.

"Well, enjoy yourself. Don't fall into the water or wander too far", Jacob called back as he moved to his car. Lori responded with an affirmation and Jacob moved to enter the vehicle.

Just before he closed the door, he heard Lori begin to talk to the water again, speaking in an excited whisper, although he couldn't make out what was said. Shrugging, he started the car and peeled away.

* * * * *

Jacob came home around noon the next day, when the cold light of the sun warmed him just slightly. He was in a better mood than usual, having introduced himself to many people in his line of work, and hoped one would put a good word in for him. He absently glanced at the lake, expecting Lori to be there.

He walked into the downstairs guestroom where they had set up Lori's DVD rig and found her sitting on the bed watching a movie. It was *Finding Nemo*, and the fish had just lost the goggles in the deep water.

"Heya, kiddo", Jacob said as he sat next to his daughter, ruffling her hair.

"Hi daddy", Lori responded, not looking away from the screen. Jacob was taken aback by such a strange reply. He looked down at his daughter closely and he had to wonder if Lori was looking especially pale today.

"So... what have you been up to?" Jacob said awkwardly, as Lori's eyes never left the movie. The light of the anglerfish was now luring in the fish characters, and Lori's voice came out slowly and sleepily.

"Miss mermaid reminds me of that fish."

Okay, well that was a strange statement.

"Your friend from the lake?"

"She is a beautiful light in the deep," Lori said slowly, but with a strange reverence in her voice.

"And is she just as scary as the angler?" Jacob asked, uncomfortable with how eerie Lori was being. She had never spoken like this before.

Lori slowly moved her eyes up to her father's face, and her eyes were heavy lidded and unfocused.

"You want to know what Miss Mermaid told me?" she asked softly. Jacob gulped and did not reply.

"She said that you would still have your job if you'd actually just done it properly." An unsettling smile grew on Lori's face as the words left her lips, but she was quickly snapped out of her dazed state by the loud yelling of her father.

"What the fuck did you just say?!" Jacob roared at Lori. "What the fuck did you say?"

Lori's face quickly morphed into one of fear and confusion, and Jacob continued to yell as she scrambled to understand what was happening.

"Did your mother say that to you?! Damn bitch is shit talking me behind my back!"

It was then that Lori began to wail loudly, and April came running in and wrapped her arms around her bawling daughter.

"Have you been bad mouthing me to our kid?!" Jacob roared at April, who looked back at him with a confused yet unamused look, a calm fury behind her eyes as she held her child closer.

Jacob felt himself getting even more angry in the face of her silent defiance and he stormed out of the room. April continued to hug the sobbing girl and rocked her back and forth.

"I'm sorry! I'm sorry!" Lori cried. "I don't know what I did!"

April stroked her hair until Lori calmed down and sat with her watching a movie. She had no idea what happened, but she would find out soon enough.

By the time Nemo was back at the reef, Lori had dozed off.

April dislodged her arm from under the sleeping child's head as carefully as possible and made her way up to the bedroom to confront Jacob.

"What the actual fuck was that?!" April raised her voice slightly but made sure it wasn't a full yell. "Why the hell were you screaming at her like that?"

Jacob lifted his eyes from the floor, standing from his position sitting on the edge of the bed.

"What the fuck have you been telling Lori?" Jacob growled.

"Excuse you?"

"I said what have you been telling our daughter?!"

April scoffed at him.

"Why on earth would I say anything to Lori? What did she say to you?"

Jacob paused for a moment, as though he thought revealing the circumstances was not actually wise. His jaw clenched, and he began his deep breaths. While bringing himself down, one thing buzzed in his brain, and it slipped out before he could stop it.

"Do you actually think that?" Jacob asked through gritted teeth.

"Do I think what?"

"That I…" Jacob paused, realising he perhaps did not want that question answered.

"You know what, forget it," Jacob finally said. "I'll go apologise. I don't know what came over me."

April eyed Jacob wearily as he walked out of the room but could not press the issue further in this case. She thought of perhaps getting him anger management therapy to curb his temper, but he would probably yell at her for suggesting it.

She thought back to the day Jacob came home with a black eye and the news that he had been fired, the sheer panic April felt at him losing his job mere weeks after she had lost hers, and the stressful days waiting for a warrant for assault, even though Jacob insisted he had retaliated in self-defence and could prove it. April didn't know if she believed him. The warrant never came, but that was little solace in the face of the reality that neither of them had jobs anymore, and had a third mouth to feed.

April sighed and sat down on the bed, trying to put together the pieces of the events, but she could not. Opening the drawer of her bedside table, she retrieved a small flask, and took a quick swig. The burn and the warmth of the booze calmed her nerves, but there was the slimy aftertaste of guilt and shame that followed the path of the fiery liquid down into her chest.

"God, this is so fucked up," April muttered, her forehead resting against the back of her hands, one of which still grasping the open flask. April closed the small container and hid it back in her drawer under the packets of over-the-counter painkillers and a variety of pamphlets.

Deciding to leave it as Jacob suggested, April picked up her book and began to read to distract herself from the strangeness and her own mind.

* * * * *

Jacob's eyes slowly cracked open as a sound resounded through the room. The silence that followed and the soft sound of April's breaths lulled him back into slumber, until he heard it again.

A loud, wet slap, followed by a dragging noise.

Jacob shot up, and April groaned at her awakening.

"What's up?" April croaked sleepily, her arms twisting above her head as she tried to orient herself in the waking world.

"I heard something," Jacob placed a hand on April's forearm. "You stay here. I'll go take a look."

He swung his legs over the side of the bed and grabbed his phone from the nightstand. His eyes burned slightly from the bright light from the screen, but he quickly switched on the flashlight and made his way to the door, April now sitting upright in bed.

His light followed the wet trail down the hall, and his nose scrunched up as the smell of putrid water and mildew suddenly washed over him. His hand quickly clapped over his mouth and nose in response. His eyes watered and his breaths came out in a shaky staccato as he tried not to inhale the stench. The smell may not have been that bad if it were not so thoroughly overpowering.

Another SLAP and the dragging sound echoed from further down the hall, causing Jacob to jump. His heart pounded in his ears as he realised that something was indeed in the house. He looked again at the trail on the floor. The trail of water was quite thick, and large irregular splashes surrounded the line.

Jacob took a deep breath, instantly regretted doing so, and began to follow the water trail. Every few steps, there would be a clump of green slime that jiggled as he walked near it. Along with the smell permeating the hall, the sight made him gag slightly, but his attention was refocused as another slap was heard, louder and clearer than before. He was definitely closer now.

Jacob swallowed his fear and stepped lightly as to not alert whatever was there of his presence. After another few steps, SLAP, drag. The sound was coming from just a few feet out of the range of his light pointed in front of him, and he froze to listen.

Silence.

Jacob raised his light from the floor to where there appeared to be a rather large puddle in the centre of the hall, the water now giving off the smell of road kill. As the light moved up, a pair of muddy feet came into view. Jacob's heart pounded as the light shone upon the face of his daughter, soaked and covered in mud, her eyes closed. He began to approach her when she began to lift her right arm. With a sudden swing, there was a loud, wet slap as a soaked towel hit the ground. The towel sprayed Jacob with a shower of debris and water. His rage rose and was about to violently chastise Lori, when she opened her mouth to speak, a smile appearing on her lips, but all that came out was garbled gibberish as Lori suddenly collapsed to the floor.

His anger vanished, replaced by concern. Jacob rushed to her side and check his child for injuries or immediate signs of illness, but Lori was just sound asleep in his arms. Jacob was no longer mad about being splashed but more puzzled and relieved as he carried the sleeping girl back to her room and put her to bed.

"Well?" April asked as he came back to the bedroom.

"Well," Jacob began, "Lori seems to have become a sleepwalker, and we need to scrub the hall tomorrow."

April cocked her head in confusion.

"Yeah, I don't know how, but Lori filled a towel with dirty water from that awful pond and was slapping it around the hall." Jacob put his palm up to his forehead. "I don't know why she had that thing."

"Maybe she soaked it during the day?" April suggested. "She spends most of her time near the water now, what with her friend supposedly living there."

The next morning, as her parents scrubbed down the floor, Lori once again spent the majority of her day by the lake. Whenever April or Carla looked out, they saw Lori standing at the shore, staring out at the water. Once or twice she was sitting, but she did not move, and she stayed there until dusk. Jacob did not check, as he did not want reminders of Lori's weird antics.

* * * * *

Once again in the night, Jacob was awoken to a strange sound, but this one sounded much sharper, as though the surface upon which it occurred was solid. Jacob did not hesitate that night, and he quickly grabbed his phone and followed the sound, irritation replacing his previous fear.

He followed the slapping down to the end of the hall, past the landing, to one of the bathrooms. The light was off, but the sound was unmistakably coming from that room, a loud, wet slap echoing across the tiles. Jacob pulled open the door and flicked on the light.

The walls were covered in smears and handprints in black, sticky mud, and the room smelled strongly of the stale water and rotting foliage of the last night. In the closed space, it was probably even worse than in the hall. The black sludge dripped down the walls and even more pond slime coated the bathroom, along with a copious amount of fluid on the floor.

Lori was up against the mirror, absently smearing more mud on the glass, and didn't even register he father's presence, until he stormed up to her and grabbed her shoulder.

This time, the words were clear:

"Miss Mermaid comes to the house at night, and I have to make it nice for her".

And with that she appeared to snap from her daze and collapsed again. She almost hit her head on the sink but was saved by her father's catch. Previously only aggravated, Jacob was now quite spooked. In the back of his mind, a nagging voice told him that this behaviour was serious and Lori needed help, the kind that he could neither provide nor afford.

As he carried her out of the filthy bathroom, he noticed some of the handprints on the walls seemed much too large and high for Lori to have caused them. Jacob tore his eyes from them, quickly trying to convince himself that his nerves were causing his mind to

Once again, Lori was placed back in her bed, and Jacob returned to his own room.

"Same deal?" April asked.

"No, actually," Jacob replied flatly. 'This time, she decided to repaint the bathroom."

"Oh, Jesus Christ," April groaned.

"With mud," Jacob sat down on the edge of the bed. April blinked.

"Mud? Where the hell did she get the mud?"

"Beats me, but that is going to be a bitch to clean up," Jacob muttered before adding, "oh yeah, and she said she had to make the house nice for the mermaid."

April stared at him in disbelief. "Well, that's creepy."

"Tell me about it."

They both dragged themselves back into bed, but neither slept well with the thoughts of their daughter's nightly episodes racing through their minds.

Lori holed herself in the guest room and watched movies through all of the next day, as her parents worked to scrub the black muck off of the walls of the bathroom. Carla had suggested she call a cleaner, but Jacob had insisted to clean it himself. By the time they finally scrubbed the last of the grime from in the pipes under the sink, all the while questioning how it got there, the sun was already low in the sky.

Dinner was quiet and awkward. Lori ate, but did so in total silence, and the stillness of the air almost made the adults afraid to break it. As soon as the meal was finished, Lori shambled up to her room and immediately laid down, although she didn't appear to be sleeping yet. As everyone began their bedtime rituals, Jacob poked his head into Lori's room, all but glaring at her.

"Tonight, this door will be locked," he said sternly. It was a statement, and there was no room for argument, not that Lori tried.

She let out a meek "Okay," and with that the door closed, and the lock was turned. Click. Jacob tested the door. It didn't budge, and he walked to his room, satisfied that he could finally get some sleep.

"Why are you not more concerned by our daughter's new habits?" April said to her husband as they settled down. "She goes into these weird states when she's awake too, so it's not just sleepwalking."

Jacob made a snorting sound. He was fed up with everything and especially Lori's new quirk. Underneath his frustration and anger was fear. Although he would never admit it, he was genuinely scared by how she apparently turned into a little psycho during her fits.

"What else do you propose we do right now?" Jacob said accusingly. "Drop everything and rush her to a psychologist?"

April let out a groan in response. "No, but I feel like locking her in her room isn't really a solution".

"Look", Jacob started, "there is nothing we can do tonight, you need to be able to function tomorrow, and I don't want to clean up another mess." He began to lean back into the bed. "So just lie down and we'll think of what to do when you get back from the conference."

And with that, Jacob rolled over so his back was to April. The conversation was over.

April pinched the bridge of her nose, but relented. There really wasn't much they could do, and as long as the door was locked, Lori couldn't actually wander off and hurt herself. April got into bed and did her best to empty her mind. She thought briefly about taking a swig from the flask in her side drawer to take the edge off, but swatted the temptation away, focusing on the ticking of an old clock on the dresser across the room.

As April's eyes slid shut to the rhythm of the contraption, and the waking world melted away, she could have sworn she heard a rhythmic thumping and dragging somewhere deeper in the house, along with a wet slap.

* * * * *

At the crack of dawn, April headed out. Jacob still slept quite soundly, as Lori had not been out sleepwalking last night, due to the locked door. April lifted her bag quietly and left the room as silently as possible. She walked down the hall and stopped by Lori's room, turning the key to open it. The door creaked open, and April sighed at the sight inside.

Lori may not have woken anyone up, but she had clearly been walking around. She was sprawled on the floor near the wall to the right of the door. As April approached, she noticed Lori was clutching her water bottle, which had clearly been emptied. Onto the floor it seemed, judging by the puddle. April once again sighed, though slightly irritated, and she picked up a towel and placed it over the spill. She then grabbed a blanket and placed it over the displaced sleeper. April kissed Lori's temple and left the room, not locking it this time.

April quietly walked downstairs and out the door and put her bag in the trunk of the car. In the dim, near-morning light, she looked over at the lake. It was just as dark as ever, and it probably still stank. Nothing stirred in the water or near it. No animal made any noises. Come to think of it, there had never been a single bird sound around the house. The only signs of life in the area during their entire stay had been the remains of that rabbit.

The realisation hit April hard, but she had no idea what to do with the information. She had to get to her event, so she opted to just push the thought away for now. The sooner she got a good job, and possibly got Jacob a job, the sooner they could get away from the creepy lake. Lori clearly had some weird fascination with it, so distance would probably do her some good.

April pushed her foot down on the accelerator and sped off down the winding forest road away from the home.

* * * * *

Carla was already up and drinking a cup of tea when Lori walked into the living room. Her skin was still pale and obviously clammy, and her she appeared to be having trouble breathing, her breaths coming in quickly and shallowly.

"Auntie Carla, can we please go for a walk?" Lori said weakly. "I need some air."

Lori looked even worse for wear than she had the night after the sleepwalking. Dark circles had appeared under her eyes and her skin was pale. If she did not improve soon, she would need to see a doctor. Why she hadn't been taken yet was beyond her. Truthfully, Carla was becoming uncomfortable and increasingly concerned with April and Jacob's parenting, or lack thereof.

"Alright, dear. If that will make you feel better," Carla said. She assumed that Lori felt worse in the absence of her mother and needed some comfort. They both put on their outdoor shoes and coats, and Lori held Carla's hand as they walked out of the house.

They slowly moseyed around the front yard, taking in the crisp, chilly air. It had gotten substantially colder in the time Lori and her parents had been staying at the house, and the last of the orange leaves had fallen to the half-frozen earth.

Walking out of the yard onto the path to the lake, Carla smiled and squeezed her hand fondly.

"Even through all the troubles that brought you here, I'm glad you came," Carla said. "It can get lonely out here."

Lori nodded and stared out at the water as they approached the shoreline. She squeezed Carla's hand back.

"I'm glad I came here too," Lori said, but her tone was not friendly or warm and it immediately put Carla on edge. "By coming here, I've found a true friend."

"Ah ha ha, is that so?" Carla laughed nervously.

"Yes, and I've brought you out here to meet her. I need you to meet her in the lake," Lori said flatly, and Carla suddenly felt very cold. She felt the colour drain from her face as the child gripping her hand continued.

"Meet her… in the lake?" Carla drawled out slowly.

"Miss mermaid says she wants to take you to her kingdom, and if I help her, I get to go there and be a princess," Lori said flatly as she turned her pallid face back towards Carla. "And then I won't have to be sad or lonely anymore." Lori lips curled into a smile, as she appeared to imagine the scene in her mind.

"Lori, dear, you're scaring me," Carla tried to back away, but felt the creak of the old dock under her feet, the wood damaged and ready to give out. She turned her head to look at the lake behind her. The water was calm, and as dark as ever.

"Come on, Auntie Carla," said the child as she gripped old woman's hand tighter. Carla couldn't help but notice how cold and clammy they felt now, and in her advanced age and frailty, she could not fight the unnaturally strong grip of the girl before her.

"Miss mermaid says Uncle George is waiting for you," Lori said with an unsettling grin on her face.

Carla stiffened at the mention of her husband, and she scanned Lori's face for any clue as to her intentions. Her eyes were unfocused, glazed over, as though she could not really see what was in front of her. Her eyes looked like those of a corpse.

Lori took a step forward, pushing Carla further toward the end of the dock, and the old wood groaned beneath her again. The child's grip on her hand was bruising and she could not muster the strength to fight it. Carla was frightened, close to panicking. Something was psychologically wrong with the girl, really wrong. Carla continued to try to pull away from Lori's death-grip as she went through what to do when she broke free. When she got back into the house, she would insist Jacob take Lori to the hospital. If he refused, she would call 911 and have the authorities take her. It would be for her own good. Despite her rising fear, Carla tried to maintain her composure and tried to reason with her small captor.

"Lori, dear, I know things have been rough with your family," Carla began, her voice wavering from fear, "but I want to help you."

"I know," Lori replied, "and that's why you need to go with miss mermaid."

And with that, Lori pushed Carla over the edge of the dock into the freezing water below.

The shock of the cold knocked the wind out of the elderly woman, but she soon regained her sense and began to attempt to swim, flailing her arms about and desperately kicking her legs. Lori watched as Carla yelled and thrashed in the dark water.

"Please, Lori! Help me!" Carla tried to yell over mouthfuls of water but spitting out the putrid liquid muted her voice. Her thick hand-knitted shawl and sweater soaked up water, weighing her down, and she began to sink. She splashed frantically as each second pulled her further into the dark depths. Tears flowed from her eyes and mixed with the murky water as her head began to go under.

"Please…" Carla garbled out as she struggled to spit out another mouthful.

"Bye-bye Auntie Carla," Lori called, sleepily but cheerfully, "I'll see you again soon."

The last thing Carla saw before her eyes sank below the surface was Lori waving slowly at her. Soon, Carla's hands sank as well, and all that was left was a stream of desperate bubbles. A minute later, even those were engulfed by the black surface of the lake.

Lori lowered her waving hand and turned away, her gaze slowly moving to the upstairs window where her father was probably still sleeping.

Sluggishly, she made her way back to the house. The grey of the sky opened, and rain softly drizzled on the girl, and on the now-calm water.

* * * * *

April slammed the door on her car, once again exhausted and dragging her feet as she shuffled to the door. The wind was still tonight, and she could hear the waves of the lake lapping against the shoreline. It had clearly rained earlier, as the dirt beneath her feet was soft and probably ruining her shoes. Had she had more energy, she may have appreciated the serenity of her surroundings, but all she wanted was a glass of whisky and to pass out.

She fumbled with the keys as she slowly made her way to the door, each step heavier than the last. With the key at last in the lock, she turned it, feeling relief wash over her as she heard the clanking of the heavy lock. She pushed the door, ready to finally rest after a long day.

As she put her foot onto the carpeted floor, April felt a cold, slimy chill worm up her spine. Her drowsiness left her as she was gripped by a sudden dread.

Why did the air feel so different? Why did it feel so damp?

April moved into the house slowly, trying to make as little noise as possible. Every step onto the carpet let out a soft squelching noise, as it was completely soaked through with foul-smelling water. Piles of green sludge were interspersed over the floor, along with twigs and dead leaves. The air felt thick and soupy.

April fumbled for the light near the coatrack, and while the light did come on, it was dim and yellow. This sickly illumination was enough for her to see the scene before her. She stared into a veritable swamp, the house flooded and filled with foliage one would find at the edge of a pond, with cattails and lily pads dotting the new landscape.

Where did all this water come from? The night outside was a still as the dead, so it couldn't have been blown in. April's mind thought back to the puddles, smears, and piles of muck Lori had been tracking around the house lately.

A sudden realisation hit April like a truck, and a deeper, primal dread came to the forefront of her mind. Where was everyone? Surely, they had to have noticed something. Was Lori okay?!

April carefully made her way up the stairs, finding them also covered in water and green slime. She gripped the bannister, trying not to slip as she headed up to check on her daughter.

The upstairs landing was bathed in shadow, and water flowed freely down the hall, like a small creek. The smell was even thicker in the tight hall, compressed by the walls into a long tunnel of stale air and darkness. April tried to flick on the light, but the bulb did not respond. She pulled up the flashlight on her phone and shone it into the cold darkness.

The light seemed to be swallowed by the dark of the hall, as though a thick, black mist hung in the air, but April's trepidation was overridden when she heard Lori's soft giggle from further into the dark.

One foot after the other, April began her trek into the hall. The water leaking into her shoes was warm, and the stench in the air around her was overpowering. Underneath the smell of old water was something else, something like the smell of a run-over skunk. Like rotting meat and musk. April suppressed a gag and quickened her pace as she could hear Lori speaking softly to someone, her feet sloshing with every step.

April finally came upon one of the bathrooms, and she could clearly hear Lori's voice on the other side of the door. Faint light glowed from within, and water poured out from underneath the soggy wood. April turned the knob and flung open the door to reveal Lori sitting cross-legged in front of the bathtub in a torrent of dark water, the light from above the bathroom's mirror glowing the same dingy yellow as the downstairs light. Upon hearing the door open, Lori turned and smiled at her mother.

"Hi, mommy," Lori said, smiling lazily up at her. Lori's eyes were glassy and unfocused, her skin was washed out, sickly, and looked severely waterlogged. A sudden wave of terror and revulsion swept through April as she made a terrible connection: Lori looked like the re-animated corpse of a drowned child. April pocketed her phone and moved to scoop up her daughter but halted abruptly as she saw movement within the overflowing tub.

Long tendrils of darkness began to flow along the currents, the crown of a head of dark hair popping up within the pool of water. Translucent, veiny, pale skin surrounded huge, bug-like black eyes. Adorning its silky locks were the most perfect white lilies April had ever seen, untarnished and beautiful, and they glowed like the full moon on a clear night. Even with the overpowering stench of decay that radiated from the thing, their sweet scent was still distinguishable.

April felt her face drain of colour as Lori's description at dinner suddenly returned to her mind.

"Hello, miss mermaid," Lori slurred from the floor. "Have you finished talking to daddy? Mommy is here now too."

April forced herself to move and grab her child. Lori's skin was cold to the touch and she shivered in her mother's hold. God, why was she so light? When had she lost so much weight? She felt like skin and bones. Her flesh squished and shifted unnaturally beneath April's grasp, softened and loose from the extreme waterlogging and fluid it had absorbed. April never took her eyes off the emerging being in the bath.

The creature's gaze did not waver from April as she held Lori, and soon a taloned hand breached the side of the tub, its claws long and scaly like those of some bird of prey. It began to push its body out from the water, more of its head exposed with every second. The beauty of its face only extended to the nose, and below was a huge, toothless, stretched maw with a dark gullet that seemed to extend on for eternity. Its neck was long and serpentine, with cartilaginous ridges along its throat where its endless oesophagus would be. Behind it, a large, long lump of twisted flesh thrashed about against the basin, covered in malformed fins and what looked to be small, undeveloped arms.

The thing continued to hoist itself from the bath on freakish, elongated limbs, its claws scraping against the porcelain, and as its torso began to come into view, April's instincts kicked into overdrive and she turned on her heel and ran out of the bathroom faster than she had ever run. She heard the thing screech behind her and the bathtub slosh and groan as it slipped out. She could hear it dragging itself along the floor, its hands slapping down against the wet floor, and she remembered those nights where she thought the noises in the halls were just Lori sleepwalking.

In the dark, without the light on her phone, April prayed that she would not slip and fall, that she would find the stairs, that the thing moaning and dragging itself in the dark behind her, slowly making its way towards her, would not prevail. April continued to run, but the weight of her daughter was making it hard to maintain her pace, and she had to slow to catch her breath. As she panted and clung to Lori, the splashing in the distance ceased.

The silence that followed was deafening. Every breath April and Lori took sounded as loud as thunder, the rush of water around her making it hard to discern if there was any movement. April continued slowly through the hall, the faint light from the entry of the house finally peaking at the end of the hall. Before relief could even be felt, April saw a shape begin to emerge from the water situated on the floor of the landing.

She could see the outline of its body in the light, and beside its long arms appeared to be another pair of shorter arms, and they were holding something. The monstrosity cocked its head and raised what it was holding up to be seen. Backlit by the light of the entry, April swallowed a horrified scream and a gag as she realised that it was a human arm. It was Jacob's arm.

The twisted thing moved the arm up to its cavernous mouth and shoved the limb in, swallowing it whole. April held in her desperate weeping, staggering back as the thing slowly sunk back into the floor. It had done that display just to taunt her. To break her spirit. To make her easier prey.

April would have dropped to her knees had the weight of Lori in her arms not brought her back to reality. She heard something moving in the water directly behind her, slowly slipping through and panting heavily, hungrily.

April took off again, as she felt rotten breath against her neck and the light brush of an arm on her back. The creature groaned from the dark as April sprinted as hard as she could into the dim light, and practically flew down the stairs. Her heel slipped against the slime on one of the stairs, and she slammed into the steps hard. A sharp, deep pain shot up her spine on impact, and she struggled to lift herself again, the strain of carrying Lori causing excruciating pain in her lower back.

She could hear thumping along the stairs above her and forced herself to move as fast as she could in her current state, her back throbbing, nausea beginning to overtake her. She crossed the threshold of the door and continued to hobble to her car, the creature behind her able to finally keep up with her slowed pace. It groaned and moaned as it dragged its unnatural form closer to the limping woman, drawing ever nearer, its second set of arms reaching out to claim its next victim.

April hissed as she held Lori in one arm, grabbed the car door, and threw both herself and her child in, slamming and locking the car behind her. As April lay on the seat, shaking in agony and terror, the thing slapped its hands on the window, pond scum flying off with each impact. It keened angrily as it circled the car, trying to slip its fingers in to gain entry, its eyes repeatedly flicking to Lori.

Lori had long since passed out, and its talons could not find purchase to claw open the windows or doors, nor did it try to smash the glass. Its black, enormous eyes showed no emotion, its jaw loose and hanging showed no change, but it lowered its hands from the car, and began to slink further back.

April sat up to watch it retreat, but it was already gone. Whether back into the house or into the lake, she was not sure, but she did not want to find out.

April crawled into the front seat, with great difficulty and pain. Something in her lower back clicked as she moved, and April gritted her teeth as she sat down. She looked back at her daughter and saw that the colour was still absent from her cheeks and she looked like a mess, sporting deep bags under her eyes and blue lips. Her clothes were soaked, her skin smudged with dirt, and strands of green goo clung to her hair. April's throat tightened as she turned away, fumbling with the keys. She turned them in the ignition, and the engine roared to life. She began to pull away from the now accursed home, shivering in fear and pain as the adrenaline began to wear off, and she desperately hoped she would not pass out on her way to the nearest town.

She glanced into her rear-view mirror a final time as the car began down the forested path away from the old house and caught a glimpse of the silhouette of a head on a serpentine neck, backlit in one of the house's windows. As suddenly as it had appeared, it sunk down from its position, out of sight. April's eyes darted back to the road quickly, not wanting to acknowledge the reality of the horrible situation. In her single-minded focus, she did not notice the heaviness building in her eyes as a soft, deep melody wafted into her ears, nor did she realise that Lori now sat upright, her eyes still unfocused, a wide but dreamy smile on her lips as the car began to swerve and skid on the soaked, slimy earth.

* * * * *

Scaly, ancient hands pulled a small, limp body from the pile of twisted metal. As the being lifted the small frame into its scaly arms and up towards its endless, unfathomably dark maw, Lori turned her head to look at her mother, although her mother appeared to be staring at her, April's empty eyes did not see anything anymore, as the branch of a tree had smashed into her head. As the warm darkness began to enclose around one of her limbs, Lori had to agree with daddy that it really was amazing how her mother's neck could bend like that.

I Found My Missing Relative's Journal by Alicia Sarazin

So, I was cleaning out the attic of my parents' house and I found a journal. According to the name on the first page, the journal belonged to someone named Silas, and some of the earlier content indicates that it's from the 80s, like mentions of politics and sports games. It's leather-bound, but not too fancy, and it's in decent condition. No pages are missing or anything, but quite a few are soiled enough that I went out and bought plastic gloves.

I've asked around and was definitely a Silas in my family, but from what I gathered, he died decades ago but nobody is sure how. Some think he was murdered; others think he just slipped off the grid. A few say he went mad. He had moved out into the boonies after his divorce, so he lost touch with basically everyone, and he apparently wasn't close friends with anyone. He wasn't reported missing for months.

I looked into it a bit, and something interesting came up: his animals were also missing. There were signs of blood all over the place, but all the carcasses or any traces of them were gone. The going theory was that someone killed him, hid his body, and then stole his livestock. Ties everything up pretty neatly, but the journal was always a mystery to the case. Poisoning was thrown around as a method of murder because of his apparent hallucinations, but without a body, nothing came of it. The journal was returned to the family after the case was dropped. No one was really that concerned with finding him, as sad as it is.

Perhaps I just wanted to play detective, but maybe the journal holds the key, thought I. I think I may have been right about that.

Most of the journal's contents are pretty mundane, talking about farm work and crunching numbers, but near the end, it gets really weird. I mean, obviously, because why would I share it if it wasn't?

I've transcribed it as best I can.

Here is what I found.

* * * * *

May 6th

Something got at the chickens last night. Not a speck of blood, nor any sign of damage to the enclosure. They're just gone. The other chickens are definitely spooked.

No sign of entry. At all. No blood, no broken fence, no hole under it. Unless some fox or coyote is the reincarnation of goddamn Houdini, I'm stumped. Hell, five chickens is just excessive, and why didn't the chickens wake me up if a predator was in the coop? It just doesn't make sense.

I'll stay awake tonight. Predators always return for easy prey.

May 7th

Stayed up. Nothing. Chores took longer than usual. Don't know what I expected, staying up like that.

Beatrice is still heavy with her calf. Should be born any day now. Definitely worried if a predator is prowling around. Whatever it is, it must be huge to nab five chickens like that. Worst case scenario, it's a cougar.

But then how did it slip through the fence?

Horses need new shoes, so I gotta go into town, but that would mean leaving the animals unattended. I'll wait until I'm sure the predator is gone, by my hand or otherwise.

May 8th

I had a strange dream last night. I can't quite remember it, but I have that feeling you get after a weird dream. I think it was about Holly, but I woke up upright like

100

it was a nightmare. Probably stress. My throat was scratchy, so maybe I'm getting sick? No fever so couldn't be a fever dream.

The horses were acting funny this morning. Real skittish. No tracks or anything, but it may be the predator.

I'll try staying up again. Maybe it got bold enough to come back.

May 10th

I don't know what happened. I don't know where the last day went. I stayed up, and I thought I heard something moving around in the bushes. And I saw Holly standing there, in her wedding dress, as beautiful as she had ever been. She beckoned me, and walked away into the corn field. I don't know what possessed me to follow her, but I did. I followed the cracking of the moving stalks, but the sound faded. Not like it was farther away. Like turning down the volume on a radio. I called out to Holly. I was so desperate to find her that I didn't notice that my vision was going dark.

The next thing I know, I woke up on my front porch, face-down, and covered in vomit a full day later. The electricity is down.

On top of that, I now have absolutely no idea what took my chickens, because they're all back in the coop. I can see them there. I counted as I walked past.

I need to sleep. I need to clear my head. I'll check on it tomorrow.

May 11th

Checked on the chickens. Three dead, two alive but look catatonic. Definitely my chickens. I cremated the dead ones and held a small funeral.

I don't know what to do with the live ones. They barely move.

Still no signs of entry. So not only did they take the chickens without leaving a trace, they returned them without a trace too? I'm starting to think a person is behind this, but even a human leaves evidence. Why take the chickens, and bring them all back? Even the dead ones.

But Mister is gone now. Maybe taken when the chickens were returned. But the barn door is heavy and loud, and there's no tracks in the dirt. Old goat didn't even kick up a fuss? I don't get it. I don't get what's going on.

May 12th

Went into town because I needed supplies. Didn't want to leave, but I still need food. Got everything I needed, but the people there were looking at me funny. Ran into ol' Raymond and he had the honesty to point out the red spots on my face.

"Like your face was made of hands that had shovelled manure for a week". When he puts it like that, I'm surprised I hadn't noticed it before. But now that I *have* noticed, they sting.

No gossip about someone running around kidnapping and traumatising animals, so they may be some recluse or a drifter.

Scribbled note, no date:

Awake. Clock said before dawn, but it's bright outside. Bright green and pink and blue. I can hear Holly. Need sleep. Mister is here.

May 13th

I don't remember writing that. Don't remember waking up.

Chickens are still mostly immobile. They just lay on their side, but I saw one dragging itself to the water bucket. It didn't walk. It just used its feet to claw its way over with its body flopping around behind it. That's definitely not normal. Maybe I should put them out of their misery.

No sign of Mister. Scoured the barn over and over. Nothing.

Horses are refusing to leave their stables.

Beatrice was crammed into the corner of her pen. She screamed at me when I tried to check her calf. I've never seen her do that.

I also remember my dream from last night. It was a whole lot of Holly. I woke up when she was giving the wedding ring back to me. I think I was crying because my face was wet. It stung the blisters.

May 14th

My vegetable patch is destroyed. It looks like everything just withered and died. Anything that was growing on the plants is gone. Tomatoes, zucchini, melons. Hell, even all the lemons from the tree. The stems look snipped, but the cut tips look like they've been scorched. The whole place smells like sulphur. It's like someone carefully Napalmed my crops.

The other chickens are avoiding the two that came back. They seem almost afraid to move too close to them.

Still no sign of Mister. Will he be brought back like the chickens? If he was, will he even be alive, or a limp husk like the chickens are? And which one is the worse option?

May 15th

I'm going crazy. I must be. That can't have happened. The two that came back changed. Something happened in the night. I think there were lights, but the chickens were going wild. I ran out, and it was a massacre in there. Every chicken ripped apart, and the two had holed up in the coop. They were definitely the chickens, but chickens don't chirp and screech like that. I shut the door to the coop and   padlocked   it.

Never used the door before. I hope that holds them.

Mister is back. No sign of entry and catatonic like the chickens   were.

Beatrice gave birth, but the calf is nowhere to be seen, and she was fucking drained of blood. Dry as jerky, but not a speck surrounding her.

I should just go beat in Mister's head, but I can't bring myself to do it. I tied him up and locked the barn.

I thought I saw someone behind my house when I ran to the chickens.

May 16th

Those things aren't fucking chickens. They grew fucking crab legs from their chests, but it's like something is wearing the chickens. The legs just drag their limp body.

They got out of the coop. Ripped the wire enclosure apart. They've been circling the house, scratching at the door, flinging themselves at the windows. They haven't broken in yet, and I'm afraid to shoot and give them a way in.

I hear screaming from the barn. I think Mister has changed too. Those restraints won't hold him for long.

May 17th

Mister got out in the night. He went straight for the horses. I could hear their screams. Goats cannot make sounds   like   that.   They   don't   roar.

One chicken has eaten the other. I heard them fighting. Their screams almost sounded like cats fighting.

I saw something pass by a window last night, backlit by the lights. It's not a person. I could hear Holly calling out for me. My skull feels like it's going to burst.

May 18th

I opened a blind and Mister was there. He isn't a goat anymore. He has too many eyes and teeth, and he had to bend down to look in. His legs have too many joints. He smiled at me.

There's something else out there now. It's crying like a baby. It sounds wet.

Chicken still scratches at my door. I'm sure other things are out there now. I can hear their screams. I see their shadows. Many more.

May 19th

I regret everything. I regret moving to this place. I regret meeting Holly. I regret letting Holly leave. I regret it all. I regret. Everything has led me here, on my floor, burning and bursting, being watched from the things outside and Holly. But Holly can't be here, because she left. But maybe she's here because she never really left.

May 20th

I can't touch anything. The blisters are forming and bursting every second. It burns. I'm boiling. It's agony to hold the pen, but I must. This is all I have. Everything else is screams and stinging and teeth and eyes.

When it gets dark but not dark, the blood and pus glows. It glows a bright blue in the lights from the sky. It's pretty and I can hear other things being dragged from the woods.

No date

It's been three days. Where did the days go? Where was I? I can't chew. My molars fell out. My skin feels so hot, like it's melting. Is this hell? I can hear hooves on the roof. It sounds like it has six legs. I counted the footfalls.

Is the devil here to collect his due?

No date

Holly was outside last night. The man behind her was too tall, and his head was too long. His eyes were too big too, and glowed like a cat's.

I closed the blinds again when the thing with antlers made of teeth walked past.

No date

It's been night. Night is rare now. No lights. When there are no lights, I can think and see. I can't bandage the blisters. The skin sticks. The other animals are dead or changed. I thought I heard a wolf's howl, but it changed onto a man's scream. Was it a changed wolf? Or a changed man?

No date

No supplies. Can't leave. Door is blocked by eyes. Eat? Eat. Eat hand? No. No teeth. The man took my teeth. How could he get in? The door is there and blocked by growling eyes.

No date

I saw the tall man again. He makes lights. He takes them and brings them back.

He doesn't want to take me. Doesn't need to. The wood on my door is wearing thin.

Need water. No water. Head fuzzy.

No date

Nails are long. Can't clip them, but it's okay. They'll fall out. Hand is sticking to pen. Paper is always wet. Wet like the calf. Beautiful baby boy. Holly's and Beatrice's and mine. Gone and buried and screaming.

No date

Holly was singing. The moon is lights.
Screaming calf. It has my face.

No date

She looks so beautiful in her white dress.

Open arms. Teeth. Eyes. The lights. Tall man. No sleep.

Why is my spine?

No date

I'll be with Holly again soon. Will open the door. Tall man isn't watching.

No date

Door open. Holly. Screams. Lights.

HELP ME HELP ME HELP ME HELP ME HELP ME HELP ME HELP HELP HELP HELPHELPHELPHELPHELP

Please make the screaming stop.

* * * * *

The next page was just a bloody handprint, like when a kid has dipped their hand in paint. It has kind of a yellowish ring around it. Given the other entries, I think that's either plasma or pus. I dunno if he moved his hand while doing it, but it kind of looks like it's been split down the middle.

Aside from the handprint, those last pages are covered in blood. This is why I bought the gloves.

I really don't know what to make of the journal. The blisters could be caused by some kind of radiation, and maybe radiation makes you hallucinate. What else would kill him and everything on his farm, and apparently in the surrounding area including the crops? But then where were the bodies?

It's all absurd, and the journal lends credence to the idea that he went crazy. But it's the only lead anyone's ever gotten, even if it was dismissed. Maybe I should head out to the farm. There may be more clues. Maybe I'll be able to find out what really happened. Maybe I can bring a Geiger counter to test the radiation theory.

Or maybe heading out there would mean running into whatever got Silas.

Foreword by Author Aneal Pothuluri

Biography: Aneal Pothuluri is an aspiring author who lives in Austin, Texas with his family and two dogs. He has a very deep love for all animals and has an affinity for writing stories with anthropomorphic characters- think *Redwall* and *Zootopia*. If that's your cup of tea, you can check out his short story, "The Medjay's Son" in the anthology, *A Sword Master's Tale* by Armoured Fox Press coming soon both online and in print. Aneal has a love for all types of fiction, and has dabbled in writing historical fiction, romance, and adventure. He is now making his horror writing debut in this anthology with more to come in the future.

Author's Note: I have been a fan of horror since I was very young. My love for the horror genre is something I inherited from my father. We would often bond watching scary movies together, which is why it has a special place in my heart. That being said, I had never actually written any horror until "The Scarecrow's Hat." It was new and exciting, and I am very grateful for the opportunity. I really love folklore, mythology, and urban legends from all around the world. I had the concept and design of this monster sitting around in my head for some time now, and the setting and story just fell into place around it. I truly hope you enjoy it!

"Whispers From the Void" was inspired by H.P. Lovecraft, of whom I am a big fan. This story was written as homage to him. I tried my best to write in a style similar to his, as well as explore themes and ideas that he often used in his works. Any other fans of Lovecraft should be able to spot the little nods and references in this story. For those of you who are not familiar with Lovecraft, I hope you will still enjoy the story, and I strongly encourage you to check out his works. Without further ado, *"That is not dead which can eternal lie. And with strange aeons even death may die."* Enjoy!

The Scarecrow s Hat by By Aneal Pothuluri

"Sarah, wait up!" Thomas shouted as he scrambled down the old weathered road.

"How many times do I have to tell you to get gone, Thomas Crenshaw!" Sarah fumed, quickening her pace.

"You gotta let me explain!"

She stopped dead in her tracks at this, giving Thomas just enough time to catch up. When he was a few feet behind her, Sarah turned on her heels and looked him in the eyes for the first time in a week.

"Explain what, exactly? Why you stood me up Saturday night, or why Mary Radley says she saw you sneaking out of Debbie Aultman's window!" It was more of an accusation than a question but that didn't stop Thomas from trying his best.

"Both! Sarah, I swear to you it's all a big pile of lies. Mary Radley's just after attention 'cause no one ever pays her no mind."

Sarah seemed to think this over for a moment. She almost wanted to believe him, but no, it couldn't be that easy.

"Oh yeah? Where were you then, huh?" She challenged him with newfound skepticism.

"I-my grandpa needed help out in the fields, that's all."

"At sundown?" Sarah's hazel eyes narrowed at the half-baked excuse.

"Yeah! He thought foxes might be gettin' in the chicken coops. He had me stay up all night tryin' to catch 'em in the act."

"If that's really true, then why didn't you just call to tell me?" Sarah asked, the frustration clear in her voice.

"I tried, but I couldn't get through to you. You know how hard it is to make calls out here."

"I...I really wish I could believe you, Thomas," Sarah weakened again, the hurt seeping out through the cracks in her resolve.

"Baby, please," Thomas started taking her hands in his and squeezing them tightly. "Just tell me what I gotta do to make things right. I swear I'd do anything for you."

Sarah stiffened at the sudden touch, but she didn't pull away. She just stared up at Thomas as if the answers she was looking for were hidden somewhere in those soft brown eyes of his.

"Anything?" her voice was soft and timid now; the lion had been reduced to a mouse.

Thomas smiled that perfect little smile that always got him out of trouble.
"Anything, baby, just name it."

Sarah pursed her lip and twirled a finger through her fiery red curls as she thought it over. "Alright I...I want the hat off the scarecrow on the old, abandoned Dupres farm."

Thomas' loving expression quickly turned to a look of confusion. "Of all the things, you want that dirty old scarecrow hat?"

"No one's ever done it before, and you know what people say about that place! If you can get me that hat it'll show me how devoted you are to me. Every kid in town'll be talking about it."

"Course I can get it. It's just a scarecrow."

"Maybe, maybe not," Sarah muttered.

Thomas tilted his head at her curiously. "You believe in all that hocus pocus?"

Sarah crossed her arms with a huff, reminding Thomas why the request was being made in the first place.

"Never you mind what I do or don't believe, Thomas! You just worry about getting me that hat!"

"Alright alright. I'm sorry."

"Just bring it to school tomorrow and give it to me at lunch in front of everyone," Sarah exclaimed. "That'll put an end to all this Debbie Aultman talk!"

That explained it all loud and clear. Sarah didn't really care about the hat or the scarecrow. She just wanted all the gossip to stop, and if there was anything that could make that happen, it'd be someone getting their hands on that damn hat.

"Alright, baby, I'll get it done. I love you, y'know?"

"I gotta get home, Thomas. I'll see you around," was all he got in response as Sarah left him alone on the empty old stretch of road.

He sighed and started his walk to the Dupres Farm. Guilt swelled up like a knot in his stomach. The truth was he had indeed been unfaithful. He still loved Sarah, at least he thought he did, but he was eager and hormonal, and like many boys his age, he had needs and urges. Sarah wanted to do the proper Christian thing and wait, something Thomas had agreed with at first, but as time went on, he found this arrangement increasingly frustrating. Then Debbie came along. Sweet, easy Debbie. She made everything so much better for a time. It was never serious. They both understood that perfectly. They'd sneak off and have their fun, and with his needs satisfied, Thomas was a much more agreeable boyfriend to Sarah. It went on like that for a month. Thomas was happy, Debbie was happy, and Sarah was happy, too. That is, of course, until she, along with the entire school, found out what Thomas was doing.

Now everything was so messy, and Thomas was beginning to realize what a mistake it had all been. He continued to think that fact over as he made his way to the old farm. It was a way he knew very well, actually. His grandfather's land was right next to the Dupres'. Thomas could remember spending many restless nights staring out of his bedroom window wondering if that old scarecrow was out there watching him, but he wasn't a child anymore. Now he saw that scarecrow for what it was: straw and cloth and dust…nothing more.

As Thomas finally made it to the small wooden fence that separated his family's land from the Dupres' he found himself more worried about the possibility of a snakebite rather than any old scarecrow. The Dupres' land was truly an eyesore; an unruly jungle of grass and weeds sprung up from every inch of the property, the worst of it stretching to two feet in height. Thomas didn't want to think about all the different types of nasty critters that could be waiting for him in there. He reminded himself that he was doing this for Sarah, and with a big gulp of courage, he started to climb over the fence. Unfortunately, he only managed to get one foot onto the property before a strong, leathery hand grabbed him by the collar of his shirt, and a rough, crackling voice rang out from behind him.

"Thomas!" The boy's grandfather shouted loudly, nearly sending Thomas jumping out of his own skin. "What in the hell do you think you're doing, Boy?!" the old man scolded as he pulled his grandson back over the fence.

Thomas tried to fight, but despite his age, the old farmer was much stronger than he. He wriggled in vain as his grandfather dragged him into the house. Once inside, Thomas was finally freed from his grandfather's grip.

"I have told you time and time again to stay away from that land! How many more times do you need tellin' before you start listenin'?"

"God dangit! I ain't a child no more!" Thomas began shouting before his grandfather's hard stare shut him up.

"Then you ought to stop actin like one, and don't you ever take the Lord's name in vain!"

Thomas mumbled out an apology as he stared at the floor, unable to meet his grandfather's oppressive gaze.

"What were you doing trying to get over that fence?"

"What's it matter?" Thomas huffed

"Boy, you better answer my question," the old man said coldly. Thomas knew that tone, and he knew better than to give any lip when his grandfather used it.

"I was gonna try to get the scarecrow's hat," he admitted, finally meeting his grandfather's eyes. To Thomas's surprise, that cold stare turned to an expression he'd never seen before. It was a solemn look with tinges of fear and something more, something deeper, the old man kept buried inside.

"Grandpa?"

"I was praying you wouldn't say that, but I knew it was coming," the old man answered in a defeated voice. "Sit down, boy. Let's have a talk."

Thomas followed his grandfather to the wooden table where they ate all their meals, and once they'd both sat down, his Grandfather spoke again.

"Why do you want that hat Thomas?" There was no anger in his voice now, just concern.

"I-I messed things up real bad with Sarah, and she said givin' her that hat's the only way I can make it right."

Thomas was surprised by his own honesty. He hadn't wanted to tell his grandfather any of it, but it just seemed to spill out. Thomas's grandfather sighed and began rubbing his temples.

"I know how much you like that girl, Thomas, but you can't do that."

"I have to."

"Go talk to Sarah tomorrow. Find another way to make things right. I won't let you do that. I *can't* let you do that."

"Why not? Why's everyone in this town so damn terrified of that dumb old scarecrow?" Thomas's voice peaked in frustration.

"Boy, how much do you know about that old farm?"

"Just stupid bedtime stories to scary little kids. Sarah's mom told her one night that scarecrow jumped off his post and gobbled up the Dupres in their sleep and that he'll do the same to any children who don't mind their elders," Thomas scoffed.

"So, you never did learn the real history of that place and that *thing*…that's my fault. I should have told you about it a long time ago. I guess I just didn't want to acknowledge it myself."

Thomas stared at his grandfather quizzically. The promise of an explanation managed to lessen his rising temper.

"It all started with Virgil and Edeline Dupres. They were a Haitian couple that moved here from Louisiana. From what people say they were kind, hard-working people. It was a different time, though, back when people didn't take kindly to seeing colored folk ownin' land, let alone see them prosper because of it. That bitterness and disgust just festered and slowly turned to rage and hate until, eventually, something evil happened. One night, the townspeople came in their white hoods with their torches and their clubs. They dragged Virgil Dupres out of his own home, and they tortured him. Then they hung him from the oak tree beside his house. Edeline had been visiting family in Louisiana at the time, and when she came back, the only thing waiting for her was her husband's remains swinging from a branch. They never convicted anyone. The police turned their back on it all and Edeline was inconsolable," Thomas's grandfather explained regretfully.

"The grief, anger, and fear all ate away at her until she just couldn't take it anymore. If the law wouldn't bring her justice, she'd get it another way. Unbeknownst to the rest of the town, Edeline Dupres practiced voodoo, and in her grief and rage, she started making that scarecrow. They say she stuffed it with talismans and mystical herbs. Wrapped it in cloth dipped in strange potions and even made it a costume out of different scraps of Virgil's clothes. And once it was finished, she put it on a post in front of the house.

She cut the throats of every last bit of livestock she owned at that scarecrow's feet, and with all that hatred and suffering and blood, they say she put a demon in that scarecrow.

Now, when word got around town that Edeline Dupres had been out there sacrificing animals and singing in a strange foreign language, people were up in arms. They swarmed the farm, planning to lynch Edeline just like her husband. They never laid a finger on her, though. They say that scarecrow sprung from its post and tore every last one of them up like an animal. Then it impaled their bodies on the branches of the oak tree Virgil was hanged by, all while Edeline sat on her porch and watched.

The people that remained in the town never bothered Edeline after that. She stayed in that house, mad and alone, until she finally drank herself to death. The bank sold the land many times over, but all the owners either died or fled soon after. Eventually people stopped buying, and the land was abandoned."

Thomas stared at his grandfather wide-eyed and slack-jawed. "You really believe that load of horse shit?" Thomas was flabbergasted. This was just absurd! Voodoo magic? A killer scarecrow? He felt like the only sane person in a town of gullible, superstitious fools.

His grandfather just sighed and shook his head before continuing. "I know. I thought it was nonsense when I was your age, too. Then one night I tried to steal that hat, myself."

Thomas' ears pricked at this. "What happened?"

The old man stared down at his clasped hands and took a shaky breath. "I didn't ever wanna have to tell anyone this story, especially you, but I can see it's something you're gonna need to hear. It was me and three other people. The whole thing had been Peter Barnette's idea. He'd always been a troublemaker despite being the son of our high school principal. Peter's younger brother, Andy, tagged along wherever Peter went. There was also Carol Ann Deats, a girl I was sweet on at the time," a faint smile spread across the old man's wrinkled lips as he remembered the girl from so long ago. "I was really only going to impress her. We were all gonna be the first kids in town to nab the scarecrow's hat. That's what we thought at least.

It was dark out when we all hopped the fence and started walking. Everything was normal for a while. Peter and Andy were walking ahead while I stayed in the back with Carol Ann. We were talking about school, joking with each other. Then Carol Ann noticed something odd. It was dead quiet out there. No crickets. No toads. No nothing. And in a place as overgrown as the Dupres' land, it just didn't add up. It spooked Andy something fierce, but we all just tried to forget it. Eventually after a good deal of walking and complaining, mostly on Andy's part, we made it to the scarecrow's post." Thomas watched as his grandfather's eyes turned glassy and his voice grew quiet and fearful as he continued. "It was so…unsettling up close. The thing was dressed in a moldy dark green shirt, ragged dirty blue pants, and a tattered maroon shoulder cape. The getup looked like it belonged more on some New Orleans voodoo man than a scarecrow. It had such an unnaturally long and thin body, and its head, *the thing's head*, was a pale, ghostly white stuffed sack tied tight with rope that coiled around its inhumanly long neck. It had long, dirty straw for hair. The only facial features the thing had was a long-stitched smile and another set of stitches higher up on the head that almost looked like a single shut eye. And on top was that damn hat. It was a large, wide-brimmed hat that was the same maroon color as the cape with two big black feathers sticking out of the side. The worst thing about it, though, was the way it was posed. The post was shaped like a large cross. The scarecrow's arms were tied to it by barbed wire. Its head was resting on its shoulder like some sick mockery of the crucifixion.

We all just stood and stared in awe and disgust at the thing until Peter finally piped up and snapped us all out of it.

The post was so tall that none of us could reach the hat on our own, so Peter had Andy climb on his shoulders to reach it while me and Carol Ann watched. That was fine by me. I didn't wanna get any closer to that thing. I was just glad we were gonna get the hat and get outta there, but just as Andy was about to reach it, he let out this terrible shriek and fell off his brother's shoulders flat onto the ground.

We all started cussing him out for scaring the life out of us when he started shivering and pointing at the scarecrow. That's when we all saw it. The thing was staring at us with a big, bloody red eye. The damn thing had an eye! It lifted its head off its shoulder with an awful cracking noise and just stared down at us with that single, piercing red eye. Then it opened its mouth with a wet tearing noise and took the shrillest, most bone chilling breath of air I've ever heard in my life. It was as if the thing hadn't used its lungs in decades. The thing started to jitter and writhe on that post until two hands burst out of its sleeves. The thing didn't have human hands. They looked more…more like giant crow's feet. I can still remember the way it wiggled those three sharp clawed fingers. Once it sprouted those hands, its back started to throb and pulse like its arms. Then a pair of big, feathery black wings burst out of the thing's back.

None of us moved a muscle the entire time. You may think us stupid for not bolting the moment that thing started to move, but understand this, until you've seen what I have, you'll never understand what that kind of terror does to your body. We were all paralyzed, and as much as our minds screamed for us to run, our legs just wouldn't listen. All we could do was watch like the helpless things we were.

As the barbed wire started to unravel and the monster dropped from its post, its body making more of those sickening cracks and pops as it stood, Andy managed to let out one more shriek that somehow freed us of our paralysis. The thing wrapped a large, clawed hand around the boy's head and leaped into the air, carrying Andy up with it. We were all in hysterics. Peter especially. He was screaming and crying, calling out Andy's name and begging for him back. Carol Ann was just mumbling to herself with this foggy look on her face. And all I can remember was screaming at the top of my lungs that we had to run. Eventually, the two of them realized I was right, so we ran as fast as we could.

We didn't make it far before Andy's body fell from the sky in front of us. Every bone in his body looked broken and there was so much blood. Peter started throwing up then, and while he was doubled over, that thing just swooped down and landed right on him. I didn't stay to watch what happened to him. I just grabbed Carol Ann's arm, and we kept running. We were so close I could just make out the wooden fence when Carol Ann's hand was yanked away from mine. I turned just in time to watch that monster drag her away." A pang of grief stabbed at the old farmer his voice grew full of shame and regret as he forced himself to keep talking. "For a moment I thought about going back for her, trying to fight that thing and save Carol Ann, but I knew that was suicide. No, I did the less noble thing. I kept on running until I hit that fence. I remember climbing over it and landing on my hands and knees on the other side, and when I turned around, there the thing was perched on the fence like a gargoyle.

I was sure this was it, that monster was gonna rip me apart, but it didn't. It just sat there on the fence staring at me with its single, bulging, hate-filled eye. Then it darted back towards the property. I managed to get to my feet just in time to watch it return to the fence with Carol Ann. She was alive. Both her legs were broken. It dropped her a few feet away from the fence and just stared at me. She tried to crawl, but the thing just pulled her back if she got too far. She was sobbing and begging me to help her. I took a single step towards her, but then I saw the eagerness in that monster's eye. I understood what it was doing. It was trying to lure me back onto the property because it couldn't leave.

I told Carol Ann I was sorry. Then I started stepping back. Once it knew I wasn't taking its bait, the scarecrow let out a wail like I've never heard before. It pounced on poor Carol Ann. It snapped both of her arms like twigs and once she couldn't defend herself, it tore into her with those talons. I watched helplessly while that monster tore the flesh off her beautiful face then it plucked out her eyes. She was alive for all of it. She was screaming my name and begging more to help her--then it took her tongue and she was quiet. Once she was gone, I watched it drag her body back towards the farmhouse." Tears welled in the old man's tired eyes. He stifled a sniffle as he wiped them away before finishing.

The police found all three of their bodies impaled on the dead oak tree the next morning. I was so scared they'd pin it all on me, but there was never an investigation. People knew what happened, and like they had so many times before, they turned a blind eye to it.

You can believe whatever you want, boy, but I know what I saw on the Dupres' farm that night. What I've just told you is the Lord's truth and it's why you're forbidden from ever setting foot on that property."

Thomas sat quietly, trying to process his grandfather's words. His head raced and his skeptical resolve started to waiver, but only for a moment. It was quite the tale, but that's all it was, just a tale, meant to scare a child into behaving. Thomas wasn't a child, and he saw through his grandfather's tricks, even if he still didn't know the reasons for it. He assured his grandfather that he understood and would never set foot on the property again.

* * * * *

Under cover of night, while his grandfather slept, Thomas snuck out and crossed the fence onto the abandoned land. He made his way to the old farmhouse where the scarecrow waited. To Thomas' unease, the thing was just how his grandfather had described, right down to that unsettling pose. His grandfather had gotten a lot of things right, in fact, like the dead silence of the area. Thomas shook away the paranoid thoughts. There was a simple explanation for all of it... his grandpa had indeed been on the farm, but he'd just chickened out... that was it.

Satisfied with that explanation, Thomas began climbing the wooden post like a tree. The hat was nearly in his grasp when he saw it--a single red veiny eye with a pale milky iris staring him down. He fell from the post with a terrified scream. As he lay there on the ground, coughing and trying to catch his breath, he realized just how wrong he'd been as the scarecrow's stitched mouth tore open into a large nightmarish grin.

Whispers from the Void by Aneal Pothuluri

To whom this letter finds its way, my name is Dr. Marcus R. Parson. I've worked as a psychiatrist at an institute known as Whippoorwill Mental Asylum for over seventeen years. My specialty was treating patients suffering from severe cases of psychosis. My time at Whippoorwill made me a confident man, then an arrogant man. I presumed to know the nature of reality and to understand the terrible delusions that plagued the men and women under my care, but now, I know the truth. I knew nothing. We humans know nothing of the world we inhabit, and believe me when I say, ignorance truly is bliss.

* * * * *

It was a patient who opened my eyes. He was a young man by the name of Kyle who admitted himself into Whippoorwill, claiming to be tormented by a creature that visited him while he slept. It was far from the most outlandish claim a patient had ever made, and Kyle did possess the clarity of mind to seek professional help, so I expected this case to be quite an easy one to treat.

My assumptions were proven wrong the moment I laid eyes on Kyle. His delusions had clearly taken a toll on him. He was severely frail and malnourished, his hair was both prematurely greying and thinning, and large patches of his skin seemed to be breaking out in a strange rash. The worst part, however, seemed to be his eyes: two bloodshot little orbs sunken into his dark, tired sockets. They regarded me with a chillingly blank, haunted, stare that seemed to steal the voice from my throat. Seventeen years, seventeen long years I worked with all manner of troubled souls within the walls of Whippoorwill, and yet, the look in that young man's eyes was one of the few things that ever truly affected me. I must have stood there frozen in that room for at least a minute before Kyle broke the silence.

"Are you here to make me sane?" He inquired in a dull drone.

I must have blinked several times before even registering the question.

"I'm…my name is Dr. Parson, and I'm here to help make you better Kyle," I answered as professionally as I could despite the uneasy feeling that lingered under my skin.

"I don't believe I can ever be better, Doctor," Kyle said turning his gaze to a corner of the room. "It has made sure of that for me."

"This monster of yours, yes? Tell me about it," I asked feeling more in control with the patient's eyes no longer boring into me so.

"Monster is too kind a word for it, but there is no word that wouldn't be. It torments me. Every night it drags me further down into madness. That's why I'm here, Doctor. It's driven me here."

"And how exactly did these episodes first begin?" I questioned further.

"I first encountered the thing one month ago, but to understand how it all started I must go back a bit further. I don't recall exactly when, but some time in my adolescence I learned how to control my own dreams. Once I learned how to tell a dream apart from reality, I was free to do as I pleased. I created elaborate fantasies for myself. I could make the world bend to my will! It was as though I became a God every night as my head fell upon the pillow. Eventually however, I grew tired of the same experiences every night. I began exploring the edges of these dream worlds just to see how far they would take me, and just like that, one month ago I drifted too far. One moment I was soaring through the bright and wonderful glow of the cosmos, then the next all was dark and empty. I was alone in a void of nothingness, with no sense of direction to get me back. I tried to will myself somewhere, anywhere, away from this horrible abyss, but it wouldn't work. I could not leave, and I could not wake up. I must have panicked because soon I found myself crying out into the darkness for help, and then I felt *it*. A presence, someone or *something*, there with me in that lightless void. I tried with all my might to will myself awake as I sensed the thing drawing ever closer. I cried out as I felt the thing's talons exploring my face, and then thankfully, mercifully, I woke from my hellish nightmare. I had never been so relieved in my tiny, insignificant life to see the familiar and utterly uninteresting sight of my bedroom wall, and yet, in that moment it was the most comforting thing I could lay eyes upon."

He gulped and starred at me pitifully. I realized he was nearly in tears.

"Unfortunately, that comfort was swiftly replaced by panic when I became aware of the fact I could not move, no matter how hard I tried. I was paralyzed, and as terrible as a feeling it was, it was just the beginning of the horrors I endured that first night. Just like in the void, I began to feel that strange and foreboding presence intrude the safety of my room. That's when I saw it for the first time: A tall, emaciated, *thing* as black as the night itself. It stood in the corner of the room watching me."

Now the young man was visibly shaking; chilled by the very memory.

"When it started shambling towards my bedside that I understood how wrong its form truly was. It had legs that bent back like a goat or dog and ended in these terrible clawed feet. Its arms were far too long, and its hands seemed big enough to wrap around my head as if it were a mere apple. It walked upright like a man at first. It was awkward and unsteady, but as it reached my bed it righted itself and began crawling on all fours like a gorilla. In the moonlight I could see its skin: black and shriveled like a mummy. It leaned forward craning its horrible head down at me. It looked humanoid for the most part, except for the face. The thing had no eyes, ears, or nose, only a small perfectly circular hole that seemed to serve as its mouth. The thing was mere inches away from my own face, and yet I still could not move. I was certain it was going to kill me. Instead the thing did something far crueler. It crouched down low beside my head, leaned in close, and whispered in my ear. It spoke the most horrible, mind warping, truths, truths that man was never meant to hear. All night it shared its cruel secrets with me, only ceasing when the first rays of sun began to peak over the horizon. Then it slipped back into the void it crawled out of, leaving my broken mind to put itself back together."

He gulped audibly, trembling like a leaf in a rainstorm.

"Every night since then it has come back repeating the same nightmarish routine. Paralyzing me, filling my head with madness, and only freeing me as the sun rose. It is killing me, Doctor! Slowly but surely it is killing me! Every word it speaks is like another drop of poison in my ear! This is no way to live. I cannot eat, I cannot sleep, I cannot silence the terrible things that abomination has put in my head! I can't go on like this. I'm so very tired. Do you understand now, Doctor? I am not here because I see imaginary monsters. I am here because of the twisted truths this cruel thing has told me."

Quite the vivid and imaginative hallucination, to be sure. I'd never heard of a case quite like Kyle's. After listening to my patient's tale, one question prodded my mind more than any other.

"And what sort of things did this creature tell you exactly?"

Kyle's haunted eyes shut tight at my question.

"I dare not repeat the things I was told for the sake of my sanity and that of anyone who might hear. No, I will take this knowledge to my grave, and it will be the greatest kindness I'll ever do!"

Despite my efforts to explain how imperative it was that I know all the details if I was to help him, Kyle was unshakable in his insistence to secrecy. In the end, I abandoned any hope of getting any more information from him, so I decided to make his physical health my priority. I had the nurses make sure he was well fed, and I prescribed him a mild sedative to ensure he didn't lose any more valuable sleep. He fought back quite furiously against the latter, but with some effort, we did manage to sedate him.

Despite our best efforts, over the following days Kyle's condition only seemed to worsen. It was perplexing, to say the least. That is, until the night that changed everything.

I was on my way out after an especially long night when I heard the most peculiar noises coming from Kyle's room. If I had known what was waiting behind that door, I don't believe I would have had the courage to open it, but that's exactly what I did. I remember turning on the light as I called out to my patient. The words caught in my throat as I laid eyes on the nightmarish *thing* hunched over the side of his bed. It was exactly as Kyle had described it, yet his words did no justice in explaining just how terrible its twisted form truly was.

Kyle lay in bed jibbering as the thing whispered to him. His eyes were rolled back into his head, and blood leaked from his ears and nose. I don't think I'll ever forget the look on his face. Fear, agony and, sorrow all showed through that pitiful expression. His body spasmed three times before he let out a single choked groan, and then he was still. The creature promptly stopped its whispering then and its eyeless face simply stared down at poor Kyle's corpse.

Then, it turned its head slowly to where I stood, still frozen in the doorway. It tilted its head at me like a curious dog, and even without eyes it felt as though the thing was staring into my very soul. With its face still locked on me, it backed away slowly into the corner. It melded into the wall and--just like that--I was alone.

* * * * *

Kyle's death was attributed to a brain aneurysm, and with no next of kin to claim him he was laid to rest in the cemetery on Whippoorwill grounds. I resigned from my position shortly after the experience. I no longer had any grasp on what was reality or delusion.

I still wonder if Kyle was the only patient at Whippoorwill who truly did experience what he claimed to. I also think of that creature far more than I wish to. I wonder about the things it told poor Kyle. What could be so terrible to drive a man to death? I am eternally grateful he never shared them with me.

Sleep rarely comes easily to me these days. I fear one night I might awaken to that blank, inhuman face staring down at me. Alcohol and morphine serve as my only solace now. They will most likely be the death of me, but I've made peace with that, and so I leave you all with a warning...

Be wary of places left unexplored. There are wicked things waiting in the darkness, and they know such horrible things that would tear your mind apart. Pray they never whisper in your ear. Pray you don't suffer the same fate as Kyle.

\

Foreword from Author Caleb Wilkerson

Biography: Caleb Wilkerson is an author from Illinois, USA. Although he has published several articles in the American online media company *The Odyssey*, the *Wicked Writing* horror anthology holds his first fictional published work. Caleb serves as a Staff Sergeant in the United States Air National Guard with one deployment to the Middle East under his belt, and proudly holds a degree in Criminal Justice from Rend Lake College. Time spent apart from military service and writing is spent drumming for the Southern Illinois based rock band Memories Made.

Author's Note: Having been a member of the *Chilling Tales For Dark Nights* community for a long while, I was very excited when the crew, along with the brilliant Meagan J. Meehan, offered the chance to take part in a horror writing class and ultimately publish the results. I honestly believe her advice has improved my writing exponentially, and I can't thank her enough. The combined motivation from my supportive friends and family has kept me from losing my dream of becoming a published author. A short story among many others in this anthology may not sound like much to some, but to me it means I'm checking an item off of my bucket list. In the time that has passed since the writing of this story, I have put several more ideas onto paper. So, if you like what you read here, keep your eyes open for more. *They Need Help* came from a part of my mind I'm sure I share with you, reader. A morbid fascination for realistic horror. The idea of a haunted "Insane Asylum" has been done again and again, but that knowledge does little to a horror fan who so much as drives past one. Thoughts immediately go to a place of ghosts and ghouls deriving from literature and cinema of popular entertainment. Every author of the horror genre has his or her own ghost story, and this one is mine. I asked myself; "What can I do different?" and They Need Help was my answer. Thank you for reading, and I hope you read my work again.

They Need Help by Caleb Wilkerson

Shawn took one last drag of his cigarette. He didn't smoke regularly, but this occasion nearly called for one. It had been years since his last job interview, and it was all he could do to stop his hands from shaking. He looked at the cigarette and remembered the time he had promised his parents to never do such a thing. Now he wished he had time to start another one. The numbers on the dash of his car read 0754. Time to go inside. Shawn flicked his cigarette and collected his papers, stepped outside, and took a deep breath. He read the massive steel banner atop the building. Although the place seemed surprisingly well kept and the banner said "Grassy Plains Behavioral Health Center," he could see only dark clouds, a bolt of lightning, and the words "Insane Asylum". He knew these places rarely called themselves that anymore, but deep down they were one in the same.

Shawn made it inside the building and was greeted by a friendly nurse at the reception desk who directed him to the security office. An older man, Shawn guessed to be around sixty, introduced himself as Earl Fitzpatrick: Chief of Security. "How are you today, Shawn?"

Shawn was almost surprised hearing this. For many years he practically had no first name. "I'm fine sir, how are you?"

"Why do you seem so shocked? Forget your name?"

"No sir, I'm just used to being called Myers. That's all."

"Ah, right, you're a military guy," Earl said, unimpressed. He stared blankly at Shawn and looked down at the paper, as if something didn't quite add up.

"How old are you again, Mr. Myers?" he asked.

"Twenty-four, sir."

"Damn, and with a resume like this? How are you twenty-four if you spent five years in the Air Force? Did you join at fifteen or something?"

"Seventeen, sir. There wasn't much of a job market where I'm from and they said they'd pay for my college so I signed right up."

"Did they? Pay for your college, I mean?"

"Yes sir. All four years. I did it all online while I was stationed in England."

"I see," he said and shuffled his papers. "Well, let's get down to it. I have to say, your resume is quite impressive. Five years Security Specialist in the Air Force, one tour in Iraq, Bachelor's in Applied Science of Criminal Justice," Earl removed his glasses and put the resume on the table in front of him. "Seems to me like you're a little over qualified to be a security guard at a hospital. What the hell makes you want to work here?"

Shawn thought for a moment before responding. "No offense, Mr. Fitzpatrick, but I've been through a lot over the past couple years and figured I would work a job with a little less stress. Maybe one day I'll go on to become a cop or something, but for now hospital security seems like a bit of a break for me."

"I see," said Earl. He looked away from Shawn and back to his papers.

"You were discharged under less than honorable conditions, Mr. Myers. Now I guess you don't have to elaborate on that but I have to say I'm curious."

Shawn heard the question Earl didn't ask.

"Well, sir, um…I was seven months into my second tour overseas when my wife, Chloe, was in an accident. She was driving during a severe thunderstorm and ran into a tree across the road." Shawn gulped and struggled to shoo away a tear he felt forming. "She didn't die. Not right away, at least. She was in critical condition though and I tried to get home, I tried so hard. But my request wasn't approved in time and she... succumbed to her injuries. I couldn't get out of Iraq. I missed the funeral. The second I saw my commander I punched him as hard as I could, right across his face, for denying my leave. I know it was wrong, I just couldn't help myself. So, when I finished my tour, they gave me the boot."

Earl looked at him with interest. He dropped his gaze and muttered something like "I'm sorry to hear that." Then Earl sat up straight again and said: "Look, we're dying for some good people here. You seem like you'll fit the bill. I'm gonna skip all the normal interview mamba jamba and say this; I like you!" He threw his hands into the air to exaggerate his point. "I want you here. In fact, I would like to make you an offer you can't refuse. I'm old as dirt, there is no denying that. I've been wanting to retire for fifteen years, I just can't find anyone the hospital admins find worthy to run this pile when I leave. Yeah, I have a few guys working under me already but *you*! You seem like you would fit the bill. This may be more than you bargained for, but I'd like to offer you my job as the Chief of Security. Of course, the hospital administration will have to approve it and all but I think I can work some magic. Hell, they'll be happy to get me out. What d'ya think?"

"Uh, Mr. Fitzpatrick, I don't know, that seems like a lot. I mean I've never even been here before. How am I supposed to run all of this?"

Earl chuckled. "It's nothing! It's mostly making schedules and other paperwork. I'll show you the ropes, you'll get it in no time." When Shawn didn't answer, he went on. "You still seem unsure, so how about this. I'll talk this all over with the admins and see what they think. If they like it, it's yours. If not, well, we'll hire you as an officer anyway. It's a win-win for you! How 'bout it?"

Shawn thought hard but not long before agreeing to the terms. The two men shook hands and agreed to stay in touch.

* * * * *

Shawn got a call less than forty-eight hours later. The admins were apparently just as impressed with Shawn's resume as Earl was, and the job was his, if he accepted it. Shawn did accept the job and returned to the hospital for the paperwork and training. In the meantime, Shawn used Chloe's life insurance to fund the seventy-mile move to Cambria from his home in Millertown. He settled down in a rather large three-bedroom house on an acre of land a short drive from the hospital. It was a house Chloe would have loved.

The death of Chloe had made Shawn what some might consider a rich man, at least in rural Pennsylvania. All of his belongings were transferred with the help of his brothers and a couple friends and after the last box had been unpacked, the group went out for a celebratory drink. It felt good to Shawn. He hadn't quite been himself since his discharge, and his friends knew it. They had a good night at the bar, but Shawn had something else on his mind. He almost felt bad for moving so far away from Chloe's resting place as it was routine to visit her grave often. But he found other ways to cope.

* * * * *

Shawn began his first unsupervised shift on a warm April Monday. While walking from his car he noticed a figure in a window to his left. About six windows away he could make out a young man, perhaps his own age, looking at Shawn from the West Wing. Shawn waved hello to the man. In return, the man motioned for Shawn, as if to say "come here". The man's face was emotionless. Shawn ignored this gesture and continued walking.

Upon entering the hospital, he was greeted at the desk by the same nurse that gave him directions to the security office the day of his interview. He learned her name was Riley. She had greeted him almost every day of his training and had once even winked when he passed by. She was beautiful: a young, thin, brown-haired woman, and Shawn was convinced she had a crush on him. He felt a twinge of guilt for being so attracted to her.

"Hi, Mr. Myers" she said flirtingly.

"Please, call me Shawn. I like it better. I went five years by the name Myers and, believe me, those weren't my best days." He said this with a wide smile, showing off his white teeth, courtesy of Air Force Dental.

With a cute giggle, she replied "Okay! So, *Shawn*, a few people and I are going to The Cozy Table for lunch. Want to come? It'll be good for you to meet more of the staff and just relax, you always seem so uptight! I know, I know, the military does that to you. Anyway, you should come."

Shawn gave his best smile. "I don't know Riley. I'd love to but-"

Shawn was interrupted by a scream.

"HELP! THEY NEED HELP! THEY NEED HEEELLLLLPPP!"

Shawn sprinted toward the source, an old woman standing at the end of the hallway waving her cane around while she screamed.

"What's wrong? Who needs help? Where?"

A laugh came from behind the woman, and Shawn bolted up to see a middle-aged white doctor approaching. Shawn stood bewildered as the man grabbed the old woman's shoulders and walked her into the third room away--all the while she kept hollering.

Shawn then realized that it wasn't just the doctor cracking up, but also Riley and the other nurses at the reception desk. Shawn blushed with equal parts embarrassment and confusion. He could hear the doctor in

141

the room quietly speaking to the old woman, who had finally stopped her rant, before he re-emerged into the hallway.

"Sorry for laughing Chief! I'm Dr. Jansen."

He held out a hand that Shawn shook, still confused.

"Uh, hi. I'm-"

"Mr. Myers! Chief of Security. The Army man!"

Shawn was about to speak when Riley came to his side and spoke for him. "That's Air Force man to you! And call him Shawn. He likes that better."

"My apologies, 'Shawn he likes that better'." Shawn laughed more out courtesy than humor.

"No, don't worry about it. Uh, what just happened?"

"Oh that?" asked Dr. Jansen as he started to laugh again. Even Riley chuckled. "That's Mildred. She's been here longer than I have." He sighed, then continued. "That's just what she does. Take your eyes off of her for more than a minute and there she goes, screaming for help. She's a permanent patient. She fell off of a horse in the early '90s and developed some brain damage. She's selectively mute."

"She sure is loud for a mute person."

"*Selectively* mute, Shawn. It means she *can* talk, she just doesn't," Riley explained. "Nobody really knows why. It usually develops at a young age in children but I guess she's a different story. Our best guess is that it's a result of the head trauma. In fact, her family thought she was completely mute before they brought her here. That cry for help is the only thing she says. It happens every day, I'm surprised you haven't encountered it yet."

"Wow," Shawn said when he could think of nothing better. Nobody said anything after this. Before the silence became awkward, Shawn added: "Well that's my health lesson for today. I better get to my office. I'll see you guys around."

"So, I'll see you at lunch?" asked Riley.

"Yeah, yeah I'll see you at lunch."

The following couple hours were quite uneventful save for some paper work, just as Earl had promised. As noon rounded the corner, Shawn leaned back in his seat and flipped open his wallet to reveal a picture of Chloe, worn from all the times he had removed and replaced it. She had made her way into his mind, as she often did, and Shawn sighed. He liked Riley. In his mind, that was not a good thing. When the news came of Chloe's passing, he had pledged his heart to her, silently promising to remain faithful to their marriage despite his widower status.

Doesn't that seem a little ridiculous now? He thought to himself and then felt guilty for even considering it. *What am I thinking? It's just lunch with coworkers, not a date!*

"Hey you!" Shawn nearly jumped out of his skin at the sound, dropping his wallet onto the floor. It was Riley at the doorway. He smiled and stood, reaching a hand to wipe a tear he just noticed was there.

"I'm sorry! Are you okay? Is this a bad time?"

"No, no it's just, uh, allergies."

"It is that time of year... Anyway, are you still up for lunch?"

Shawn bent down to retrieve his wallet. "Yeah, I suppose so."

The pair walked out together and made it to the lot before Shawn realized they were walking alone.

"Where's everyone else?"

"Huh? Oh, they couldn't come. Tyrese got tied up with a patient and Maddison brought her lunch, which is weird. We always go to The Cozy Table on Mondays."

"So, it's just us."

"Yep. If that's okay. I don't want to make you uncomfortable. But I know you've been here since seven o'clock cooped up in that office all day. You've got to be dying for something to eat."

Shawn couldn't help thinking just how beautiful Riley really was. He had never seen her in good light, and she seemed even thinner, athletic even, with a gorgeous smile and picture-perfect teeth. The scrubs she wore seemed like they were made for her, fitting tight to her body. Standing about three inches shorter than Shawn himself made her a tall woman, and if he had to guess her age it would be no older than twenty-three. He shook off the guilt building up.

"I'm starving."

* * * * *

They took Riley's Ford Focus after Shawn stated he had no clue as to the route. The Cozy Table was a small family diner in town, and in it the two ate. Riley spoke little about herself, more interested in Shawn's story. In all fairness, his was more interesting. Shawn spoke little about his early life, sparing Riley the boredom, and instead started his story with his military career. He talked about his time stationed in Europe and his tour in Iraq, sparing the details of his wife and her death. Not because he didn't want her to know, rather because it pained him to talk about. Especially to another girl on what had mistakenly become what seemed like a lunch date. He ended it with the moment he first walked in the doors of the hospital, assuming she knew the rest, purposely jumping over the part of the story which he left the military hoping she wouldn't ask. All the while Riley remained as upbeat and flirty as he knew her to be. Shawn made a conscious effort to not reciprocate the flirting, while subconsciously being friendly and not fully turning her away. To the uninformed individual this may have seemed like Shawn was playing hard to get, but in his mind, he just couldn't bring himself to resist her temptation.

Riley's demeanor grew serious. "Shawn, do you believe in ghosts?"

Shawn nearly choked on his food.

"Uh, yeah I suppose I do," he replied, "Do you?"

"Well… I don't know. Have you ever seen one?"

"No."

"Then why do you believe in them?"

Shawn gulped and prepared himself for his answer. "See… I once lost someone very close to me. Before then I never did believe but," he fought back a tear, "after their passing I guess I *wanted* to believe. I wanted to believe in spirits because, well, maybe she was one. And maybe she follows me around. Maybe she's still right next to me. That's why I believe. It just makes me feel a little better knowing her soul is still around me."

"Oh. That's deep. Have you tried to contact them? You know like a seance or a Ouija board or something?"

Shawn shook his head. "See, I wasn't there when she needed me. I'm afraid of what she might say if I did communicate with her. Besides, the only thing I would know to say is that I'm sorry, and if she's a ghost that follows me around, she already knows that."

"That's so sad. Do you mind if I ask who it was?"

Shawn was silent for a moment before lying. "My grandmother. We were real close."

"I'm sorry to hear that, Shawn. I didn't mean to bring anything up. The only reason I ask is because, well, there are a lot of people who believe that our hospital is haunted."

"It's an 'insane asylum' of course it's haunted. Have you ever seen a horror movie?"

She blushed, perhaps a little embarrassed. "Yeah, I guess. But I have to say that it can get pretty spooky at night."

"Have you ever seen a ghost?"

"No. But I had to cover one of Maddison's night shifts one time. And I swear I kept hearing noises from the West Wing. Not footsteps or stairs creaking but, like, screaming and crying. I know that stuff like that isn't uncommon in a hospital, but this was different. I don't know how but it was. It was only me and a couple other nurses and Dr. Jansen. I tried to talk to them about it but they acted like they had no idea what I was talking about. But I swear it's true."

* * * * *

When the bill came, they both reached for it, touching hands for only a second. Their eyes met, and Shawn quickly removed his hand, the check still in it.

"Oh Shawn, let me pay! It was my invitation. Besides you're new. Call it a welcoming gift."

Shawn almost argued that it was the gentleman thing to pay for a meal. But he didn't. *This isn't a date.*

He slowly handed the bill back to Riley, expecting a surprised look that he had given up so easily, but no such look was given. She simply smiled and took it to the counter.

* * * * *

The following two weeks yielded nothing out of the ordinary. Warm days kept coming, Mildred kept screaming, and Riley kept flirting. They had gone to The Cozy Table two other times, and she had even come to Shawn's house after a particularly busy day under the guise of returning the office keys he had dropped in the lot. She had been exiting the hospital just behind him when his keys dropped. She tried to yell for his attention but was unable to get it. Shawn was shocked to see her pull into his driveway moments after he did.

"Hey handsome! Hope you don't mind I followed you home, you dropped your keys!"

Shawn stopped in the doorway and took them from her hand and thanked her for bringing them.

"My mom used to say I would lose my head if it wasn't attached. Thanks again, really, I appreciate it."

"Don't mention it," she replied. "I'm sure you would do the same for me."

She took a step back to admire Shawn's home. "Wow! Shawn, you have such a nice house! How many bedrooms is it?"

"Three."

"Oh my. And you live here all alone?"

"Yes."

"I see. I know how it is to come home after a long day like today. To an empty house. Eat dinner alone. It really gets to me sometimes, you know? You ever feel that way?"

Shawn knew the feeling all too but only shrugged in response.

"Well I'll leave alone," said Riley after a deep breath, hanging her head and playing with the gravel at her feet, "I'll see you in the morning."

As much as Shawn tried to refrain from giving in to her flirty persona, he couldn't help it this time. Inviting her in, at least for a little while, seemed like it was just the right thing to do, even for a man with a dead wife.

"Hey," he said just before Riley got back to her car, "I can't just not invite you in. Why don't you come inside, just for a bit? I'll give you a tour, maybe you can stay for dinner if you'd like."

"Well…," she said with a sarcastic thinking face, "I guess I could stay for a little while." She excitedly hurried to the door, and Shawn let her in.

* * * * *

After a tour of the two bedrooms he used for a study and for storage, they moved along to the living area, the screened in back porch, the dining room, and lastly the kitchen. It was at this point that Riley asked: "So you aren't going to show me your bedroom?"

Shawn didn't want to explain to Riley that he had pictures of Chloe and other personal items in the room he wasn't sure he wanted her to see. Instead he decided to make an excuse something along the lines of the bed was unmade but before he could, she said playfully: "That's alright. Maybe you can show it to me after dinner."

He couldn't be sure if she was genuinely interested in seeing the room or if she meant that sexually, but the latter scared him.

Maybe scared isn't the right word. In fact, he wanted her. Despite his best effort, he just could not resist Riley's charm. She was just so… perfect. It almost felt like his high school days, when he and Chloe had first started seeing each other. In another world Shawn would have pounced at the opportunity to have a relationship with such a fine woman. But these were special circumstances. He had already pledged his heart to another woman, and that is what scared him. He may not be able to fulfill his promise; if Riley tried to sleep with him tonight, he would oblige.

Shawn threw together his mother's recipe for Manicotti. He ate it slowly. He was still playing out what possible scenario might occur after they were done. Riley had removed her blouse and now sat across him in a white tank top. She stated that it was warm which struck Shawn as odd; he liked to keep it cool in the house.

"That was delicious, Shawn!"

"Well, what can I say, my grandparents are Italian."

Riley giggled loudly at this. They sat for a moment, just smiling at each other.
Suddenly, Riley leaned against the table and played with her hair, revealing at least two inches of cleavage.

"So… about showing me the bedro-" she was interrupted by Shawn's work cell. He was both relieved and frustrated to hear the ringing but answered it nonetheless.

"Hello," he said into the phone.

"Chief? Chief it's Payne. There's been an emergency at the hospital. It was Mildred. God, she went bat shit crazy! And I don't mean crazy like normal crazy, that's why the old bitch is here in the first place!"

"Well? What's going on? Do I need to come over?"

"Yeah Chief we're gonna need ya."

Shawn looked at Riley, who seemed disappointed. He pulled the phone away from his ear, pointed at it, and mouthed *It's work. Sorry.* She waved a dismissive hand before getting up to put on her top.

"Alright Payne I'll be there soon. And god damnit stop calling me Chief. It's just Shawn!"

He hung up the phone and walked Riley to her car. "I'm sorry about this. I still hope you had a pleasant evening."

"I understand," she said, "duty calls."

They stood awkwardly for a few seconds before Riley hugged Shawn around the neck, standing on her tiptoes to do so, and then saying goodbye.

* * * * *

Payne was standing outside the main entrance when Shawn pulled in. Payne was a short lanky man of twenty-one years that Shawn didn't much care for. He seemed lazy and rarely shaved his face no matter how patchy his hair came in. He was hired as a security guard just days after Shawn started his new position and seemed a little intimidated by Shawn.

"What's the deal, Payne?"

"Well Chief, uh, I mean Shawn, Mildred. She was screaming 'Help, they need help" over and over! So, when Dr. Andrews went to go talk her down, she stabbed her! The old bag stabbed Dr. Andrews right in the face with a fork from dinner!"

149

They started to run into the building. "Where's Andrews now?"

"EMS took her as I was calling you. She's at the ER now, I'm sure she'll be fine, but Mildred got her right in the cheek. My God you won't believe the blood."

They rounded the corner into Mildred's room to find her missing.

"Well where the fuck is she?"

"She took off. She still had the fork and before we could get Dr. Andrews out of the room, she busted her window with her cane and booked it."

Shawn kicked his foot against the bed.

"You expect me to believe a woman who can barely walk jumped out of the window and ran off?"

"We weren't exactly worried about that, Shawn, we had a bleeding doctor to worry about!"

"Alright make sure this mess gets cleaned up. Call in the rest of the security team, ask them to come in. We have to find her."

Only four of the six officers cared enough to roll out of bed to aid in the search. The first evening yielded no results. Shawn knew the woman couldn't have gotten far. She was old and brittle and walked with a cane for crying out loud. The search during the second evening was composed of local PD and volunteers who had more luck. Shawn received a call Wednesday night not two hours after his chaotic shift. They found her.

* * * * *

Shawn met a Cambria police detective in front of the hospital and explained that Mildred was found in a field just shy of two miles from the hospital. She was discovered at the bottom of a steep hill with a broken neck. The story was that she must have walked the distance, an astonishing feat for a woman in her condition, until she met the steep decline,

150

where she lost for footing and tumbled down like Jack and Jill. It was the detective who made that comparison, laughing while he said it. The detective had likely seen dead bodies before, but Shawn had seen the process. More than once during his time in Iraq had he seen a man take his last breath. Shawn didn't laugh.

The following evening, Shawn's day off, Payne called in. Shawn wasn't surprised that all other officers were "unable" to cover, so he took it upon himself. Payne was set to work a night shift, something Shawn had not done yet. He had also never done a routine patrol, outside of the military, of course. His job so far had been just as Earl Fitzpatrick had told him it would be: a lot of schedule making and paperwork. The thought of actually getting to patrol the grounds excited Shawn, he was just beginning to think he couldn't handle sitting at the desk anymore.

He got there at ten that evening and began walking along the East Wing of the hospital. It was storming horribly; a storm like the one that took Chloe.

Walking along he told himself he wouldn't, but he couldn't help stopping when he passed Mildred's room. He looked up and down the hallway to check for any observers before unlocking the door and shutting it behind him. Turning on a flashlight, Shawn scanned the room, not sure what it was he hoped to find. He looked at everything left to right before something caught his eye. A white piece of paper stuck out from the end of a pillowcase. Puzzled, Shawn picked it up. From what he knew, Mildred had lost her fine motor skills years ago.

The chicken-scratch handwriting read: *West Wing needs help, THEY NEED HELP!!*

The paper interested him. He could count on one hand how many times he had gone into the West Wing of the hospital. From what he understood, those patients were the worst of the worst as far as condition. Most of the patients

151

on that side had such severe mental health problems that they were so doped up until they couldn't walk or talk.

But then Shawn remembered what Riley had told him the first day they went to lunch. That she heard screaming and crying. Was it possible that Mildred was hearing the same sounds, all the way in the East Wing? Surely, if an old woman could hear it, it would be loud enough to alert the staff. Unless she was right about the ghosts. This was an old hospital, and surely many patients had died there.

Putting the piece of paper in his pocket, he thought: *Maybe I'll go check it out. After all, it is my duty to investigate.*

He exited the room as stealthy as he entered and made his way toward the West Wing. An older nurse was just walking out of the wing when Shawn approached and he decided to wait until she was out of sight before he went in.

After walking down the hallway, he immediately realized that this area of the hospital was not kept up as nicely as the rest. Dust covered the floor and a faint putrid smell filled his nostrils. Sure, this section wasn't visited as often, but it should still be treated the same by maintenance. Shawn had just stepped passed the fifth room when the lights flickered. From outside he heard a loud crash of thunder just before the lights went out completely. It only took a few seconds before they came back on, but they were much dimmer now. *Must be the backup generator.*

He kept walking. He could definitely tell what Riley was talking about. Of course, the dim lights had something to do with it but it was creepy as all hell in that place.

Shawn turned a left corner to see a boy around age twelve about twenty feet down the hall. Shawn jumped, startled by this. The boy had long scars all across his stomach and was bleeding from the head. A grown man with a medical uniform painted with blood and a face that was impossible to see in the darkness stepped out from an open door behind the boy and the boy began screaming loudly before charging at Shawn. He turned quickly and fled the way he came, only to run into a middle-aged woman slumped, seemingly dead in a wheelchair. She hadn't been there just moments earlier! Her hair was white and her eyes were sunken deep into their sockets. Shawn jerked in time to avoid falling directly onto her but tripped over the footrest on the front of her chair and caught himself just before his face met the floor. His flashlight flew from its place on his belt and rolled away from him, but Shawn paid it no mind. The woman in the chair began to scream just as the boy was. The screams were so loud!

Shawn kept running. Every room he passed revealed a face at the window, all beating on the glass and screaming: *"Help! We need help!"* except one black man who laughed maniacally while pounding his head on the small window, leaving bloody cracks in the glass. Ahead a hand busted through the glass of a door and caught Shawn by the shirt. Shawn desperately fought to get it free and pulled himself away so hard that his shirt began to rip. The man on the other side of the door released his grip and Shawn fell to the floor. Another rip of thunder crashed and the lights went out again.

Shawn laid on the ground in a panic. It was pitch black save for the emergency exit signs on either end of the endless hallways. All around Shawn could hardly hear himself think over the roar of cries for help. He could hear the boy he ran from getting closer and this was the motivation he needed to finally get to his feet and run blindly toward the distant red glow. He wasn't even sure he was running in the right direction, but was too afraid to run along the wall for fear that he would be caught in another man's grip. Trying his best to run in the center of the hall, the glowing exit sign grew closer and Shawn knew he was approaching the end.

The lights flickered on, and Shawn had never felt so happy. He bolted out of the hallway doors, passed the reception desk, and out into the parking lot. He stopped only when he got to his car. He couldn't just leave, could he?

He took a moment to catch his breath. He was breathing dangerously hard and could feel every beat of his heart thumping wildly in his chest. He tried his hardest to calm himself and slid against his car until his bottom hit the pavement.

I didn't even run this hard on my last PT test.

"Shawn! Shawn are you okay?" It was Dr. Jansen, running worriedly toward Shawn from inside. He was followed by a nurse Shawn had never met before. Shawn said nothing at first. He wasn't sure what they had seen.

"Sarah said she saw you running like a bat outta hell, right out the door!"

Shawn assumed the worried nurse behind Dr. Jansen was Sarah. "Is everything alright? Now don't tell me you're afraid of the dark."

Shawn forced a fake chuckle. "No, no I'm fine. Just, uh, felt sick. Didn't want to barf on the floor so I ran outside."

What am I supposed to say? That I just saw a ghost? An entire hallway of them? They should have heard that God awful screaming, but they didn't. If they did, they would have done exactly what I just did; ran for their fucking lives. But they didn't. From the looks of it, they were completely oblivious. And my guess it, the same goes for the rest of the night staff.

"I see. Why don't you just take the rest of the night off? You look like shit, man."

Against his own will he said, "No. I can't just leave the hospital with no security."

"It's midnight. Nothing ever happens at these hours."

Shawn laughed. If only. "What about my relief?"

"I'll tell him you had an emergency. He'll understand. We'll keep it on the downlow from the admins. You don't have to but I would sure recommend it." Grinning,

154

he finished with; "I am a doctor after all. Besides, you're the boss. Who are they going to tell?"

Shawn took the doctor's advice and went home. He felt terrible for leaving but could imagine he would feel worse if he had stayed.

The next morning, Shawn texted Riley to ask if she was working. Coincidentally, she wasn't. He asked her to come over.

Within the hour Riley had arrived, dressed in a yellow floral sundress.

"Hi! Is everything okay? When you called you sounded... *off*. Didn't you work overnight? You must be exhausted! What are you doing up?"

Shawn sat on his couch in the living room, and Riley sat next to him, ignoring the recliner adjacent to them in which he expected her to sit.

"Riley please just... let me talk. Something happened last night. In the West Wing."

"Oh my God no. Don't tell me you seen a-"

"Please don't say it. I don't know. But there was something."

Shawn hesitantly recounted the entire story to her. From the note he found in Mildred's room to when he got home. A part of him thought he was stupid for telling this to her, but she remained interested throughout his story and he appreciated it.

"That's so crazy! And you're sure nobody else heard anything?"

"I'm sure. They had no idea what was happening."

Riley sank into the couch cushion. "You know, I used to watch this show when I was younger. About the 'paranormal' or whatever. I don't remember which one. Anyway, I'm sure it was all a load of bull but I do remember them saying that some spirits just take to people, just like they would if they were alive. Maybe they just think you're special and they want to send their message onto you and the other people who have heard things."

"But why me?" Shawn asked.

"Like I said, special people. I think you're special. I've experienced some things there too, remember? Don't you think I'm special?"

My God, don't start this now, thought one part of him. *Not at a time like this.* The other part of him thought: *You know, she never has gotten to look at the bedroom. Maybe if I show her the bedroom, she'll show me what's under that dress.* The crudeness of the thought physically made him shiver.

"Yeah but who else has been through this?"

"Honestly I don't know. We don't rotate days and nights anymore. Night shift is given to basically anyone who wants it. And the people on it now are the freaks who would rather be there at night. It's been the same people on nights for months. And none of them seem to notice it."

Shawn looked out of his window into the yard. "I don't know what to do."

"Maybe you can go to someone for help. Like a psychic medium or something. Maybe she can help make sense of all of this."

The idea seemed ridiculous at first but after some deliberation it seemed like the only option they had. It wouldn't hurt to try it out. After a long search online, Shawn and Riley drove for forty miles to find a medium near Philadelphia by the name of Madame Woodrow. The drive over seemed silly to Shawn, but Riley seemed rather excited. Which is why Shawn felt bad for asking her to stay in the car.

"What? Why? I want to hear what she has to say."

"Look she's probably full of shit anyway but... I have some demons, okay? And if on the off chance that she's legit, I don't you to be there when it comes up. Please, just trust me."

156

Riley slowly leaned over and held Shawn by the face with her small, soft hands. Then kissed Shawn on the cheek. Shawn made an effort not to quiver. It wasn't her fault. She didn't know about Chloe.

"Okay. But when you come back, you're telling me everything. Good luck."

Shawn went inside. He approached an empty table in a small room. It seemed so different from what he had seen in movies. It wasn't a dark purple room with long drapes or even a crystal ball.

"Hello?" he asked.

"Have a seat honey, have a seat."

Shawn still couldn't see Madame Woodrow but he did as she said.

"You have come to see me because you are troubled, right? Something is bothering you deeply, I feel it. Something quite worrisome. A conflict in your mind, am I right?"

Shawn was becoming frustrated that he could hear the voice but not see its owner. He began to stand up when a hand touched his shoulder, guiding him back into his seat.

"Now, now," she said, suddenly standing behind him, "not so fast. Tell me what brings you to see me today."

"Shouldn't you already know that?" Shawn replied.

She looked at him with an annoyed face, one that said *ha, funny.*

"I'm sorry, I don't mean to be rude. Look, I believe there are some, uh, troubled souls that may need my help. I'm not sure what to do about it because-"

"Give me your hand."

Shawn was taken aback by her request but nonetheless surrendered his hand to her. She held it tightly, running her thumb back and forth across the back of his knuckles. The woman closed her eyes and pointed her nose to the ceiling.

"Why yes, I'm afraid there is a troubled soul."

157

"*A* troubled soul? As in just one?"

"Yes, it would appear so. A girl. A young girl."

Shawn tried but could not remember a young girl during his encounter.

"She has something she would like to tell you. Would you like to hear it?"

Shawn gulped. His hand was shaking but the medium didn't loosen her grip.

"I-I-I don't know honestly."

"She says your friend is very beautiful."

Shawn froze.

"She says she misses you oh so very much. And she says she hopes you stay as happy as you can be for the rest of your life. 'Love that girl', she says, 'she loves you! Almost as much as I did!'"

Shawn ripped his hand from the woman's grasp. "Chloe? Is that Chloe? Oh my God Chloe, baby, I miss you! Quick, Madame Woodrow, tell her this for me, tell her that I love her so much and I am so sorry for not being there when she was dying." Shawn was screaming now. "I tried to leave Iraq, I really did, but I couldn't and I just felt so horrible but I came home as soon as I could, and I visited her grave every single day for weeks! Oh, baby you have no idea how much I miss you!"

Madame Woodrow was quiet. "Well?" asked Shawn. "Are you telling her?"

"That'll be two hundred dollars."

"What?"

"That will be. Two hundred. Dollars." She said, pronouncing each few syllables as if Shawn spoke English as a second language.

"Are you kidding me? Are you FUCKING kidding me?!" Shawn stood and flipped the table he was sitting at on it's top. "Fucking tell her, you old cunt," he shouted through tears, "tell her what I said right now!"

"You think I do this shit for free, asshole? You better get the hell outta here before I call the police!"

Shawn thought better of arguing and stormed out, punching a hole into the drywall as he left. He stopped outside the door and rested against the wall to collect himself before walking back to the vehicle. When he got to the car, Riley asked "Well? What did she say?"

"Nothing. She was a phony, I could tell from the start. Waste of time. Let's go home."

* * * * *

They made it back to Shawn's house just before sunset. The two had hardly spoken a word the entire ride home, and when they arrived Shawn silently removed himself from the vehicle and walked up to the door. He had thought long and hard about what Madame Woodrow had relayed to him.

"Mind if I come in, Shawn?" asked Riley. Shawn sighed and let his head fall against the door. "I don't know Riley. I'm pretty tired."

"I think we could both use the company. Besides, you never did show that bedroom of yours."

Shawn didn't respond nor did he look back at her. She continued: "Shawn, look. You were up all day and then worked a night shift. You were tired. Maybe you fell asleep and it was a dream. A terrible, terrifying dream. Maybe when I told you about some people's belief that the place is haunted, I planted a seed that bloomed in your sleep. Let's just go inside and relax. You deserve it."

Shawn was more than confident that he hadn't been dreaming. But maybe she was right. It was the closest thing he had to a reasonable explanation. He wanted to ask Riley to leave, but couldn't muster the courage. Instead he unlocked the door and opened it wide enough for her to walk in next to him. "You're right, let's go see it."

159

The two went straight to the bedroom and Riley sat on the bed while Shawn spoke about the various objects he had on the shelves and floor. It was pleasing to show someone new his knick knacks and souvenirs. Although she politely nodded and acknowledged what he was saying, Riley seemed a little distracted.

"You're pacing, Shawn, or stalling. Either way, you need a break. You just need to sit down and relax for a while. I know all of this is going on at once but can you just forget about it for five minutes. Please?"

Shawn sat next to Riley and hesitantly kissed her. It felt good. It had been almost a year and a half since he had kissed a girl. It didn't bother him anymore that that girl wasn't his wife. All he had on his mind was Riley. He had been debating with himself for so long, and he had finally done it. According to Madame Woodrow, it was the right thing. It felt right. Like Chloe had gone away and brought the most beautiful angel God had created and put her in Shawn's path on purpose. That's what Shawn chose to believe.

They kissed for a long time before Shawn recruited the courage to put a hand on her thigh and slowly reach it further up her dress. It took less than two minutes for them to take each other's clothes off and find each other under the covers before they made love.

Following the love session, Shawn lit a cigarette, stale as it was likely from the same box that he had bought the morning of his interview. The staleness didn't bother him. It's not like he smoked enough to really know the difference. He offered the smoke to Riley, who happily accepted. She took a long drag and coughed the cutest laugh Shawn had ever heard. They giggled and rubbed noses before hearing the doorbell ring.

Shawn sighed, then gave Riley a kiss before lazily getting up to put on a pair of sweats and get the door. Beyond the door was the detective from Mildred's case.

"Detective, may I help you? Something new with Mildred's case?"

"No, Mr. *Chief of Security.* How do you even call yourself that, huh? How do you sleep at night?" He spat on the ground. "You need to come with me."

"What the hell are you talking about?"

"You heard what I said. You're comin' downtown, let's go."

"No, I'm not going anywhere until I know what the hell is happening!"

Several Cambria police officers appeared from behind the detective and pushed passed, grabbing Shawn by each arm. Shawn didn't resist as they cuffed him and dragged him to the car. No questions were answered on the way to the station. Shawn found himself being led to an interrogation room in the department and was on the brink of tears from his anger and confusion.

After what seemed like an eternity, the detective made his presence in the room.

"Alright, now tell me why I'm here. I haven't done anything! What's the deal?"

"You know damn well what the problem is. You're a damn coward."

"What?!"

"All of those poor defenseless patients were getting their asses kicked by your crooked staff and you didn't do a goddamn thing about it. In fact, you fuckin' ran!"

Shawn couldn't speak. His head was spinning.

"All of those poor patients. The ones in the West Wing of your so-called hospital. We know what you people did to 'em. You drugged them all up so they can't hardly think let alone defend themselves. Then your crooked staff raped and tortured every one of them."

Shawn's jaw dropped.

"That's right, the jig is up. We have footage of it too. You know that simpleminded little boy who you met in the hallway? Someone had just knocked his teeth down his throat. All those scars on his body? They whipped him *that* bad. He comes stumbling around the corner and you *ran* from him. Anyway, his mother had been suspecting something fishy was going on for a while so on her last visit she hid a camera in his room. She went back today and got it. She brought it to us and we watched it, along with all the surveillance footage we could get our hands on from *your* office. You know what was in that footage? You, running down a hall lined with victims begging for your help. Oh, and one of our officers found this in your house."

The detective threw a piece of paper on the table in front of Shawn. It was the note he had found in Mildres's room that read: *West wing needs help, THEY NEED HELP!!!*

"Sir", Shawn started, "you don't understand. This sounds crazy but... I thought they were ghosts." He felt ashamed for having said this and felt tears forming behind his eyes. "You don't understand. The night I was there, nobody else in the hospital even reacted to the noise! It doesn't make any sense! I swear I never touched anyone! I was honestly scared but when I ran outside, some staff members followed me out to make sure I was okay! They didn't seem like anything was out of the ordinary, I thought I was just going crazy!"

"Are you an idiot? Who do you think tortured and raped all of these people? Ever think the other staff members were just trying to save their own skins? You don't get it do you? It was the night shift! All of them! Every night when the last day crew member left, it was hammering time for these sick freaks. We've already arrested most of them. Dr. Jansen, Sarah Fowler, the lot of them. Now I can't prove that you physically assaulted these patients, yet, but I can clearly prove that you knew all about it and you ran like a roach and didn't do a thing about it. That's enough for me to put you up for a long time."

162

Shawn couldn't believe what he was hearing. *How could I be this stupid? Have I stooped this low? How can I blatantly see someone in need right before my eyes, and not even know that it's real? Am I insane?*

It took Shawn a moment to realize that this wasn't the first time he wasn't there for someone who needed him.

Chloe would be so disappointed.

Foreword by Author Corbin Eichhorn

Author's Note: As the saying goes "write what you know" and this story is loosely based off my very own (thankfully short lived) experimentation with the drug K2. The utterly nightmarish experience I endured haunts me to this day, chilling me to my core, and I captured a little fragment to show in this story. This is also a cautionary tale, showing what might happen when you are left with nothing but your unrestrained thoughts, at the mercy of a mind melting substance.

C-9 By Corbin Eichhorn

"I don't give a damn where you go! Just get the hell out!"

A powerful voice boomed from the doorway and several random objects flew through the air, missing Alex as he stormed off down the driveway. His father had always been a raging alcoholic and had a habit of throwing tantrums, but this one was the worst yet. Alex had failed history three grading periods in a row, breaking his promise to at least pass his classes.

"It's not my fault Mr. Thomas is the most boring and confusing teacher ever..." Alex muttered under his breath as he pulled on his hood, fighting off the chill of the mid-November air.

Pulling out his phone, the steaming teen dialed up his good friend, Red.

"Yo, dude, I need a place to crash for the weekend, my parents kicked me out again," Alex sighed into the phone.

"No problem, bro, I've gotcha covered," his friend replied on the other end. "Just come on over to my place, my mom's gone on another week-long bender, so she won't be home to care."

Alex could always rely on Red, ever since they were merely nine-years-old. Coming from similarly broken homes, Red and Alex had a mutual understanding of each other, finding comfort in each other's company, along with any mind-altering substance they could get their hands on.

By the time Alex arrived at Red's beaten up shack of a house, Red had already invited other guests. Upon opening the door, Alex saw who had shown up. Before him was Red, a short and lanky ginger with skin as pale as paper. He was smiling widely, showing off the gaps in his teeth from one too many fist fights. Inside the house Alex spotted Eric, a massive, stout eighteen-year-old who was like the older brother of the whole group. His beard grew in when he was twelve, so Eric had always looked like a huge mountain man. Lastly, but certainly not least, there was Patricia, or Patty, as Alex called her. Patty was Eric's little sister of two years, and while he didn't enjoy what she did in her spare time, he wanted to keep her safe, since she had a bad habit of catching the attention of thug types. While younger than the rest of the group, Patty stood a good six inches taller than Alex, but she never wasted time rubbing that in his face.

"Hey shortie! Glad you could make it to the party! Red's got some good shit for us tonight," chimed Patty as she sat on the stained couch, sipping from a flask.

Smiling softly, Alex stepped in as Red closed the door behind him.

"The lady speaks the truth, my good man. I have procured a new brand of substances from yonder pipe shop! Behold!"

Red held out several packets, all labeled the same.

"C9! Cotton Candy Clouds! Read the packaging, depicting what would look to be clouds made of cotton candy, as the name suggests."

"C9? What on Earth is that?" Alex inquired, just as Patty draped her arms over his shoulders.

"Ah! C9 is the newest and hottest thing on the block, daddy-o! One puff of this and you'll be as high as the peak of Mount Everest!" Red replied while giving Alex the finger guns, changing his mannerisms as per usual.

"It's a synthetic, supposed to mimic the effects of pot, but it's crazy cheap," Patty added and Red nodded in agreement, tossing the packages to Eric who sat in the oversized recliner, which still looked small compared to him.

"Eric! My man! Do me the honors and stuff those pipes for me!" Red chimed as he strikes an overly dramatic pose. Eric grimaced, signing to Red that he was tired of him bringing in new things around his sister.

166

"Chill, bro, it's totally safe, it wouldn't be legal if it was dangerous, right?" Patty retorted with a chuckle, drawing sigh of defeat from Eric; he couldn't say no to his little sister. While Eric started stuffing the pipes with what looked like saw dust, Patty pulled Alex to the couch and pushed him down, sitting next to him, but clutching his arm.

"My friends! Tonight, we explore new territories," announced the overly zealous Red as he took a stuffed pipe, wasting no time in lighting it up and puffing hard. The foul stench of burnt cotton candy filled the air, making Alex's nose scrunch up.

Receiving his own, Alex placed the pipe in his mouth, Patty lit it for him, and he inhaled. Burning smoke filled his lungs, scorching everything it touched all the way down, eliciting violent coughs from Alex. Drinking water to expel the horrendous taste from his mouth, Alex watched as Patty and Eric joined in, taking puffs of their own. For many minutes, the group felt nothing, taking repeated puffs on the pipes in hopes of speeding up the process.

"Ay, Red, I thought you said this was good shit!" Alex scoffed, dumping out the ashes from his chili-pepper-shaped pipe.

"Shit, man, I was told this was the hottest shit right now. Maybe we just can't feel it since…"

Alex looked up at Red, expecting him to finish his sentence, but all Alex could see on his friend's face was…nothing. It wasn't that he was expressionless, but he had no face.

Blinking rapidly, Alex realized Red still had facial features, but they were blurred out, as if he was in one of those police shows where witnesses wanted to keep their identities concealed. Alex couldn't remember Red's face for the life of him. Looking around, he realized that the same occurrence was happening with Patty and Eric.

Numbness overtook Alex, he neither felt nor heard anything, aside from a steady and rapid thumping from his chest, like a muffled drum. Soon after, his vision started to fade to blackness, it was a warm and comforting darkness like when one falls asleep. The tranquil feeling of security was quickly lost as Alex realized he was back home, staring into the scarred door to the hallway closet. A sturdy looking board leaned against the doorframe, looking to fit in metal hooks screwed into the wall on either side of the door. Dread overtook the boy as he felt an imposing force behind him, pushing him towards the slowly opening closet.

"I told you, boy, you mouth off to me again, I'd put you in the Locker! Consider yourself lucky!"

A deep, rumbling voice bellowed from the force pushing him through the doorway.

Panic set in as Alex struggled against the force, but much like an animal fighting against the current of a river, his efforts were in vain. Behind him, the door swung shut and the loud thud of wood hitting metal rung out, casting Alex into silence and darkness. Pounding on the door, Alex cried out in fear, begging for freedom, but the old-world wooden door held fast, not relenting to the boy's feeble attempts to break it down. Alex screamed until his voice went hoarse, and then all he could produce was a pathetic squeak. With the will to fight broken, Alex slumped against the door and silence fell upon him. Within the claustrophobic closet, which acted as Alex's prison, no light shone from under the door, drowning the boy in a sea of darkness as thick as pitch. Hours upon hours of solitude in the endless void of shadow took its toll on him, scrambling his sense of time and reality. Just as countless memories of days spent in the prison of the closet flooded Alex's mind, suddenly, the imposing claustrophobic grip on him was gone. Quickly, he got to his feet, scanning his surroundings.

Much like in the closet, Alex stood in a smothering darkness, until he turned to see the azure glow of a fountain. An oddly out-of-place fixture in the dark, it stood tall and proud, a spire resembling a steeple to a gothic cathedral with many gargoyles that spewed glowing water from their mouths, but made no splashing of water on water. Atop the granite fountain stood a figure, human in shape, but completely devoid of any features. No hair, clothes, nose, ears--not even any eyes. Just a wide grin, a row of bleached and jagged teeth splitting open the tightly pulled onyx colored skin on the face, an expression far too wide to be anywhere near human. In the faint glow of the luminous water, Alex could see the skin on the being's forehead split open with a sickening tear, putrid gray fluid leaked from the newly formed wound. Splitting further open, the break in skin revealed an inhumanly large eyeball, the size of a baseball, glaring back at Alex.

Before any words could be spoken, the solid footing under Alex gave way, plunging him into murky water forcing him to hold his breath. Coldness gripped Alex as he heard faint voices, though he could not make out what was said. Somehow, the voices seemed oddly familiar. Several hands pushed against his face and chest, growing more frantic as time went on. Alex couldn't move to fend off the groping hands, they felt like they were griping every part of him. A burning sensation grew in his chest as his lungs ache for air. Voices grew frantic and jumbled, like a crowd of people yelling over each other. Suddenly, the hands grabbed him all over and Alex felt them pulling him through the water quickly. Overpowering force slammed him on his back at the bottom of whatever body of water he was getting dragged through.

As quickly as it all began, the water vanished, and Alex took in a breath of stale, musty air. Looking up, he saw ceiling tiles, and felt the cold, hard tile of the school hall floor. Many students muttered to each other in tongues Alex had never heard before. Having pulled himself to his feet, he swung his head around to see all the students staring at him, their gazes piercing straight through him. The stares surrounded Alex, he could feel himself getting impaled by judgement as the muttering rose in volume. Through the cacophony of noise, Alex could make out one word, "Face."

His hands immediately shot up to his face, and he felt something like slime, with bits of something floating in the ooze. With haste, Alex bolted to the restroom, which was luckily unoccupied, and once inside, he flipped on the light. Horror struck Alex as he finally saw what all the other students were talking about. His face was melting, much like a candle in front of a blow torch. His skin turned a sickly gray and began to peel off his face, his nose dangled from a thread of muscle as a rancid odor filled his open nasal cavity. Though Alex watched in horror, he felt no pain, the decaying flesh of his face felt alien and wrong. Fingers dug into flesh and tore it away in a frenzy, globs of decaying skin and muscle covered the porcelain sink in a gray fluid. His heart pounded painfully hard as he frantically clawed at his face, the same gray fluid oozing from between the muscle fibers and dripping onto the sink. Vision in his left eye faded as the eyeball melted into a jelly, slipping from its socket and into the sink. Nails scraped against bone as the last remaining shreds of flesh melted away. Using his index finger, Alex pried out his right eye, and with an audible pop, the eyeball was ejected from its home and fell down the drain. Alex's vision followed the eyeball down the drain into complete darkness.

The, once again, Alex stood before the fountain, the ominous figure was still standing motionless atop it. His hands frantically groped his face in an inspection, finding his features to be untouched, as normal as usual. Returning his gaze to the ebony figure, Alex saw that several more wounds tore their way through the being's skin, revealing piercing eyes all over the body, from the head to the legs, no part of the figure's body was left untouched by the multiplying eyes.

"Alex!"

A familiar feminine voice cried out as Alex was shaken awake, the bright kitchen light blinded him temporarily.

Patty? He thought to himself, covering his eyes with his hands. All Alex could feel was a mind-crushing headache, it felt like his skull might split open from internal pressure. The cold tile floor under him felt foreign and new, as if it was the first time he had felt it, or anything for that matter.

"I told you he smoked too much! He passed out right away! Damn it, Red!"

The feminine voice barked as Alex's head was cradled in jarringly cold hands. Forcing his eyes open, Alex peered out into the room around him. Having expected his friends, Alex was instead greeted with the same blurry figures from before, all three stood above him. There was one feature on each figure he could make out--those inhumanly large scowls, the mouths stretching ear to ear.

"What a loser, it only took a few hits and he was out like a light. Pathetic!" A male voice sneered as Alex's head was violently twisted and forced to face sideways. It felt as if an inhuman force was holding him down and pressing on the side of his head.

"Loser! Nobody likes you! We only let you hang out with us because we pity you! Do yourself, and everyone else a favor, and just die already!"

Agony swept over Alex, the pain he felt no longer a force pushing out, but an even mightier force pushing in. Alongside the pressure on his head, Alex felt jabs and kicks to his sides, and his ribs audibly snapped under the force. Pain shot up his spine. Alex tried to fight back, to break free and escape, but the pressure on his head was tremendous, keeping him pinned to the cold, filthy floor.

"Your parents hate you! We hate you! Why are you so pathetic?!"

"Waste of skin..."

"Worthless!"

Words of hatred filled Alex's ears as the boot on his head pressed down like a vice, bolts of pain ripped through his head as his skull splintered and cracked under the pressure. His vision faded to red as the pressure in his head ruptured all the blood vessels in his eyes; the sanguine fluid seeped from his nose, mouth, ears, and eyes.

Any urge to fight was crushed as a sickening crack filled his ears as his skull gave way.

With a blink, Alex was back, once again, to the fountain. While his head was very much in one piece, the pain of the skull crushing still lingered, keeping Alex from standing. Water rippled and splashed around Alex's prone form and he felt movement in the shallow sea. Suddenly, a long, slimy tentacle wrapped itself around Alex's leg, and hoisted him into the air. Catching a good look at the tentacle that held him, Alex saw onyx black skin, much like the figure atop the fountain, it was even adorned with several sporadically-placed grinning mouths and glaring eyes.

"What is real?"

"Is this a dream?"

"Will you ever wake up?"

"Do you even remember how to?"

A swarm of whispers bombard Alex as he ascended. Having been hoisted up, Alex hung upside down in front of the dark figure, their faces were mere inches apart. Alex gagged as a new eye split open from the forehead of the being, the stench of rotting meat slapped him in the nose. Within the same socket, the grapefruit-sized eye split, like dividing cells, into smaller eyes, repeatedly, until the singular socket was filled with hundreds of tiny writhing eyes, all looking in different directions.

A hole opened up under Alex and water rushed into the new pathway as the tentacle loosened its grip on his leg and he fell landing hard on his back in a heap. Dazed, Alex looked around and felt something familiar, grain. All around

172

him, grain. Realization hit him, and Alex knew he was inside a grain silo.

One summer when he was six, he had played with his cousins on his uncle's farm. He had climbed on top of the silo, trying to hide from his cousin by jumping into the grain silo. What he had not realized was that grain can act like quicksand, and it engulfed him rapidly. Alex kicked and screamed as he sunk deeper into the dry grain, he heard his cousin's voices calling to him from the top of the silo. Each kernel of grain put a tiny amount of pressure on Alex, each trying to push him down, all together they forced the boy deeper. Having flailed his arms, Alex tried as hard as he could to free himself from the impending prison, only succeeding in burying himself deeper. Taking a final breath, Alex's head plunged underneath the grain.

The grain faded away from grain to soil, and Alex's eyes snapped open, only for him to be blinded by freshly disturbed dirt. Clarity hit him as he clamped his eyes shut, trying to wipe his eyes but his hands were held in place by the earth around him. His lungs began to burn for air, each attempt to draw in breath was met with more dirt. A chorus of voices screamed at him to escape, to go up. With burning muscles, Alex fought to lift his arms. Though it took all his effort, he managed to shift through the loose soil. Next came his legs, the dirt proving a formidable foe to overcome. Worming his way up, Alex felt the surface just out of reach.

Then, once again, Alex stood before the fountain, but with eyes of various sizes surrounding him on all sides in the darkness. The entire shallow sea was alive with swarms of giant rotting tentacles, each with their own mouths all spouted hateful insults and mockery. The fountain ran gray with the same putrid fluid pouring from the black figure that was now perched atop the highest gargoyle. All the statues in the fountain turned their heads in unison and stared directly at Alex, all yelling in alien tongues. A deafening cacophony of screams barreled into Alex, forcing him to clamp his hands over his ears. The floating eyes glowed red with hatred as the grin on the black figure grew wider and wider, splitting what remained of its face until Alex heard a sickening crack, and the bottom jaw flopped open, revealing thousands of rows of undulating razor-sharp fangs extending all the way down the abyss that was its throat.

Alex sat up in bed and screamed, flailing his arms in a cold sweat.

"Whoa, whoa, whoa! Calm down there, buddy!"

A familiar voice sounded and a door opened. Alex stopped and saw that he was in Red's room, lying in his bed. Turning, Alex saw that his best friend standing at the door with a steaming bowl of what Alex presumed to be soup.

"You alright buddy?" Red inquired, walking over to Alex and sitting on the bed. "You scared the shit out of all of us, man! You completely passed out."

Alex rubbed his eyes as the haze started to lift from his mind. He suddenly recalled that the night before he and his friends had tried that new C9 crap.

"Bro, I think you need to sober up a while. That fucked you up. You've been out for two days," Red added as he looked deep in Alex's eyes, checking to make sure his friend was all right. A rumbling sound came from Alex's stomach, malnutrition setting in.

"I knew you'd be hungry by the time you woke up, so I made you soup," Red said with a smile as he handed Alex the bowl.

A wave of relief swept over Alex as he took everything in. He was out, out of that hell, done with that trip. Maybe he should take Red's advice and sober up for a while, could do him some good. Alex had this thought as he brought the spoon into his mouth, then immediately spat it out. Dirt! Alex was eating dirt. The once mouth-watering scent of soup was replaced with the musty scent of soil.

Alex blinked and he was instantly back in darkness, gasping for air only for his nostrils to be filled with more loose soil. He had never left his hole in the ground, he had imagined all of the events in his friend's room. His lungs burned for air and his muscles ached from lack of oxygen. Panic set in as Alex flailed in the dirt, digging his way up once more as his mind swam.

Visions of moments flashed before his eyes. The long nights spent in the Locker, the beatings his father never spared him from, the apathetic looks his mother gave him, the time he soiled his pants in class by accident, walking down dark alleyways at night with a homeless man following him in search of drugs; these and many more flooded Alex's mind while he fought for survival. He felt cold evening air on his hand as he broke to the surface, gripping stable ground as he pulled with all his might. His muscles began to fail him, deprived of oxygen and overtaxed from the effort. All thoughts slowed to a crawl as a biting cold slowly enveloped Alex, drawing him deeper into a sleep he couldn't fight anymore.

The sound of birds chirping stirred Alex awake, his eyes fluttered open as golden sunlight poured through his window and into his room. Sitting up quickly, Alex felt the clean linens of his bed.

Am I out? For good? Is this just another dream, a figment of my imagination?

Well, it felt real enough, so that was good enough. Alex spent the next half hour collecting his thoughts, remembering the events of the previous night in vague detail. He honestly couldn't tell whether or not what he went through was a hallucination, a dream, or--even more haunting of a thought--reality.

After dressing himself and grabbing his phone, Alex noticed the small light signaling a new message. Clicking on the screen, Alex saw the new message was from Red.

"Hope you made it home alright! Last night was nuts, bro! Be sure to come grab your hat!"

175

Alex rubbed his eyes as he shut off the screen, pocketed the cell phone, and stood up to dress. It was then that he noticed he was in a new, clean, set of clothes. Disregarding questions surrounding the origin of his new outfit, Alex set off towards Red's house. When he arrived and knocked on the door, Alex quickly realized that Red wasn't home. Using the spare key under a rock near the door, Alex let himself in.

Man, the place is trashed, more so than usual!

Broken glass and candy wrappers laid scattered all over the floor, painting an odd picture of what had occurred merely a few hours earlier. Spotting his hat on the couch, Alex walked over and picked up his cap. Then he stopped, frozen in place.

Slowly turning his head, Alex looked out the back-sliding glass door, noticing a large hole in the backyard, complete with scattered and freshly dug dirt.

Alex's heart sank. That hole wasn't there the day before.

Foreword by Author Erin Miller

Biography: At a very young age, Erin decided she was going to be a wizard. She has been working steadily towards goal that ever since. She has written many things since then, some of which is readable. When not working, she's usually found with her Imaginary Friends online, where they grumble about certain famous authors and try to make sense of magic, listening to audiobooks, or indulging in her podcast addiction.

Mission Bells by Erin Miller

Will and Ben were in Mission Viejo thanks to Lou, the directional app on Will's phone. *Short for 'Loser,'* Will had said, and Lou lived up to the name, leading them to try and make U-turns, move into southbound lanes, and occasionally bringing Google Voice in to remind them: "I can't find what you're looking for."

They thought they had found the mission by sheer luck when they stopped at the GasUp - formerly Mobile, formerly Shell, formerly Esson, according to the overlapping fading signs – to buy a paper map from a bored looking woman with earrings in the shape of small bells whose name badge read Debbie. Will had taken the risk of using the gas stations lone bathroom while Ben filled up the Cherokee and walked out into the shadow of the mission's wide sandstone walls. He shivered. It felt as cold as a desert night in there and it was only in the 80's in the sunlight.

Ben joined him as he was stepping back into the sunlight. Will smiled and gestured at the facade, decorated with the campanile with spaces for six bells. Planters full of citrus trees flanked heavy looking doors. "Didn't I tell you?" he said. "I said I'd find the next mission before dark, and I did. You owe me a Coke."

"I don't think this is a 'Historic Mission Trail' type mission," Ben replied. "That Debbie girl didn't mark it on the maps."

"It's got one of the bell wall things, an ugly, heavy door…"

"…and no sign saying what mission it is."

Will sighed. It had been a long day of driving, Ben's retelling of ghostly war cries, men with red horns and statues that wept blood alternating with Lou's antics. Will had grown up in a haunted house, but this was too much; apparently, God had carefully placed ghosts in every

179

building along the 101 freeway. When he'd came up with the idea of seeing California like a tourist, he must have forgotten how much he hated tourists. "It can be a Pepsi instead of a Coke."

Ben shook his head as he scrolled through his phone. "The place is not on *any* maps, man."

Will shrugged. "Maybe they just forgot to put it on."

Ben looked at his friend in disbelief. "The entire internet. Forgot to put this place. On a map."

"All right fine, so it's a shopping center. Congratulations, Mr. Home-Care Detective, you've solved another one. When Audrey calls to check on us, ask her to make you some congratulation cookies."

"I am not eating anything Mrs. Beech made, even if she is my favorite client," Ben said with a shudder.

"Isn't it illegal for a live-in caregiver – "

"Aide."

"- not to eat what their patient feeds them?"

"Isn't it illegal to wear red shirts three days in a row when you're on vacation from Target?"

"I like red," Will protested.

"You're brainwashed. Come on, maybe they'll have a Best Buy or something."

"In 500 feet, use any three lanes to turn left, then turn left," Lou offered robotically.

"Someplace that will humanely kill our buddy here and replace him with someone better." Will grumbled.

"Rerouting," said Lou.

"He sound smug to you?"

Ben was already opening the heavy wood and iron door. It led into a patio with a cobblestone floor and plants growing brittle against the cracked walls. They walked across to the arched corridors, where they could get some relief from the sun.

"Okay, yeah," Will said "See, *this* place is definitely haunted."

"Surprised you didn't say that about the gas station bathroom."

"Nah, that place is possessed."

"There's usually fountains, right? When there's business."

"Probably can't afford the water."

"We don't normally get visitors this time of year," said a cheery voice from behind them.

Ben jumped and turned to face a woman wearing a dark blazer, white blouse, slacks, and a wide-brimmed hat, standing in the corridor, near one of the doors leading indoors. "And a fountain, being purely decorative, isn't really in the budget."

"Hi," Ben squeaked.

"I'm Myrna. And you?"

"Ben," he gestured, "And this is Will." His friend nodded, hands firmly in his pockets.

"Nice to meet you," she said. "Have you been here before?"

"First time." Ben said, putting down the hand he'd been holding out for her to shake. We're touring the mission trial. For a blog."

"Dude," Will hissed. *Weird Shit Just Happens* was a way to keep in touch with friends and family; he didn't want this woman reading it.

Myrna clapped her hands together. "How exciting! Well, you're on the right path. Would you like a tour?"

"Tour?"

"It's something new we're trying out. Everyone else likes to let people just wander around but we think there's a certain intimateness to having a tour guide. Would you like one? It's free."

Myrna widened her eyes and stood slightly on her toes, looking like a puppy begging for a walk. Will frowned. There was something about the slight tilt of her head and the false peppiness of her voice that made him wary. A long career in retail had given him an instinct on the various flavors of crazy a person could encounter. Customers like this were Flavor 6: the ones who threw the largest tantrum when their expired coupon wasn't honored. As much as he hated it, they had to agree.

"Sure. Sounds good."

"Great!" Now the peppiness sounded real. Never a good sign. "It's my first time too. Not being here, I mean, but being the first tour guide. Ahem."

She stood up straighter, adjusted the hem of her blazer and rolled her shoulders. "Okay, here we go!"

Myrna breathed in deeply and then gestured to the general area. "This is our mission. Building began in 1816, but we weren't officially designated 1820." She led them down the left end of the arched walkway and around a corner. "We had the benefit of skilled craftsmen and suppliers to help our construction. Thus, we have the strongest sandstone and in here…" She opened a rustic door, "you can see that our buttresses are made from the finest alder wood."

"Really?" Will said, warily.

"Being temporary is no reason to skimp on proper work. It's for God after all." Myrna smiled, standing in the aisle between hand carved pews. Ben, trying to play the tourist, snapped a picture with his phone and took another one when she flourished an arm in a pose.

"Uh-huh, and where is *here*, exactly?" Will asked, gesturing to the plain, simple walls, decorated only with the same paintings of Jesus's walk to the cross that every single mission seemed to have identical copies of.

Myrna tilted her head, putting her arm down. "What's that?"

"'Here,'" Will insisted. "Which mission is this?"

She looked at him blankly. "It's on the sign just outside the patio. You must have read it as you came in."

"There wasn't any si-"

"It must have fallen; if you'll follow me through here…"

Myrna disappeared through a door behind the altar they hadn't noticed until then, making sure to gesture to the baptismal font by the altar. "That's a bowl."

Will and Ben shared a look.

"We should not go in there," Will said.

"Dude. It's a room, like every other room."

"Not feeling it, man."

"You're as bad as Mrs. Beech."

"And I'm one thousand percent okay with that. It means I'm not stuck in a clearly abandoned building with a Flavor 6 crazy."

"What's a…no, you know what? I don't want to know. Stay here then, with the totally not scary 'statue of a dead guy.'"

Ben indicated the Jesus on the cross behind the altar and headed towards the back, where Myrna had apparently been talking regardless of their presence.

"…and on your right is the Sanctuary. This is where the book is kept when it's not being used," she lowered her voice to a whisper, putting one finger to her lips. "You can look in if you want, but you have to be quiet."

Ben leaned forward to peer into a room as white and brown as the rest of the building with an ornately carved box in the center. His ears rung in the silence.

"It's very nice," he whispered. Myrna looked relieved and headed towards the room on the left. "This is the wardro—sacristy. This is the sacristy. It's where all the vestments are kept. Look, don't touch!"

"How long have you worked here?" Will asked as he caught up. Ben tried to surreptitiously check the time on his phone. He noted that he wasn't getting a signal and that it'd been over an hour already.

Myrna thought about it. "About a week. Or maybe three days. Everything gets really *samey* after a while. It could be years for all I know."

"And this is your first time giving tours?"

"Yeah-huh."

"What'd you do before?"

Myrna paused. "I…worked at a restaurant. Or a café. Do you want to see the gardens?"

"Make a U-turn."

"What?"

"Nothing," Will said over Lou's "Recalculating."

Myrna led them through an antechamber to the left of the sacristy and out into the air again. They toured both the priest gardens and the communal gardens, each filled with what Myrna described as "some plants" and "some other plants" and "some trees." She paused again to describe a chipped altar to Mary hidden in a corner, in front of a wall of prickly pear plants. "She doesn't get many visitors these days either. Though we should be grateful that they left her intact."

"They who?" Ben hadn't meant to ask, but the words felt pulled from him.

"Those... *people*." Viciousness temporarily twisted Myrna's voice and face but was gone before either man could comment. "You see, San Cipr-- *we* only operated as a functioning mission until 1848, when we were raided. There'd always been rumors: war riches hidden behind the walls; holy worship in the day, devil worship at night, all that nonsense. Then some Maria or other goes running off with some ranch hand. People start saying she was lured away with love spells and kidnapped by the padre as a sacrifice. That's all the excuse *they* needed. Storming the place in the middle of the night, breaking, burning and taking everything. Awful." She huffed and tugged again at the hem of her blazer. "After everything we'd done for them."

Will silently upgraded Myrna to Flavor 8 as Ben carefully asked "That's why there's no bells in the campanario? They broke?"

"The what?"

Ben gestured to the wall that stretched upwards beside them.

"Oh, that. No, they're in the tunnels." Myrna answered, overly peppy once more.

"What tunnels?"

"Under the floor."

She said it like that was normal and Will found himself trying to find a gate in the wall, so they could get back to the car. Their tour had been scratching away at the back of his brain since the beginning and he was now thoroughly irritated with Myrna's general lack of usefulness. Someone must have been wondering where they were by now, right? Their absence had to have been noticed, at least by Debbie the gas station girl.

"They put them here, in the gardens – well, under the gardens – and under the buildings. Tunnels that go all the way up and down the road, connecting all the missions together. It's said that they were built to provide a quick escape in the event of an attack. They were only used once, during the raid of 1848, and the bells were buried to keep them safe. They're real silver you know?" She looked around then leaned close to her guests. "I'm not really supposed to do this, but I can show you."

The *Twilight Zone* theme rang out in the still air, causing the boys to jump and Myrna to scan the air curiously. Ben silently thanked the spirits of cell phone signals. Out loud he said:

"That's my fault. I should really take this. It's my job."

Myrna's shoulders drooped a little. "Oh."

She turned to Will.

"What about you? Or we could wait for your friend…"

"Uh, no. Tunnels and Ben are not on good terms. Or small spaces in general."

185

"Oh, they're very spacious. And quite nice."

* * * * *

Ben headed to the far side of the garden, phone to one ear, hand on the other to hear better. "Hello, Mrs. Beech. How are things?"

"As well as can be expected," the carefully practiced refinement in her voice was refreshing.

"Things not going well with Cindy?"

"She's a very nice young lady, and quite… proper in her manner."

There was that clipped voice that indicated the struggle to find something nice to say. "She's been helping me with the laundry."

"Sorry." Ben said automatically.

"It's not your fault. I told you to go. You needed a proper vacation. Though, if you wanted to make it up to me…"

"Museum of Death's two-headed turtle, I know."

"I've seen the pictures on the Yelp. It's less of a two-headed turtle and more two turtles joined at the butt. It's just so adorable."

"Don't worry, we'll get plenty of pictures. It's on the way to the San Gabriel Archangel, we'll make it our pit stop."

"Good. Now there was something else. I can't quite…"

"Did you have a visitor today?" Ben encouraged gently

"Aren't you clever? That Cindy girl went to change the wash and while she was gone, that man came in, you know the one."

Ben nodded. "That man" or "him" or "he" was the strongest of Mrs. Beech's hallucinations, but as she never seemed frightened by his appearance and he didn't stay long,

186

Ben had never pressed the matter.

"So, we got to talking, I do at least, and I mention you and William going on the trip. He told me –" she paused, then asked "You aren't going into those places at night, are you?"

"No ma'am."

"Good, because it still gets very cold and dark at night and I don't want you two getting lost. Anyways, he said that the sound of bells leads towards the light."

"Okay. Anything else."

"Not really. He seemed in a hurry. Probably has a very busy day."

There was a longer pause Ben recognized as Mrs. Beech temporarily losing focus with the world, then returning.

"You should let William know, and fairly quickly. I don't want you two being kidnapped."

Ben looked over his shoulder to see that both Will and Myrna had vanished, with only a gap between the prickly pears lining the north wall to indicate where they might have gone.

"Yeah, I'll go do that now."

"Good luck, dear."

The prickly pear plant was a dull green with a slightly waxy look to them. That, Ben thought, should have been the first clue. Or that Myrna's "we" – who he was beginning to suspect was like Mrs. Beech's "him" – hadn't been able to get bells reproduced for the tower, even for the aesthetic. He brushed aside a clump of green with plastic spikes and looked down. A gap in the wall stretched downwards with the vague, illusionary outline of steps.

Ben considered himself stupid, but not horror-movie stupid. He checked his phone. The battery was at a healthy 80%. He put it back in his pocket. He pulled out the flashlight he always carried with him, considered that by going down a set of stairs in a mysterious hole in a wall, he probably was horror-movie stupid, and stepped into the dark.

* * * * *

Myrna was right, the tunnels were absurdly spacious. There had been a camping lantern on a hook inside the doorway, which she had taken down and lit.

"Like I said, we don't get a lot of visitors, but it doesn't hurt to come down occasionally to check for rats, cave-ins, or just keep the place tidy. Here."

She took a strip of rope with a carbine attached to it, hooked one end to a belt at her waist, and handed him the other end.

"Even with a light it can be dangerous. Hold onto this and you won't get lost."

Will was grateful for the lantern as they went, although it was only a pinprick in the darkness and his her from sight. Her voice echoed off the walls, making directionality a chore. It felt like they were twisting and turning as they walked and he found Myrna's lead tugging him in the opposite direction he thought they were headed. It would have been easier if she would only slow down, but she didn't stop talking long enough for him to ask. She was also surprisingly strong.

"Easy to get lost in here," he said, interrupting Myrna's explanation of the Mexican-American war.

"Yes," her voice came from somewhere up and to his left. "There's no point in escaping if your enemy can easily follow you. You don't need to worry. We're down here a lot."

"You keep saying 'we.'"

"San Cipriano is too large for just one worker."

Now it was on his right. He followed the turn and heard an excited "Ooo, over here" in front of him.

"So, you know how I was saying there's treasure down here?" asked Myrna's voice.

Will didn't remember, but he doubted she could see whether he nodded or not. "This is the room where they keep--they *kept* it, plus the bells, you remember those don't you?"

"Signal. Lost," said Lou.

"Oh, really?" Will said in the tight, high-pitched tone he reserved for when he wanted a Flavor 6 or 7 crazy to throw a tantrum, so he could call security and get on with his day. The cold down here had been seeping and the lack of any distinguishing smell was bothering him. It didn't matter if the sunlight blinded him as long as he was outside.

"Now, you have to promise not to tell anyone that I showed you, all right?"

"We don't have to look. We can just go back up and see how Ben is doing."

"After travelling all the way down here? Come on, just one little peek?"

Will sighed, and the spark of light led him under an arch that was twin to the corridor outside.

Each wall of the room was lined either casks, or shelves stalked with bottles. If Will had been a betting man, he'd have bet that the wine was just pruno made by monks. If he sold the bottles during their trip, he could probably buy enough gas to get them to San Francisco.

"This counts a treasure?"

"Of course not. You can't fit the spoils of war into a bottle. I mean you could, but that sounds really hard. It's in the casks."

There was an expectant pause by the archway. A thought was itching at the base of Will's skull. He needed to leave, and he needed to leave now.

"Do y—"

"I'm afraid we don't have time for more questions," said the light in Myrna's voice.

Then it vanished.

A minute later, the rope slackened. It slithered in his grasp like a living thing. Will instinctively dropped it in disgust. He reached down to pick it up again and found only stone floor.

* * * * *

Ben could never explain why he felt in such a hurry to rush down there. It wasn't just Mrs. Beech's call. It wasn't just that he wanted to leave. The moment he moved from the last step to the dirt floor, he felt like he was being followed. If he didn't keep moving forward, all was lost. So, he walked quickly; he didn't dare run. His light showed walls, turns and nothing else. He thought of calling Will, but his phone had no signal down here. He thought of shouting but was stopped that by the insistence that others would hear. More than once he thought the crunch of his shoes on the ground were the sound of other footsteps, moving at a much faster pace and he quickened his.

His stopped when his light flashed across cloth. Someone tall, covered in brown or black cloth.

"Will?"

The figure gave no indication that it heard him.

"Myrna?"

Still nothing. Ben followed.

Like Myrna, the figure wore a wide brimmed hat, but the brim on the side of the head curled upwards, spiraling into the darkness. As it turned again, Ben could see the flame of a lantern, but not the hand that held it.

"Hey," he called. "Excuse me. I need help." His voice sounded odd to his own ears, as though he was speaking a language he didn't know. *Maybe if I tried I in Spanish?* he thought. *Because, ya know, high school level is super useful in real life.*

The figure turned where there was no turning and Ben stood still, listening to the sound of footsteps running to catch up with him as the space around him began to close in.

"We're fine," Will told himself. "Everything is fine."

"Signal. Lost."

190

"Shut up Lou, I said we're fine." He raised his voice: "Myrna?"

He reached his hands forward and took a few steps towards the archway. After ten steps, he turned and tried to find a wall. He assumed the wall couldn't have been more than thirteen steps away. After step sixteen he turned again. He hoped it was towards the first way, but the room could have been upside down and on its side for all he knew.

"Recalculating."

"Lou, stop."

Will tried to turn on his phone's flashlight. It lit up one inch of darkness.

"Rerouting."

Will groaned and walked in what he hoped was a forward direction until he felt the heavy presence that came with passing under the archway. It was a start.

"Which way?" He asked himself.

"Turn left."

"I hate, you goddamn piece of crap. Shut very much absolutely up."

There was silence then. "Turn left."

"Ugh. Fine!" Will huffed and went right.

By now Ben was certain there were more than three people in the tunnels. He had to have been minutes away from Will and Myrna, tops. In that time, he'd followed two more of those brown clad figures and one more in red and he was certain he was nowhere near wherever Will had gone.

This doesn't make any sense, he said to himself. He'd scanned the walls whenever he lost track of a figure, hoping to find some indication of which way to go and only noticed vague rounded shapes scratched roughly into the walls.

He shouted "Will!" and winced at the way the dark swallowed up his words. *I really don't feel like dying down here. I have a double-headed turtle to look at!*

He could feel his ears and eyes straining, searching for some indication that he wasn't alone, afraid to be proven right. He thought he strained too hard, because there was a tinny ringing in his ears, like the sound of distant bells. It was quickly drowned out by shouting voices and the clink of metal. Ben followed the sound and found three men huddled in coats, having a rapid discussion that made his head ache to try and translate. The oppression of increasingly stale air was getting worse. A gasp to Ben's right caused the group to turn towards him. He had trouble recognizing Myrna standing next to him, blazer-less and having traded the slacks for a round skirt, but there was no mistaking the wide, puppy-dog look of surprise in the eyes. She looked at him, and her shock melted into a sly smile.

"Isn't this fun?"

Ben looked at her in disbelief. "No."

"Oh." She looked disappointed, then brightened up. "You'll get used to it. See?" She indicated her blouse, where a dark stain was blossoming, spreading onto the sash that marked the beginning of her skirt. "After the first, like, six stabbings, it starts to tickle. A little. Maybe. Not really. But then, you get to lead a tour. Or tend the gardens. Oh, maybe you can make a fountain! Fun, right? Do you have any gold? They like that. It's why we were down here to begin with. Oh, look."

The men in coats stalked towards them, sharp knives in their hands. The air grew thicker, walls drawing closer together with each step they took. Myrna leaned towards Ben. "This is my favorite part." She whispered.

Behind them, Ben could hear a distant ringing. The floor beneath him shivered with the sound. He turned and ran.

"In 1,000 feet, turn right."

Will took another left. The last three turns against Lou's directions had led to dead ends, but there was only so often the buggy brick could be right. A force slammed into him, knocking him backwards. He pushed forward as far as he could, but it was like fighting against a riptide made of people: silent, pressing.

He heard Myrna's voice, moving from what he hoped was his front to what he thought was his back, sounding like she was leading a tour.

"This is Will. He's going to help us rebuild. He doesn't know too much, but he asks a *lot* of questions." The rush paused. He felt the crush of bodies stop moving, turn towards him. "He's just got first day jitters; I'm sure we'll make him feel right at home." Slender arms draped themselves over the front of his shoulders. Will's shout was twinned by a delighted yelp that started the crowd moving again.

He tried and failed to find a way forward, eventually collapsing against a wall until the pressure around him lessened enough that it was safe to move again. He stood shakily and listened for some sign that Myrna was hiding somewhere, waiting to jump out at him. When nothing happened, he headed in the direction Lou had previously sent him. At least one of them could pretend they knew what they were doing.

"We're getting out of this," he told Lou. "We're getting Ben. We're going straight to L.A. We'll never trust a woman in a blazer again. It'll be fine."

An un-Lou-like ping sound made him glance at his phone. Low battery. Shit.

"Hang in there, dummy, we're gonna make it."

"Make a U-U-U-turn."

Ben stopped. It was faint, but he thought he heard: "Head east. For. 3.1 miles."

Relief washed over him. He ran towards the noise and ran straight into Will, who yelled when he slammed into something not a wall.

"Where the hell where you?" he shouted.

"Looking for you dumbass," Ben replied.

"Where's Myrna?"

"Don't know, don't care."

"Recalculating."

Ping.

Will looked at the Ben-shaped darkness. "Please tell me you know the way out."

"Yeah it's...uhm..."

"Lou?"

Ping.

"Head east."

"Which way is east?"

Ben pointed. "Over there...I think."

The tinny ringing had was growing quieter in that direction and Ben turned and took a few more steps in Possible West, then Maybe South, where the ringing got louder.

"This way."

"I wouldn't," a cold feminine voice said suddenly.

Ben's light illuminated Myrna.

"Well, you're not. We are." Will replied.

Myrna smiled. There was a tinge of regret to it. "If you go that way, the devil will get you."

"The what?" Will started to ask, before Ben interrupted him.

"Nope. Not hearing this."

"He got everyone else," Myrna said.

The tinny sound had changed to an ascending of scales and clangs. Ben pushed past her.

"Bye, crazy lady. Thanks for the tour."

"But we're not done!" She called after them.

Will grabbed onto the back of Ben's shirt as they ran, as the latter started moving faster.

"Do you know where we're going?"

"I'm hoping out."

"Why are you shouting?"

"Recalcu-"

Ping.

Rings became clangs, became peels and they

followed them until they reached a wall.

Oh, fuck off! Will thought, too out of breath to say it.

Ben shined his light around. "This has to be the way out."

"Stop shouting! I'm right here, dude."

"'The bells to the light.' That's what he said. So, there's got to be a light. A lamp. A flashlight. A friggin' lightbulb!"

Will took the flashlight as Ben frantically pounded on the wall. In the small pool of light, Ben stopped and turned to Will with a pale face.

"They've stopped," Ben whispered.

"What has?" Will whispered back.

"Shh!" Ben strained his hearing, but the ringing in his ears wasn't tinny.

Footsteps approached. The quick swish and clomp of running shoes on linoleum was audible. It came with the tinkling of bells. Ben back away as a door-shape part of the wall swung inward. Fluorescent light flooded the area, outlining a tall figure with crossed arms.

"What the hell are you doing?" it asked, as though this was the latest in a series of the day's ridiculous events. "Get out of there!"

When neither Ben nor Will moved, the figure sighed and stepped aside. "Let's go! Out!"

They stepped out, taking a moment to take in rows of chips and candy, a wall of cigarettes, and a slushie machine.

"...the hell?" Will managed to ask.

"You the guys who left the Cherokee here for like an hour? Because this is a gas station, not a rest stop" The unimpressed woman said. "And whatever you were doing, don't do it in the maintenance closet. That's just gross."

She looked different without the wide-brimmed hat. Tiny bells served as earrings.

Will hesitated "Myrna?"

She pointed to her name badge "Debbie."

Will blinked and only then noticed her face was too round, and her eyes too far apart to be the tour guide.

"Your car's out back. More security cameras. Boss says I wait two hours, then call the police. Store policy." She shrugged. "Whatever. $24.50 for the gas. Ten bucks for making me wait. That's *my* policy. Sodas are two for four dollars right now."

As she led them around the back of the GasUp, Will ventured to ask. "You...don't happen to know anything about the mission, do you?"

"What mission?"

"The one across the parking lot."

She looked where he pointed and huffed. "Yeah, dude. It's dedicated to Saint Petco, patron saint of kibbles and treats. There used to be one, Saint Sippy's, you know, the creepy one who raised the dead. It burnt or something. Heard it sucked as a mission though." Another disinterested shrug.

Will and Ben sat numbly in the car after she'd left.

"This is why I never take vacations," Will muttered. Ben nodded. "What did you hear back there?"

"Drink your Coke."

The *Twilight Zone* theme played. Ben stared dumbly at his phone. Will answered it.

"Hi, Audrey."

"Hello, William. Still in Mission Viejo?"

"Uh-huh."

"Well, don't stay there too long. It's almost rush hour and you know how the freeways get."

"Uh-huh."

"Are you okay, dear?"

"We're fine, Mrs. Beech," Ben managed. "Uhm, you haven't had another visit, have you?"

"No, dear. I just had a feeling I should make sure everything was okay."

Ben ignored the warning look Will was giving him.

196

"Yeah, *everything's* fine." He turned on the engine to prove it. "We're just on our way to see the turtle now. Should be there before d- before seven."

"Head north for three miles," Lou encouraged.

Footsteps of Giants by Erin Miller

As a kid, I would lie in bed listening to the sounds that always occurred around 9:30pm.

Boom. Boom. Boom.

A steady sound, plodding with slow inevitability towards my house, my room. I could count to five in between each step.

Boom! Boom! Boom!

But there was a barrier; at one point, when the count reached four, there would be a flash of green, and the booming would devolve into multiple frantic pops and squeals that faded into barely audible of music and cheering. The giant was defeated.

My parents made good money and had clear ideas of what it was for: buying a home, yes, buying theme park season passes, no. I only went there three times: once on a class trip, once because my school marching band was playing there, and once because a cousin of some sort from out of town insisted that we *had* to go. My parents were not the sort that let their kids run around out of their eyesight, so I left each trip with the profoundly adult impression of going somewhere overrated. I saw the actual fireworks show on the band trip. The air around it was filled with crowd noise and canned music that made the display seem quieter than back home. They were, disappointedly, just background to a light projection show, only there to keep people awake enough to leave the park afterwards and find their cars. There was no way these were the things that came around at night.

As I grew older, I taught myself to distinguish the pattern of booms and what made them, based one of Dad's many "Family Time" video tapes and the halos of colored lights that I could see from my window when I dared to look. There was the pair of long, screeching whistles from comets-- red and gold in winter; blue and white in summer, and an unimpressive yellow the rest of the year. Then the crackles, and a handful of spiders. Then, all too soon, the willows, rings and glitters; a barrage of color, accompanied by one or two last loud kabooms amidst all the popping and creating of makeshift clouds in its wake. During an anniversary, or a holiday, there would be a waterfall with its soft shhhh mimicking and encouraging polite applause below it. After that, everything would fade to silence. Some nights, there would only be the quiet pop and sparkle of a late arriving cluster of crossettes.

Even knowing what they were didn't stop me from hearing the booms as the approaching giant, but the number of them and their meaning varied night by night. One night it was two coming to destroy the house, crushing us all under its bulk. The next night, it was one guardian, stalking the outskirts of the barrier and keeping the neighborhood safe. A passing car, a possum on the fence, and an unpruned citrus tree in the neighbor's yard would combine to throw large, distorted shadows on the wall. The gibbering nonsense and thumping beats of a party down the block became a reminder to my young mind that the world outside was full of monsters, just waiting for their chance to break through. I sometimes wonder if I ever actually slept during my childhood, or if I just let terror wash over me until I passed out from fear.

I learned to ignore the sound as I grew up and began treating it as simply the nighttime background noise to my life. On the Fourth of July, they reached higher and peppered the sky with color, but otherwise were unobtrusive. When changes in the wind forced them to be cancelled for the night, there would only be a niggling suspicion that something critical was missing.

I grew up. I moved away. City regulations changed after too many complaints about noise pollution and ashes damaging far too expensive cars, forcing the theme parks to be quieter and less celebratory. When I visited, it was just barely a grumble in the sky. Thunder was more frightening than the footsteps. It was sad.

Which why it's strange to hear it now, miles from where my family used to live. Still in the path of the fireworks, but further away. It is here, though. Not just a rumble, or a crackle, or a whoosh--but the loud, thudding, boom of armed giants.

* * * * *

It started at 9:30 at night. I wasn't in bed. I'd barely gotten in from work, another day of long, difficult, and ultimately meaningless effort. There are days I can't even remember what exactly my job is. Today I was too aware; I'm here to fill a seat and be part of a headcount so that someone I'll never actually meet can get a bonus for my efforts.

As I debated as to whether there would be enough hot water and pressure left to take a shower with, the first boom hit. I waved it off as a car backfiring. The second boom was someone with shit taste in music and a shittier opinion of what other drivers thought of it. The third was the neighbors upstairs, unused to apartment acoustics after a lifetime of living in a lovely suburban home where you might actually know the names of your neighbors. I don't know their names. They're just "the new ones." No one here bothers with real names. Our own lives are enough, no one has the time or energy to share it with others. I have nicknames for all my neighbors though. Across from me is "Damnitall Sharon," Yappy, and Mysterious Roommate. Next door is Podcaster, with visits from Sound Design via Skype every other Thursday. Last month their theme was the minutiae of some internet puzzle conspiracy. This month it's either audio drama or porn. Possibly both.

Each Boom is a five-count apart. I stood still in the kitchenette and counted.

One.
Two.
Three.
Four.
Five.
Boom.

That's how it worked, how it had worked for years. Count to five. Then count to four. Then the barrage. Then silence. It would all be over in ten minutes; then I could move on with my night, and not think any more about it. I didn't bother to look out the windows. The trees and street lights blocked any view I would have had, even of hints of color.

Within three minutes it had stopped. Obviously, one of my theories was right. I could bring it up tomorrow, when I was forced into conversations at work. Or I could lie and say that I was stupid drunk, or high and hallucinating. No one ever noticed I didn't smoke, or drink. They didn't notice I hated making conversations.

* * * * *

I brushed off the idea of standing in a small shower while the remains of the booming still echoed in my head. My time would be better spent cooking up the hard-boiled eggs for next week's meals. There had to be a way to freeze eggs so they could be reheated in a microwave at the right time without exploding everywhere and making the office smell like…well, eggs.

Boom.
One.
Two.
Three.
Four.
Fi-
Boom!

203

In the silence afterwards, I slowly became aware that I was holding my breath. I let it out. I got the eggs in the pot and got it boiling. I put the timer on for twelve minutes.

Boom.

One.

Two.

Three.

F-

Boom!

There were no crackles, no comets sizzling upwards to reassure me that it was just a light show, everything was under control, everyone was safe. There was no barrier keeping us from the giants.

The hair on the back of my neck prickled. The last time I felt like this I had been twelve and knew that the last boom should have been over by 10pm. The boom that woke me had been so loud it couldn't possibly be in my ears.

In later years, my mother insisted that it was "Exploding Head Syndrome" brought on by the flu I'd been recovering from, because she had just discovered what that was.

I remember waking up on the floor by my bed, turning towards my window, and seeing the orange streetlight behind my curtains flash green entirely too close. I jumped up and stumbled towards my parents' room, trying to shout about giants breaking through the barrier without alerting whatever was outside. I reached their room at the other end of the hall just as a crack appeared in the wall.

That was when I noticed the ground beneath me was rolling; as if the giants had woken a beast that lived under the house.

My mother grabbed everyone's spare shoes and a suitcase, my father grabbed me. We huddled under the sturdiest kitchen table ever created with a radio that played mostly static until everything stopped.

Then people wandered outside into the street, with tentative steps, as though any wrong move would dislodge a power or phone line.

It wasn't even a proper earthquake, I learned when I was older. We had been merely a victim of an aftershock. That's why our house was still standing. The green light turned out to be a transformer blowing by the apartments behind our house. Repairs and free piles of glass for everyone!

* * * * *

It's 10 pm now. The eggs overcooked.

There hasn't been another footfall in five minutes. It should make me feel better.

It doesn't.

I'm hoping that, out the living room window, beyond the palms and street lights and the Norms restaurant, there's a hint of blue willows or golden spiders. A stray comet to tell me someone found a firework from the 4th and decided tonight was the night to set it alight. Or perhaps it was spotlights to announce the opening of the newest Mexican takeout place. Just one thing, anything, to tell me that giants aren't real.
One.

Two.

Three.

Boom!

I silently wished for the comforting shhh of a sparkling, multicolored waterfall.

There's nothing.

One.

Two.

Three.

Boom!

Standing near a window in an earthquake is stupid, I remind myself. Not even a rookie mistake, just a mistake. There's nothing to see there.

This apartment wasn't built when the giants broke through. Architects may have taken more care in its construction. I doubt it. This is a place where people go to ignore the world and be ignored by it. No one is here voluntarily. Construction was down to the minimally passing specifications. I've been considering my exit points. I don't trust the stairwell doors that always seem to be locked, or the decorative escapes.

One.

Two.

Three.

Boom!

I don't have a three-day supply of non-perishable food or water...or a fire extinguisher...or a waterproof container. I don't even know where I would keep all that. The garage, where it will be useless once this all topples down? In here, where I could not carry more than my duffel bag full of clothes, band-aids and gym towels?

One.

Two.

Three.

Boom!

There are no fire drills in apartment buildings. Why are there no fire drills in apartment buildings? I was twelve the last time this happened. I didn't have the attention span to really understand what was happening. All I knew was that our house was under attack, and my father was bravely squeezing the air out of my chest as he tried to protect me from a collapsing world. I've seen the pictures and video of the epicenter since. At our house, it was merely "strong", barely a four on the Richter scale.

Can this building handle a three?

One.

Two.

Thr-

Boom!

Don't stand in the doorways. Don't hide under the particleboard kitchen table. Don't stand by the windows.

There's nothing to see.

Not the flash of green and white and showers red-gold sparks, entirely too close.

Not the shadow the height of the Norms restaurant, outlined in the afterimage of colored lights.

Shadows. More than one.

I manage to take three steps backwards.

I feel Dad's arms again, squeezing the air out of me, reassuring me even though he's pale.

One.

Two.

Boom!

Did I leave the stove on?

Is there time to check?

Should I warn my neighbors?

How do I even start?

One.

Two.

Boom!

I should be scared.

I don't have time to be scared.

One.

T-

Boom!

Foreword by Author Jacen Bishop

Author's Note: For Idle Conversation, I would like to thank Meagan and Kim, for your invaluable feedback and help in taming the grammatically challenging beast known as English. And to John, for the many hours of horror movie conversation that helped spawn this story. And Then You Remember is dedicated to my first-grade classmates whose hysteria over Bloody Mary lost us access to the restroom for an afternoon.

Idle Conversation by Jacen Bishop

"I'm tellin' ya, just destroy the head and take out the brain. That'll stop 'em," John says. Ever the Romero devotee, that one.

"That's your answer?" Jay has that look. The one that tells me he's not gonna let John slide on this one. "We've been over this! Just because practically everyone that makes a zombie film follows Night of the Living Dead doesn't mean it would work."

"Anthony would agree with me."

"The fanboy? Yeah, we should ask him," Jay snorts. "Of course, he'd say that. He's a zealot when it comes to that series." His tone changes into his best attempt at a mimic of Anthony's nasally voice. It's not even close. "Zombies don't run, they shamble; and they're not sick people, they're reanimated corpses. That's why all those new 'it's a virus making people crazy' movies aren't zombie movies."

I rub my eyes as my vision starts to blur, tuning Jay out. I've heard this rant before, including the non-sarcastic version. God, my head hurts. I force my eyes to focus on the clock above the fridge. Almost midnight.

That can't be right, seems like it should be later, like the four of us have been sitting around my kitchen table for hours, maybe because I'm so exhausted or maybe because this discussion has been chasing itself in circles. Everything since the restaurant's a blur.

"Well he's right. They're not zombie movies." John's clearly trying to resist the urge to scratch at the bandage on his arm. "They're not relevant now."

Jay has the look of a man who just found out he's not the real father.

"What?!...How can... " he stops and attempts to regain his composure. "The point is that they have the overall feel of a zombie movie and that's what matters."

Could be a good counter, depends on how he backs it.

"They force you to look at the genre in a whole new light. Shamblers are only dangerous in numbers. Runners take the threat to a whole new level. What do you do if they can run? Or can't be put down with a head shot? Or still have the ability to think and reason?" That's definitely a good point, what do you do when they can run or even reason?

"Well Anthony's not here. So, what does it matter what he'd think?" Dan says. He's been quiet so far, leaning against the fridge not saying anything.

He comes over and takes a seat at the table. He moves slowly, like his muscles are sore, and I can't tell if he looks tired and haggard or just pissed at the other two.

"You feelin' alright?" I ask. He briefly glances at the table in front of me.

"I'm fine," he says.

Dan never was big into zombie flicks like the rest of us. Jay bought him one as a gift, but he never got around to watching it, much to Jay's annoyance. I suspect it's a point of perverse pride on Dan's part. I always wondered what he got out of the group. Jay's about to retort but Dan's not in the mood.

"All I know is, it's good that zombies eat brains," he says, cutting Jay off and putting an end to the no doubt masterful point he was about to make. "Otherwise you two'd be in some serious trouble."

"Real funny," Jay says, turning to Dan, his volume increasing. "We're trying to have a serious discussion here..."

"Hey," I cut in, gesturing upstairs.

"Sorry...I forgot," Jay mutters.

"How is she?" John asks.

"Resting," I reply. "Sleeping I think," I add as I realize I haven't heard anything from upstairs for a while now. I should go check on her but can't bring myself to.

Dan laughs softly. "I remember when we met Jessica," he says. "I still say a guy like you had no right bringing a girl that good looking to a party." I shake my head and smile slightly at the memory of him saying that at said party, in front of Jessica, then I give him the finger.

I think back to that night. We were headed to Anthony's birthday party. It was the first time I'd seen her in the black flared dress she favored. As we pulled up to his house, I noticed she was fidgeting with her handbag, a rarely seen sign of nerves, no doubt anxious about meeting my friends for the first time. "They'll love you," I had reassured her. "Gorgeous and a walking encyclopedia of zombie movie facts; how could they not?" at that the left side of her mouth had pulled up into the crooked smile I'd come to adore.

"Zombies don't eat brains," John's voice is barely audible.

"What?" Dan's instantly annoyed again, his comment already forgotten.

"You said it's good they eat brains. That was only in the Return of the Living Dead series, in all the other ones they eat flesh."

Dan looks at me for confirmation.

"It's true," I confirm. "The general consensus in Hollywood seems to be that they eat flesh, not brains."

"Well, I don't think you're gonna get much help from zombie movies when it comes to the real thing." I've never seen Jay look so hopeless.

"Yeah," John shrugs, "all the movies would give you is a bunch of dead ends."

I laugh quietly despite myself. That pun was awful and John's always had a habit of making them unintentionally, but that's what happens when I'm exhausted

-- the stupidest things are far more funny then they should be.

And then it happens: the one thing that's destined to happen in any conversation.

The Pause.

You know, that moment when everyone runs out of things to say at the same time. You know what I'm talking about. I'd bet everything I own it's been part of every conversation since the beginning of time, and it occurs to me in that moment there's true silence for the first time since we went out.

No quiet questions of concern from the staff to the ill-looking man at the table next to us that we hadn't noticed until then, questions that quickly turned to panicked shouts for help and doctors when he started violently convulsing. No screams that quickly spread through the crowd when he suddenly lunged at Jessica and mauled her. No more screeching tires and crunching metal of car wrecks as panicked drivers bolted through red lights into oncoming traffic. No gunshots from the responding police officer as a group of things that had once been other diners violently dragged him down. None of the hysterical yelling from Dan for me to grab the gun the officer dropped. An absence of Anthony's cries of shock and pain when that same, now mangled, officer got back up and tore into him. No chaotic din set to a backdrop of wailing sirens. An end to my begging Jessica to stay with me as I fight to stop her bleeding. No more reasons to continue this conversation.

I turn to look at Jay and he stares at me a moment before slowly nodding. This is what he and I had secretly agreed to at the beginning of the discussion. At the beginning, before we realized that no amount of horror movies or hypothetical discussions could have prepared us for this.

I pick up the pistol that's been laying on the table in front of me, point it at John and shatter The Pause with a

214

trigger pull. That possibly dead cop had taken a small chunk out of John's arm. I'm gonna trust the movies on this one. Dan stares at me, the shock on his face almost comical. He tries to stand, but I pull the trigger several times before he can protest. He was done too…wasn't bitten but was definitely showing the signs of infection... at least I'm pretty sure he was, looking a lot like that guy in the restaurant.

It's as he slumps back into his chair that I notice I didn't score any headshots; I don't know if it will matter; I don't think anyone does yet. Maybe they'll both come back. Maybe Romero knows. My arm falls to my side, hand shaking from the recoil, my ears ringing with the discharge. I never realized something could be so loud.

"Now me," Jay whispers. I'm caught off-guard by that, we had agreed on John and Dan, but not this. I raise an eyebrow. "Yes, I'm sure," he says." His voice is shaky, eyes watering. "I can't do this; I won't make it. I don't want to end up like they are."

I realize this is one thing the movies got wrong. I don't experience any moral dilemma in the moment. With all that's transpired tonight, I can't feel anything besides an all-consuming numbness. I raise the gun towards him.

"Wait," he says suddenly, and I pause. "Do you think Return of the Living Dead got it right?" he asks.
He sees my confusion and clarifies: "That it hurts, ya know... being one… one of them, I mean…do you think it hurts to be dead?"

"I don't know," I whisper. It's the most honest answer I can give. He processes that before looking up at me. He nods. I pull the trigger.

In the silence that follows, I find myself wondering what happens next, if I can do this, where the script will take me. I think of the scene Jay was referring to, where the zombie explains why they eat brains. Because it hurts to be dead, that they can feel themselves rotting. I must've seen

215

that movie a dozen times and for the first time I shudder in horror at such a monstrous concept.

My thoughts are interrupted by an uneven clicking that's slowly growing louder, the sound of a woman in just one high heel walking across a hardwood floor. The kitchen door opens and I turn to find myself looking into Jessica's face. She's still wearing the black flared dress she wore out to dinner tonight. She's so beautiful. I hear a clatter as the gun slips from my grasp.

Jay's question comes to mind.

I bet Jessica would know.

So, I ask.

Her remaining eye slowly focuses on me.

Her lips twist into a mockery of the crooked smile I always adored.

It looks like I'm gonna get my answer.

And Then You Remember

Jacen Bishop

Sweat rolls down your forehead and into your eyes as you take quick, shallow breaths. You squeeze your eyes shut in an attempt to both block out the salty sting and focus on taking deep breaths to regain control of your respiration and try to fight back the rising bile in the back of your throat.

It's a futile gesture.

Your stomach rolls and seizes, kickstarting a wave of convulsions that send another surge of the half-digested contents from last night's revelry rocketing up on a reverse trajectory. You grip the sides of the bowl as abdominal muscles continue to rebel until there's nothing left to give up. The cramping of abused muscles moves in time with the pounding behind your temples as you slowly wipe your mouth on the back of your hand.

"I pray to Siva, let me die."

The line from that Harrison Ford movie surfaces unexpectedly from the recesses of memory. It's funny the connections the mind makes at times. You haven't seen that movie in years. No...it was on in the background last night, wasn't it?

Regardless, you find yourself echoing its sentiments for a moment. Please God make it stop! you pray, but it's an insincere plea. The only time you pray, if it could be called that, is in these moments of self-inflicted misery. Prayers that are always followed by vows and internally declared commitments to never put yourself here again...vows you know damn well will be broken the next time your friends want to go out.

Feeling the worst of the storm has passed and sincerely hoping you're not just in the eye of it, you flail weakly and blindly at the side of the tank until your hand finds the lever. The sound of the exiting water filling your ears seems far too loud and that's when you become aware of the figure in the doorway. No doubt, it's your friend coming to check on you after hearing you being sick.

"I'm sorry," you mutter. "I didn't mean to wake you. I'm okay, just need..."

You trail off as you realize no one's there and your pounding headache prevents you from devoting anymore thought to it. You get shakily to your feet and move over to the sink. You reach out to turn on the faucet, but suddenly recoil in horror at what you see.

Streaks of crimson run down the wall from the ledge at the top of the sink and pool in the bottom of the basin.

"What the hell?" You gasp aloud as your eyes try to focus on the dark stains in the dim early morning light filtering into the bathroom from the tiny frosted window. Hesitantly, you reach out to touch the liquid, run a finger across it. It's soft but solid and realization dawns on you. It's wax. A deep red wax. Relieved, you look up and, sure enough, you see the remains of three candles on the ledge just under the mirror.

Candles? Did the power go out? no...no, you're certain it didn't. You stare at the melted stumps for a moment. You can't remember why you lit them, but vaguely recall it was important that they were red.

Turning the faucet on, you splash water on your face. Your mouth and throat are painfully dry so you try cupping some in your hands and tentatively take a few sips. Your stomach grumbles a bit in protest but, in the end, accepts. You shut off the water and begin to make your way unsteadily down the hall. Passing the open door to your friend's bedroom you stop as you catch something in your peripheral vision.

Your friend, the one that you just saw in the bathroom, is sprawled across her bed. Her loud snores inform you that she's been out for a while. You stand there for a moment before shrugging it off.

You make your way down the hall and then carefully navigate the stairs; your dizzy state presents a challenge with each step. The pounding inside your skull is unrelenting and your body begs you to forget going home and just find a couch to crash on. Stopping in the foyer, you glance hopefully into the living room only to have those hopes dashed. You see other guests from last night sleeping it off on the couch, the easy chairs, and the floor. Going home to the comfort of your own bed is the only option left you and you feebly attempt to psych yourself up for the long walk back.

Sighing, you dig your coat out from the collection overwhelming the wooden coat tree, knocking several jackets to the floor in your search. You can't be bothered to hang them back up. Pulling your coat on is a struggle, but eventually you prevail and then proceed to pat your pockets; it's an almost ritualistic behavior you perform each time you're about to leave a place. Wallet? Check. Keys and phone? Check and check. Satisfied, you grab the doorknob and then jump backwards, startled by the reflection of a figure in the decorative window at the door's center.

Long dark hair frames a pale face, features distorted in the multi-paned glass. Whipping around reveals nothing behind you. You grit your teeth in pain, hand going to your forehead as your headache takes revenge for the sudden movement. You turn back to the door feeling stupid for jumping at what had to be your own reflection and quietly let yourself out.

* * * * *

The mid-morning sun shines with a high-noon intensity that pains your poor hungover mind to the point that it forces you to close your eyes. After what feels like an eternity, your eyes adjust enough so that you can open them just enough to see where you're going. Then you stumble off the porch and begin the half mile walk home.

You keep your gaze on the sidewalk in front of you to combat the sun's glare; the crisp October morning brings no small amount of relief to your aching head. Your route brings you onto Main Street, the many shops unusually quiet for this time of morning. As you walk, you gradually become aware of a presence in your peripheral vision. Looking to the right, you see a young woman with long dark locks standing in front of the hair salon directly across the street from you. Between the shadows from the salon's awnings and your squinting, you can't make out her face at all, but know on some primal level that she's watching you. Your walk slows to a stop as you stare back. She's not someone you immediately recognize, yet there's something vaguely familiar about her…

Bzzzzzzzzztttt!

The buzzing of your phone in your back pocket nearly gives you a heart attack. Pulling out your mobile, you see a text notification. Your friend must finally be up.

Where u at?

Walking home, you text back. Looking up, you glance back across the street. The woman's no longer there. Your phone buzzes in your hand.

You okay?
Besides the massive hangover? Yeah, I'll live.
You sure? After all, you didn't say goodbye. 😊

Before you can respond, you get the feeling that you're being followed. Looking over your shoulder you swear for an instant that you spot a swath of dark hair behind a line of hedges. You stare intently, watching for any movement, wondering if someone is hiding back there. No, it's just shadows cast from the branches moving gently in the breeze.

You shake the sensation off and start walking again, but can't help continually glancing over your shoulder. You unconsciously quicken your pace as a hard, cold knot of dread begins to form in your gut.

A blaring horn yanks your attention forward as you step off the curb, causing you to scramble backwards onto the sidewalk as a strong rush of air blows past. Your gaze follows the pickup that seemingly materialized out of nowhere and almost splattered you across the road. You internally chew out the driver for speeding. Finding fault in their driving helps you excuse the inattention that almost got you killed. The light turns and this time you make a point of looking before crossing and continuing past the row of shops and restaurants that line this block. The shot of adrenaline from your near miss has done wonders for yanking your brain out of its dehydrated house of pain, as you become aware that you're shaking slightly.

Bzzzzzzzztttt!

You jump and almost drop your phone. Get it together! You scold yourself.

Suddenly, the door right next to you opens and you start as someone exits. The young man stepping into your path is too engrossed in his phone to even notice you let alone how close he comes to running into you. He continues down the sidewalk utterly oblivious to the near collision he almost caused. At least you're not the only one. The normally pleasant aroma of coffee follows him and you realize you're in front of the Brewhaha Coffee Shop. Your queasy stomach begins to roll slightly at the smell of your favorite beverage. You begin to debate. The thought of being sick again is a strong argument to just keep moving. However, the incoming withdrawal symptoms from your caffeine addiction is the last thing your poor head needs right now.

Why do you keep putting yourself in this situation?

The sidewalks are strangely empty for this time of day and the sudden urge to be around others seals the deal and you quickly head inside. The ding of the door chime and the familiar sounds of the cafe calm your nerves. The hum of activity around you stands in stark contrast to what you left on the other side of the door. Getting into line, you remember your phone and check your texts.

> Hello?
>
> *Sorry, was busy trying to throw myself into traffic.* 😵 *you text back.*
>
> LOL! Headache that bad, huh?
>
> *Definitely a contender for the number one spot.*
> *Well that's the least of your problems now, you didn't say goodbye* 👻 *lol*
>
> What? I couldn't. You were passed out.
>
> ?

A voice cuts into your thoughts. You look up to see that you're next in line and the barista is staring at you expectantly.

"What can I get you?" He repeats patiently.

You place your regular order, digging out your wallet. You hand him your card, knowing the price before he tells you. He moves to take it and stops. A sudden look of confused concern spreads across his face as he looks over your shoulder. You scan the room behind you and then you see her by the door. Pale skin standing out against her dark dress and even darker hair that falls down either side of an expressionless face that's staring right at you. You turn back to the barista, your arm still outstretched. He takes the card, eyes flicking back to you before shaking his head slightly. Does he see her, too?

"That'll be right up," he says before you can ask.

Pretending to look out the large bay windows that line the front of the shop, you casually glance over to see if she is watching you. She is and you drop your eyes to the floor as soon as you make eye contact.

"Here you go," the barista says, interrupting your thoughts as he hands you your drink.

"Thanks," you mutter, taking the cup, while simultaneously attempting to stick your wallet back in your pocket.

You hurry out the door, stealing a glance to the side. She's still there, black dress and all, her unblinking gaze following you. Back outside, you hurriedly put a couple of blocks between you and the coffee shop. Stopping to catch your breath, with your headache angrily complaining about the sudden physical exertion, you pull out your phone and begin to text frantically.

I think I'm being followed.
Sure you are. She's gonna get ya, LOL
How'd you know it's a she?

222

I was there, remember? I told y'all not to play that stupid game.

Game?

You struggle to put the pieces of last night back together. What game is she talking about? You don't remember playing any game, but that doesn't really matter as it dawns on you that last night's book has a lot of missing chapters. Your phone buzzes again.

It's a picture. You're standing in front of your friend's bathroom mirror. Your drunken state is obvious even in the photo. You're posed with hands on your cheeks, an overly-exaggerated expression of mock horror on your face. The three red candles on the ledge under the mirror cast distorted shadows across the background.

Your phone buzzes again.

I don't care if it is a stupid kid's game. I'm still not going mess with that stuff. My luck it would work. Lol. The last thing I need is some dead chick cursing me, the new message reads. And then taunting her that you took her baby! That's some intestinal fortitude right there. 💪

Dead chick? You vaguely remember a discussion last night about an old town legend and wonder if that's what she's referring too.

You start to respond when you hear the rustle of fabric. You look back to see the pale woman from the cafe moving briskly towards you. She's here! Is all you have time to text. Her arm extends toward you and you flinch and squeeze your eyes shut.

"Hey," she says, "you dropped this."

You open your eyes and see your wallet in the hand of a woman in a black dress, face covered in makeup to darken her eyes and make her skin more ashen than normal.

"Man, you burned out outta there like your hair was on fire!" She says. If you hadn't stopped, I wouldn't have caught ya. I can't really run in these things." She gestures down at the

223

clunky oversized combat boots she's wearing. Then it hits you--the dress, makeup, pale skin, darken eyes. You didn't realize the Goth look was still in around here. Your cheeks start to burn in unison with how stupid you suddenly feel.

"You okay?" She asks, head cocked to the side, a quizzical expression on her face.

"Yeah," you respond. "I'm sorry, just...it's been a rough night and rougher morning."

"I've been there," she laughs.

"Thank you for returning this," you say taking the proffered wallet.

"Anytime," she replies with a smile. "Have a good one, get some sleep."

You put your wallet in your coat pocket, taking care to make sure it's secure this time.

"Thanks again," you call after her.

She acknowledges your call with a wave as she heads back to The Brewhaha. You look at your phone to see several missed texts. Ghost emojis surround the words.

Oooooo you're in trouble now!
Hello?
Quit playing. You there?
Seriously, not funny. Is someone there?
Sorry. False alarm keep freakin' myself out.
You ok?
I'm fine. I'll explain later.

Within ten minutes you're walking through your front door. You set the paper coffee cup you emptied on the stand near the entrance and promptly knock it over as you remove your coat. Right now, picking it up seems like far too much effort. You fall onto your couch, but no sooner

224

have you sat down than your body issues the alarm and you rush to the bathroom. In hindsight, you realize you should have listened to your stomach about the coffee.

Moving to the sink, you start cleaning up when your phone begins buzzing, rapid fire notifications illuminate the screen.

OMG! Look at the picture!

You pull the picture up again, but nothing stands out to you. Another text pops up.

You didn't say goodbye! I TOLD you to say goodbye!

Confusion reigns in your mind as you text back:

And I TOLD you, you were asleep when I left.
Not me! The rules! You didn't follow the rules!
What rules?

Your thumbs fly across the screen as you start to get frustrated and demand answers.

Just look at the picture!

Is all you get back.

You go back to the picture, but still you don't notice anything special about it. Wait... there is something in the corner. It's in the tub, standing just over your left shoulder. A pale face framed with straight dark hair...and an expression of inhuman rage on its face. You begin to shake uncontrollably. With a great deal of effort, you steady your hands enough to text back a question, one you're not sure you want the answer to. You ask what you did last night.

Movement reflected in the phone's screen catches your eye; it's as if someone else is also leaning over the phone too. You don't want to look up but, in the end, you can't help yourself.

225

There, in the mirror, is the same face from the picture complete with the matching expression. Once she sees that she has your attention, her cracked lips twist into a grim parody of a smug grin, and then she screams. You drop your phone as you cover your ears. The mirror shatters under the force of her voice, shards of glass fly everywhere, but you don't move. You can only watch as she reaches out and grabs either side of the mirror's frame. At that moment, the door slams shut and the ceiling light blows out. You're only vaguely aware of the blub remnants falling on you.

In the blackness you hear your phone vibrating, no doubt a text telling what you did last night, but it no longer matters. Because as you listen to the crunching of broken glass signifying a childhood tale now pulling herself into your world, you suddenly remember everything.

Foreword by Author James Close

Author's Note: I wanted to write a simple short horror story that anyone could place themselves into. We all have memories of traveling down long dark roads at night. I wanted to capture the feelings I felt, wandering what was out there.

Keep Awake By James Close

The numbers shine 1:39 AM in the crimson light of the car's dashboard clock. You've expended your supply of soda, and the bag of lollipops your parents taught you to bring for long road trips, but you're still struggling to keep your eyes open. Even the last resort of blaring music only serves to worsen the headache of sleep pounding angrily against the windows of your eyes, demanding entry.

The windows to your soul, you muse.

Man, you think of the stupidest shit when you're tired.

You've been on the road for fifteen hours, and with another six to go before you reach the next town, you decide to stop, or risk falling asleep at the wheel.

It's the intelligent thing to do, you decide.

It only took you slightly swerving into the opposite lane to come to that conclusion, not that it would've mattered much, you haven't seen another car for miles. On a regular road it might not be so bad, but you might as well be driving on a treadmill. Repeatedly driving passed the same barren expanse. You're getting low on fuel anyway so you figure you might as well rest now and use one of the spare gas cans you keep in the trunk to refill the tank in the morning. So, you pull over to the sound of dirt shifting beneath the tires. The relaxing noise almost lulls you to sleep right then and there.

The pounding of sleep becomes a welcoming knock, more a friendly face than an unwanted visit from the relatives. You check your phone out of habit before bed. No signal, of course. So, you just reread your last conversation:

I'm leaving now, should be there by sometime Tuesday.

Or you could just buy a plane ticket and save a day.

You know I hate flying. My feet aren't leaving solid ground.

229

Whatever. You'd better just be here in time, or we'll start without you.

Okeydokey.

You wonder if they could feel the attitude through text, or if they just thought you were an idiot. Finishing, you turn off the engine, lay your head back and let yourself be engulfed by sleep.

You don't know how long you slept, only that it wasn't long enough. You find yourself kicked awake by the feeling of the car suddenly lilting forward. You lazily look out the windscreen to see a squat silhouette on the hood of your car. Too braindead to feel more cautious, you reach out your hand towards the car's ignition. Half turning the keys, the headlights flash on and every ounce of sleep is washed away by a cold wave of fear. What you see, sitting crossed-legged on the hood of your car, is so close to human that it can't be described as anything but wrong.

Its body is too thin, too long, and too gaunt. Its skin is too sallow and glabrous. It gives the air of a coyote whose body has been broken in a metal frame, to force a resemblance to the shape of a man's. It's just sitting there, staring down at you, head tilted slightly to the side like a curious puppy, unblinking. Its shallow ribs show no signs of breath. It's completely motionless, except for its hands. Its arms are at its sides, palms flat against the hood, but its fingers are slightly shaking. The languid motion is the only thing that betrays any sign of life.

At first you thought it had long black claws, but you soon realize that the fingers themselves are long and the skin at the tips runs a deep blue, as if the blood couldn't quite make the distance. Not that you're too concerned with its fingers, its face is what really holds your attention. The skin under its eyes is dark and the veins beneath them, darker. The eyes themselves are small in their sockets, like black marbles glazed over by a thin film of milk, with more of the residue collecting around the edges. The mouth is dry and cracked and looks as if it has been torn open by the teeth within...teeth that are now sneering down at you. Yes, it was that face which held you. Your gaze stays centered on it as you slowly lean over to the glove compartment to grab the pepper spray you keep there for emergencies, afraid a sudden movement might startle it.

Startle it...

You don't chuckle.

And its gaze stays centered on you. Head laggardly turning, as if on rusty hinges, to follow as you move, eyes disinterested in what your hands are pulling from the glove box.

Its eyes never leave you as you return to your position in the driver's seat, pepper spray in hand. It was a small comfort to at least have something to defend yourself with if the creature tried to break in.

Dear God, what if it tries to get in?

As any trapped animal does, you begin to try and think of an escape. You contemplate just throwing the car in reverse as quickly as possible and hope it falls off, but you remember how low the tank is. And you don't want to have to stop and get out to empty a couple of cans in half a mile-- not while that thing is still out there somewhere. You think about honking the horn to try and scare it away, or turn on the windshield wipers, or the sprayers--something to cause a distraction so you can make a run for it--but you realize that, in the middle of nowhere, you'd have nowhere to run. No, the car is the safest place; you don't know for how long, but the car is your safest place.

I just need to stay awake until sunrise, you think. This doesn't look like the sort of thing that likes the daytime.

You find yourself wishing your pepper spray was garlic instead and with that stupid thought, you remember just how bone-tired you really are. You glance down at the clock as quickly as you can, not wanting to take your eyes off of the creature for too long. 2:21 AM it reads.

Okay, I just need to keep my eyes open, and pointed at this thing for the next...four hours.

The minutes crawl by at an arthritic pace.

3:52 AM: your vision begins to blur in and out as your eyes sting at their edges.

4:09 AM: you begin to feel physically ill from exhaustion, as if you are running a fever. And that numb pulsing sensation is running throughout your body, just under the skin, like you're going to throw up.

You know you can't take much more without help, so you turn on the radio, low so not to disturb... that thing, but you're desperate for anything, anything--even back-to-back infomercials--just something else you can focus your mind on.

5:11 AM: You haven't noticed it blink once, not even a squint in the three hours it's been staring down at you, while white tears run down its face, like dripping candle wax. The fingers are still the only things that show this broken creature is still alive.

5:36 AM: this time you do notice something different. The creature's sallow skin seems to be growing even more yellow and sickly, but not just ...whatever is sitting on the hood, the landscape behind it is growing dimmer as well.

It's getting closer to sunrise, it shouldn't be getting darker, you think to yourself.

Your heart sinks with the realization.

The battery!

You turn the radio off in a panic to buy as much time as you can. It slows, but doesn't stop. The creature is becoming harder and harder to see as it becomes lost in the shrinking light.

"No, no, no, no, no!" you whimper, almost in tears now, "please last!"

Foreword by Authors Taylor Kuykendall & James Otis

Biography: Taylor Kuykendall and James Otis are partners in both life and writing. They crafted this story as a team.

Parts & Pieces By James Otis and Taylor Kuykendall

The sun was just starting to rise above the city skyline, but Greg and his wife Emily had already been up for hours. Emily was packing to go on a trip to see her family. Greg and Emily lived and worked in the greater Washington DC area. Greg's family lived relatively close by in Maryland, but Emily had moved to DC from Oregon and hadn't seen her relatives in over two years. Emily had been saving vacation time for over a year and had been looking forward to introducing Greg to her family.

Unfortunately, Greg had recently started a new job and didn't have much vacation time to
spare for a large trip. He and Emily talked about it and they decided that she should go home to see her family and he would be able to meet them another time. Emily had been disappointed by the decision but she could see the practicality. The only alternative would be to wait another year until Greg had enough vacation time as well, an alternative that didn't suit Emily or her family.

Greg had to be at work early to attend a meeting so Emily would be taking her car separately to the airport. When they were done loading Emily's suitcases into the trunk, Emily came back inside to give him a hug and kiss goodbye.

"I love you. See you in two weeks," Emily said.

"I love you too. Tell your folks that I'm sorry that I couldn't come but I'll try to come next time," Greg said, giving Emily a kiss goodbye. Emily then left while Greg went about making a cup of coffee from their Keurig coffee machine. A moment later, he thought he heard Emily say something from the driveway.

"What's that?" he called.

235

There was no answer. Greg waited a moment but didn't hear Emily's voice again. He guessed he had just imagined it. Still he listened in case she had said something, only giving up when he heard her car start and pull out of their driveway.

Greg left for work a few minutes later, grabbing his coffee and a bagel so he could eat breakfast on his way to work. His work day dragged by, probably because he knew that he would be going home, not to the love of his life, but to a dark and empty home.

Not that Greg was entirely upset to have the house to himself for the next two weeks. The life of a bachelor could be a lot of fun after all, as long as you know it is only a temporary situation. Greg was looking forward to playing video games all evening, going out fishing, and maybe inviting his buddies over for a poker night without having to worry about Emily's approval.

Still, when he got home that night, he couldn't help but notice how empty the house felt. There was nobody to share a meal with, talk about his day to, or cuddle up next to in bed at night. Greg imagined he would have a certain amount of fun for the first few days that Emily was gone, but he knew that he would spend most of those two weeks desperately missing her and looking forward to her return.

Later that evening, his phone chimed, indicating that he had gotten a text message. He had been expecting one from Emily a few hours earlier to let him know that she had arrived safely. When he hadn't received one, he tried calling her phone, but it had gone straight to voicemail. Her phone was either turned off or dead. Greg was annoyed. Emily was known for being forgetful about things like that but he sometimes felt that she didn't take his feelings and worries about her safety all that seriously.

When he checked his phone, however, the number that had texted him was not Emily's. It was a number he had hoped to never see again. The number belonged to Rachel,

Greg's psycho ex-girlfriend who had stalked him for months after he had broken things off with her. Rachel's pattern of strange behavior had dwindled over the past year and Greg had hoped that after marrying Emily, Rachel would have finally moved on.

"Hey, would you like to meet me sometime this week?" Rachel's text had read.

Greg looked incredulously at the message. He considered just ignoring it, but knew that Rachel would keep persisting until he gave her an answer.

"What do you want?" he texted back at her.

"I just want us to be together again," was her reply.

"I told you I'm not interested in seeing you again. You know I'm married now, don't you?"

"I know."

"Then why don't you move on and find someone else?"

"I want to be with you."

Greg was frustrated and unnerved. He thought he had put this relationship and all the baggage that went with it behind him. But here she was, starting up the same shit all over again. Instinctively, Greg glanced out the window to see if he could see Rachel's car outside. He looked up and down the street but didn't see her vehicle anywhere. At least she wasn't watching him right now.

"Listen to me. I never NEVER want to see you again. Is that CRYSTAL CLEAR to you?" Greg texted to Rachel again.

She replied "Don't do this to me. I love you and I need you. I can't live without you in my life."

"Just stop. Go away and stop trying to contact me."

"You're mine. I will have you with me again."

"I'm not yours. I haven't been yours for three years. You need to stop this."

"If you won't be with me, I'm going to do something drastic."

This last message caused a quiet unease for Greg. Rachel had always been strange and obsessive. She had never tried to do anything to hurt him before, but this last message seemed to be a thinly veiled threat or perhaps an escalation in her behavior.

"What is that supposed to mean?" Greg asked.

"If you don't agree to be with me, I'm going to cut off a body part and mail it to you every day until you do."

Greg couldn't believe his eyes. He reread the message twice to make sure he wasn't just imaging this strange scenario. What the absolute fuck? She was going to mutilate herself and mail pieces of herself to him unless he agreed to go out with her again?

"She's fucking lost it," Greg muttered to himself.

Naturally, Greg considered the possibility that she was just bluffing. How many times had she threatened to kill herself if he hadn't come back to her before? A dozen times at least, but she was still alive and well from the looks of it; using the term 'well' liberally, of course. He decided not to play this particular game with her. He decided to text her one last time.

"You're fucking nuts! I'm not doing this with you. I'm turning off my phone and going to bed. Get the fuck out of my life you psycho bitch."

Greg didn't wait for a response; he simply turned off his phone and tossed it onto the counter beside the dishwasher. No doubt she would continue to text him, but he was done listening to anything Rachel had to say. Greg turned his phone on again later that night and listened to it buzz as a slew of texts popped up. Greg let them come but refused to check any of them.

Sleep didn't come easily to Greg that night. He tried taking his mind off of Rachel's threat by watching movies and playing video games, but she was still there in the back of his mind. By the next day, though, Greg had largely forgotten his strange conversation with Rachel. He had a busy day at work and was commended by his boss on giving a very successful presentation of their latest product to their clients.

Considering the good work he had been doing so far, Greg thought he would be a shoe-in for his company's yearly bonus and perhaps even an early promotion. However, his good feelings were dashed when he checked the mail that night and discovered an unmarked, unaddressed envelope. There was no stamp, only writing on the front that said "For Greg."

Curious, he opened up the envelop and let the small item contained inside fall into his hand. Instantly, he screamed and dropped the object onto the ground.

"Holy fucking Christ!" Greg exclaimed, utterly horrified.

The envelope contained a bloody human ear. By the amount of blood in the envelope, it looked like it had been sawed off the side of someone's head while they were still alive; blood from the envelope and the hacked off ear had dribbled onto Greg's hand, causing it to become slick and grimy. Greg, nauseated by the sight, rushed to the side of his house, collapsed against the front stoop, and vomited into the grass.

Rachel had made good on her threat. She'd hacked off her own ear and sent it to him in the mail. Although no, she hadn't sent it. There was no address or return address, and no stamp. She had to have delivered the letter in person to his mailbox. Greg got shakily to his feet, wiping his mouth with the back of his hand. He breathed heavily, leaning against the side of his house. Once he decided he wasn't in any danger of passing out, he considered what his next move should be. Obviously, he would have to contact the police and tell them what had happened. The ear was still laying in the grass next to the mailbox, so he would have that as evidence. Probably calling nine-one-one was a bit of a stretch. He nor anyone else was really in imminent danger;

239

mostly he was just freaking out. He decided calling the non-emergency police number would be the practical approach.

Greg went inside and immediately dialed the local police department and explained to the dispatcher what had happened. She took down his address and informed him that she would dispatch an officer to the scene. Greg asked what he should do with the ear and was advised to leave it where it was until police arrived on the scene. Greg thanked her and hung up the phone. Greg than shakily poured himself a whiskey on the rocks and went out onto his stoop to sip it where he could keep watch on the mailbox and wait for officers to arrive.

Later that evening, a marked cruiser pulled up in front of his home and two police officers got out. Greg stood, thanked them for coming, and proceeded to tell them everything he knew about Rachel, the text message conversation the previous evening, and the severed ear by the mailbox.

Both officers listened and took down the information he gave them. One of them inspected his phone, briefly scanning over all of the text messages that were sent back and forth. One of the officers--Williams according to his badge name--advised Greg that he could keep his phone in his possession if he wanted to but advised Greg not to delete the text message exchange between Rachel and himself in case they needed to use it for evidence later on.

The other officer, Greg didn't get his name, produced a pair of what looked like long tweezers and an evidence bag. He then placed the ear into the evidence bag and marked the bag with a bio-hazard sticker.

"We'll take this into evidence and put it on ice to preserve it. You did a good job responding to this person. Once we have Rachel in custody, we'll have all the evidence we need to charge her with stalking and make sure she doesn't bother you again. In the meantime, if you don't have a court order of restraint, I'd strongly advise you to seek one out."

"Thank you, I'll definitely look into that," Greg said.

Officer Williams gave a card to Greg containing his direct number.

"Give me a call if anything else funny happens or if you get any more body parts from Rachel. We'll step up patrols in your area as well."

"Thank you," Greg said again. After the officers had left, Greg found that he could focus on little else beyond the latest and greatest sick game that Rachel was playing. Putting her hacked off ear in his mailbox? That was quite literally Vincent van Gogh level crazy. Who knew what she might do next. One thing for sure was that he had no intention of checking his messages or talking to her again tonight. His only comforting thought was that, at the very least, Emily was far away visiting her parents in Oregon, probably the safest place she could be given the circumstances.   Rachel was true to her word. Over the next few days, Greg continued to receive body parts in the mail from Rachel. The next day had brought the other ear. The day after that had been a finger. The day after that, a thumb. Rather than visiting his mailbox in person again, Rachel had taken to putting the body parts in plastic storage bags, placing them in envelopes, and mailing them to him in the traditional way.

The police had kept their word as far as Greg was concerned. Each time a new body part turned up in his mailbox, they came and collected it. The police checked the postmarks on each envelope and determined that Rachel had been dropping them off at different post office boxes within town or in a neighboring town each day. Because the police didn't know which dropbox she would use next, there was no way for the police to stake out his mailbox or any given dropbox and wait for Rachel to show up.

The police went to Rachel's address, or at least the last address Greg remembered her living in, but when the police checked they had discovered that Rachel had moved out a year earlier and left no forwarding address. The police then checked government records and discovered her current address, however they found it abandoned when they went to investigate.

An APB was put out for her registered vehicle which had also turned up nothing. Greg couldn't help but feel frustrated by the situation. The police were all looking for Rachel, but despite all efforts, they couldn't find what would now be an extremely disfigured woman who somehow found a way to keep mailing body parts to him.

Greg was still refusing to look at his text messages the whole time in order to avoid seeing any messages from Rachel. Emily would probably be worried sick about him by now as well. She would undoubtedly been trying to text him at some point over the past several days, but if she had, he hadn't responded to her. Even if she had contacted him and knew of the situation he was going through, she would probably be even more worried about him.

Finally, the day came when Greg, feeling a great deal of trepidation, checked his mailbox and was greeted with the sickest present yet. Greg stared in horror at what Rachel had done. There was no envelope this time, so Greg knew Rachel had come to visit his house directly. There, in the mailbox, was an eyeball that Rachel had obviously carefully positioned so that it would stare directly at him when he pulled the mailbox lid down. The eyeball had been crudely cut out, and the optic nerve was still attached like a limp, bloody noodle. Greg felt the urge to vomit again and forced it back down.

Greg just stared at the eye; something wasn't right. He looked closer at the eyeball. He noticed the iris was brown, but that didn't make any sense because Rachel had blue eyes. Greg went inside to get his phone and, for the first time in days, checked his messages. He was unsurprised to find he had gotten dozens from Rachel all demanding that he talk to her and meet her or risk getting more body parts. He didn't bother reading most of them. He finally texted her back.

"You are fucking crazy, you know that?" he asked.

"OOH! You've been getting my gifts I see!" was her response.

"I've been getting the body parts you've been sending me. But something doesn't make sense. You sent me an eye today, but the iris of the eye is brown. Your eyes are blue."

Greg waited a few seconds to see Rachel's response to his observation.

"Oh my God! No wonder you haven't been responding to me! You thought I was cutting body parts off myself and sending them to you?"

Greg stared at the phone completely nonplussed.

"What, you haven't been," he asked?

"No! Those body parts I've been sending you weren't MY body parts. Those body parts came from your wife!"

Greg felt an icy chill go down the entire length of his body.

"My wife? My wife is in Oregon, you stupid bitch. What are you talking about?" Greg texted.

"No, she isn't. I have your wife here. I was waiting outside your home and I heard everything you both said to each other. I overpowered her by her car while you were still inside and I took both her and her car to my special place. I sent a text to her family telling them something had come up and she wouldn't be coming to Oregon this week after all."

Greg dropped the phone onto the floor and ran back out to his mailbox where the eye was. Now that he looked at the eye more carefully, he realized that what Rachel had said was true. He recognized the eye as belonging to Emily. Greg collapsed to his knees and began to scream over and over again while his neighbors came out to see what was going on. He was still screaming insanely as the police arrived.

Foreword from Author Jim Roderick

Biography: The only member of his thoroughly proliferated family to be born out of state (AZ instead of TX, for the curious), Jim has managed to continue that tradition of silent alien observer on into his adult life. A latchkey military brat raised in the electric nurseries of late '90s television and video games, and forever tormented by the unceasing ebb and flow of potential Armageddon's on the horizon, Jim never truly felt at home amongst his immediate, early-realized ersatz vicinity instead taking refuge in critic and artist-curated "Top [number divisible by 10]" retrospections of past pop ephemera in the forms of old avant-garde and horror films and the dated sounds of the mundanely labeled "Classic Rock" search engine keyword, effectively, yet intimately, entombing his existence in the reposed dirt and dust of the past and forever relegating him to hapless spectator to its insatiable devouring of all things, a process paradoxically sped up and slowed down by the ever ubiquitous world wide web -- he also has a dog and plays drums in a vacillating Jazz trio on occasional weekends.

Author's Note: This quick excursion into the mind of a man haunted by a recurring nightmare was inspired by my desire for wanting something more out of a particular film I had watched prior to writing this story which was completed virtually that same late night. I also wanted to explore just how horrifyingly dreadful it must feel to lose a child at such a terribly young age and to what extent that anguish might manifest itself in one's life, whether through dreams, drug and/or alcohol abuse, degraded social interactions, or even a loss or compromise of faith. I would even say that there's some subtle hints of my own perception regarding my father

and his relationships with myself and my sister especially--
but I'll save that can of worms for therapy one day.

The Last Five Years by Jim Roderick

"Where are you, Daddy?"

The child was rightfully distressed given the current predicament she and her father found themselves in, for the room they had shared involuntary occupation in for what seemed a lifetime had become as dilapidated as a forgotten home whose entropic disposition would result in decades of urban myths regarding spinsterial shut-ins, supposed spectral sightings, and crack-crazed denizens. Father, still in shock from what his confounded eyes beheld, fell to his knees in hopeful despair. Was this shivering spirit hobbling over to him truly his daughter? How could she be? Was it not true, then, that a mere five years had elapsed since he found himself in similar genuflexion atop the fresh mound of upturned dirt that separated him from her heart-wrenchingly small casket? Were those seared images that haunted his every morning and night of his precious daughter's pale body, so delicately swathed in her favorite flower-pattern sundress as she lay as inert as a photograph in that satin eiderdown, but mere nightmarish fantasy?

"Is it -" he choked a little, his eyes growing bloodshot from the crying. "Is it really you, baby?"

"I can't see you, daddy!" she cried out in panicked desperation. "I can't see you!"

His daughter finally stepped out of the eclipsing shadow revealing a gaunt and distraught face, tears coursing down her checks from tightly shut eyes curtained by long unkempt hair.

"Daddy, why can't I see you?" she sorrowfully protested.

"Oh, sweetie..." Father gasped hopelessly. With a hard sniffle, he continued, "...you need to open your eyes -- open your eyes for me, baby, please!"

"Daddy, I can't see you! Where are you!?" The girl was now extending her arms out in Marco Polo fashion as she feverishly groped at the air for a heard yet unseen daddy. "Why can't I see you?" she tearfully reiterated under terribly painful existential strain.

"I'm right here!" Father answered, his arms a vacant harbor for his daughter's safe return from the dark sea surrounding them. "Sweetie, please!" Father cried out. "Please, open your eyes for daddy. Open your eyes for me -- oh god, please open your eyes!"

He now found himself lying along the open edge of his far too young daughter's casket again, his tears raining down upon her rosary clasping hands as they had on that insufferable day and the uncountable recurrences that played out in his recalcitrant mind virtually every night since then.

"Why did you take her from me? Why?" Silence. With a heave, he bellowed, "Why, dammit!?"

"Daddy...?" Her trembling voice sounded from just behind his left shoulder, causing Father to spin around in heart accelerating surprise.

He could see his daughter again in the shadows, still draped in her final outfit now tattered and torn from the insatiable mastication of earthworms and maggots in primal conquest for another cold cadaver.

"Daddy..." once more, her voice growing in intensity. "...I can't see him. Why isn't he here?"

"See who, baby?" Father asked as puzzlingly as any parent might upon hearing such a childish statement of unsettling vagueness. "Who can't you see?"

"You said he would be here to help," the girl continued, her voice becoming strained from inconsolable sobbing. "You promised that he was here!"

Father's gut was slowly sinking from the ensuing trepidation. "Who's not there, baby?" he asked, confused and discomforted. "Who can't you see? Tell me."

"I can't see God, daddy!" she replied, now in full breakdown. "Daddy, I can't see him -- where is God, daddy!?" The child, eyes still shut tighter than reposed earth, began to wander around the decrepit living room feverishly, her arms flailing every which way in frantic search for her promised savior. "Daddy, why can't I see God!?"

"No!" Father yelped as his tears began to blur his dubious vision. "No... don't say that, honey. Please, don't --" cut off again by an unrestrainable sob.

"Daddy, you promised!"

"No, don't say that... please, don't tell me --"

"Where is he, daddy? Where is God!?"

The room had undergone an undetected transformation into a stifling black void. Father remained kneeling as he helplessly watched his daughter meander blind and aimlessly through the nothingness.

"I'm so scared, daddy," she said.

But just as her words reached Father, he then witnessed his once jubilant and nimble daughter, whose dancing radiance could brighten up even the heaviest of dreary moods that lurked in every corner of their quaint mundanity, was now taken down to her hands and knees by a darkness that she could not fight, that she could not understand; a darkness that shattered her steadfast belief that daddy and his benevolent deities would always be there to pick her up; a darkness that Father could not bring himself to traverse through as if frozen torturously by his own betraying will.

"You promised he was here!"

"He is there, honey..." Father said with about as much confidence as a trapped fly might have in a spider having a change of heart. "He is there... he's gotta be there, baby. Why would he take you away and leave you here in this awful place?" The question was posed mostly to himself, but also to any god that could be listening.

"I wanna go home, daddy," his daughter cried out. "Why can't I come home with you?"

"I want you to come home," Father replied with slowly shredding sanity. "I want you to come home with me. I just need you to open your eyes. Open them for daddy. I beg you, honey!"

He was now hunched over his daughter's closed coffin again, arms laid across in a futile embrace.

"Open your eyes for daddy, please." He turned his head upward to direct his pitiful petition to the apparent absence. "I beg you, God... open her eyes. Give me back my little girl!"

Suddenly, a clamoring of bangs from inside the casket, and Father was flung back as he heard his little girl's lightly muffled screams of torment and fright.

"Daddy! Daddy, let me out! I can't see anything. There is nothing here!"

Father slowly backtracked away from the bucking coffin, his eyes widening as he brought a hand to his agape mouth.

"Don't leave me, daddy, please! It's dark, daddy. Why is everything dark? Daddy!! Please!!!"

"Let her out," he squeaked almost inaudibly. He took another breathe and repeated, "Let her out of there. Get her out of that thing - can't you hear her crying!?" He looked around for any sign of empathy from within that black anti-place, crying out once more, "Can't you hear her screaming!? Let her out!"

"Daddy! Daddy, please!" His daughter's desperate pangs for freedom were growing harried and shrill as her frantic banging continued. "Daddy, why can't I leave? Help me, daddy!"

Father watched in total, guilt-laden surrender as his little girl's subterranean container slowly retreated to the darkness. Yet, he was still able to hear her cries as if they were occurring right inside his head, as they always had every night for the last five years.

Foreword by Author Leon Jaques

Biography: Leon Jacques enjoys writing horror stories and drawing.

Inari by Leon Jaques

The movement of the water caused the water spirit to stir from what he considered a meditative state of mind, he couldn't quite sleep but he also required rest for his own well-being. He was well aware that his mental health could be affected by not resting but it had been many days since he had actually gone below to try and slumber. The rain was pushing against the surface of the water, stirring it to the point that he could not stabilize himself within the bottom of the lake.

It was something that was eating at him that caused him to be unable to rest completely, he was well aware of what it was and yet he didn't know what to do about it. He pushed himself against the muddy bottom of the lake and gave himself an initial boost up towards the top of the water. He yearned to see if she was there... perhaps then he could try once more to reach out to her, to try and communicate with her. He didn't think that it would be such a hard task, but even he could feel the hole in his heart that she had left him. He missed the carefree conversations, her smile and the way the wind caused her brunette hair to tangle. Her skin had been so soft that he had nearly thought she was a just another flower from below the surface that had formed into a human. He knew that it was probably not possible, but she had been the only human he dared to get close too.

He couldn't help but mix up the thoughts of humans with things below the water, his natural dwelling place. The lake was his home and he had not really been able to venture far from it. Although he couldn't recall it, he knew he had been birthed here and raised with neither siblings or family. It was lonely and the fact he had even learned to speak was due to the various people that came to him from many years beforehand. Had he not had the chance to learn he would have never been able to approach her, to ask her about the water and why she thought it was safe to swim. He could recall the event of their first meeting in faultless detail.

* * * * *

She was scared because he came out of nowhere and considered him to be a pervert; the high tension in her voice at that time had never been repeated until her death.

He held regret hearing her scream even as he dragged her beneath the surface where her screaming became nothing more than muffled gurgles that no other human would hear. He remembered the fight that she had in her but his own determination kept dragging her lower and lower into the water until she finally took her last breath.

He hated that she died with her eyes open because the scared vision of her lifeless face haunted his memory; he would never forget her. He was doomed to be cursed by the last vision of her and even though he had never felt guilty about killing a human before, he didn't think he should allow such a thing to start bothering him now. After all, he had her to look forward too.

* * * * *

He finally rose towards the surface of the lake. His chin and lower body remained covered by the water as his eyes scanned past the light rainfall and towards the water's edge. He didn't see her down near the cove and so he shifted his body a bit to stare towards the lush green trees that surrounded his lake; he liked the summer time. It brought what he considered to be immense heat but it also brought about nature and he liked watching as the once-dead-ends of the forest were brought back to life with just more sun and rain. It provoked him to go walking, to venture down towards the other nearby pools of water although he was aware of the risk. He normally liked going back and forth.

As of now, however, he just wanted to reside within his home where he had taken her life.

He knew that remaining here would offer him little justice to his actions, but he just wasn't ready to let go of it yet, so he kept thinking of those memories. At least this way he could recall certain conversations at certain locations.

It was surely unusual for a creature to be thinking such things but, alas, it was just how he was. Even now his eyes were looking for just the slightest bit of color in the forest and when he finally narrowed it down just what he was looking for he came up from the surface a bit more.

As usual, she was standing close by, eyes cast out towards the water as if she was waiting for him. He moved his figure towards her within the water. Surely, she had to be waiting for him to come closer, this ghost of his. He wanted to talk to her today and see if he could reach out to her just a bit to try and have some of those old conversations. It had been so long now that he was afraid that remembering just wasn't going to be enough for him.

How long had it been since she died? He held no conception of time or days as it was never important to him. Yet seeing her made him wonder just how long she had been waiting for him to notice her.

He did what he thought was best and roamed the bottom of that lake after eating. He recalled that, in old times, many people came in search of loved ones. He didn't want to risk being caught and killed--after all, he was no human.

He sighed mentally at the thought of what might happen the day he would be caught. He did feel it could happen... it brought dread to him due to the new technology that had come about. He didn't quite understand it nor want too as the idea alone bothered him deeply. It drove him to wonder what someone might due to him to find her now.

She had a family after all, they were easily able to make time for her and she had always been with them. It was a situation far different than his own, but he had always

257

admired her venturing spirit and willingness to accept what he was. It was perhaps that spirit of her that caused him to want to be closer to her even with that fear in mind.

* * * * *

After reaching the edge of the water near the cliff that let him see his friend, he stared at her with a gentle expression on his face. He didn't know what would happen if he called out to her but he felt the desperation swelling within his chest. He could feel the anxiety spreading over him like a wildfire at the mere thought of her turning away from him calling out to her, what little heat was in his body rose at the pressure in his chest. He could have sworn the feeling was something other than nerves but he was merely trying to rationalize the situation.

"Eeva!"

He called out to her watching her lips curl into a wide smile as if she was happy to see him. He wanted to believe that it was possible but something in him told him that wouldn't be the case. He let his eyes rest upon hers looking for some kind of sign but instead, he was met with a look of pure hatred in spite of her happy smile. It wasn't what he was looking forward to and he quickly looked away from her thinking that he had made a mistake in her appearance. Looking back at her he realized that it was still Eeve from before this was no illusion.

He moved within the water trying to come up with an idea. If she wasn't going to run away from him, what else could he do? His eyes rested on the edge of the water near the end of the cliff where a makeshift beach resided there.

"Why won't you talk to me, Eeva?"

His eyes glided back towards her; his cerulean hues tried to connect to her emerald green eyes to search for some kind of answer from her. Eeva didn't respond, she just turned

258

her head to look at the edge of the bank that he too had been staring at.

He moved down further as she looked back at him and her smile dropped as if she was anticipating something. He decided to move towards the land since he could walk upon it in the rain. It wouldn't be hard for him to breathe so long as he had something to keep him wet. He wanted to do this to answer his own questions about her and to wipe away the uneasy feelings that were gathering in his chest. If he could get to the shore and join her, perhaps he would be able to put to rest the decision that he had made. He didn't feel like what he did was wrong, he felt like everything he did was a step further to ensure that they would be able to remain together.

* * * * *

The memory of the day was still fresh in his head. He could remember the soft hum that emitted through her closed lips and the way she bounced down the path towards where he was. He had been relaxing against the cove's edge, his body leaned up against a rock as his hand held the flute near the edge of his lips. His music had always been something that she liked and he had promised to teach her that day but it was just another lure to get her closer.

He had planned to get Eeva close enough to the deep end so he could drag her down without worrying about her getting far away from him if she got free. He knew the moment she took her last breath he would have to consume her and his mind kept telling him that was all that mattered, but he refused to want to accept that. He knew he had not had a decent meal in a very long time but this was not something that was pushing the decision in his head, he just wanted to be with her forever. Humans were fragile creatures and they could die at any given moment from anything around them--or, even worse, from the people they were near every day.

He felt as if he was giving her a better option to become a part of him, to live on through him as they would become one from him consuming her. He wanted to be able to show her another way even if that meant she had to die, but this way, she wouldn't age and she would never have to worry about the what-ifs of life. He would release her of all her future pains and heartbreak and he convinced himself that this was the path he had to take to ensure it all for her.

In his head, these final moments were all that seemed to matter. The sound of her bones crushing beneath the weight of his teeth and the thick blood that thinned in the water were all secondary issues. Anything that had been dwelling in the water ran away at the first sign of a struggle leaving them alone as he devoured her.

* * * * *

He could not take pride in what he had done, just that he had known that it was the right move to make

"She has to understand that," he said to himself with determination as he reached the shore and emerged from the water. His webbed feet pushed into the wet sand as he left his lake behind him now. He had never liked the way it felt on his webbed feet. Even now he wanted to wade back into the shallow side of the water and clean himself off but that was not an option at the moment. He lifted his head to look at Eeva who was facing him, he moved his hand to push his blond hair to one side. Her pale skin stood out among the brush and she almost seemed to be glowing in the mid-light of the afternoon storm. She waved him forward in silence as if beckoning him to come towards her, to follow her as she eased back a few steps.

Taking his first steps forward in her direction his knees wobbled a bit from his own weight. He was small and what Eeva often called "anorexic" due to his appearance. It was one thing that had always made Eeva worry, but water spirits weren't meant for the land. They were just like the mermaids of the sea built to remain in water forever... at least that is what he assumed; he could have been wrong. He had never really met a mermaid and had only heard about them in stories. Eeva had told him and taught him everything that he valued which only made the pursuit of her even more important to him. He just wished things had not ended up this way.

He should have considered it was a bad idea to follow her when she crossed away from him at the cliff and waved at him to come forth. Instead, he chose not to think about it. He kept moving forward until the lake became a background shadow to the trees. He had no idea of how far he had actually traveled but the deeper he went into the forest the more he felt a sinking feeling of dread crawling over him. He felt out of place and quite vulnerable out of the lake; he periodically paused in his steps searching through the trees for something. He could only hear the sound of the rain against the leaves as he stopped. He felt like he was losing a part of his sanity out here, and a shiver ran down his spine as the sinking feeling that he was going to be left alone out here entered into his mind. She had been merely guiding him somewhere and he had yet to know just where it was that they were going. Perhaps Eeva would continue to toy with him before making a fool out of him sometime after...

He didn't know if he felt more fear or anger. He had just wanted some kind of answers and now he was stuck nearly straining himself in every direction to try and catch a glimpse of her to know where to go next. Would she lead him to her grounds where she could remain stable enough to speak?

She'll leave you here alone!

His own thoughts became tangled between what he wanted to bury out of fear, and what he should consider as a possible outcome.

She gave you a name and you ate her!

Guilt was tearing into his soul and he couldn't stand the way it hissed in his mind, so he tried to shake his head to gain control of his own thoughts. He had done what was right. He fed himself the same old line.

This was to save Eeve, I know what I did was right!

He felt himself calming a little but it wasn't enough to ease the tension he felt in his chest. His legs forced themselves to carry him forward again, the sight of her body illuminating from the rest of the darker forest colors was all he needed as a guide to get by. He didn't like the fear that settled into his bones and told himself that it was never going to work out the way he wanted it to. He didn't want to believe that all this was going to be for nothing, he was positive in his own actions and path that he would be able to finally feel a sense of peace about everything. He just had to keep going, he didn't have to let the vast forest close in around him, it was just a mere illusion built up from his mind from the stress of being on land…at least, that was what he told himself.

* * * * *

Eventually, he found himself face to face with a swamp. He wasn't really fond of these areas since the last time he tried staying in one he almost messed up his back completely. He could feel the entanglement of his own hair trapping itself within the thick algae that covered the water and, because of that, it would stick to the exposed side of his back which caused irritation and irregular growth. His time in a swamp had not been enjoyable, but if you had brought him to a marsh, he would change his tune. Suddenly, in the forest with hardly any noise at all, other than the rain, he heard a twig snap--and it was not off in the distance but quite close to where he was. He turned feeling a chill travel through his body just as a sharp pain rippled through his left side where his rib cage was.

262

The connection of the blade to his skin made him realize that it was something that could indeed harm him. It was not often that he came across something that could leave a mark on him, let alone cause it to burn. He faced what he had thought would be something else but instead it was his ghost. He stared at Eeva in confusion as he did not want to wrap his mind around the fact it had been her that tried to hurt him. Even looking at her now he could tell the look in her eyes was serious, was this really Eeva? The question was quick to leave his thoughts as she went to stab him again. It was now that instinct decided to take over as he had caught her arms within his own hands. This had come to a surprise not only to her but to him as well, he could touch her. He could put his hands on this so-called ghost and that he had been chasing. He felt like the thing he had been chasing was something else. It wasn't who he wanted it to be. This was not Eeva because he had killed her, this was not her ghost either. It was this conclusion that caused him to roughly shove her away from him.

In that moment he tried to calm the panicking feeling that rose in him as he stumbled back, nearly falling into the swamp as the wound on his side burned from the touch of the iron blade she held. He didn't have much time to think before the girl quickly went to lunge at him again as he struggled to get his balance in the muck.

"Kyösti!"

She shouted his name loudly enough that his body nearly froze. He rejoiced in hearing the voice that he desperately wanted to hear, but this was not the person he desired. He tried to stop her as her blade nicked the inner parts of his rib towards his heart. He didn't know if she was close to killing him or not but, right then and there, he decided that he was going to kill her first.

Like the flip of a switch, his instinct took over as his jaws unhinged and came down onto her left side. He twisted as he pulled her close throwing both of them into the swamp.

He was confident that he would be able to drag her down with him and break her. He wouldn't let this person--this thing--ruin his image of Eeva, this had to be an imposter another monster. He bit harder breaking the clavicle and he was sure that he going to win, at least until he felt the fire spreading from his chest. In his earlier movements of twisting them both into the water, he had given her enough leverage to force the blade into his chest. He released her with a scream beneath the water as she pushed herself away from him. He didn't want to let her go but he could no longer feel anything as his eyes became clouded and his life slipped away from him.

* * * * *

Emerging from the water, the girl coughed and gasped for air; trying to rid her mouth of the taste of blood and water. She knew she had risked too much. She tried to pull herself up through the mud but the moment she tried to lift her left arm she could hear the grinding sound of bone. It had to be the one he broke. She groaned as the pain lashed through her violently. She decided to focus all of her strength into her right side and pushed herself along the bank with her only working arm and forced her legs to help her stand. This was not at all how she was hoping it would have gone. She had nearly drowned, all for the sake of Eeva.

She had been hellbent on getting revenge... she had thought that Kyösti was good but the moment her twin sister went missing she knew who to blame. She knew that it had to be him; the way he looked at her the first day she found him told her everything. His look of longing had made her stomach turn. Even after her encounter with him, she found it hard to believe he might have been a Nacken or Nakki, these typical legends were usually nothing more than stories told to keep kids away from the water. She should have been more cautious from the beginning and she had been a fool to let her sister do what she wanted.

Despite her successful revenge, she still felt regret in her heart, but she hoped that her sister's spirit would be at peace knowing her killer would never rise from the depths again.

She let her emotions out in short cries and laughs and felt accomplished despite the pain and dirt and desire for cleanness and rest. The idea of getting freshened up appealed to her more and more as she started on her journey home outside the forest. Her skin was itchy and her throat felt horse. She shifted about in her shirt, trying to itch at the skin that continued to irritate her. The bone felt flat as if the surface of the skin had nothing to show for the wounds beforehand.

When she got home, she ran into the bathroom down the hall and stared at herself in the mirror. The surface of her skin was just as smooth as it had been when she woke up. She trailed her fingertips over where her back itched, and then dug her nails in. It quickly coated in blood.

She pulled back the moment she felt her flesh move with her nails, and she quickly lifted her shirt. Her soft pale skin was turning purple and black, rotting as if it could no longer stay together. She felt herself take a deep breath and heard the ghostly voice of her twin sister tell her that what she had done was wrong, but she knew what she had done was right.

"What I did was right!"

The same thoughts as Kyösti circled into her mind... perhaps the two were more similar than she realized.

Foreword by Author Marissa Haynes

Biography: Marissa Haynes is an emerging artist and writer. She loves to read and discuss the art of storytelling.

Shattered by Marissa Haynes

Rip, tear, scream, splatter, death.

The dream slowly fades away as I come back to the waking world. I want to go back to the dream though, at least being in that surreal landscape was comforting compared to facing what is out beyond these four walls. It is savagery. Everyone has gone mad and I am the only one who has some sense left. God, what a disaster.

I was a man of science, striving to bring a whole new world in chemical engineering. It is amazing what the molecular compounds and atoms can do without even being seen. From that small structure, you make anything, build anything as long as it applies to the laws of science. I was going to make the world a better place. At least, that was what I had thought.

My workplace was nestled in the middle of lush forestry, at the outskirts some godforsaken town. The company I worked for wanted us to be far away from any possible distractions along with their competitors being unaware of the company's projects and experiments. This suited me just fine. I had no need for social gatherings; besides, I was there for a greater purpose. I was hired for my work ethic and my employer shared similar visions of the use of science to make the world progress into a better state. What more could I possibly ask for? Well, absolute, 100 percent full credit obviously, but better not to bite the hand that feeds you.

I remember that day clearly. When everything went so wrong. The laboratory was sleek, clean, everything in order to the task at hand for the latest experimentation and drops of liquid dropped into the glass beaker. There was soon a flash of light.

Afterwards, the world wasn't the same. I saw things, horrible things. Malformed shadows, ugly, mutated creatures who could barely pass as a humanoid. They were many, so, so many. Such animal like behavior where it caused these mutants to act like savage beasts without any moral compass or conscious mind. I was the bringer of this new world and now I had to fix it.

Each day that I would leave the sanctuary of my room in order to scavenge the ruins of the structure, I had brought a sharp object as a weapon of choice. Guns were not accessible to me plus the noise would bring more of them. A herd would overwhelm me and what good would that do me then? As days passed, I saw less and less of the monstrosities. Then it came to pass, where when I explored the entire building, there was no one else but me. Just me, the silence, and sometimes at the corner of my eye, malignant shadows crawling on the walls. Sometimes, when I lie down in the empty office space that is my safe haven, I hear whispers. Soft hisses, ruthless, small attacks to my ears that won't give me peace of mind when I wish to sleep. Sometimes there are cruel words being given to me where it was all my fault. My fault. My fault for bringing about the end of everything. And that when I die, I will die alone and with nothing. Then, when my eyes close, the dreams begin all over again.

This day, I had decided to venture outside of the building. Despite the destruction caused in the interior, the outside looked the same as I remembered it, except the atmosphere was bleak. Even worse, I couldn't hear the wind, or birds. No bird song to make this place seem natural and inviting.

BANG! BANG!

No, wait, how? How did they come in? The door. Oh god no, the door...it's opening…

Foreword by Author Michaela Smith

Biography: Michaela Smith is a lover of horror ranging from old slasher movies to creepy pastas (especially audio renditions). Her favorite movie is Sinister and her favorite creepy pasta is The Russian Sleep Experiment.

As Long as You Feed It by Michaela Smith

This morning before I left for work, I went out to refill my bird feeder on the balcony. To my horror, there was blood and feathers underneath...for the umpteenth time that month. As always, I briefly wondered if maybe a cat or something had gotten them, except I didn't have a cat...and my apartment was on the third floor with no trees in sight. This frequent occurrence had plagued me for some time, but I decided there wasn't time to figure it out and be on time for work, so I left with a sick feeling in my stomach once again.

Work was kind of hazy. I walked around in a bit of a daze as I went through the motions: putting on my apron, taking orders, etc. The diner that I worked at was fairly laid back and rarely very busy, so my almost robotic act was of no consequence.

As closing time rolled around, I went into my default-mode of wiping down the counter. No one was in the diner, so I continued to let my mind mull over what kept happening to those poor birds.

"Miss?"

I jumped. The man who walked in and sat down on a bar stool startled me out of my daze.

"Long day?" he chuckled.

"Yeah…" I sighed and half-heartedly chuckled back, slightly annoyed that someone had come in only a half hour before we closed. "What can I get for ya?""

He smiled and asked, "Do you have any pie left?"

Without hesitation I listed them off. "We have apple, cherry, blueberry--"

"I'll take a slice of that apple pie."

"Whipped cream?"

"Yes, please." He smiled again. I promptly went back into the kitchen and returned with a crudely cut slice of apple pie covered with a hefty amount of whipped cream. "Thank you," he said as I set the plate down in front of him, "and I'm sorry for coming in so close to closing time." I must not have been hiding my annoyance very well, which kind of made me feel bad because the way he said it made it seem obvious that this guy wasn't a total asshole. I continued my closing duties as he ate. When he finished, he left the money for the pie and a rather gracious tip and left without saying a word.

"...ok, then." I muttered to myself. I took care of the leftover dish, locked up, turned the lights off, and headed out the back. As I proceeded to walk out to my car, I heard a familiar voice.

"Miss?" He startled me again. This time because it was dark and no one was around rather than just me zoning out. I turned around as he bent down and picked up my keys off of the ground. "I think you dropped these." He handed them to me and I thanked him. Suspicion rose in me, but before I could finish my thought of wondering why he had followed me to the back of the diner, something hard was slammed against the back of my head and I was out cold.

*****

I was awoken by a bump in the road.

"Jesus, Alejandro! Slow down!" complained the voice of whom I had originally thought wasn't an asshole. Alejandro--who I assumed to be the man driving--said nothing. He drove on for a few more minutes before the car jerked to a halt. I heard the rear doors open and I was dragged out of the car by my restrained arms and forced to stand upright. The bag over my head was yanked off. I looked around frantically, but all I saw was greenery. No houses, no people, not even a city skyline. I tried to scream through the duct tape over my mouth, but it was no use. No one came.

272

My captors didn't even try to stop me. My heart sank. I was terrified.

When they turned me around, I saw a small church in the middle of the clearing. It was one of those gothic-style churches. It wasn't as grand as a cathedral, but I still admired the design. I was dragged in its direction by a man who wasn't the one I had met at the diner. I thought maybe it had been the driver until I heard the driver side door open. The man who was dragging me looked back and grinned at me, but unlike the man at the diner this one made my skin crawl and probably would've had the same effect even if he wasn't kidnapping me.

"I'm glad we got a pretty one for this," he said.

"Steven..." the man from the diner, who was walking ahead of us, warned. Steven ignored him and pulled me close.

"I'm gonna enjoy watching you scream while it rips you apart," he whispered menacingly. Not two seconds after trying to intimidate me, Alejandro came up from behind, grabbed Steven, and lifted him up by the collar of his shirt. Our driver was rather tall and looked to be a bit of a brute. "C'mon, man!" Steven pleaded. Alejandro stayed silent and glared at the smaller, rather scrawny man.

"Are you two done fucking around?" the man from the diner asked impatiently. Alejandro dropped the scrawny, and now also trembling man on his ass. He then scooped me up in his arms and carried me the rest of the way. My quivering ceased slightly as I felt oddly safe...well, not really, but you know what I mean. I can't really say that I liked any of these bastards, but I can safely say which one of them I disliked the least.

"Hey!" I yelled to the man from the diner, but it came out muffled and incoherent through the duct tape. Alejandro painfully, but quickly ripped it off and I followed with a loud ow! and then thanked him kindly. "What...why did you bring me out here?" I could hear my voice shaking, but I did my best to sound more angry than scared; I didn't want to give Steven the satisfaction of my terror. "What are you gonna do with me?"

The man from the diner made no effort to face me and kept on as he answered, "Be patient, my dear."

I cringed as Steven cackled and said, "Oh, David. You're no fun." David opened the door to reveal a white tile floor and several rows of polished wooden pews. As we walked down the aisle, I realized how nice and well-kept this place was for being out in the middle of nowhere. The stain glass windows were striking as they were lit up by the moonlight and I briefly wondered how pretty this place must look in the daytime. Alejandro laid me down on the altar and walked away and up the staircase on the right side.

"So, now that we're all settled, would you still care to know why you're here?" David asked.

"Oh no, no," I replied sarcastically, although less confidently now that the big guy that had kept me away from Steven was gone, "I actually enjoy being kidnapped and then placed on altars like some sort of satanic sacrifice." David chuckled very much like he had when I first met him.

"Well, sacrifice is certainly close enough," he began. "You see, we have in our possession a rather interesting thing," He paced around the altar and continued. "We were out and about one day--never mind what we were doing--and we stumbled upon a rather...fearsome looking thing." He nodded towards Steven, who scoffed when he said, "This one pissed himself." He rested his hands on the altar on either side of my head. "It was very menacing the way it was...looking at us. When the thing lunged at us, we ran and

274

decided to take shelter in the back of our van. Then, I got an idea." He looked down at me, smiling again. "You see, we had a...let's call her a stowaway...in the back of our van. I wanted to be sure exactly what this creature's intentions were, so I uh...let her loose." Steven was off in a corner chuckling darkly to himself. "As you can imagine, the things we heard and saw were...rather gruesome."

Steven gave me that bone-chilling grin again. "It ate her."

David continued on, "We soon realized that once it had fed, it didn't seem interested in us anymore, and it ran off," he paused and thought for a moment. "Actually, I think I should clarify that what it had lost interest in was eating us. The thing was interested in us, but more as a...supplier. What made us realize this is that we would run into it from time to time and--since we're in the business of collecting stowaways--we would end up presenting its food much like we had before. Over time, we realized that as long as we fed it, it pretty much just left us alone."

Steven chimed in, "Why don't you tell her what else we figured out about it?"

"Ah," David said, "I forgot the most important part." He took his hands away and started pacing around again.

"We found ourselves being followed one day after collecting our stowaway, and we don't really care to have witnesses around. I found my curiosity piping up again, so we let him follow us while we did our usual routine of feeding our new pet. Once it had had its dinner, I spotted our witness in the trees out there and simply...pointed in his direction. Our problem was taken care of without any hesitation," David chuckled again, "A very useful asset in our line of work." He stopped his explanation and sighed.

Steven continued for him, "Unfortunately, we haven't seen our pet in a while and it's starting to worry us. We would like it if it would continue to not eat us and do us favors when we need it. So, that's what we've got you for." He smiled that unsettling smile again. My heart was trying to pound its way out of my chest. In a panic, I rolled myself off of the altar, landing hard on the marble floor. I scrambled to my feet and made a break for it. Steven started to come after me, but David stopped him.

"Let her go. It won't matter."

Bong!

I stopped running.

"What's the hell is that?" I asked with a tremble in my voice.

"The dinner bell," David answered. I realized where Alejandro had gone off to and my dislike for him immediately leveled out with the other two.

Bong!

I looked around the church frantically. My heart stopped as I saw something moving in the corner by the ceiling. A large, dark, arachnid-like thing crept out from the shadows. It crawled down from the wall, over the altar, and straight down the aisle towards me. I couldn't move. As it came closer, I could see hands at the end of every black appendage, except for the praying mantis-like front claws that looked metallic and sharp. Its body and head, other than the abdomen, which was very much like a large spider's, was long a pale...almost human. The face had two human-like cloudy eyes, but no nose or mouth. I fell back as the thing towered over me. I opened my mouth to scream, but no sound came out. The thing's claws slammed down, digging into and cracking the marble floor on either side of me. It lowered its face down to mine as the bottom half of its face began to rip apart revealing a countless number of fangs. Its mouth hung open for me as if to make sure I could see each and every one of them.

The brain is a funny thing sometimes. In this moment of absolute horror and bracing myself for my doom, my mind flashed back to the blood and feathers that I had found underneath my bird feeder this morning...and the morning before that...and the morning before that.

As long as we fed it…

The thing was still standing over me but wasn't making any more advances towards me. I prayed to a god I wasn't sure I believed in and pointed in the direction of my captors.

* * * * *

I watched as Alejandro walked back down the stairs. He screamed upon seeing the remains of his friends strewn out over the church floor, the only sound I heard him make all night.

Tears were streaming down his face when he turned his head towards me in disbelief as I politely asked, "Do you think you can give me a ride home?"

Foreword by Author M. J. Lambert

Biography: M.J. Lambert is a Magna Cum Laude graduate of the University of Pittsburgh, PA, with BS in K-6 Education and minoring in Performing Arts. She currently teaches 6-8th Creative Writing and Science, and 6-12th Chorus and Technology and is the Head of Artistry Development at Lambo Studios. She also runs the music program at a local preschool. Since moving to Nashville in late 2010, she has pursued her music career by playing bass, keyboards, synths, and being a lead vocalist for a variety of local rock bands. In 2012, she was recognized as a Grumbacher Fine Arts Instructor. In 2015, she opened her handmade aromatherapy doll business called Potato-Babies™. In 2018, she received her G-Suite Certification and CK-12 Educator Certification, and at the end of the year became a first-time mommy! Ever since a young age, M.J. has always had a passion for writing, especially horror and suspense stories. With inspiration drawn from R.L. Stine and other horror greats of her youth, she is proud to finally get back into writing scary stories as an adult.

It Comes from The Hollow by M. J. Lambert

"This is the judgement: the Light has come into the world, but men still loved the Darkness rather than the Light, for their deeds were evil."

- John 3:19

There is a stillness here now, as if an arm is wrapping itself around me, muting any sound that tries to intrude. The night air is crisp and chilled. I can feel it climbing through the recently broken window pane as I turn to stare out at the dark, bruised sky. I close my eyes for a moment then hang my head to look back down at the old J. Stevens single-shot pistol I placed on the table in front of me. Trembling, my fingers slowly glide over the cracked wooden handle. I inhale deeply, absorbing the overwhelming pungent smell of mountain ash.

She's here.

* * * * * THREE DAYS PRIOR * * * * *

DAY ONE

I first came upon this old secluded coal mining town when trying to research oddities in southwestern Pennsylvania for the Pittsburgh Press. I was tired of being assigned to "local yocal" stories and really wanted to make a name for myself as a reporter. After reading about Fallen Ash and its afflictions, I knew I had something tethered. Over the last century, more than sixty reported mysterious disappearances and at least twenty recorded suicides have taken place. With a current population of only about four hundred, I was sure I could find someone there that would talk to me and want the cause of these tragedies exposed.

The town itself was established in 1801, mainly for the search of thick peat deposits and for transport of bituminous coal by railroad. Fallen Ash was located conveniently on the edge of the Pittsburgh Coal Seam, and its railroad connected to the main stretch of the Appalachian Basin, bringing in resources to the town. However now abandoned and run-down, the railroad, like the town itself, is just another reminder of economic doom.

I lost cell service in the mountains about a half hour away from Fallen Ash. After driving through miles of wooded backroads, I finally saw a break in the forest, and there it was, Fallen Ash.

At the entrance of the town, there was a crooked and cracked wooden sign stating "Welcome To Fallen Ash, PA" with paint chips clutching on for life. The road was full of potholes and eventually turned to just gravel and scattered shell. I only saw one entrance to the town, so I assumed it was also the only road heading back out. Driving further down the main street, I looked around at the exhausted vernacular buildings and old Colonial style homes in much need of care. I pulled over in front of Smitty's Market and Deli and decided to venture in.

A bell rang above the door as I stepped inside. No one was behind the front counter. Just then, a gruff male voice shouted out from the back of the shop. "I'll be with yins in a minute!" Soon after, a man in his late sixties came walking up the center aisle with another man dressed in a suit who appeared to be about in his mid-fifties.

"Oh, a newcomer?" the elder man said with surprise. "My name is Earnest Smith, but folks 'round here call me Smitty." He extended a worn hand, and I accepted the greeting as the other gentleman spoke.

"And I'm Randall Schaffer, Deputy Mayor of Fallen Ash."

I firmly shook his hand. "Mark Rochland, Pittsburgh Press."

Smitty raised his eyebrows and looked at the mayor.

"Well, Mr. Rochland, what brings you to these parts?"

I could tell by his demeanor that he already knew why I was there or at least the basis of my visit. I cleared my throat and smiled at the men, "I was reading about your town and found its history fascinating and thought I'd write up a little narrative for our paper." I smiled at the men.

"History?" laughed Mayor Schaffer. "I think you mean legends. Am I right, son?" he asked as he tilted his head accusingly.

"Well…" I began but was interrupted.

"Nevermind that, Randall," Smitty said as he placed his hand on the mayor's shoulder. "What's important here is that we finally have a visitor! Someone new to try my famous scrapple in the morning! Isn't that right Mark?" Smitty widened his eyes at me in suggestion.

I nodded and smiled even though mushed cornmeal and pork scraps didn't sound amazingly appetizing, but I knew that I had better go along with the change of subject.

"I'll take care of 'em, Randall. You just go along home and thank Ada for that shoofly pie." Smitty gently slapped his friend on the back and walked him outside.

I could see Mayor Schaffer saying something to Smitty through the shop's front window logo, but quickly turned away to get a better look at the inside of the quaint market. It was obvious that I wasn't welcome, or perhaps any outsider that stopped by was automatically deemed suspicious. I reached down and grabbed the local town bulletin. It included church service times, the deli's weekly menu, a change in postal service deliveries, and a short message from Mayor Schaffer.

The shop's bell rang as Smitty made his way back in. "You have to forgive Randall. He's not used to socializin' with anyone besides the townsfolk." Smitty made his way behind the front counter and grabbed a set of keys. "I, on the other hand, am more neighborly," he smiled. "I'm gonna assume that you need a place to stay, so here are the keys to the house right across the street from me. It's been empty for years, so no need to worry about keepin' it up."

I reached across the counter as he handed me the keyring. "Oh, wow, thanks a lot. Yeah, I figured there would be some kind of motel nearby that I could ask about. I also brought some camping gear just in case."

Smitty just smiled in amusement. "Camping is always an option. Lots of forest 'round here. Keeps growing every year it seems."

"I think having a roof over my head instead of a tent is more preferable, so thanks again." I held up the keys in appreciation.

Before I lost the opportunity, I decided to ask Smitty a little about the town and the locals that resided in Fallen Ash, since he seemed slightly more relaxed without the mayor around. He mentioned that the residency of the town decreases every year because there are no jobs to bring in new faces and the current population is mostly made up of the elderly. I asked about the multiple disappearances, but he just shook it off as if the ones who went missing just simply got lost in the woods and were picked up on the highway leaving town. He didn't seem to believe in any local legend as the mayor had called it. I also asked him about the suicides. Once again, he just contributed them all to logical facts, such as deep depression from living in Fallen Ash - a town slowly failing without a future.

"If you lived here as long as some of these folks, you'd want out too. And there are only two ways of leavin' Fallen Ash according to most, if you know what I mean. Except for Merv Keller that is. If you want to hear some hogwash, that's the man of a thousand stories. But mind you, he's crazy. Probably from breathin' in all that mine dust."

Smitty finished sweeping the floor then propped his broom in the corner and turned toward me. "Anyway, I'm headin' home now for the evening if you want me to show you the house."

I nodded and followed him out of the market.

* * * * *

The house was much like the other Colonials on the street, warped and worn. I was actually surprised that the old knob and tube wiring still brought life into the dark rooms. After Smitty had shown me around, he left me with a few groceries from his shop, then retired across the street into his home.

I unpacked my sleeping bag and air mattress and put them in what once was a formal dining room, but soon changed my mind and went upstairs. Since there were no curtains, I didn't want to be secretly spied on in the middle of night, and an upstairs room just sounded more private from wandering eyes. I found a room at the top of the stairs to the right that had a small desk in the corner. It was perfect. I set up my sleeping arrangement in the center of the room, then placed my set of writing pens and notebook on the desk. Call me old-fashioned, but there is just something about physically writing a good story that gets to me.

I sat down at the wooden desk and began to take note of my day's observations and thoughts when a sudden chill trickled down my neck. I reassured myself that I was just being spooked from being alone in such an old house. I rubbed the back of my neck with my left hand and looked over toward the window. A tree limb quietly tapped the pane in the wind. I stood up to go over and open the window to get some fresh air, but on my way across the room, the tip of my boot got stuck in a loose floorboard causing me to fall flat on my stomach. When I turned around to look back at the damage, I noticed something gold glistening in the light. I inched my body toward the new hole in the floor and pulled out what appeared to be a leather-bound journal wrapped with a gold locket around the cover.

I blew away the dust and cobwebs from the journal and slowly massaged the small oval locket between my right thumb and forefinger. The initials LB were etched into the metal. I tried prying the locket open with my thumbnail and hissed in pain as it slipped and cut through the top of my cuticle. Quickly sucking off the small drop of accumulating blood, I reached inside my backpack to look for my pocket knife to unhinge the old piece of jewelry.

Inside the small relic were two grayed photos, one on either side of the piece. A young man and woman, I'm guessing in their late teens, stared back at me with an expression that I could only describe as simply stoic. I stood up and carefully set the necklace on the desk and then sat down to further examine the journal.

I shivered as I read aloud the date of the first entry, exactly sixty-two years ago to the day.

MAY 26TH, 1956

It has been about a month since Father has gone missing and three since we lost Brother George. I can see the burden their disappearances have left has fallen upon Mother. She hardly leaves her room, but when she does, she walks without purpose.

There is an evil presence here that is forbade to speak of, but I need to let someone know. It comes from the center of the eastern woods. There is a clearing there that I have been to before with George. He showed it to me right before he started having his nightmares. He would wake up screaming about… "Her"… slowly seeping out of the forest into his window at night, filling his thoughts with darkness as She fed.

I can hear Mother walking now. I must go tend to her.

-Leona

The lights flickered in the bedroom. I gasped, quickly shut the journal and turned around. The wind outside was beginning to pick up. What exactly did I just stumble upon?

As much as I had to resist curiosity, I decided to wait to read the remaining journal entries in the morning amongst the sunlight's safety. Although I am a sucker for a good ghost story, living one wasn't exactly what I had in mind. I left the journal next to the necklace on the desk and went to sleep.

* * * * *

DAY TWO

I woke bright and early to the sound of some rooster crowing in the distance. I couldn't stop thinking about the journal and wondering about the eastern woods. I climbed out of my partially deflated air mattress bed and headed toward the desk to grab the journal, but it was missing from the desk along with the necklace.

What the hell? I thought. There was no way that I dreamt everything. I went back over to inspect the loosened floorboard, and there, lying in its place, was the journal once again wrapped with the small chain. I could have sworn that I left them on the desk, but logically trying to justify their new resting place, I must have put them back for safe keeping and simply was too tired to remember. I reached down and picked them up and headed downstairs to make breakfast.

Thankful for the groceries from Smitty, I fried up some eggs with toast and poured a glass of orange juice. I sat down at the vintage formica top table in the kitchen and ate while I read another entry.

MAY 30TH, 1956

Mother says that she hates the smell of the little white flowers outside. That was the last thing she had said to me. She hasn't spoken in weeks. I miss her voice. I miss her smile.

She's not the only one being affected by disappearances in the town. Mr. Jackson's wife also went missing three days ago. We were praying for her in church when he said that she had taken ill a few days back. Then at Sunday's mass, he said she was just gone. He woke up, and she wasn't anywhere to be found.

Kel says it's just my imagination, but I know she was taken like George and Father.

-Leona

I finished wiping up what was left of my eggs with my toast and turned the page.

JUNE 5TH, 1956

Mother hanged herself yesterday.

-Leona

Damn, I thought to myself. I downed the last of my juice and wiped my mouth on my shirt sleeve. I read one more entry before deciding to head out for the day.

JULY 15TH 1956

Kel came over after mass today. I told him that I think I'm next, that She's coming for me. He told me that I never should have went to the Hollow, that I'm only in lament and still grieving the loss of my family. I told him that I had started to smell the disgusting aroma of the small white flowers. Kel says that the white flowers always stink when they bloom, but they had finished blooming weeks ago.

I noticed that I also feel lost every now and then, even when Kel is around. He gifted me a gold necklace today with a locket. He said that no matter what, we'd always be together, and I wouldn't be alone.

I'll never take it off.

-Leona

I sighed as a closed the journal and rubbed the textured cowhide binding. I took one last look at the two photos inside of the locket. "Hello Leona. Hello Kel."

I jumped into my car and headed down Main Street. I drove past the closed Smitty's Market and Deli and continued to the town square. As I pulled around the circle, the bells of St. John's Catholic Church began ringing. Time for 8 a.m. mass. I haven't been to church in years except for the traditional Christmas Eve gathering with the family, so I decided against going in. It seemed, however, that that was where everyone in the entire town was at the moment. Just before I looped back around the circle, I saw Smitty walking up toward the church. He smiled and waved at me. I rolled down my window.

"Good morning Mark!" Smitty called out. "What a morning, ay? Did you get to taste those eggs I gave ya?" Smitty walked over to my car and rested his hands on my window ledge.

"Oh, yes, they were fantastic," I smiled and nodded. "Is this where everyone is?" I motioned toward the church.

"Sure is! Care to join me? Plenty of space in my pew. I like to sit t'wards the back in case I start dozin' off. Heh!"

"Uh, that's alright," I smirked.

The second set of church bells tolled signaling the start of mass.

"Well son, I best be gettin' in there. Don't want t'keep the Lord waitin'." Smitty tapped the roof of my car and began to turn around.

"Hey Smitty," I said to get his attention before he left, "could you tell me how to get to Merv's? I wanted to interview him today. You know, to hear some of his tall tales?"

Smitty squinted and rubbed the front of his beard almost as if I had thrown him off guard with my request. "Of course," he resumed his smile. "He lives in the small cabin near the old mine entrance. Take the first right out of the circle and just follow the road until it forks. Take the left near the big hemlock and you'll eventually come to the mine entrance. You'll have to park there and just walk the rest of the way. His cabin's not but a few yards west."

"Thanks," I said.

Smitty nodded and headed into the church.

I rolled up my window and followed Smitty's directions until I reached the entrance of the old mine. It looked like a cave, slightly grown over with weeds. I could still see the mine cart rails going into the dark abyss. Who knew what could be hiding down there now. I made my way through the tall brush and overgrown greenery hoping that I wouldn't run into any poisonous plants and soon saw a small path that lead up to a quaint cabin.

The cabin itself, much like the rest of the town, was very tired looking, but the landscaping around the front porch was well maintained. I walked onto the front porch,

288

passing a "No Trespassing" sign and "Violators Will Be Shot" warning, held my breath and knocked on the door.

A shotgun cocked just as I heard, "Get the hell off my property! I told you delinquents to stay off my land!"

I jumped back and stepped off of the porch. "Mr. Merv Keller," I yelled, "my name is Mark Rochland! I'm a writer from the Pittsburgh Press, and I just wanted to speak with you about Fallen Ash!" I continued to back slightly away from the cabin. "I don't want to intrude! I really just want to figure out what has been taking place here over the past century with all of the tragedies!" I finished yelling at the closed door, anticipating a bullet to fly by my head at any moment.

Just then, the front door cracked open and a long gun barrel poked around the corner. A tall, stocky elderly man in overalls was at the other end.

"Merv Keller?" I asked with my hands up and eyebrows raised.

"You alone?" he asked as his eyes scanned the land behind me, his gun never lowering.

"Y-yyes sir," I stammered slightly, hands still raised.

He looked around one last time, lowered the shotgun, and gestured for me to come inside.

Merv leaned his gun against the wall next to the door as I walked in. I briefly looked around the small living room before settling my eyes upon Merv, who had walked into the even smaller kitchen to the right.

"You're never gonna write that paper, son," Merv scoffed as he picked up a coffee mug. "Cause you're never gonna leave." Merv took a sip from the mug and pulled out a chair from beneath the table and sat down.

"Excuse me?" I asked quietly.

"You heard me." Merv motioned for me to sit down.

I pulled out the other chair and sat down across from him. Merv looked to be about in his late seventies, but still very stout. Along with wearing the old denim overalls, he had on a Vietnam Veterans hat, sitting high on his head tilted slightly to the right. For some reason, it seemed like I had met him before, but couldn't place the face. I took a breath to start to explain my reason for coming, but was interrupted by Merv's hand slamming onto the table causing me to jump.

"Fallen Ash is corrupt!" Merv asserted. "It's been harvesting an evil locked within the surrounding woods for centuries. Once you've come through town, they ain't gonna let you out."

"They?" I asked.

"Those asinine townsfolk down there," Merv shook his head in disgust and pointed out the window.

"I haven't met many but Smitty and Mayor Schaffer, and Smitty seems like a really hospitable guy," I said in his defense.

"Well then, they have you fooled. They're all a bunch of idiotic half-wits working in cahoots with the devil." Merv took another drink from his mug.

I reached into my backpack and pulled out my notebook and pen. "Do you mind telling me your perspective on Fallen Ash and its history?"

Merv chuckled through pierced lips then took another sip from his mug, set it on the table, and readjusted the brim of his hat. "My perspective, huh? They told you I was crazy, didn't they? Well, they're all the liars."

"I'm not here to make judgements, sir. I just want the truth, no matter what form it takes."

Merv raised his thick white eyebrows and leaned back in his chair. He sat there for a moment in silence, then turned to look out the window.

"Mr. Keller?"

"Some call it a witch; some call it a demon. I just call it 'Her'," he started, and my mind instantly referenced back to the first journal entry I had read.

"People gradually started losing their minds and eventually would either kill themselves or disappear. The

290

hollowed are now growing in the eastern woods, feeding the darkness," he continued.

"Hollowed?" I asked as I looked up from my notebook.

"The disappeared. They don't just go missin', son! She takes them! Slowly sucking out the soul! As long as that forest grows, She thrives."

"I don't know if I follow," I squinted at Merv.

"I didn't understand it either until She took someone very precious from me," Merv looked at me then down at his mug. "The soul's energy is never destroyed, just... I don't know... recycled. Once She attaches herself to you, you start to become less of yourself, just empty inside until one day, you're just gone. Some people go through such detriment and torture that they end up killing themselves as the only escape from becoming."

"Becoming what?" I swallowed.

"Part of The Hollow, part of the forest, part of the fuel, part of Her," Merv grew quiet and shook his head. "She comes to feed off of the living, harvesting their fears. And those damn townsfolk are all part of it!" He raised his voice with revolt.

Merv seemed to think that the people in town had made some kind of agreement with the presence. If they continued to provide sustenance, their families would go untouched. He said because of the time spent between feedings, the entity's hunger has increased.

Merv stood up from the table and went over and opened one of his cabinets. From within, he retrieved a small pistol. It looked extremely old. He held it in his hands for a moment, perhaps reminiscing. Then he sat back down at the table, slid the gun forward, and looked directly at me. "You'll know when She's coming. It all starts with the mountain ash."

I smiled uncomfortably. "You think that this thing is going to come after me?" I almost laughed, but Merv continued, ignoring my question.

"The smell is repulsive. Funny thing is… mountain ash is pollinated by flies. The tree actually contains a substance that is found in rotting bodies. Ironic isn't it, son?"

A familiar chill went down my back. I cleared my throat and began gathering my notebook and pen. "I best be going Mr. Keller." I stood up.

"I wouldn't be leaving without that J. Stevens. Might be your only way out," Merv pointed at the pistol.

I reluctantly took the single-shot gun and put it inside of my backpack.

Merv smiled and nodded in approval as he stood and walked me over to the front door. I stepped outside and breathed in the much-needed spring air. I started to walk off of the porch toward the path to my car, but stopped and turned back to Merv.

"Mr. Keller, one more thing. What does the tree look like?"

Merv stepped out onto his porch. "It has white flowers."

As I drove back into town, my mind kept replaying Merv's story, then jumped over to the journal entries. White flowers…

I decided to drive over toward the eastern edge of Fallen Ash and have a look around the infamous Hollow. Leona's journal entry described the location of the Hollow as in the center of the eastern woods.

I trekked through the overgrown brush and thick pines, eventually arriving at a small circular clearing. I could see newer saplings growing on the inside rim of the opening, but nothing too out of the ordinary.

Maybe this isn't the place? I thought to myself. Just then, the sun ducked behind a cloud causing the area around me to gray and cool. Shuffling noises and twigs crackled from behind me. My heart began to thump. I jumped as some crows cawed and fluttered out of their limbed prison cell. I sighed in relief, but quickly choose to turn back as a feeling of anguish settled over me.

When I arrived back at the house, I made a quick lunch and sat down with the journal.

JULY 29TH, 1956

Kel convinced me to let him stay. He wanted me to come with him and his daddy, but I didn't have the heart to leave the house and all of my memories behind. He still doesn't believe in the darkness residing over the town. I can feel it at night, watching me when I sleep. I see movements in the shadows.

-Leona

I turned the page.

AUGUST 13TH 1956

I can't sleep. I can't stop shaking. I am slowly being torn apart from the inside. Kel is asleep next to me. I tried to wake him but without success. I write as tears soak into these pages. A set of eyes is watching me. I can see them over by the window in the corner. The hairs on my arms are standing on end. My heart races. I'm having trouble breathing. God, please save me. Have mercy. Have mercy.

-Leona

AUGUST 14TH, 1956

Morning has finally come but without relief. Kel had to go back home for the day to help around the house. I'm sitting on my bed as the shadow in the corner waits for me to move. I can barely look up. Writing is my only escape. I rub the locket around my neck. Just go away.... Please just go away.

-Leona

I was startled by a knock on the door. I stood and put the journal on my chair which I pushed under the table, then went to find Smitty smiling and waving on the other side of the kitchen door. He came to see how my interview with Merv went, and I told him that Mr. Keller didn't even let me onto his property. Smitty didn't act surprised, but instead almost seemed relieved. I decided to keep it at that and told him that I was in the middle of prime writing time and excused myself. Smitty was reluctant to leave at first, but then went on his way after inviting me over for dinner.

I never ended up making it to dinner that night.

* * * * *

DAY THREE - 2:15 AM

I woke abruptly in a cold sweat. I must have had a nightmare, but I couldn't recall any of the details. By the light of my cellphone, I decided to make my way to the bathroom to wash off the remains of restlessness. I made my way down the dark hall casting a mockery of shadows between the banister.

When I reached the bathroom, I filled up the small glass on the countertop with water and chugged it down. I exhaled and let my hands run under the cold water, watching it glisten in the moonlight, then closed my eyes. I splashed the water over my face as I leaned forward, staying there for a moment to feel the tiny droplets fall from my nose. Blindly, I reached for the hand-towel to my left and patted my face dry, then opened my eyes. Staring straight back at me was my reflection… which soon began to warp into a horribly disfigured version of myself.

My eyes poured from their sockets as the flesh from my cheeks withered and fell. My nostrils twisted and stretched until only a rotted hole remained. The reflection immediately reached toward me as I shut my eyes and threw the towel at the horrid vision. Then once again, I was staring back at myself.

I quickly returned to my room, shaking off what had just happened, attributing it to the nightmare from which I had previously awoke.

8:30 AM

I headed downstairs to begin my final day in Fallen Ash. I thought that some coffee and toast would help me relax and to jot down my last thoughts for the article. It was gloomy outside, absent of the sun's rays because of the incoming storm. When I reached the kitchen, I hurried to turn on the light as if it would somehow sooth my uneasiness.

There in the corner of the room, hunched over in a deformed mound of flesh, was my other self. His neck twisted and snapped as he looked up at me and smiled with a toothless grin. His eyes turned back into his skull as his spine popped and cracked as he began to unnaturally crawl towards me at an unearthly speed, bending and distorting with each movement. I was frozen in fear and couldn't move, watching this deformed doppelganger race for me then suddenly vanish, but not before I smelled its sour decaying breath.

I immediately grabbed my backpack and ran out of the house. I jumped into my car and headed into town as the first boom of thunder rolled. I wasn't sure where I would end up, but I just knew I had to get out of the house, away from myself, away from being alone.

It started to rain heavily as I drove around the town circle then down Main Street. I parked outside of Smitty's Market and Deli and ran to the door. 'Closed for Town Meeting - back at 11AM' read the sign.

Who holds a town meeting at quarter till nine in the morning?! I jumped back into my car and drove to the north end of town and parked at the old railroad station. I reached into the front pocket of my backpack and pulled out Leona's journal and began to read the final two entries.

SEPTEMBER 9TH, 1956

Emptiness. All I feel is emptiness. No remorse… no love… no fear. Black wisps float around me, circling above my head like flies on a rotting corpse. That is what I've become - a nothing.

Dearest Kel,
Please forgive me.

-Leona

SEPTEMBER 16TH, 1956

Yesterday I buried Leona next to her mother. It's already been a week since I found her with my pistol laying in her hand. Damn it I never should have left her alone! I should have listened to her sooner about that damn witch! She took everything from Leona, everything from me! This whole Godforsaken town is cursed.

To anyone who finds this, get out now. Do not go into the clearing. Do not trust anyone. You'll start to turn on yourself and won't be able to getaway once it's begun. You can't escape Her because you can't escape yourself.

I love you Leona.

Forever Intertwined.

-Merv Keller

I closed the journal and reopened the locket to look at the photos of Merv and Leona one last time before wrapping it once again around the leather cover. I jumped as lightning struck behind the tracks. I began to feel nauseous and had a sudden urge to leave town. I started my car and headed back towards Main Street, gradually picking up speed as I grew closer to freedom. I sped past the Fallen Ash welcome sign and never looked back until I reached my apartment in Pittsburgh.

5:30 PM

After eating a late lunch and settling back in, I was relieved to be back at home, away from Fallen Ash. I turned on the television for some background noise while I took out my notebook from my backpack, brushing my fingers across the forgotten pistol from Merv. I didn't even want to write this story anymore.

Just as I was picking up my pen, a large bird flew directly through my living room window, flopped around on the floor a few times, then died. My heart was pounding again.

Why the hell did I get myself into this?

I grabbed a garbage bag, disposed of the bird, and went back to the table to write. Small splatters of blood speckled my fresh white sheets. All of a sudden, I felt extremely claustrophobic, almost choking on the air around me. I tried taking a deep breath but could not fill my lungs. Gasping, I headed toward the shattered window and cut the palms of my hands as I leaned outside.

Shit!

I ran to grab a towel from the hallway closet, but there was a dark figure standing in my way. It seeped out of the shadows, oozing like pus from a wound. I turned away and ran to the kitchen to grab a knife, but when I returned it was gone.

* * * * *

PRESENT TIME - 7:00 PM

I am writing this to warn readers about the evil that resides in the forest of Fallen Ash. It induces a psychological fear where your own fear rots your mind. The legend slowly lurches into real life, crossing the boundary between story and reality where there is no escape. You slowly become less of yourself, witnessing the new and demented self slowly appear and take over until you become ultimately hollowed, consumed. I will not let Her win. I sit here as an intelligent man telling you to somehow destroy that town before She escapes…

There is a stillness here now, as if an arm is wrapping itself around me, muting any sound that tries to intrude. The night air is crisp and chilled. I can feel it climbing through the recently broken window pane as I turn to stare out at the dark, bruised sky. I close my eyes for a moment then hang my head to look back down at the old J. Stevens single-shot pistol I placed on the table in front of me. Trembling, my fingers slowly glide over the cracked wooden handle. I inhale deeply, absorbing the overwhelming pungent smell of mountain ash.

She's here.

Foreword by Author Nicholas Gray

Biography: Nicholas Gray is an aspiring author from the Great Lake state of Michigan. After reading authors like Stephen King, Ronald Kelly, and Richard Laymon, Nicholas knew that he wanted to tell stories of the macabre just as his heroes have told before him. He wanted to enthrall his readers with stories of horror, whether that was giving the reader a chill up their spine or giving them a good laugh. Nicholas loves reading and writing, but he also loves his pets! He has a pet dog named Lula and a tortoise named Chester. Nick hopes to one day write a novel that readers enjoy and will recommend to others. Being a cancer survivor (Hodgkin's Lymphoma) Nicholas knows what true horror is, and hopes to give an escape from the real world to his readers with his stories of monsters and other macabre things.

No Smoking by Nicholas Gray

Tom placed his timecard into the punch-clock; 3:14pm was stamped onto it, just a minute before the afternoon huddle. Placing his punch-card back into its rightful slot, he headed over to the breakroom for the afternoon huddle. He never looked forward to the afternoon huddles. They usually always brought bad news, and today was no different.

"From this day forward, H&G Machining will now be a smoke free company! No longer shall anyone smoke in the vicinity of the property," his boss, Mr. Mason announced to the grumbling employees. He said this with a slight smile. Russ, a second shift employee scoffed. Mr. Mason beamed at him, as if to shut him up. Russ looked down and didn't say a word.

Most of the employees were smokers, and this news brought no joy to them at all, especially Tom. Tom spoke up in a voice that had become raspy from years of heavy smoking.

"Why, all of a sudden, are we being punished for our God-given right to smoke?" Everyone looked at Tom, and then back to Mr. Mason. The boss put a hand to the right side of his head and started to massage his temple.

"You know why, Tom."

"What? Because of Steve and Benny?"

"Yes, because of Steve and Benny."

Steve and Benny were two second-shift employees that were presumed dead. Benny went missing from his shift three months ago, and Steve disappeared more recently. They both went missing after going outside for a smoke break. The two of them, plus Russ, rounded out the night shift.

With Tom's interruption, the breakroom broke into a rumor mill. The grumbling employees went on about how Steve and Benny weren't missing, but dead! Others said they just left town to get away from their wives, which was a very strong possibility.

"I heard a bear mauled Benny to death on a hunting trip and Steve got mowed down by a bus," one coworker said to another.

"Nah man, I heard they both died on the job, right in the back alleyway," the other coworker whispered back.

Tom overheard their conversation and grimaced. He couldn't speak for the bus, but he knew a bear wouldn't stray this far away from wilderness. Being a hunter, he knew a thing or two about bears.

Even though juicy rumors swam around the breakroom, all Tom could think about was the dreaded second-shift with its new-implemented no smoking rule.

Two days after Steve's disappearance, Tom was informed that he would have to replace Steve on the saw. After all, someone had to keep the saw running during the second shift or else they would never hit the projected numbers that the company demanded. Tom wasn't too fond of working second-shift. He usually went out on a drinking binge around 8pm with his buddies. He used the time to complain about the two strikes he earned at work and lament that if he received one more it would mean automatic suspension, or even worse, getting fired! Tom enjoyed his drinking sessions. It was a good opportunity to shoot the shit; complain about ex-wives, the boss, and what the libtards were doing to the damn country! Working second shift was akin to a punishment. Tom couldn't drink, or shoot the shit, and now he couldn't even smoke. This was crossing the line; prisoners had more freedom.

"Steve and Benny were chain smokers!" Tom sneered at his boss. "We shouldn't get punished for their... their..."

Tom was drawing a blank. The word was at the tip of his tongue. "Dumbassery!" he finally shouted aloud. That was not the word he wanted to use, but it got his point across suitably.

Stern looks flashed towards Tom from his fellow coworkers, but he didn't care. In fact, he actually enjoyed the attention.

"Oh, and you're so much better?" Mr. Mason retorted and leered over Tom, seemingly attempting to send a message with his eyes, but Tom was oblivious.

"Well, yeah!" he replied heatedly… damn well knowing that there were four or five cigarette butts laying on the ground outside the driver's side door of his car. He had smoked all those cigarettes in the spare ten minutes he had before punching in for the meeting.

His truck was the jacked up four by four, that was probably compensating for something, parked in one of the two only "handi-capable" spots at the company. It reeked from a few years of accumulated cigarette smoke. He always got to work on time, so he could have some time to smoke before having to deal with whatever work had in store for him. He typically smoked about two packs a day, which was an improvement from his previous record.

Tom had a smoking habit, if that's what you wanted to call it. He smoked any time he could. When he was anywhere besides work, Tom always kept a cigarette butt hanging out of his mouth. His pearly whites had yellowed from years of smoking and two of his front teeth were missing. The veins on his arms had become so prominent that he could almost see the blood pumping throughout his body. He had a bad cough that could scare anyone in his vicinity. When the company asked for checkups, he went to his doctor's office where he was informed that if he continued his bad habit it was only a matter of time before he collapsed from a heart attack or worse, lung cancer, but Tom didn't care. It was his body and he'd do whatever the hell he wanted with it.

* * * * *

Three hours passed and Tom itched for a cigarette. He looked up at the clock and saw it was 6:30pm. It was time for his first break.

Just one cigarette Tom, just one. It won't hurt ya, Tom, just smoke one.

He went outside and pulled out his lighter. He put the cigarette into his mouth and was about to light it when he saw a security camera turn his way. The camera looked as if it were focusing on him; zooming out, then back in again.

Becoming paranoid, Tom put the cigarette back into its pack and stuck it in his back pocket. As he turned his back to the camera, he noticed another camera zooming in on him. Tom cursed, punched the door to the breakroom, then went inside. He needed to take out his aggression on somebody.

Russ sat at one end of the breakroom, spinning his wedding ring on the tabletop. Chris sat beside Russ at the table reading a book that Tom didn't recognize... although Tom wouldn't recognize any book he came across.

"Chris, what the fuck're you doing?" Tom yelled out.

Tom didn't have an indoor voice, so Chris jumped a little then shook his head in annoyance.

"Oh, it's just a Ray Bradbury story about--"

"Does that book got any pictures in it?" Tom interrupted.

"Um, no. Just the one on the cov-"

"Then how y'know what's going on?"

"Excuse me?"

"C'mon Chrissy, you ain't fooling no one here"

Chris look puzzled for a second, then realized the charade Tom was carrying on.

"Look, I don't appreciate--"

"We know a dumbass like you couldn't get through a book unless it got pictures!" Tom roared out in laughter. His laugh gradually turned into a wheeze, then a tear started to form in his right eye. "Y'know, cause ya can't read and all!"

Chris refused to take the bait. He was enjoying reading *Fahrenheit 451* for the G.E.D. class he was taking.

He was the shop bitch, at least that was what his coworkers called him-- Tom chief among them. When someone clogged up the toilet, Chris had to clean it up. When the local cats started shitting in the parking lot, he had to pick it up. He crawled inside the machines and cleaned them from within.

He wanted to be a full-time machine operator! The company said they would pay for his school tuition if he aced all of his tests, and he knew he could do it. He just had to get one thing out of the way, his G.E.D. He needed to work nights so he could go to class in the mornings. When an opening became available on the second-shift he jumped at the chance... the major downside being that he was exposed to Tom night after night.

"Just leave me alone Tom, I'm trying to read."

This, for some odd reason pissed Tom off. Tom grabbed the book from Chris' grasp and started to flip through the pages.

"Hey, I'm gonna lose my place."

Tom ignored him. "Yup, I don't see a single picture in this book!" Tom said before hacking up as much phlegm as he possibly could and spit in between the book's pages. Then he walked to the trash can and dropped the book in. He laughed a hardy, yet wheezy, laugh.

Russ looked over at Chris and shook his head.

* * * * *

A few more hours passed. Tom was approaching his next break. The withdrawals were getting worse. Normally, he would have already smoked one pack by now. A voice in his head kept repeating the same thing over and over.

Just one cigarette Tom, just one. It won't hurt ya Tom, just smoke one.

The need for nicotine was really getting to him. When his lunch break came, he hurried to his truck in a now nearly empty parking lot. Other than his truck there was only Chris' van and Russ' motorcycle. Yet when he made it to his truck cameras were pointing at him from multiple angles. He cursed. Instead of lighting up a cigarette, he tried to get a nap in, but all he could think about was smoking.

He thought about the good old days, the days before rules for smoking indoors were created. Back then he'd burn through more packs then two people could put together.

Smoking was a part of who Tom was. *Smoking is in my genes,* he'd say. His father, and his father before him all smoked like chimneys. He received his first pack of smokes from his dad on his twelfth birthday. He had been smoking cigarettes well before then, but that moment was like passing of the torch, and it was Tom's time to puff.

Tom leapt out of his gas guzzler and landed in a grey puddle. Disgusted, he lifted his boots, cringing as the grey muck slid off his heel. He didn't know what he landed in, but the scent it delivered was nauseating. His gaze glanced upwards at the truck's door where he saw a smudged handprint smeared across it. He touched the substance and brought it up to his nose. Appalled, Tom wiped his hand onto his pants.

This must've been Chris' doing!

It was an odd way to get back at Tom, but it was the only logical answer at the time.

I'll get him back tomorrow.

How he would, Tom didn't know, for all he could think about now was his need for a cigarette.

Lunch ended, and he headed back inside. A couple of more hours passed unbearably. He thought about going to the restroom for a smoke, but the last time he did that a coworker ratted him out resulting in him earning his second

306

strike. And it was people that didn't smoke, like Chris, who rat. Tom didn't want to risk it, although the need for tobacco was strong enough for him to chance it! He could go into the restroom, turn off the fire alarm, and puff up a storm until all his problems went away. The headache that was making home inside his head would be evicted as soon as he had a few puffs of that sweet, sweet cigarette.

Last break finally came, and Tom was at his breaking point. He entered the break room and sat down at Russ' table.

Russ was a tall, scrawny biker, but you could never tell by his demeanor that he rode with a biker gang. He was a pretty nice guy. Never had he snitched on anyone, including Tom. He mostly kept to himself; a characteristic that made Tom trust him.

"I don't know how you did it!" Tom said, hands twitching slightly.

"Did what?" Russ asked, unwrapping paper revealing the concealed gum inside. Russ knew where this conversation was heading. "You're talking about how I quit smoking, aren't ya?"

"Yeah, how'd ya do it Russ? I can't even last an hour! I need a cig like a whore needs a big ol'-"

"It was hard," Russ cut him off before Tom could get any further with his attempt at a joke. "There were moments where I thought about smoking and how one cig wouldn't, couldn't hurt."

He closed eyes, as if to remember the sensation of smoking, and let out a big sigh. "Smoking is like a ball and chain, it won't let you go, just make you work harder to live."

This was all nonsense to Tom. He simply wanted to know how to make it through the rest of the night without losing his mind. The rest of what Russ was saying was little more than unnecessary gibberish.

"Right… well anyways, do you know of a spot around here one might be able to, y'know…"

Tom paused to look over at Chris, the rat, who was deep into reading his book. Tom leaned in closer to Russ, just to be careful. Russ could smell Tom's gnarly breath, as he attempted to whisper, even though his whisper was about the same volume as someone's normal voice.

"Where a guy could get in a quick smoke break?"

Russ gave out a low chuckle. "Sorry, can't help you there."

Tom frowned and pushed his seat out with his back as he got up and began to walk away.

Russ looked over at Chris, remembering what Tom had done to his book. He recalled Chris spending his lunch break cleaning the slime out from between the pages. It was a little hard to watch. Russ managed a smile, and a change of mind turned in his head.

"You know what Tom, as an ex-smoker, I know what you're going through. I'll tell ya a little secret."

Tom was instantly reeled back in.

"Back when Steve and Benny were still around, we used to smoke in the alleyway out behind the shop."

Russ looked over to Chris to make sure he wasn't paying any attention as Tom sat back down beside Russ and leaned in closely. Russ' voice lowered a bit, just to make sure Chris wasn't listening.

"Back when we'd take our smoke breaks in the back alley, I noticed that there's no security cameras in or around the area. You could probably pop a death stick and smoke one without Mr. Mason catching ya on tape. Just grab a trash bin so the cameras inside the shop don't catch ya going outside for no reason

Man, Steve, Benny, and I would smoke so much, the fire department would get called to the scene! Those were the days," Russ laughed, then continued. "God, I miss Steve and Benny. Ya know, they're reason why I gave up smoking in the first place? I quit cause-"

Russ looked over at Tom and noticed that he wasn't interested in this bit. His leg was bouncing like crazy, like an addict without his crack.

"Looks like you need to smoke badly, huh?" Russ popped the gum into his mouth and began to chew.

Tom looked at him yearningly. "I'll die if I don't get a cigarette in me!"

He got up from his seat and thanked Russ profusely, even hailing him a life savior.

* * * * *

Tom was looking forward to trying out the new spot. Other than his truck, the only other place he smoked was in the restroom, which ended after a rat snitched on him and he received his second strike, something that kept going through his mind repeatedly, just like that one phrase.

Just one cigarette Tom, just one. It won't hurt ya, Tom, just smoke one.

He had an hour left of his shift till it was punch out time. His lungs were begging to him for a cigarette.

Just one cigarette Tom, just one. It won't hurt ya, Tom, just smoke one.

His head pounded, and the room began to spin. He felt as if he were on a Tilt-A-Whirl ride at the carnival. Tom felt as if he was going mad! He tried to concentrate on his work, but he found himself looking at the clock every ten seconds, thinking at least ten minutes had gone by. His hands were shaking, and he couldn't take it anymore! He needed to smoke! Tom remembered what Russ told him and grabbed a trash bin.

It wasn't really filled with anything; two empty chip bags and a torn rubber glove, it didn't matter though. Bolting his way towards the door, he excitedly sprinted into the dark outside. It was a little chilly, but not winter weather. A fall jacket would be seasonable, but Tom was tough--at least that's how he rationalized his unwillingness to wear something with sleeves. If he wore sleeves then no one would be able to see his ink, which he always kept covered up during his day shift.

On his arm was a tattoo from Guns N, Roses *Appetite for Destruction*, the original cover art as Tom liked to point out. It depicted the aftermath of a graphic sexual assault perpetrated by a robot, and an otherworldly, ferocious metal-beast, with knives for teeth, about to devour the mechanical assailant. When he was younger, he was in love with that album, and the art it held immersed him. Lots of people scorned him for his racy ink, but he didn't care.

He began walking to the dumpster at the far end of the shop, right next to the holy spot, the back alleyway that Russ told him about.

Just one cigarette Tom, Just one.

He was going to give in. Tom lifted the lid of the dumpster and chucked the bag inside. He slammed it down and walked over to the dark alleyway. He looked around to see if Russ' story held true. He scanned the wall, one end to the other, and decided that there were no cameras in sight. He looked past the corner of the wall to see if there was anyone outside. He didn't see Russ or that supposed rat, Chris. Tom smiled. He almost jumped up and clicked his heels.

He whipped out his pack of smokes and stuck the butt of the cigarette into his mouth. The lighter came out next. He put his thumb on the wheel and struck down. A flame erupted from the lighter. He pulled the lighter to his mouth and burned the tip of the cigarette. He inhaled deeply as smoke filled up his lungs. He held it in for a few seconds and then released. A white cloud filled the air and Tom let out a big sigh of relief. The cigarette's smoke pacified him instantly. He put the cigarette back into his mouth and took another long drag. Again, he held it in his lungs for a few seconds before releasing. Other than the light being emitted by his cigarette, the only other illumination in the dark alley was high up, near the roof of the building.

Tom took a few more drags of the cigarette. It was bliss. He didn't care if he spent the rest of his shift outside; he had almost hit his numbers anyway, which was better than what he usually did. Sure, he could go back inside and work for another hour, but then they would start to expect it from him. And he would hear it from his boss for sure! Mr. Mason would laugh at him and tell him:

"See, this is what you could accomplish if you weren't taking a five-minute smoke break every twenty minutes or so!"

To have to work harder without the help from his cigarettes? Tom didn't want to think about that. All he wanted to think about was, well, nothing at all. He just wanted to inhale his cigarette and let his shift pass on by.

Suddenly the light in the alleyway began to flicker. Tom looked over his shoulder and noticed the silhouette of a man just beyond the circumference of the light. Tom quickly threw the cigarette to the ground and stomped on it, grinding it into the pavement with his steel-toe boot. He turned toward the man and went to say something, but there was nobody there. Tom became a little uneasy. He knew damn well there was a man standing just past the light. Hastily, he started walking toward where he saw the figure standing and turned just to make sure nothing was following from behind. He turned his head back toward the other end, where he originally saw the silhouette, and saw a man walking toward him.

"Russ, is that you?" Tom called, with a slight quiver in his voice. "Hey, uh, you finally decide that the Nicorette gum just wasn't doing it for ya?"

The man walked a few more paces, then dropped to the ground.

"Hey, you alright!?" Tom cried out.

The man on the ground didn't move. In fact, Tom could barely make out the body from where he stood. He crept toward the man but stopped a few inches short. Something was *off*, Tom could just feel it. He got the same feeling once when he was out hunting deer with his buddies. A bear came from his rear and startled them. He'd never admit it, but he'd damn near wet his pants. They remained as still they could and eventually, after looting their food and destroying the tents, the bear left them alone. But this thing--this figure--didn't seem to have any intention of leaving him alone.

Tom reached for his lighter and flicked a flame out of it. Waving the lighter towards where the man apparently fell, he discovered that it wasn't a man at all--it was just a puddle of muck. But the smell was oddly familiar to him. Tom knelt down and dipped his fingers into the puddle that smeared the ground. He rubbed the thick liquid between his finger and thumb. Its texture was slimy, yet rough at the same time. Tom brought it up to his nose to smell it. He couldn't pinpoint what the aroma was, but he knew it was familiar. He turned his phone over to check the time. It read 11:42pm. It was getting close to closing time.

My mind is playing tricks on me, he thought and started to make his way out of the alley.

He got to the light and it suddenly went out. Caught off guard, Tom jumped and cursed from the surprise. He put his back to the wall and took in several deep breaths.

It's the lack of cigarettes that has me on edge, that's it! That's all it was!

He realized he needed to calm down before going inside, so he reconciled with himself and decided another smoke was necessary to carry on with the rest of his day. Putting another cigarette into his mouth, he began to pull the lighter toward his lips. He lit the cigarette, closed his eyes, and took a long drag, holding it deep in his lungs and finally exhaling out a big cloud of smoke.

That's when Tom heard it: a deep guttural growl at the end of the alleyway towards where the muck lay. He turned his head to see a man languidly walking toward him.

"Hey, I-" Tom muttered, but stopped mid-sentence. The outline of the thing seemed way bulkier than before. As it crept closer, it became larger in height, until it was standing nearly seven feet off the ground! Tom took a few steps backward, remembering the bear and the fear it had struck in him. He remained perfectly still as if he were dealing with a T-Rex. He considered running, but the thought trailed off as the light in the alleyway began to flicker back on. Now Tom could just make out what this thing was, and it was just that--a *thing!*

Standing underneath the light, was an inhuman figure. Its bones protruded outwards, revealing a rib cage that extended much larger and longer than a human one would. Its entire body was covered in sludge. Its arms and legs were clumped with something, as if the thing was covered in black tumors. Its face was the worst part of its skewered anatomy. It had long, darkened yellowed teeth that came to jagged points. What little hair it possessed was thin and greasy and the thing had no eyes! Its hands morphed into four long fingers, each ending in a knife-like claw that extended too long. The thing was wheezing; it was a deep and ungodly sound.

The creature stood over Tom. His cigarette dropped to the side of his mouth and fell to the ground. The creature was taking deep breaths, as if it were taking in his scent. Tom took a few more steps backwards, then turned to run, but it was no use. The creature went for one of Toms legs, grabbed his ankle and swept him off his feet. The monster was extremely agile. Tom kicked at the thing's arm, but its grip didn't loosen. The thing let go, and before Tom could attempt a crawl to safety, it borrowed its nails into the middle of Tom's chest like an Olympic dive. Its claws broke through Tom's breastbone. Tom let out a wail, and grabbed at the thing's arms, but again it was no use. It had its nails underneath Tom's ribs now. It let out a huge roar and its arms moved apart from one another as if it were performing a breaststroke. Blood splattered on the ground and wall, and Tom's face was one of agonizing pain. He whimpered, for that was all Tom had left in him to do.

Tom's chest was exposed. His beating heart thumped near lungs that were blackened from years of indulging in a bad habit. The creature grabbed at both of Tom's lungs and ripped them from their place in his chest cavity. Tom lost the ability to breathe. Before life left him, he looked up at the monster one final time. The beast took one lung and hovered it over its mouth, then squeezed it like a sponge. Blood and a tar-like substance poured into the monster's mouth like an expunged orange. As it gulped it down and swallowed, the creature tossed the lung to the side, then it moved onto the other lung. Tom's eyes fluttered, then closed shut, and everything went dark.

* * * * *

Chris swiped his timecard through the punch clock and hollered at Russ to have a great night. Russ nodded to him and stuck his card into the machine. He walked outside to the parking lot, saw Tom's truck, sighed, and made his way towards the alleyway.

Russ fully expected to find Tom in the alleyway-- instead, he found what was left of him. Lying on the ground resided Tom's ransacked corpse. Russ immediately pulled out his phone and dialed his bosses' number.

"We got another death due to smoking."

"Lemme guess, was it Tom?"

"Yup, the sorry bastard went outside for a smoke break. Guess he couldn't help himself."

"God dammit Tom! That insubordinate, stubborn piece of shit."

Russ went over to Tom's body and nudged it with his foot.

"Did it leave everything except the lungs?" Mr. Mason asked.

"Yup, it left the rest of him in the alleyway, just like Steve and Benny."

Russ unwrapped a stick of gum and popped it into his mouth. Nicorette gum tasted God-awful, but the way he saw it, it was a lot better than getting your lungs ripped out of your chest.

"Well, Russ, you know the drill," Mr. Mason said calmly into the receiver. "Call in the cleaning crew and make sure that they clear all signs of the incident off the property. I'll inform the owners about the mishap in the morning."

"Aye-aye captain," Russ said in a monotone voice.

He hung up the phone and proceeded to dial in the next number. Before he hit the call button, he looked down at Tom's body. Russ felt no remorse for what he had done. He knew what he was doing when he told Tom about "The Spot." He knew he was sending him to his doom; like showing a rat a piece of cheese, then leading the little critter to a fox's den and tossing the cheese in. But did he feel bad for Tom? Not really. Tom was an ass to just about everyone in the company. That little gag he pulled in the lunchroom with Chris pretty much sealed his fate.

Yet Russ was having a difficult time dealing with the loss of his fellow coworkers Steve and Benny. And quitting cigarettes was slowly eating him away inside. He missed that damn feeling smoking brought to him. Even now, seeing the pack of cigarettes lying next to Tom's corpse had him itching.

Just one cigarette, Russ, just one. It won't hurt ya, Russ, just smoke one.

Russ looked away in disgust at the realization that he could even consider risking his life for one drag from a death stick. That's what he called them now, death sticks. Three murders now…all due to the death sticks.

Russ knelt and picked up the pack of cigarettes. Tom was still clutching the lighter in his cold hand. Unfolding Tom's fingers, Russ took the lighter from Tom's dead grasp.

Just one cigarette, Russ, just one. It won't hurt ya, just smoke one.

Russ grabbed his head.

Just one cigarette, Russ, just one. It won't hurt ya, just smoke one.

The message kept repeating over and over. Russ took a deep breath.

"What the Hell, one cigarette can't hurt, right?"

Highway to Hell by Nicholas Gray

So, there we were, playing Highway to Hell for what seemed to be the tenth thousandth time. The song was playing on repeat, with the occasional *Hells Bells* and *Hell Ain't a Bad Place to Be*, all performed by AC/DC, my favorite band. This playlist was on for a special occasion though, for we were literally going to Hell.

Hell is a small town in the great lake state of Michigan. My brother, Wesley, and I were on our way to Hell, so we could say we've been to Hell and back! We were also heading over there to get a T-shirt for Wesley, which was a major reason why we were making this trip in the first place.

Oh, I forgot to introduce myself. My name is Sydney, and I had just gotten out of my last year of high school and was working at a local pizzeria for extra money. That all was displayed by my shirt that read, in bold, 'Give me a pizza that pie,' with the name Joe's Pizza arching over the saying. I didn't like my job, but I figured nobody does and muscled through my days of rolling dough and baking pizzas. Besides, it was better than being at home, I figured.

I became sick of pizza, just the smell of it made me ill, but occasionally I would bake myself a free pizza, which Joe allowed, and take it home for my family to eat. My family wasn't great on money at the moment, so any time I could bring home free food, it made a great day.

One Friday, while I was getting off my shift to enjoy the weekend, I fixed myself a pizza for the road. I drove home in my old silver minivan with a Joe's pizza box sitting in the passenger seat. Rock tunes booming out of the car's speakers, I pulled into my family's driveway, slammed the car door behind me, and approached the house door with slight unease.

I could hear my parents arguing inside. It was never fun to be stuck in the middle of my parents' fights. I felt like a referee in a cage match; sometimes being part of the fights and actively taking sides and, at other times, breaking them up. Their fights were always petty too.

You were supposed to take out the trash, she'd say.

It was your turn to pick Wesley up from school, he'd say.

They'd argue, throwing insults at each other, then mom would slam the door to what was supposed to be their bedroom, while dad would head to the old, familiar confines of the couch.

Who knew why they were fighting this time; I intended to race past that mess and go to my brothers' room, who was probably looking forward to my return.

I opened the door and ran up the stairs, slipping past the argument ensuing in the kitchen. Walking past the bedroom, I was now facing my brother's door, which was covered in horror movie monster stickers. I knocked at the door gently and slowly opened the door, emerging into Wesley's bedroom.

Wesley was my small chubby brother, who at that moment was playing video games, but I could see he wasn't fully into the game.

"Hey buddy, how's it going?" I said with a caring face, their parents still could be heard yelling at one another downstairs. He paused his video game and turned to me, but just looked down to the ground. I shut the door behind me, muffling our parents fight downstairs with the shutting door.

"I… I started this one," Wesley said, referring to the fight happening downstairs.

"No, you didn't buddy. Mom and Dad are just… going through some things. It'll get bet--"

"No, no I started it this time!"

"Why do you think that?"

"Because I asked dad if he'd take me somewhere and he said no, which got mom to yelling at him and he started yelling back and, and…" He trailed off, wiping his eyes with his sleeve to clear them from the tears falling down his cheeks.

"Where'd you want to go?"

He sniffed a few times, then began to talk "Well, you know the small town called Hell. I thought it would be cool if we all went to Hell, like that one time we did when we were younger."

He was remembering a happier time. A time where they took a family trip to Hell, Michigan, to say our family could survive a trip to Hell and back. But it didn't go well. Wesley begged mom for a shirt and she said no. Ever since then he's wanted to go back and get a shirt; specifically, the one that says 'See you in Hell' in bold, with Michigan in small text just under the word hell.

I frowned. I understood where my younger brother was coming from.

"You know what, we'll go to Hell! Just you and me. It'll be fun! And we'll get you that shirt you've always wanted!"

He got his chubby body off the ground and slammed into me, clasping his arms around me for an embracive bear hug. I set the pizza box on the bed and held him tightly.

"Thank you, Sydney," he said, his voice muffled by my shirt, which was covered in flour.

So, we packed our things up, got in the car, and hit the road.

We drove for quite a while. Eventually, we turned onto M53 while jamming out to Hells Bells. It was known as the high way to Hell, for it was the last road you hop onto till you reach Hell, Michigan. I was banging my curly fro' side to side, while my little brother head banged off beat in the passenger seat. He wasn't much of a rocker like me, but my music was perfect for this occasion. I was paying little attention to the road in front of me, but then something caught my eye. I was seeing something weird up ahead.

"What is that?" I said, staring at what seemed to be a red fog off in the distance.

"I don't know. Maybe it's a flare," My little brother said while paying no mind to what I was seeing, switching the song over to *Highway to Hell*.

"It could be a flair… but what if it's a fire?"

I kept driving, and when we got closer it wasn't any easier to figure out where the fog was coming from.

"I don't know about this. Maybe we should turn around."

"No! We're almost there Sydney. Just drive through it," Wesley said, looking up at me with a face you just couldn't say no to.

"Okay, but if I sense any danger, I'm turning this car around."

He nodded, and we pursued towards the fog.

When we reached the red fog, it was dense. It was hard to see through, but I could just make out the road in front of us. My biggest fear at the moment was that I was driving on the wrong side of the road, and that an oncoming car might hit me if I was not careful. I started to drive under the original speed limit, going about ten miles an hour, just to make sure I didn't get hit by any cars that could possibly be coming from up ahead that can't see us. I also turned on my fog lights, since visibility was low, but it didn't seem to make much of a difference.

Then something changed. I didn't notice it at first, but it became noticeable the deeper we went into the fog. The road was unusually bumpy, like we were driving on a brick road or something. As I squinted to the little bit of road, I could see in front of me, I realized that the road did indeed change; we were now driving on a path that was cracked a bit, with a bright red light piercing through the ground.

"I really don't like this," I said nervously.

Then, as Wesley was turning the volume up, the music suddenly stopped in the middle of the song, looping the word 'hell' repeatedly, like a broken record. Wesley struggled to turn off the radio as it pierced our ears. I winced at the increased volume and yelled for him to turn it off. He hit random buttons and twisted dials till it finally stopped as he switched it off from blue tooth to FM radio. Relief hit us both as the volume seized. I looked over at the station playing now. 66.6 FM was the station it ended up landing on. Weird, I thought, didn't know such a station existed. A slight shiver went down my back at the thought of the sign of the devil, three sixes. Even though I wasn't a firm believer in the afterlife, it still made me a little uncomfortable to be on this station.

"Hey, is there any other stations other than this one?" I asked.

He hit the seek arrow and it flipped through a bunch of numbers until it landed back on the same station.

"Nope," Wesley said nervously, looking over at me with a concerned look.

"Is the volume down?" I asked, wondering if the station was naturally silent or the volume was just low.

"I tried turning the volume down before," he said, testing the dial to see if it was turned all the way down, "and it looks like it's on mute."

"Turn it up."

He slowly turned up the volume and I instantly regretted asking him to do so. Screams screeched through the car's speakers and nearly deafened my brother and me. I almost let go of the wheel to shield my ears from the violence being put upon them.

"Turn it off Wes!" I yelled. Wesley reached for the dial and spun it in the direction to mute the screams, but to no avail. The screams sounded horrific and blood curdling.

"I can't turn it off!" Wesley yelled, as he stopped attempting to silence the screams and instead covered his ears, the only defense he had against the banshee noise. Then the red fog lifted, and what we saw was, well, hellish.

The sky was dark red. Before, it was a little gloomy outside, but you could just make out the sun in the sky up above. Now, there was no sun in sight, just an all red sky, with a few black clouds. The road up ahead turned into a red bricked path, the car bobbed up and down as it lumbered across the cracked road. But that was only the tip of the iceberg in changes we perceived as we continued to look around.

Large spikes speared into the red sky, and as my eyes followed the spike to its peak, I noticed something was on the tip. I squinted, then made out what it was. It was a naked man! A naked man that was impaled on the giant spike! And it wasn't just one man. There were people impaled on spikes as far as the eye can see!

Wesley whimpered in the passenger seat.

"I don't like this, Sydney!" Wesley said, sinking into his seat.

"Close your eyes, Wesley!" I demanded, and he quickly followed the command, covering his eyes with his palms.

I checked the rearview mirror, but all I saw was the red bricked road; no red fog that we drove through before. I looked forward, making sure I wasn't going to hit anything, then peered back into the rearview mirror. That's when I noticed something was starting to emerge a good distance behind us. It peaked over the horizon. Whatever it was it was getting closer, and fast!

I kept my eyes on the road, but constantly was looking out the rearview mirror, trying to ignore the scenery around me. My ears adjusted to the screams through the radio. It was just background noise. As we kept driving forward, hoping to reach our destination, if that was even feasible at this point. Then the thing behind us came into view.

"What is that!?" I said in an alarmed tone. The thing behind us appeared to be a skeleton. A Skeleton with black wings. In its hands was a scythe. Its wings flapped vigorously as it approached closer and closer. Wesley was now tuned around in his seat, peering out the back of the van to see what I was petrifyingly captivated by.

Fuck speed limits, I thought. At this point I knew it was time to floor it.

I slammed my foot to the pedal and the car shook as it switched gears. The van wasn't use to going over seventy miles per hour.

"Hurry Sydney! It's gaining on us!" Wesley yelled, aware of the danger I sensed as well.

"I'm trying, I'm trying!"

The thing was just behind us now, no more than twenty feet away.

"Fuck, fuck, fuck, fuck, fuck!" I finally said, releasing the panic I was holding within.

The thing was now fifteen feet away. Ten feet away. Five feet away.

Crack!

The car began to halt. I turned to the rearview mirror and looked as the skeleton was holding its ground behind us; its scythe piercing the top of the trunk, getting stuck there. I'd have to find a way to explain that to mom if we made it out of here alive. If this thing didn't kill us, she would.

Sparks flew up from the back of the car as the bumper made contact with the brick road. Our speed was dropping quickly. I had to think fast, or we were doomed. That's when I hit the brakes, causing the van to lurch forward, before I threw it into reverse.

I contorted my body, so I could properly see out the back window and slammed on the gas. The skeleton behind us got into the pushing motion. We were in a tug-of-war; we were going in reverse and he was pushing us forward. The car's tires released smoke as the wheels turned in place, but we were slowly backing up. The skeleton switched positions, shouldering the weight of the van. Then he collapsed underneath the vehicle as the van overcame the skeleton's strength and reversed two tons of minivan on top of him.

I hit the brakes. Wesley and I were breathing heavily as the lights of the minivan shone onto the skeleton.

"Is he... dead?" Wesley asked.

The skeleton twitched a bit, got to its knees, then it began to prop itself back up.

"Run him over! Run him over!" Wesley yelled.

I hesitated at first, then threw the van into drive and slammed on the gas again. The skeleton pushed against the hood of the car, pushing us backwards a bit. I could tell it was using all of its strength to stop us from moving forward.

"Run him over!" Wesley yelled again.

"I'm trying!" I yelled back

Smoke appeared from the van's tires once again as the skeleton pushed against it. This time the skeleton was winning. I cursed, then began to think on my toes. I threw the car into reverse. The skeleton fell forward onto its knees, then stood up, preparing for the next move I had planned on doing. It probably thought I was going to ram him again. Fuck that, I thought.

I slammed on the gas, making my way towards the skeleton. Then, right before making contact with it, I veered. I veered like I would for a deer. I floored it and we made our way past the skeleton, or at least I thought we did. I took in a deep breath as we drove forward onto the brick path. I could hear my heartbeat in my ears, that's how much adrenaline was flowing through me at that moment.

Then I heard footsteps coming from the roof. It was on top of the van! The skeleton was on top of the van!

I hesitated again as my brain lagged in a dire situation. Then I whipped the wheel back and forth, hoping to get the thing to tumble of the side of the van. It was fruitless.

I then heard the scythe being expunged out of the top of the trunk. Shit, I thought. I looked over at Wesley, who was in tears at this point.

"It's going to be alright Wes. We got this." I gave him an unconvincing smile as thuds on the roof could be heard, until the thuds stopped just above me. I veered the car again and again, but it remained on top of the car. There was only one thing left to try...

Suddenly, the windshield was impaled by the scythe, which missed my face by mere centimeters. The scythe retracted, and I could feel another swing coming soon. That's when I had to make my move. I slammed on the brakes, causing the car to skid and rumble to a halt. The skeleton went flying forward and tumbled to the ground. I hit the gas and ran over it. This time I looked into the rearview mirror to make sure he was left in the dust. The skeleton stood up and stared at us, wings starting to flutter.

The car started to sputter, then it stopped.

"NO! No, no, no, no, no, NO! I yelled.

"What's happening? Why aren't we going?" Wesley asked.

"I can't believe it right now! We're out of freaking gas!"

That's when a loud thud landed on top of the roof. The skeleton was back.

He walked onto the hood of the van, turned and knelt down, peering into the van's windshield. He looked at both of us, then a deep, disembodied voice burst through the car's speakers.

"You don't belong here," the voice said, as the skeleton pointed a boney finger at me.

"NO, we don't!" I screamed.

The skeleton looked back and forth at us. Then it turned and hopped off the hood. It walked a couple of steps forward, then lifted a hand in the air. A red fog began to appear, covering the area around it with its eeriness.

327

"Go," the disembodied voice said.

We sat silently, not knowing to trust the skeleton or not. We really couldn't move anyways, since the car had no gas left in it.

"LEAVE!" It yelled, and I quickly hit the gas pedal, which moved the van forward into the fog. I looked over at the gas gauge, which still read empty.

We journeyed into the fog for a few minutes; the fog turned into a pinkish color, then turned white, until it finally lifted and a normal paved road came into view. Just ahead of us was a sign that read "Welcome to Hell." Our van sputtered then came to another halt as smoke began to emerge for the hood.

"What the hell was that?!" Wesley said, breaking the silence between us.

"I think Hell is precisely what it was."

We let out a nervous laugh, hopped out of the car, grabbed a gas can from the trunk, and walked into Hell, where a restaurant and souvenir shop were calling our names.

Author s Note by Oliver Dace

Biography: Oliver Dace can be found buried between a blank page and his overdemanding dream to become an author before thirty. When not trapped in the pits of creativity or procrastination, this rare specimen of the writer genus can be found daydreaming around Wellington City while, at the same time, sketching his characters. He calls this trilogy of horror stories "The Crush Course Series."

Author's Note: In order of story appearance:

Black Marigolds. This was an accidental story. *Black Marigold* was the last story written in the series. It was originally meant to be a sequel to *Sweet Whispers behind a Stall* but was pushed aside from an imagery of talking lips glued to a wall (Amazing what showers can do). Similarly, the original theme was an addiction to haunting where the main character enjoyed the attention that the ghost gave. The role of incest became apparent when I asked on how I can twist the relationship between the ghost and its victim.

Ember Smell of Winter. The next two stories involved Maori mythology. The original concept was based from a short story I had written in 2013. The current version was a product on how I can twist New Zealand's love for nature and renewable resources. The idea of human corpses being the primary building material felt fitting to the story. This was strengthened by the usage of Maori mythology to explain the cause behind the curse. Think it as an attempt to create cosmic horror.

Sweet Whisper behind a Stall. My personal favourite! Keeping with the use of Maori mythology, the story was created as a challenge to create a monster that was both cruel and monstrous but at the same time appealing to the reader. The result was a lovesick serial killer couple stuck in an abandoned hotel while being hunted down by faeries. Both of whom became one of my favourite characters I created at this point.

Black Marigolds by Oliver Dace

My cousin, Ryan Magiver, was in love with my twin sister, Marielle.

She was a spoiled demanding girl with bright brown eyes that matched her side ponytails.

And, when she died five years ago, our cousin was found asleep on top of her coffin.
He had always been a little weird.

I remembered my dad wrenching him off my sister's coffin and giving the poor sob an hour's worth of lecture. It was not as if it was going to change anything; scolding the incestual bastard was like throwing water on a rock and expecting it to melt. Ryan was not going to change anytime soon.

He wasn't a bad kid.

Dad said that he acted the way he did due to a messy divorce between Aunt Selly and her husband. There was a rumour among my older cousins that Ryan was a quote-and-unquote, "main source of support" for our estranged aunt. I had no idea what that meant in my early adolescence. Ryan, for me, was the short chubby kid who spent most of his time near the buffet table with a full plate in one hand and using the other to push a slice of cake into his mouth. Marielle thought that he might end up as one of those hoarders she had seen on TV. That turned out to be half true.

Ryan's home located in a small seaside village called Makara – twenty kilometres west of the capital – was easy to spot. No other house was a castle for metal sculptures. I counted fifty last year. Now, the number doubled.

Not that his habit gave off an I-watch-you-sleep vibe. I, myself, enjoyed collecting bird feathers to create miniature Christmas trees. The problem with Ryan's hobby, however, was that many of his collections were cheap ten-dollar trinkets that he bought from a nearby scrapyard. It was a big hassle when eighty-kilometre winds kept blowing his toys into a wide stream beside his property.

Ten tin statues had piled up against a thin chicken fence by the time I parked in front of his car.

"I'll smack you with the full bill if any of your cheap dollies scratched my car, Ryan!" I said as I removed a small suitcase from the backseat.

He waved me welcome from his porch wearing the standard local yokel uniform: a black hoodie over brown baggy cargo pants. "No love for your relative, Mabielle?" He said while munching on a half-eaten strawberry cake on top of a guardrail. Two seagulls squabbled nearby.

"The only love you're getting from me is like the metal statue you gave me last year: cheap and plastic."

"You didn't have to chuck it off in a ditch," Ryan replied as he stuffed a handful of cake into his mouth. He pointed to a small metal statue of my twin holding a netball. A corner of her head was scraped off. A wooden pole replaced the statue's right leg. There was a deep gash on the chest that formed cracks along the body.

"You actually took the effort to haul the rubbish back. Cute." I spat. "Next time, try hauling that rubbish inside your car. Mark my words, it will sound like nails on a chalkboard."

"It would have been a better addition to your parent's place," he said and licked the plate clean.

"My mom doesn't need it." I shrugged. "My parents hang up so many photos of my sister that there's barely spare space for me. I don't even know what I look like sometimes, so what made you think that I'll take a dumb statue of my twin?"

"Because I can't tell you two apart."

I stared at the statue. "Looks better with rust."

"But it wouldn't be Mari without her signature look!" He tossed the plate passed the front door. "I can polish it,

Mabielle. I can paint it with black-and-gold, Marielle's favourite colour scheme."

I made my way towards his house. "I am surprised that you're not pissed at me for chucking a prime example of contemporary art."

"Is that a yes?" He walked down the porch steps; arms outstretched for a hug.

"Do you think my parents want to be reminded of what Marielle looked like after she fell off a goddamn cliff?" I stopped in front of him with a finger against the tip of his chin. His breath was moulded Hawaiian pizza with a dab of mint and wine.

"At least you are here for her anniversary. Mari really wanted to see you." He enclosed his stocky arms around me. The scent of an unwashed stained sofa clung on his hoodie. I let him, wiggling my nose away from the scent of his clothes.

"Just don't hump on coffins while I am here, Dead Sleeper."

"I don't have to, Mari – I mean Mabielle! Yes. Mabielle." He squeezed tighter.

I pulled myself away. I threw my bag at his hands to cease any further comparison on how my dimples weren't as deep as Marielle's. "Tell me you've cleaned my room properly this time. I found three cockroaches last year. Not to mention that you forgot to give me my breakfast in bed!"

"Anything for Mari's sister," Ryan said as he hugged my luggage close to his body and walked back inside late Aunt Selly's home.

Only Ryan could live in a place that should have been a decent wooden bungalow.

The sob bastard barely changed.

My first encounter with my weird cousin was when I was twelve. There was a rumour, that our older relatives spread, that Ryan had a thing about my sister, Marielle. As a

335

naïve twelve-year-old, it made sense why he liked my sister, Marielle. Mari had always been a family favourite ever since I decided to play at our local pool rather than be at home in time for my late great-grandmother's visit.

She wasn't prettier. If you held a glass panel between us, both of us would believe that we were staring at our own reflection. No. Mari had more attention. Mari this. Mari that. I got called "Marielle" more times than my actual name.

I decided to assert who I was after my sister refused to sit beside Ryan. It was a dare. Our older cousins decided to check if the rumours were true. Would our short weird cousin say or do something if he found Marielle sitting right next beside him? Fifty dollars were at stake if Ryan did something. A touch on the shoulder, sharing his meal, or granting an invitation to walk with him to the buffet table would be more than enough to win the money.

Marielle refused.

I decided to go instead. I was so sick of being referred to as Mari that I thought I could make our family realize that I – Mabielle Magiver – was braver. To prove the point, my older cousins tied my ponytail to the side and asked me to dress up in black-and-gold– Mari's signature colours. Smiles and twirls were the last ingredients to mimic my twin.

I had seated myself beside him. My cousins signalled at me to scoot closer. I compiled.

Not a word came from the chubby boy's lips except for the smacking and slurping sounds of the food that he was devouring. The house that his mother had given him was consumed by his new obsession.

He had a metal table and a crafted steel sofa set on his lounge. The kitchen counters had bright silver paint layers that fit well with his metal stools, dining table and a cutlery set that hung underneath a top drawer. Corrugated tin panels covered the dark brown walnut timber that aunt Selly had preferred.

Ryan nudged me when he walked inside. "Do you like the new project?" He said, pointing to a series of metal lips or buds that lined the walls of his hallway. They were positioned above eye level. Each was jet oil black with a touch of yellow that complimented a small black-and-gold gown that hung in my room for the night.

"It's stupid," I said aloud. "And please don't tell me what you were thinking when you made them."

"Mari told me to make them," he pulled out one of the metal lips beside the door.

"Really?" I gave out a small laugh. "Mari?" She always said that she had excellent taste in art. I guess being dead has left with two choices: rot and ugly. "What? She told you to make these?"

"She did." He nodded as he passed me. I followed, stepping over empty pizza boxes and soda bottles.

I wanted to ask if Marielle had ever called him a pig? If she had ordered him to clean up his act and get a proper job rather than be the oldest trolley boy in the country? I doubt it. The only advice that my sister gave me was to take on a scholarship to prove how much cleverer she was.

It was a smart move if Marielle had indeed demanded that Ryan clean up his act. A whiff of passion fruit and vanilla wafted out and flew up my nose. It commanded my feet to walk faster. Empty chips bags were stepped over until I stood before a five-star room amongst the clutter.

There was no trace of litter. The sheets were dusted off. The towels were rolled tight on top of a counter. A bar of soap, a small bottle of shampoo and a dozen lollies were tucked over a pillow. It was the only space where the timber walls were immune from the metallic disease that infected his home. That bastard even had a wrapped Dom Perignon champagne – something that went over his budget. Ryan prepared well. He must have been determined to get me inside that tight little dress I pulled from the doorknob.

"Do you like it?" He raised his head with a smug smirk.

I pointed to a metal lip above my bed. "Get rid of that thing."

"But it wouldn't be perfect! Marielle said she needed it in each room!"

"Yeah. Nah. I'd rather have Aunt Selly's corpse than that cheap tin over my head." I laughed.

Ryan grabbed my arm before he backed me against the door frame. Alcohol oozed off his breathe when he muttered: "I can't. Marielle told me to keep them when she visited me last night."

I grinned, shaking my head. "Was she crying again?" I asked. "Screaming? Moaning? You can tell her to piss off the next time you hear her

"She's excited to see you again." He leaned his head forward.

"What? So, she can ask me to dig out her coffin and hump its side as you did five years ago, Ryan – I mean Dead Sleeper." I said.

My cousin grinned in response lifting the dress in front of me. It was new. The poor sob hadn't pulled off the one-hundred-dollar price tag in one of its straps.

I pushed a finger on his forehead and threw back the dress towards the bed. Ryan watched as it landed at the edge before falling off outside of sight. "Don't force me, dear cousin. I know our little bargain. You will have your kink tomorrow night, I promise."

"Good." He winked. He backed off to the lounge, picking up a bottle and set himself upon a thick dusty recliner. I shut the door, grabbed rags from inside a drawer and threw them over the metal buds I found inside.

* * * * *

I had always enjoyed jumping out of our parent's car and running alongside the Makara shoreline when Marielle and I were young.

My parents usually brought us there every few weeks. Each time was spent racing against my sister to the top of a cliff, playing hide-and-seek amongst ruined houses or walking along a stretch by the shore in hope of finding a seal or a penguin.

Dad explained that the reason behind the visits was to connect with our Aunt Selly. She lived next to a wide stream at thirteen Estuary Street. A strange woman with thick black hair and an apple gut, I confessed that I never saw her outside of a witchy light. Dad said that his sister had stopped contacting the family after her divorce. No other relative except my father was willing to take back the past.

That was what he claimed each visit, but Marielle and I knew that was all nonsense, even way back then. Half an hour was the longest record our dad spent inside his sister's house. He spent much of his vacation time flying his handcrafted kites.

He had always told us that Makara was an ideal spot because the beach was a raw essence of nature. I choked up whenever my mind replayed my father's words. He wasn't wrong. The place was very much in touch with nature that the whole village was as developed as a mud brick. The location barely had anything to offer.

It was a backwater site – one of those middle-of-nowhere places – to the west of Wellington. Wooden cottages with back lawns the length of a bus was a common architectural staple. A small seaside café that fed the local inhabitants was as old as the songs that the fifty-kilometre winds enjoyed singing every night.

I can hear them.

Anyone could.

If you rolled yourself towards the window, you could hear a siren choir of hundred-kilometres winds luring the corrugated metal roof to join them in flight. Pebbles steamed through the roof valleys like boulders. Branches from nearby trees scraped its corners. Pounding waves from a nearby stream joined in a chorus that sang to the tired roof: "Fly! Join us! Sing with us! Lift your bearings and Soar!"

* * * * *

Sleep became useless after the roof creaked for an encore. I rolled to either side of the bed. The fluff of my pillow was a poor tool to block the whistles and applause that the window emitted in reaction to the siren winds. I threw a towel at it. I sat up. I wrenched my phone from its charger. 1:00 a.m., it notified me before its screen darkened.

Above me, the metal lips greeted me with a curved smile that seemed to stretch to the wall upon which they were attached. Ryan really has a way with his obsession. Who knows? Maybe I will find a set of metal boobs hanging on my room's wall next year. It didn't help that lights streaming from a gap under the door illuminated all his sculptures.

The little perv was awake.

Who was I kidding? Of course, he was.

He must be rocking himself on his recliner with the same amount of dribbling drool as he had when he had been found sleeping on top of my sister's coffin.

The Dead Sleeper sleeps again, I shook my head, making my way for the kitchen drawers with a small hope that there was a clean wine glass for my Dom Perignon Champagne.

"Enjoying my sister's concert?" I asked.

He forced a finger on his lips before he cupped a hand over his ear towards the window. "Can you hear it, Mabielle? The winds. The waves. It's always the loudest on the night of her death."

"Marielle always has been a noisy brat. She can't keep her mouth for a second, I swear."

"See? Hear that? A break in the wind? That's her taking a pause between her sobs."

"Tell her to text me. I don't answer calls from strangers or dead siblings after midnight," I said, taking out a small wine bottle with a smudge near the bottom.

"You should try and have a go listening."

"Why?" I turned back at him while rubbing the smudge off with my shirt.

"Don't you miss Marielle?"

I gave a short laugh. I walked to my cousin who was slumped on his seat. Two metal lips rested on each leg. They weren't coated in Mari's signature colours like the rest but were painted in rose, carmine pink and a touch of desert sand on the edges. "I hear that spoiled harlot's name, every day."

"Do you?! What is she saying?" He turned his head towards me.

"Hear this?" I pointed to my lips. "You're listening to her every time I speak, Ryan. What's the point of listening to some deadbeat corpse when I got myself to remind me of Marielle?"

"No remorse for your sister?"

"Remorse?" I pulled back his recliner until his face was centimetres below mine. "You listen here, Dead Sleeper. People are still calling me by that hoe's name even after she died. You know how much it pisses me off that she's still infamous? I can't say a word before some random idiot calls me by that –"

Ryan pushed my chin until I stared at buckets of stream waters thrown against the window.

"Calm your little pecker." I brushed his hand off, releasing my grip on the recliner. The poor sob nearly jerked out of his seat. Pity, it didn't happen. "It's just the wind tossing out leaves and bird shit like dumb drunk pigeons."

"I know you can hear her." He narrowed his eyes and mouth. "Mabielle … if you really want to mourn, you should have gone to where her body is buried but … oh, dear cousin …

341

we both know how she died. That's why you come here. She is calling you, isn't she?!"

I moved to the side, knelt and gave him a quick peck on his lips. "It is? And here I thought we were creating an anathema between two relatives. I still must get into that outfit. Maybe with side ponytails and rose berry lipstick to complete the look."

"Can you sing?"

I brought my hands on his cheeks and held it tight. "Mabielle is not Marielle, Ryan. Am I not good enough for you? Here …. Another kiss …. I gave you what you desired all these years, but I guess you won't be satisfied until I end up possessed by that witch! Not that it won't be a problem for you, eh? You'll be ecstatic. See? You're smiling already."

"I miss her you know," he mumbled. His eyes were glazed as he turned to me and then to the two metal lips on his legs. He brought his arm over one and caressed his fingers at the valley between the two lips.

I walked back to the kitchen to pour myself a glass full of champagne.

"And thank you again for sitting beside me all those years, Mabielle," Ryan said. His voice was low and mumbled. The banging winds drowned the words that came after.

"Thank my sister for refusing," I whispered, brushing my lips before I took a sip.

He was asleep after I drank half a bottle. His head slumped. The wind breathed its last not long after. There were no cries or wails of a long-dead family member. It was going to be a quiet night, an odd turn of events in this wind-swept little village that lay at the very edge of the country's capital.

"Mari …" he mumbled. Drool dripped from his lips. The siren choir stopped playing.

"She will be here tomorrow," I whispered, giving him yet another peck on the cheek before I left. I tucked him into his chair with a duvet that I pulled out of my bedroom. I didn't need it anyway and despite the weirdness of his fetish, Ryan deserved more than the soiled unwashed blanket found in his room.

* * * * *

If only he had known what kind of girl, my sister was.

I guessed Ryan was just a stubborn naïve mule who perceived Marielle as everyone's favourite niece at each family gathering. She was everything that he was not. Marielle was loved, cherished. She got what she demanded. Marielle had a future. I couldn't say the same for our cousin.

Yet, Ryan still loved her despite all the shouts, the name callings and the pebbles that Marielle had thrown at him. He would walk outside of his house each time we visited and wave. Neither Mari nor I understood what he was saying under his lips because, for both us, Ryan was a socially awkward boy with no one aside from his mom. That was what Marielle had taunted him with on the day of her death.

She had stopped her car in front of his house. As fate would have it, Ryan walked out with an arm already raised. Sweat had fallen to his upper lip as he tried to utter another dribble. He held something in his hand – a rock or a metal sculpture.

Marielle hadn't cared what it was.

"Go die, basement dweller!" She shouted before she grabbed a full can of coke from the back seat and threw it at him before he reached the fence. Our cousin trampled back. Aunt Selly rushed forward screaming.

"Mari?!" I shouted as my sister raced away and sped up until she parked to the edge of the village. "What the hell was that for?!" I raised my voice louder when the car stopped.

My twin pushed her hand over my mouth as she choked in laughter while saying, "Oh, don't tell me you're getting soft on the basement dweller. How so unsurprising of you, Mabi. No dignity."

I pulled off her hand. "What are we doing here anyway?"

"Celebrating," she answered, stepping out of the car. "Five more weeks and high school is over! We're finally getting rid of all that time sitting at our desk and listening to our teaching fanning over imaginary numbers or some other bullshit."

"Do you think it's early for that?" I stepped out.

"Always the spoilsport, Mabi? God, no wonder no one likes to be around you. Cheer up, sis. I got something for both of us. My future will be bright, and I need you to cheer me up." Marielle pulled out a set of twelve cans of beer from the trunk.

"Heineken?" I asked after she set the pack on my arms. "Where did you – "

"Just drink up. You can't always be straight-up, Mabielle," Marielle said as she took and emptied a can in two huge sips. "There. Not that hard, eh, sis? We better head up before Beelzebub's fat ugly mother will come running this way."

"You shouldn't have hit him," I protested.

"Why?" She threw the can to the sea. "You like him?"

"Marielle?" I paused. "What the hell are you – "

She wrapped her arms around her sides and laughed. "Oh, fuck! Is that a confession? And I thought you weren't low enough for me. Our family really is cursed with incest. Did it get to you too, Mabi? Have a desire to make up and breed children with webbed feet?"

"Will you just shut up?"

"Will you join me up to the trail?" Marielle took a second can and made her way to the same trail that we had walked countless of times as children.

I had hoped that she would make a sudden dash to the top. That was her only way to win over me. Marielle would grab pebbles along the way and throw them at me once I had managed to catch up. My sister had always been a sore loser. She could never get it in her head that I was faster than her, making up excuses liked how I wore running shoes or how I hadn't eaten a full meal.

She bounced the empty can on her hand when she stopped and stared at me from the trail's welcome sign. I followed her, raising both my hands to say, *I'm not running, sis.*

Despite being the summer months and with night-time to come in another hour, there weren't a lot of people at eight o'clock. Most – if not all – of the hikers we encountered were making their way home. The temperature had gone down since we left our car. The sun was still up but would soon make its own trek down the horizon.

"Remember what our father used to say?" Marielle said as she walked in front. "That Makara would blow away our past if we looked straight dead-eye to it? I always thought it was super cringy."

I gave a short laugh. "Well, he has to make some use with the six thousand dollars he spent on a Philosophy major."

"The liberal arts are all ideals and no work," she stared at me. "But you know what, Mabi, since school is almost finished, dad's saying has a new meaning."

"Like what?"

"What do you think?" She ignored my question. "Any thoughts."

"I asked first, Mari."

My sister persisted. "I don't care. I want to know the thoughts of the girl who got the highest score in our scholarship exam. Must be nice, isn't it?"

"It was a mocks exam."

She shrugged. "So?"

"That means that the test doesn't mean anything, you idiot. Its only use is for the teachers to find out any weak points on the subject. I bet none of those questions will appear in the real test anyway."

"But you are still the first," she said. Gone was her smile when we left the car. She pursed her lips and kept her gaze as she emptied her fourth can. "Must be a nice feeling, right? You weirdo."

"Of course," I winked at her. "Being a sore loser again, Mari? Fuck. You're cranky. How about we head down and get ourselves some real food?"

"Shut up," she stomped her foot.

"Is this what this is all about? An exam?" I asked.

"It's not just an exam you imbecile. It's our future!" The Makara winds blurred out my sister's screams. I got it why we came here. An argument as loud as this was a phone call before the police could intervene.

"Calm your tits, Mari! Are you deaf? I already said that the test will be worthless. You got a chance anyway."

"You're right. You're right," her voice trailed down. I watched her chew her thumb and threw the emptied can over the cliff once she finished. *There she goes again,* I thought. She was giving me the silent treatment once she realized she lost.

"It's quite the money though," I said, trying to cheer my sister up. I picked up the pace until I managed to walk beside her. "A thirty-thousand-dollar scholarship for the person with the highest score. I heard that eighty percent of all students are taking the test nationwide."

"But none of those twats are going to beat us," Mari said, chewing her thumb.

"That leaves with only you and me. Who will be? Hmm? Me, the future veterinarian who will one day operate on lions, tigers, and bears or the future celebrity psychiatrist for the big names in sport? We could lose, but that is where student loans get in the picture though." I said. The old ruined house was coming into view.

"I am not going to spend my prime years in debt," Mari said.

I shrugged. "One of us might have to do it."

"And I think you're going to take that burden, Mabi."

"Me?" I pointed to myself.

Marielle stopped. Her back was turned against the cliff. "Drop it," she ordered. "Drop the test."

"Why the hell would I do that?"

She grinned. "Because no one is rooting for you, Mabielle. You're an introvert, an airheaded who hates people because you don't have any real friends."

"And you're just a stuck-up bitch who wants to get things her way. Friends? People only hang out with you because you're hiding your shitty personality from them," I answered.

"At least I got people. Do you, Mabi?" She shook her head covering her mouth to hide her laugh.

"What's your point? You know I am not going to quit just because my entitled sister says so."

She raised her phone and brought up the number of some random guy named, Darren Welsh. "How about a bet," she said. "I can help you reach your goal if you quit the test. See this number? He has connections with an established veterinarian school overseas. He promised to show you the ropes if you do what I asked."

"And I bet that rope is under his pants," I laughed.

"Is that a no?" Marielle looked back at her phone. "I shouldn't be surprised from an antisocial freak like you."

I cleared my throat before saying, "That why I want to work with animals."

"Are you into bestiality, Mabi?" She smiled, flicking her phone. "You're quite the sexual deviant, eh?"

"Just give it up, Mari, and let me do the test as usual. Let's keep it level playing field. Who knows? You might take the first prize and get to achieve your dreams."

"You know I am not going to risk that. Level playing field. You? Don't talk horse shit to me."

"Scared?" I crossed my arms. "Does little Mari need a pat on the head?"

She looked at me hard before setting her sights on her phone. Her finger stopped scrolling and she glared at me with those sharp bright brown eyes of hers. "No other rope to take you off the test?" She said slowly, "Nothing. At. All?"

"You know I am not fond of ropes."

"Really?" She leaned forward with a hand cupped over her ear. "Am I really hearing that? Mabielle not fond of ropes. Oh! That can't be true because I know someone who has your legs up on a noose."

I stepped forward. "Where are you getting at?"

"Give it up," Marielle commanded as she showed me a photo depicting me and our science teacher inside one of the bathrooms.

"Marielle?! Where the fuck did you get that!"

"You looked like you were having fun! Do I spot a moan there, sis? Was the rope too fucking tight for you?!"

"Mari!"

She grinned, pointing a finger at my chest. "Don't. Underestimate. Me. A girl like you has no chance for connections." She grinned.

"All this for a test? You can't be serious! This will ruin both of us." I stepped closer to her.

"I didn't take the picture, Mabi, and this phone isn't even mine," she said, lifting one foot over the other while seizing me by the collar. "I'll be scot-free if I push this button. So? Let me hear you say that one word. Say it. Say that you surrender."

I held both her shoulders screaming. "We are sisters, Marielle. For God's sake, we shouldn't treat each other like this!"

"Say it." She flicked her tongue over her lips. "Let me taste those words,"

"Marielle!"

"Say it!!"

"Don't you dare!"

"Say it now or your future is damned!"

* * * * *

Had I meant to push Marielle off the cliff?
Of course, I did.

But why risk what was left of my future for the truth?

I had told police that she had fallen off by accident after we got ourselves intoxicated. One moment we were getting excited about what to do after graduation. The next, she was gone. Her body – and more importantly the blackmail – was torn by the rocks at the bottom of the cliff.

I told them that it was not meant to happen; that we celebrated the end of the year too early. The police doubted my story, of course. I was the only person present at the time of her death but my tears and lies won out in the end. They ruled my sister's death accidental and charged me with one years' worth of community service.

Happy Ending?

Far from it. Mari won.

She got what she wanted. It was because of her death that I had been unable to attend the actual exam. I couldn't even enrol in my university of choice and I ended up going to some lowly-rated school that I had picked at random.

Five years later and that girl was still as demanding as she was persistent. I could hear her as I stood in front of a stone memorial. The winds had a soft murmur with them. Listen to it. Face the ear towards the sea and there was a chance that a plea can be heard.

Bring me justice. Listen to my story. Help me. Help me, it says.

Each new gust made her cries louder. It made me sick. I balled both hands into a fist and stomped on her memorial until the stone sculpture tilted backward.

"You don't deserve peace you wretch!" I screamed.

My feet pounded it until the sides of my left shoe cracked opened. Marielle had always been a selfish, spoiled bitch who wanted everything with a snap of her fingers. She ruined my career, my future, and my reputation, and now was the time for her to act like a victim? Give me a fucking break.

I could have been traveling the world giving aid to endangered species rather than being stuck at a job I never wanted. She doesn't deserve peace and I am willing to spend what is left of my own life to hide that truth.

"You can have your peace after I am dead!" I shouted to the empty air, my sister who wasn't there. Then, from my position at the top of the cliff, I spotted our cousin heading towards the beach. He looked up. I waved and laughed as he raised a black-and-gold dress over his head.

Ryan had always been a weirdo. He was our strange, unkept, cousin with a fetish for his relatives. I wondered what Mari must have thought now that the only person who listened to her cries and believed in her was the one person she hated. I love the bloody irony in that.

He had told me that he knew the real story: that I had pushed my sister off of the cliff on purpose because I didn't want anyone to shed light on my short affair with a school staff member. He also claimed that my sister called out for help from within her coffin. That was why he had climbed on top of it.

When I asked what I should do to buy his silence, I realized that it was a win-win situation.

I don't mind at all. I am going to live the rest of my life free from the repercussions of my sister's ego while Ryan enjoys the benefit of me dressing and acting like his favourite, beloved, departed, cousin for a few days. Why not? He listens to the cries and wails of my sister every night. That was the closest he could be to his true love. A peck on the lips and some skin was a small reward for his silence.

I started to walk down towards him, then stopped and stared back at my sister's stone memorial. "Keep haunting him more, Mari. You know the Dead Sleeper loves it."

The Ember Smell of Winter by Oliver Dace

Emilie, Stan and I enjoyed our grandmother's tales.

During school breaks, Mom and Dad drove the three of us to her home in Plimmerton. It was a small coastal village, an hour's drive north of Wellington. Everything about the place was tiny. It was simple. There were three cafes. There was a floral shop, and a small dairy shop that served fish and chips on warm Saturdays.

On each journey to our grandmother's home, the three of us glued our faces against the car windows. We watched as the tall dark looming shapes of the saw mills were replaced with empty flat lands. The rush of salt to our nostrils replaced the saw dusts that rained constantly over our heads. The green sky followed us though. Whether it was in Wellington or Plimmerton, the sky was there to remind us. It wanted to tell us the truth that each and every one of us will turn to wood when we die.

That was fine.

The stories that our grandmother enjoyed telling us pictured a time before the curse of a wooden death struck every inhabitant of New Zealand's capital, Wellington. She told tales of strong winds that battered the city. We craned our little heads at each painting that decorated her walls. She had even showed a photo of herself as a young girl walking with two legs. By her storytelling days, however, our grandmother couldn't even move of her chair.

It was depressing.

Who wanted to see their family member degrade into an immobile husk? Her condition was worse every visit. Grandmother's lower waist had been transformed into a thick bark. Her arms hung heavy on her sides. Her legs seemed to merge, even fuse, with the wooden floor of her home. Even her voice had started to sound croaky, like two boards rubbing together.

Her condition grew worse each visit. Every time Mom and Dad told us that we were heading home, I wished, I hoped, and I prayed that we would get another chance to see our beloved grandmother. Emilie, Stan and I wanted to see more pictures. We wanted to listen to more tales of a Wellington long past.

For Emilie, she wanted to hear about the lifestyle. My brother, Stan, was fascinated with the landscape. I, for one, was curious about the museum, Te Papa.

"The Te Papa Museum was a wonderland", my grandmother described.

She said that every day, different people from around the country and the world filled the museum to the brink. It was impossible to walk inside without bumping into five or a dozen people. Some days, she said, it was best to stand still and let the crowd guide you to your destination.

The reason was simple; there was a lot to take in. Once a person stepped inside the museum, they were bound to be lost. Whether it was the natural exhibition on the second floor, New Zealand history on the third floor, or the Maori culture on the fourth floor, one simply could not walk around without stopping. My grandmother said that she could feel her pupils racing back-and-forth inside her eyes. Each pupil wanted to take in as much information that the museum provided. It was a giant building filled with laughter, joy, awe and a great sense of local pride.

I wished so badly to see what my grandmother had seen.

The Te Papa that existed today was no more than an extravagant mausoleum. Its corners were sharp. Decapitated wooden heads of the museum curators looked down from the building's large wooden doors. The creamy brown paint that had once decorated the façade had been replaced with the wooden bodies of people. Each one was strung up against the others like dolls.

It was disgusting. It was a mockery of the beauty that had once been.

Before my grandmother died, she had told us that she had forbidden herself from visiting the city. There was no point ever going back since the curse of the wooden death appeared. It would have simply made her depressed. Wellington was a husk of its former self. The current city was nowhere near like the beautiful wind-swept paradise of grandmother's stories.

She had wished that one day, the three of us would be alive to see Wellington in its glory days. Yet, even back then, I knew that the chances were already stacked against us. The side of my neck had already started to harden. The skin of my brother's back felt thick like bark.

As for Emilie, my youngest sister, I still cannot believe that *she* passed away.

* * * * *

I remember the last I saw her; it was on a cold Autumn night in May, a few days before her death.

Emilie and I went for drinks in the old *Harbour and Sea* bar in Lambton Quay. It was a celebration. Emilie had gotten a position as a receptionist for one of the largest sawmills in Wellington, a two-hundred-metre-tall behemoth at the centre of the city. The pay was very good. Her hours were reasonable. She even got the option to take three weeks' worth of paid leave per year.

I wasn't sure how Emilie had managed to get the job. She had only completed a bachelor's degree in accounting and had a few temporary jobs at various call centres. Had she impressed a top dog from the sawmills? Had one of her friends given a good word to someone in the company? Or was it all just plain luck?

Whatever the case, Emilie would be paid nearly as much as my position as a secretary for the City Council. She should have been proud and excited. The Emilie I knew could have yelled out to every person in the bar that she had secured a big gig. I was surprised – almost worried – to watch her lean down against the bar table. A half empty cup spun in her hands.

"I never really enjoyed the thought of arranging people's wooden remains to be sent to the sawmills." She confessed.

I jugged a glass. I hiccupped. "You can always give the position to me. I'd do anything to avoid crossing paths with that pig of a councillor, Jonathon Wales."

"And let you have my pay." She slammed her palm on my back. "Yeah…nah, sis, I'm keeping it thank you very much. Just because I hate the kind of work I must do doesn't mean I hate the pay. Plus, I heard that my table was crafted from the body of an All Black."

"My option still stands. Working for the City Council will be great." I hiccupped again. The bartender with a wooden jaw passed me two glasses of water.

Emilie raised her cup. The bartended answered with another pour. "It is transitional anyway. Once, I save enough money, I'll buy a huge property near Plimmerton, and set up a business where instead of chopping people up, we can make them a…I don't know…human trees?"

"You're just trying to live like grandma, eh? That's so cute." I said, drinking my glass. "Her house is still standing if you want it."

"Yeah but no," Emilie said with a smile as I caught a few guys staring idling at both of us from the far corner.

"You were always her favourite," I patted her shoulder. It had been twenty years since grandma passed away. Emilie was only six when Mom and Dad brought the three of us to the nearest sawmill to watch our dear grandma be sawed and hacked to pieces.

357

"I guessed I get why grandmother exiled herself," she said, gulping her glass in one go. "It is too depressing. I don't want to spend time in this city here any longer. I don't want to see mangled corpses in the middle of the streets. I don't want to watch them hauled onto the back of trucks or chopped up as firewood."

"You can always...err... try being a model." I said as I hiccupped. "You know...to cheer people up."

Emilie tilted her head.

"I was being serious there." I insisted. "You can start by not being so gloomy all of the time, Emilie. Come on, cheer up! You'll start a new job next year. You'll be rich in an instant. We can plan the celebration party now, if you want. Let's leave all these problems for the future, Emi. We have enough trouble as it is without thinking that we're going to end up as furniture. Plus, you still haven't had any physical trace of bark in you yet."

"So, you're saying that actually should become a model." She pushed her hair behind her ear. "Am I really that...well...sexy?"

The same guys from the corner glanced down at her soft, fleshy long legs. Emilie giggled, raising a glass up her head. "I hadn't realized that I was drop dead attractive. Everyone! I apologize for looking so sexy. Maybe it was my looks that gave me a position as receptionist for a major sawmill!"

"Emilie..." I groaned.

She sat. Head lowered, and cheeks puffed in pink. "Sorry, sorry, sis. Ego got the better of me. If it makes you happy, you're still my favourite sibling. You're not a dickhead like Stan. God, I hate our brother's guts. He thinks he is so great and mighty. I almost wanted to feel sorry when I heard that his back is turning to wood...*almost*"

"It's everyone's burden." I called the bartender for another round.

"Seriously, just for once, I just want to know who or what did Wellington fuck up so badly that it left us with this stupid curse," she muttered and let a lock of her blonde hair to fall over her face.

"Grandmother said that the God of the wind was defeated by the God of the forest. That's why *everyone* is turning to trees," I replied. "That's why everyone is turning into trees."

"I wish it was that simple." Emilie said. "How do you kill off the god of the forest anyway? Wellington was better off when it was scorched with hundred-kilometre winds. Like in the old days, you know…"

I sipped my glass, nodding.

"You're really not taking me seriously, eh, Natalie?" Emilie elbowed my shoulder. "Anyway, after one more drink, I'll call it a night. You were right, we have enough shit to worry about. I'll do my best with my new job and work my way to get a property near Plimmerton. I still have a few forms left to fill out tonight though. Fuck, I hate doing this at the last minute."

"Don't forget to sleep early," I said pointedly.

"Of course, of course." She said and craned her neck back. "I heard enough of that scolding from you and Stan to last me a lifetime. I'm not going to sleep at 3am like I use to. 11pm is my latest, that's a promise."

I later found out that Emilie indeed tried to keep her promise.

It was overdose.

That was what my brother, Stan, had told me over the phone. I felt my stomach lurch. My throat smelt like vomit when I learned that Emilie had been found dead. A bottle of sleeping pills lay beside her bed. It was no surprise how she did it. At age, twenty-six, Emilie Riche *would* have been another young victim. The local obituary *would* have labelled her as part of a growing number of people who wanted to escape the fate of watching their own bodies transform into a bark.

Yet, she hadn't.

That was the worst part. When Stan relayed the information that our youngest sibling had died with no trace of wood in her body, I heard distinct cheering on the other end of the line. It sounded like twenty or thirty people laughing in the background. My brother told me that I should be happy that Emilie had died this way. Normally, it would have taken no more than three hours before the corpse would resemble a mannequin. Even the morgue staff kept a twenty-four-hour watch for any sign, any trace of bark inside or outside her skin.

There was none.

Emilie had done it. She had beaten the impossible.

At this point, I suppose I should say that I should have celebrated. My brother reminded me that Emilie wouldn't have to face the towering sawmills that dwarfed every building in the city. The thought of my youngest sister being chopped into pieces and turned into furniture was whisked away. There was no longer any need to worry about that.

Emilie will be safe. She will be preserved. She will be the new "chosen one" who will be displayed among the decaying corpses within Te Papa. All my relatives cheered out at the news that one of our own had beaten the wooden curse.

The City Council was quite quick to proclaim the good news to the people. Not only had they given us one-hundred-thousand dollars as a gesture of gratitude, but they set up a new exhibition at Te Papa.... All as a token to Emilie's death.

* * * * *

In the beginning, Tawhiri, the Maori God of the Winds waged war against his brothers. He attacked Tane, the God of the Forest, and forced the God of the Sea to wage war against the former. The Gods of Food took refuge and hid from Tawhiri's onslaught. It was only the God of War, Tumatauenga, that took a stand and forced the god of winds to withdraw.

Ever since that day, my grandmother had said that Wellington was Tawhiri's home. It was obvious. Wellington had been considered as the windiest city in the whole country. The strong 100-kilometre gale force that could batter numerous towns in New Zealand was an everyday occurrence that everyone had gotten used to. A day within Wellington wouldn't be complete without watching an army of thick giant clouds spiralling around the city like a whirlpool!

Those were Tawhiri's children. The winds and the clouds were the god's army against his brothers. Tawhiri commanded them to storm the seas. He ordered his children to uproot trees and scatter the crops off the ground.

Whether the God of the Wind was defeated by an alliance of his brothers, or not was uncertain. It was only obvious that their presence was now gone. Wellington was no longer the windiest city of the country. It was dry. It was still, like some forgotten ruin left to decay on its own. The great fleets to clouds that had once proudly sailed the city had been replaced by an inky dark green sky. The showers of sawdust that poured out from the sawmills took over from the winds.

The only trace that Tawhiri and his children were ever here being faint fleeting clouds in the shape of a silent scream. There were quiet breezes. A gust came and went. Pitter patter of rain held on for a morning. Yet, none of them shook off the dry humid weather that had devoured the city.

There was no god to welcome me to the first day of Emilie's exhibition, only Stan.

"Kia Ora, Natalie, I'm glad to see that the curse hasn't taken you yet!" My brother greeted me at the museum's entrance. His brown hair, which he had once tried to grow, was shortened. He combed it back revealing a wooden crack on his forehead. He had grown bulkier since the last time I had seen him, almost stiff.

Maybe it was the large brown jacket that he wore. It was May, after all, and winter was just around the corner. I could already sense, almost smell, the roasted wooden bodies who were chosen to be firewood for Wellington.

"It's good to see you again, Stan." I hugged him, feeling the hardness of the wood that consumed his back. "How are you keeping up? How's the family?"

"They are doing great. The kids are being babysit now. I don't think they have realized that their auntie Emilie has died. They heard about her becoming the city's newest darling, but they still don't get that people need to die to achieve that honour. I brought my wife though. She's upstairs with the rest of the family. Mom and Dad must be gushing her about their grandkids."

"And you?" I asked. "How is your condition going?"

"You sound like I'm going to die, Nat. This is your brother you're talking to! It's all sorted out. My local carpenter told me that even though I my back has been taken over, I won't have to worry for a decade or two until the curse takes me! My wife got the gall to schedule me an appointment with a cabinet maker. I swear that I married the most awesome woman in the city." He paused, placing a hand on my shoulder. I felt the tip of a finger rubbing the thick bark at the side of my neck. "I realized that it's hard for you to be here, Nats."

"I don't think I am ready to see Emilie's dead body, and the last thing I wanted is to join some sick party. I am only here because the rest of the family is here. You know me, Stan. I can't stand being the oddball."

"I'm not surprised. You're the motherliest type between the three of us. But that's fine. That's fine. Emilie's the spoiled little princess while I'm the more…well…let's just say –"

"Extravagant? Show-off?" I cut him off. "Seriously, Stan! Did you really put on a show when you called me that day? I can't believe you! I know that you and Emilie didn't get along well but that…really?"

"My colleagues decided to come over after work for a few beers," he said and shrugged.

"Right…right….and they started shouting, 'Emilie will decay' because…."

"Because that's what people do when they hear that someone has beaten the curse." He placed an arm around my shoulder and led me inside the entrance hall of the museum.

The place was empty except for a headless wooden body at the centre. It pointed its arm towards a stack of stairs in front of us. The figure's stump was bathed by the warm blue lights of the ceiling. The low hum of the air conditioner drowned the buzzing sound of the sawmills from outside. I could even see a faint flicker of a fire off the Wellington harbour, and the shadows of trucks near the docks. Soon, the Lambton Parade will be on its way. Soon, the corpses of those deemed unworthy or useless by the sawmills will be spread across the city. I can also imagine, almost hear an army of Wellingtonians marching towards the streets with axes and machetes. All ready to be hacked by their former city folk as firewood.

For now, it was too quiet. It felt as if I had stepped inside an empty church dedicated to the holy decaying bodies of Wellington City. Each wall dedicated to a painting or a photograph of Wellington in its glory days. I wondered if the people in these pictures knew what the future of their city would be like. Their smiling faces and quiet laughs were different from the sighs and grindings that I saw every day. Were there any signs of Tawhiri's defeat back then?

363

Grandmother told us that the city was unaware of any warning that would bring its downhill. Maybe there was none. Maybe everything that is happening now was beyond our limit. *The Maori gods have done this to us, maybe they would fix it*, my grandmother used to say, *we can only hope.*

"Where is the rest of the family?" I asked as I scratched the wooden bark of my neck.

"They are on the fourth floor. That's where the exhibition will take place. Mom and Dad got a bit worried that you weren't here yet and asked me to fetch you knowing you'll be conflicted over Emilie. You won't believe how many people turned up for this day! I don't even know most of them or how they are related to us."

"I only wish grandma was here to see this," I whispered.

"Do you think she'd be proud?" Stan asked as we climbed the wooden stairs, passing over a series of old photos of the Te Papa Museum in its glory days. "She would still be rooted in her old home at Plimmerton. She had said that she was in self-exile."

"I like to think that grandma would make an exception." I said. "Emilie was always her favourite. She used to give her the first taste of cookies since she was the only one small enough to sit on her lap."

"I remember how you and I used to fight for that position!"

"We even made numerous alliances to get Emilie off grandma's special list," I smirked, catching glimpses of dark silhouettes of the sawmills from a window.

"I bet she wasn't planning to die that night," Stan said as he chipped off a piece of bark from his head. "Emilie was a klutz. I bet she must have taken one pill too many."

"I told her to stop that," I said.

"You can't really blame all of it on yourself, Nat. It's Emilie's fault for drinking all those energy drinks non-stop during university. We kept warning her that it would affect her sleeping pattern, but that girl was too stubborn and pretentious to listen. Just because she was pretty doesn't mean she had common sense. You remember how she caught me taking away her valuable caffeine drinks?"

I forced a smile. "Emile ranted a whole night saying how you were the worst brother ever."

"She even avoided me for a whole month," he chuckled. "I ruined that by popping by at her place one night. Oh, that girl wasn't keen to see me."

"And now Emilie is dead," I clenched my fist. "Stan...I...I was with her a few days before she passed away. If I had known something was wrong or if she told me about her sleeping problems, I could have...."

"There was nothing we could do."

"We could!" I said. "I was there!"

"Natalie...." My brother gripped my arm. "Please. Enough. You're not the only one who is grieving. I may not look like it, but I miss Emilie as well. We used to hate each other's guts, I swear our brother-sister rivalry was a bloody comedy sketch but now that she's gone, I'm not even sure what to do."

"Stan..."

He continued, eyes narrowed. "Did you want to see her being turned into timber, Natalie? I can still remember how men in white uniforms took our grandmother's wooden body and turned her into a piece of chair. I still have nightmares thinking about how her body was hacked by a buzz saw. Seriously, Nat, who would want a grave like that? No one! Be happy, Nat, please. It's too late for us already. We will face those damn sawmills one day, but Emilie...she will be here as long as time passes! She will be a model; a light for everyone who faces the chainsaws."

I smiled a little. It was ironic, almost a sick parody that my advice to Emilie in becoming a model rather than a receptionist came true. Her beautiful young body would be displayed for all people to see. I imagined the public gawking with wide eyes as they approached her. It was no surprise. Those who had achieved the state of natural death were people either in their seventies or late eighties.

It was rare, almost unheard of, for someone so young to defeat the curse of a wooden death. The youngest person before Emilie was a forty-year-old man who was found drowned off the coast of Red Rocks. Since then, it had been elderlies. It was clear that the city folk were baffled.

Prior to the exhibition, the City Council declared that Emilie's body was a Rank One relic. Rather to have her body slowly decay, like most of the inhabitants of the museum, she would be perfectly preserved. She will be a still frame. Generations into the future, people will ask the museum staff who she was. How had she done it? What did she eat? What was her secret?

I'll be pissed if the local news reports a huge sale in sleeping pills. If that happens, I'm going to whomever made the report and tell them that just because my sister had defeated the curse, doesn't mean that people know everything about her. It's already bad enough that our youngest sister will permanently reside within the wooden walls of this museum!

******

When I was a young girl, I played a game called, "head hunting."

The rules were simple. For every visit to the museum, my classmates and I aimed to count as many heads that we could find. It was an easy game since there were countless faces that jutted off from each stack of timber.

We gave one point for the heads with blank expressions. Two points went for the faces who were sad or afraid, and, finally, a total of three points for those with a smile, a frozen semblance of laughter etched in their wooden faces. It was a fun game. Most children and some of my teachers were happy to sacrifice an hour for a few rounds of Head Hunting. My biggest record was a two-hundred and six.

I was slightly tempted to try and beat the number as Stan and I made our way upwards. The faces that I had counted when I was fourteen were mostly gone. That was the beauty of the head hunting. Every year, a hundred or two of these wooden boards were replaced. It was always fun darting around the tall steep walls of the museum to find new faces that hadn't been there before. The constant smell of decay and the sight of peeling flesh from old bodies that suffocated the second and third floor was nowhere near the thrill of finding a new face.

I wished I had that same excitement when Stan and I reached the museum's fourth floor.

Boarded shut by thick wooden panels, the top floor of the museum was the beating heart of Te Papa. It was the holiest of holy places for Wellington City, a site where a selected few were granted the right to be a still image forever. Though it wasn't exactly closed to the public, a normal person must pay a hefty three-hundred-dollar ticket, and even that was limited for only three hours.

I had been there once as part of my work with the City Council. It was a short visit. I think it was only half-an-hour at most but even then, I could still picture myself basking under a soft white-and-yellow glow from the ceiling. The floor was white. A scent of sweet incense lifted me off my feet.

"Tena koutou, tena koutou, tena koutou katoa! Greeting to the proud families of Wellington's newest treasure! Tena rawa ata koe!" The pot-bellied figure of Councillor Jonathon Wales stood on top of a makeshift stage. A giant statue of Tawhiri, the God of the Wind, stood silently behind him.

The councillor welcomed an army of wooden bodies below him. It was a mangled contortion of wood and flesh that ruined the serenity of the fourth floor. Branches sprouted from necks. Whole legs were entombed by soft carpets of algae. The army cheered. They shouted my sister's name over and over, raising their arms and craning their heads back.

I rubbed the hardened part of my neck. Nails tried to claw the bark from my flesh. I felt sick. The thought that I would join this army was...*unimaginable*. I wanted to get out of the building at that very moment! I didn't want to see the perverted sight in front of me. I didn't want to listen to wood cracking and turning. My grandmother was right. Emilie was right. There was no point staying in the city that was a shadow of itself.

I didn't want to see my boss running his bony fingers over a large curtain-covered glass case beside him. He caressed it. He lifted the bottom part a few centimetres up before letting go. Each moment, he described the beauty of Emilie Riche. He told everyone that she was a prize worth dying for, how her flesh was serene, soft.

"You want to touch her hair! To rub her lips! You wish to whisper to her ear that she is beautiful! Waiwaia!!" The councillor shouted. His bloated belly hugged the case as the crowd cheer! "This is our city' newest treasure! Our puipuiaki! Emilie Riche!! Tena rawa atu koe! Thank you very much!"

He paused. His beady eyes scanned the room before he rubbed his head. He lowered his voice. "And...no, no, no...I almost forgot...heahea...we cannot celebrate the rerehua, the beauty of our beloved daughter without thanking the parents, the whanau, that gave her to us. Nau Mai Haere mai."

Stan grabbed my arm at this point as Mom and Dad walked up to the stage. Their bodies were woody and stiff; their heads were the only part themselves untouched by the curse. Yet, they smiled. Their faces were covered with tears knowing their wish, their hope that one of us would defeat the curse had come true.

"Let's go, Natalie," Stan said, walking forward. His breath was ragged. His eyes were glued to the glass-case upon the stage.

Stan became a man possessed. I could tell that he badly saw what was behind the curtain. He didn't mind if he walked straight through the army, bumping, crashing, and bruising both of us against the hard surface of our wooden family.

I wanted to tell him to stop. I wanted to beg him to slow down. He was hurting me! There was no need to rush! There was time! The City Council had informed us that Emilie's immediate family would have unlimited free access to the fourth floor as gratitude.

I wanted to protest but all I could muster were gasps. The back of my neck became flustered, almost hot. In the back of my mind, a little voice told me to celebrate. It told me that I could once again see my dear sister, that the three of us will be united. And as Stan and I reached the front, wooden hands pushed us forward.

I fell on my knees only to look up at the beautiful, nude corpse of my youngest sister. I opened my mouth. A uniform gasp of all my relatives conquered whatever words I mustered.

She is beautiful, declared the voice in my head.

"Emilie Riche is beautiful," I repeated, my face now fully infected by the wide, toothy, smile of everyone around. "Tena rawa atu koe!"

Sweet Whispers Behind a Stall by Oliver Dace

Do I know where Annie Vee is?

That was what I asked myself when ventured into the Akatarawa forest one late afternoon.

The forest itself was one of three major bushlands that surrounded my hometown, Upper Hutt. Up north, underneath the shadow of the Tararua Mountain Ranges was the Kaitoke Regional Park. On the right, facing the eastern end of New Zealand, was the Pakuratahi while the Akatarawa forest stood at the opposite end. All were more than an hour's drive away from the capital city of Wellington.

Though the Upper Hutt region possessed one of the largest areas in the lower North Island, it has the lowest population with no more than forty-thousand people. The city itself was landlocked. Two mountain ranges were at either side. Forests, bushlands and hills occupied much of the region with most of the population residing within an open sea of grass where the city was located.

That was fine.

I made the most of my hometown as much as anyone who had lived here. I preferred living here, surrounded by nature's skyscrapers rather than be blinded by the constant stream of lights that the capital city normally gets. There was also a rather intimate vibe that covered the city from border to border. Though I wouldn't say that everyone knew each other, I can honestly say that each person recognized something about the others.

The woman ordering a Pavlova each Friday night; she was an English teacher at the local high school. The man who filled his petrol every morning at 6am was an owner of a local business. Each person knew something about the other.

That was the nature of Upper Hutt. It also helped that most residents spent their weekends almost at the same time and at the same place. There were always familiar faces whether it was rugby, cricket, football or the classic Sunday barbeque in one of the parks.

As for me, I was more than glad that there were not any faces during my explorations. Abandoned structures within the Akatarawa Forest were hidden gems. It was common knowledge that somewhere within that vast and tight bushes were empty settlements.

These places would have been quite an idyllic site nearly a hundred years ago. They were made by people who wanted nothing more than quiet solitude. The only company they sought were the songs of Tuis singing their hymns during spring. These settlers had tried. They had failed. They had tried again. New structures, bigger and grander than before, were created to tame the land. None of it was successful. All that remained were empty husks that I was more than happy to break inside.

I'd like to say that it was illegal to enter these properties. A local representative for the government's ministry of cultural affairs had issued a law claiming that anyone caught trespassing would be fined three thousand dollars with a possibility of two months in jail for damages. That was fine on paper. Then again, who on earth would dare enter these settlements?

The Upper Hutt Council may have hired a team to patrol the first three kilometres of the Akatarawa Forest but that was a small portion. It was impossible to count how many houses lay dormant within the thick bushlands. Even if the patrols had managed to track every run-down building, what were the chances that they were present after dusk?

No one was out in the forest at eight o'clock. I was sure of it.

The only one's present were me, and Annie Vee.

* * * * *

I loved Annie Vee.

She was an unusual but attractive girl with long black hair, velvet eyes, and a set of freckles that I enjoyed counting during long quiet nights. If not for her habit of venturing into the forest, I was sure that she would have stolen the attention of Upper Hutt. Annie had explained that the main reason why she enjoyed venturing into the Akatarawa was that of the mysteries.

"There was more than meets the eye," she said.

A week wouldn't pass without me finding a note from her saying that she was doing some exploring. That girl loved her adventures among the three forests that surrounded Upper Hutt. That was perfectly fine. I, myself, was guilty of disappearing into the thick undergrowth of my region. Most of my leave from work was discovering ruined settlements after another. It was also during one of my explorations that I had stumbled upon Annie Vee. I was a very, very lucky to meet her. I'd also want to confess that despite doing these expeditions for over a decade, that girl knew more than I ever could.

I eventually found her on the second floor of an empty four-storey lodge.

The building was one of the largest settlements inside the Akatarawa. It had once served as a resting stop for travellers who wanted more than a pile of leaves as their pillow. The building was nestled near an abandoned track. There was a well at the back end. A stable that could house four horses were a hundred metres to the right. The current decayed state of its front hall exceeded far more than most three-star hotels.

"I knew you would come for me, Daniel," Annie Vee said, lying cross-legged on the floor. The redshirt and knee-length skirt, that she had worn when she left, were no more

373

than torn strips. She hunched herself forward, pressing her hands over a large exposed wound near her thighs.

I pulled off my backpack. "I brought a first aid kit, Annie."

"I loved how much you care about me," she brushed her palms over her mouth. "It's nothing, Daniel. I heal fast remember? Something as puny as this won't kill me. I just need a moment. Even the best of us need some rest, eh? You do that as well after you work out in the gym."

"Right, and I'm pretty sure that everybody has a girlfriend that can devour anything she liked," I dropped the bag. One kick and it slid towards her. "Here, I got also you some new clothes."

Annie giggled as she opened the zip and rummaged through its contents. "You always think ahead, darling. Ah! You even brought my favourite sweater with you. The one with the pictures of the tiny deer. I should really give you a hug."

"Just put some clothes on, Annie."

I strained my attention towards a thick mist that was slowly marching its way towards the building. I had seen bits and pieces of it from my search of Annie. It was not unusual for that to happen. Between the months of June to August, the winter clouds from the Tararua Ranges would descend over my town in the early morning. The city was drowned under a sea of fog at those time. The mist that slithered towards us was almost similar.

"I guessed this is the part that I'm supposed to say sorry," She apologized, pulling her long black hair off from the sweater. She limped towards me and gave me a short kiss.

I responded with a longer version. My hands were on her shoulders. I felt her nails clawing against my jacket.

She let go. Her index finger pressed against the tip of my chin. "I miss you, darling. It's been what – two days since we last saw each other. Times goes fast when you're out hunting in these woods. How are things back home, Daniel? Is the head librarian still pissed at me? I bet she is. She hasn't met anyone who kept requesting for leave nearly every week, hmmm. But just like my sisters said, you can't let the hunger starve itself."

"I'm just glad that I found you." I rubbed her shoulders. "It took me a good four hours to find you in these thick bushlands."

"You mean you went searching for me today? After work? Wow. Dedication, Danny. That was fast. I loved that about you. How did you know this was the right place to look?"

I laughed and brushed her hair. "Because you're Annie Vee! I knew you long enough that your top three favourite places in this building, an abandoned railway, and a clearing near a stream."

"The last one is my favourite." She wrapped her hands around my sides. "That's the place where I nearly killed you. Remember? Ah! What a perfect setting. Pity that it has no roof though. Not the best place to stay in winter."

"I was planning to go there during the weekend if you hadn't decided to leave."

"Sorry," She pushed herself off me. She limped four steps back, nearly stumbling at the third. Blood soaked through the fabric as she placed both hands on her hips. "But I left a note on the kitchen three days ago along with some sweets that I tried to bake that day."

I scratched my head. "We'll plan something else for the weekend then."

"How about the Sunday barbeque that your parents are preparing for their local bowls club? I heard that they're quite eager to get to know me more. Want to go?"

"I doubt you'll be hungry after this," I sighed. "I swear, things would be easier if you at least notify me when you're going out. Even a text message would be useful. You don't know how many close calls I had with the police to find you. I nearly stumbled with one of the mayor's cronies on my way."

"I said I was sorry," She puffed her cheeks.

I sighed. "I know. There are some things that you must– "

Annie's ears twitched before I finished my sentence. She paced towards a barred window. Her ears stretched back. The whites of her eyes turned black. She bared her teeth. Long nails made deep scratches against the wall.

Outside, basking under the shadow of thick trees, the mist had stood still amid the building's property. It didn't fade or thin out. Its outline reminded me of dying neon light. It blinked on and off. A carpet of cloud was there in one instance and gone at the next.

"The hunter becomes the hunted," I said out loud.

She chuckled. "I know. Isn't it exciting? I knew they would come for me and I was right."

"What is it this time, Annie? Pakehas? Ponaturis? Maeros?"

She leaned her face against the glass. "Turehu…."

"Those little things," I crossed my arms. "I thought they pose no problem for you."

"They don't until I learned too late that they had invited their two-metre cousins from the Waikato. There must have been twenty or thirty of them when I attacked their camp. All were protecting their smaller cousins. Those bastards fought a bloody good fight though. This wound was caused when they sent me flying down a small hill. Lucky hit, I say. The Giants then ran down the hill to try and finish me off. Bad mistake. They underestimate my breed since I took most of them down. My injury was worth it because they were simply delicious! I can still hear their whimpers as I gutted their bellies open. Oh! I want to relive to have their organs running down my throat."

"And let me guess, a whole army of these white-skinned, red-headed fairies are here to get revenge against you."

She grinned. "You say like it is a bad thing, Daniel. Just watching them makes my stomach growl. If you could taste it like I did, I swear you would hunt every one of them. That's how good they are, but, then again, I can't spoil myself to eradicate my food supply. I left the scene off as soon as I had my fill but as luck would have it, they managed to track me down here. Not bad for creatures no bigger than children, hmmm?"

"And I suspect that you want me to drive them away with my torch. The Turehu hate light, eh?"

"True or you could tell them that it was all a misunderstanding. Tell them I got carried away a bit. You can give them two sacks of raw kumara to eat. They like that." She said this whilst pushing her face off the glass. Light tapping began to echo from the ground floor.

"Yeah, nah, Annie Vee. I'm not sure you noticed but the whole forest floor is covered with them. There must be hundreds of those faerie-folk waiting outside."

"More the reason to devour them until they leave the two of us alone."

I pulled my bag off the floor and tapped her head with it. "Or…we could wait it out until dawn. There's a makeshift bedroom that I made months before at the back end of the fourth floor. It's my emergency shelter if I'm doing long explorations. There's a mattress, heaps of can food, and a good supply of torches."

She shifted her features back to – I would say – normal. "Boring! Can't I just go out and eat them? Can I?"

"Annie, you're bleeding. You can't even walk right. What would your sisters think if they knew that their youngest sibling was killed by Turehu?"

She rolled her eyes. "Fine. You have a point."

"Come on, we'll be safe behind my shelter. A few more hours and it will be dawn."

She puffed her cheeks again. "You got something to eat while we're there?"

I lifted my bag. "I'm surprised that you hadn't checked the back pocket. I got food. Venison. Your favourite."

Annie Vee snickered before she wrapped her arms around me. "You have always been the reliable case. I'll play your game, Daniel. Four hours you say, darling? That's a lot of time to enjoy ourselves, hmmm?"

I placed her right arm around my neck. "Think of it as a date, Annie."

"And if the worse comes, you'll be my moral support. I hope it does. I hope that the Turehu do attack us. The thought of quartering those albino fairies with you by my side is exhilarating! I can see it! I can taste it! Give me your hand, Daniel! Here? Can you hear it, darling? Can you? My heart is racing at the thought of that!"

* * * * *

I had encountered the Turehu before.

The Maori called them Patupaiarehe and claimed that these pale-skinned folks were the original inhabitants of New Zealand. They were primitive, territorial, and secluded. The countless children books of my local library described they a lighter complexion than the Maori with bright red hair and standing no bigger than a human child. That was the general rule, though the Turehu that Annie had encountered were most likely from the central regions of Whanganui.

How or why the Turehu resided among the forest of my region still escaped me. Nearly every tale or information that I heard had told me that they primarily lived in the central regions of the North Island. The beauty-lusted plains of the Waikato, the thick bushlands of the Te Aroha Range,

378

the hills of Rotorua and the lands surrounding Urewera and Wairoa; these were the home bases of the eluded faerie folk. I had never been informed that Upper Hutt and possibly other regions of the Lower North Island were home to the Turehu.

Was it because these folks were more secluded than their central cousins? It was common knowledge that they avoided people. For nearly every encounter with them, it was they who dished it out first. Even my own fair share with these creatures was often a good distance away. I had only seen traces of them during my explorations. It was usually at night, twilight hours at best, that they appeared. Often it was in the form of a mist that faded off as soon someone gets too close. Sometimes, it looked like as if a cloud had decided to rest within the thick bushes of the Akatarawa before flying off the next day.

There was no hiding this time.

From outside of the building, the Turehu filled every nook and cranny until it felt as if night had turned to dawn. Their bright red hair replaced the trees. I couldn't hear the howling Southerlies that passed through Upper Hutt from the South Island. Such was the nature of living in mountains. My home city was a bottleneck for the gales, not as powerful as the capital city but strong enough for fleets of clouds to sail through a windstorm.

The only noise heard from the inside of the building, however, were the constant tapping that filled my ears until my brain wanted to explode. There was also sounds of a flute ringing through the forest's floor.

The Maori had numerous tales of what the Turehu do to trespassers. The numerous bodies that had been dug up around the Waikato proved that the fairies enjoyed burying people alive. Most of these victims were young men who had been found underneath a thick patch of Kumara which the creatures feasted.

There weren't a lot of cases of female deaths saved for one or two over the last fifty years. Even the women who were presumed to have been captured held the account that they could not remember anything. Which was fine though the numerous accounts of Maori tribes who claimed to be descendants of the Turehu was a stab in the back of the former claim. It was a weak cloak that poorly hid away the creature's lust.

I think Annie Vee was going to have neither.

The midget fairies had their own specific execution in mind. What it was, I don't know. I can only imagine the punishment being long and torturous.

I was going to have none of that.

I held Annie Vee close with one arm was over my shoulder. She grabbed my other hand and pressed it around her waist. She limped. She stumbled. The wound on her thighs failed to recover. All the while her ears twitched at each sound. She growled, hissed. Her eyes turned coal black. Her mouth began to stretch ear-to-ear. Deep scratches littered the building's floor as her feet turned to claws.

When I asked her if she needed a break, Annie Vee simply told me that she was fine. Typical.

She explained that while hunting for deer or wild boars, she had stumbled into a large community of Turehu near the northern ends of the Akatarawa. Like I said, that was unusual since these creatures primarily resided in the central plains of the country. Sure, there were fragments of them sighted around, but not as many as she had seen. Annie guessed that they must have numbered near a thousand.

Was there a celebration? Was it a mimicry of a flat-warming party? Was it a reunion of different families around the North Island?

It didn't matter, though.

The taste of these faeries was leagues above than the typical wild game. Annie's need to satisfy her hunger was all there was to it. She had lunged into the tribe. She had killed

380

most of their two-metre cousins and devoured over a hundred faeries. When the Turehu finally managed to repeal her, they had lost a good number of their kin. It was no surprise that they had decided to give chase.

That was a bad idea.

The sight of an army of fairies simply made Annie hungrier. I had seen her in her true form. I knew what she was capable of. A deep scar near my neck was proof that Annie was more than happy to eat people. She could break the backs of ten men piled on top of the other. A family of six could easily fit inside her jaws. She was as dangerous as she was beautiful.

Yet, despite her strength, Annie was only one against an army. The Turehu could storm the building, dragged her out and taken her back to their tribe to exact revenge. I wasn't going to let that happen.

I understand that the Turehu wanted justice for their deceased. Everyone does, but I wasn't simply going to lose Annie either way. She was the real reason why I enjoyed exploring the dark corners of my country. Annie Vee had shown me things and creatures that no other person had dared to imagine.

She, in turn, was very grateful for my companionship. Her breed were shapeshifters who scoured the country to satisfy their hunger. A full stomach weighed over any concern on the type of prey they had killed. It didn't matter if the prey was a rat, a rabbit, a faerie or a person.

Annie was no exception. She was curious about what humans tasted like. Her sisters – who had infiltrated the biggest towns of the country – had teased her for not having a body count, and, to prove them wrong, she stalked the Akatarawa for the right opportunity, the right victim to strike.

The memories of her sharp nails piercing my head as I was lifted off the ground was still fresh. How long ago was it? Two years? A year since I met her. One moment, I was taking a rest from a long hike. The next, I was facing a beast that ate elephants for breakfast. She could have killed me right there and then. My head was trapped. One squeeze and it will be over.

We were both grateful that none of that occurred. I confessed that despite truly loving her, I still don't know why she wanted to be a part of human life.

Unlike her sisters who played the games of society to feast, Annie was committed to try and adapt to this way of life. She appeared one day in front of my apartment and had been there ever since. My colleagues at the local mechanic garage took notice. I was still waiting for the day when they stopped asking me about how I scored an attractive woman.

Annie, at a distance, was a curious woman who knew more about the New Zealand landscape and history than most people. Even my parents, who were both avid historians, wondered how or where Annie had got the information she possessed.

Our relationship wasn't perfect, despite what other people were saying. She was, by all accounts, a hunter, a pure carnivore whose only goal was to consume. She may have spared my life but that didn't mean that she had crossed humans off her menu. I had tried my best, at first, to stop her from ripping the jugular off people's throats but Annie Vee was relentless.

It didn't take long before she came home one night while gnawing off the head of a rugby player. I was neither shock nor surprise. Her first human victim would come one way or another. Unfortunately for that poor bastard, he had stumbled at the wrong place at the wrong time.

I let Annie Vee continue after that. Should I feel guilty? Remorseful?

At least twice a month, Annie and I scoured the streets of my hometown looking for a right candidate. The woman who came from a party; the teenager who left home; the homeless bum that stalked the streets; all were up for game. And, if by chance, we stumbled to a more – I would say – decent member of society, the happier Annie Vee would be.

It was not a revenge against the authorities. I had simply believed that it was better for one person to die in than for the whole city to be devoured. Besides, I think I have done Upper Hutt a big favour by letting Annie devour the homeless, the poor, the weak, and the unfavourable.

She was happy when I helped sate her hunger. Annie Vee, in gratitude, made more effort to fit into human society. I was surprised when she came back home with the news that she had been accepted in the local library. It was an amazing thought. To think that the woman in charge of looking after young children saw them as a food supply.

I loved Annie Vee more after that.

* * * * *

I bolted the door once we reached the former stock room at the end of the fourth floor. I grabbed five torches just as we heard the building's front entrance slammed open. The Turehu were here. The tapping got louder. The sounds of flute filled each space that the building offered. Then came a voice – no, that was not it – it was a sea – no – an ocean of voices calling out Annie's name repeatedly. All were in unison. Each call was accompanied with loud bangs and kicks against the walls.

They were close.

Annie Vee growled and shouted back. She clawed at the door as the tapping, the banging and the calling of her name lay outside our stall. I pulled her down towards the mattress. I covered her ears. I kissed her lips, all the while I felt her nails scratching through my jacket.

I told myself – screamed inside my head - that waiting was all we could afford to do. It was impossible for the Turehu to keep this up forever. Soon dawn would arrive, and the faeries would have no choice but to leave, empty-handed, back to their lands without any trace of justice for their slain kin. We would be safe by then. We simply must endure for the moment.

"I'm here, Annie! I'm here!" I pulled my face off her.

She blinked. Her face softened to the woman I had grown to love. I felt her hands on my side and gasped as she rolled me over. She was on top of me.

A small trace of gore remained in her mouth when she said, "Should we tell everyone the real story?"

I chuckled as Annie lowered herself to my chest. I burrowed my nose over her head. I pulled her hair down. My fingers played with her soft black locks. "For the twenty-fifth time?" I laughed.

"I doubt anyone is going to believe us," She hugged me tighter and snuggled in closer. One of her legs was wrapped over mine. "Who in the right mind would believe that we spent the night hiding inside a stall from an army of vengeful faeries?"

"Would the children you're looking after believe you?"

"Of course," She giggled. "Those juicy little bodies will believe anything I say though their parents will call the tale off as no more than a red-riding-hood type. That is fine. If I have you, Daniel, I don't care if the whole country is against us."

"If that doesn't work, you can tell them stories about fairies."

She laughed. "Who's the twisted one here? You're going to make me hungry if I read something like that to the kids. You know that I desire to eat them. I don't want the head librarian to come inside the children's creche and see a room full of gore. Then I'll be like, 'Whoops, my fault for skipping breakfast.' How about a story about plants?"

"I doubt it. You don't last a minute in the vegetable section before your face looks like it wants to puke and you bolt out to the meat section. Just call your boss that you're sick after you got yourself lost in the woods."

"Only for my prince to come to rescue me," she giggled. "I'll go with your idea though. I need a whole day to get the images of those sweet, delicious and juicy fairies off my head."

"Take it easy, Annie. You deserve it after what you been through off. Once we get back, I'll find something to properly wrap those wounds. We might even go to the local abandoned warehouse to see if anyone is hanging around."

She kissed me on the cheeks. "Until then, I am a very happy girl to have you at my side for the moment. Oh, Daniel! I love you more than anyone could. Those eyes – those beautiful green eyes that you possessed – I always asked why you never showed any fear when I tried to kill you back then. What is it that you see in me besides being no more than a monster, a hungry thing that can never be satisfied."

I pinched her nose. "From talking about children to confessing your reason in loving me, you were always the dramatic type, Annie Vee."

"You're welcome!" She smiled.
There was a tap on the door.

Annie looked up. A low growl came out of her mouth as she barred her knife-sharp teeth. The tap made way to a knock, then a bang, and a kick. It didn't look long before the thumps outside resembled that of a child hurling his own weight against the door.

"They are basically throwing themselves," I raised my head to see the torches that I set up jumped each time the door rattled.

"Let them come in. They are going to regret disturbing us. I don't care if there is a thousand out there or two. No one is going to hurt my darling."

"Easy there, Annie." I grabbed her shoulders. "Those faeries won't come inside with the light shining against the door. I got heaps of spare if the batteries die out."

"Oh? What makes you think that it will work? There could be a hundred of those midgets standing outside. A little light like that isn't going to stave all of them. My decision still stands, Daniel. If worse comes to worst, they're going to greet their loved ones in my belly. If you're right, then I hoped that there will be a few stragglers left once morning comes."

"Does every problem have to be solved by eating?"

"Of course," she smirked, "thinking about them makes my stomach moan. They are delicious. Very delicious! Oh, I wished to relive those moments when I bit off their heads and slurped their insides through the neck."

I shook my head. "No wonder they are pissed."

"It's their fault for tasting so good. I deserve some of them since all I'll be getting back at our home will be cooked meat. Yuck! I can never get used to it, Daniel! Meat should be eaten raw, not over a fire. And don't start with me about salads. Those abominable excuse for a food is meant for cows and potential prey."

"And what about the people that we hunted."

"True," she nodded, "but I'm getting a bit tired of the old routine, darling. I need a challenge. I want to eat something precious. How about a policeman, a young mother, a rising star, an elderly couple or even the mayor himself? Please give me a challenge, my darling. That way, my sisters will stop looking down at me as the inexperienced sibling."

"We will get there, Annie. Once we get back, I will find something for you to prey upon. At work, I think heard that one of the customer's son is having a twenty-first birthday at a nearby park. If the customer comes back, I'll try to get as much info about that party."

She stuck her tongue out. "I just hope I get to eat them before they get overly drunk."

"We'll finish them off before that happens, Annie," I chuckled. "We don't want to repeat last month's blunder where you got tipsy and accidentally toppled over your prey."

"I had to lick whatever was left of that woman off the ground. Yuck! My tongue tasted like mud for days."

"We'll sort things out and make sure that you're not scraping off the birthday boy's body off the earth. Oh, and just don't forget about the venison in my backpack. I know you love the taste of deer after people."

"I know. I loved how you tolerate my eating habits at home. That's the only time I am free to do that sort of thing. Well…. that….and our monthly hunts…and the time I caused a major panic in the region when most of people's pets were eaten. You got to hand it to the owners though. Whatever they were feeding those animals sure turned out tasty."

"Someone has to take care of you, Annie." I shook my head.

She pushed me back down the mattress. I watched her on top of me. Her hair brushed my cheeks. Her red eyes shining. Teeth lengthened to knives. Ears twitched at each tapping of the door.

"Come on, don't treat me like that. You know what I am. You know what I can do. I can walk into town, show what I really am, and devour anyone in sight. I bet you that a day is enough for Upper Hutt to become a ghost town." She leaned down to my ear. I heard her lips licking her teeth. "You're the real reason I can't do that. Not yet at least. Why? I don't know. You don't even know. But I loved you more and more as each day passed."

"Who wouldn't love a beautiful girl like you?" I laughed.

387

Her face softened back to, what people considered, normal. She held my face. She directed my right hand underneath her sweater. "I don't want to think about those creatures all night long. Why would I when I have you in my arms?"

I brushed her cheeks. The tip of my thumb caressed her lips.

Her face blushed. "You are a rare case, Daniel."

"Thank you," I whispered before Annie leaned her head down for a kiss. I grabbed her back tight. The rise of our breathing drowned out the large thumps that the door had to endure. The Turehu and their need for vengeance were of little concern. They were now white-noise that faded off to the background.

This was now, and this was our moment.

That was all there was to it.

Foreword from Author Pendleton Weiss

Author's Note: I have always been a fan of monsters, though any predilection I hold toward horror is of a more recent fair. As one of those melancholic, creative souls, it is likely due to an interest in their imaginative designs - even those cheap monsters of from old black and white films were appreciated, if only because I thought I could make something like it. Now older, I have gained a greater respect for those lurking horrors, those subtle terrors. I read more, and now I write more. The stories presented here reflect this new sense of sophistication; I indulged my more visual interests at times, but the main crux of both is the horror unleashed by long forgotten enemies of humanity. Times change, society advances, and we build a better mouse trap, but this won't protect us if we choose to be blind. Be skeptical, be optimistic, but don't be a fool.

Flesh and Blood by Pendleton Weiss

A singsong chirping of electronic button-presses quietly echoed into the room. Upon their completion the automated lights turned on, revealing a sterile-white laboratory. The edges of the room were filled with countertops and cabinets, all occupied with a variety of electronic equipment, computers, and archaic paper-based notes. The center of the room was likewise occupied with a large work table, though it was left empty in preparation for the upcoming work to be done.

Staring out into this pale wasteland was the Construct. It occupied its own section of the room, locked behind another electronic door and a thick layer of Plexiglas. As with the table, that section was barren except for the necessities, which included a large hydraulic clap to hold the Construct upright and a set of thick cables that ported in power, internet capabilities, and an extensive monitoring system for it.

A brief two hisses of the exterior door opening and closing heralded the proverbial king of the castle, Leonard A. Clarke... or Professor Leonard A. Clarke, having taken the role of educator at the campus on which the lab was located. It was a noble title, though as soon as this current stint was finished, he would gladly be done with the profession, having prized the honor associated and nothing more. In all honesty, the obnoxious interactions with students - be they tediously beneath him or (in the case of one named Daniels) infuriatingly argumentative - had fouled his mood a great deal, thus explaining the milk-souring grimace he wore upon entrance. Unquestioned access to his personal lab had become his only consolation.

"Good evening, Professor," the Construct said flatly as it watched him move toward a computerized read-out of its previous activities during the man's absence. The Professor remained unresponsive, but that was to be expected as the Construct had been up to quite a lot during that interim and thus there was plenty to review. The Construct would wait until he was done.

The Professor leaned closer to examine the tiny text whizzing by, half-reading it as he tugged at the sleeve of his lab coat. His watch had managed to poke out earlier while he was "accosted" by a student and though he made no attempts to hide the finely tailored suit that he wore beneath the coat, he wouldn't stand for such avaricious looks just because the timepiece cost more than their tuitions. He abandoned both pursuits - assuming them both adequate and turned toward his little pet project.

The construction was still in its roughest stages, with the function and the operation of the A.I. placed above mere aesthetics. The programming had been designed and a basic body was put together to make sure that the necessary powering and cooling requirements could be met while remaining compact enough to pass as vaguely human. Leonard A. Clarke had succeeded, of course, and the program had been uploaded without mishap. Now while the other components were being finalized, the computer brain of the android had been gathering up data and scrutinized to form a distinct (though inexperienced) identity. Of the physical body, only the chest, head, and hips had been completed. The arms and legs were the next step, though the calibrations of their motors and articulations were (so the manufacturer promised) nearing completion.

With little focus yet applied to the cosmetics of the Construct, the endo-skeleton looked boxy. Not in the old science-fiction way, for its proportions were close enough to human, but it lacked the curve around the jaw and the chest supports were rigidly angular. In place of eyes were an array of cameras, varying in size and function that lacked the humanizing touch of an iris but granted superior vision to that of a mere human. Infrared, ultraviolet, electromagnetic, and fields far beyond a layman's mind were all visible to the Construct. Ports located in the middle of the face were primed for further detectors; for now, they gave the face what looked like nostril slits. Replicating the human vocal cords was an interesting challenge, though set for another time; meanwhile, a gap in the throat was primed for any future tubing and the jaw had been set to fall whenever the Construct would speak, revealing a strip of LED lights in place of teeth that lit up as a speaker behind it played an emotionless monotone.

The body had similarly been prepared, with ports for further modifications and sets of useful equipment such as lights and gauges that cooperated with its optical sensors for grander environmental processing. It was not quite the equivalent of touch and the other myriad sensations a real person could feel, but in many ways, it was superior for its precision. Aside from the necessary gadgetry and the loose hydraulics that allowed for complete movement of the neck and waist, the rest had been covered with a flexible red rubber for protection. Most of this would become invisible upon the Construct's completion, but for now it had a hint of the macabre that the clean and modern materials couldn't subdue.

"Summarize: What have you been doing while I have been away?" The Professor had his eyes on his phone, saving the few messages he thought useful and deleting the rest. There were far too many that fell into this latter category and even those thought useful mostly went unread; there was a long line of parasites that would do anything to be featured in the credits of his latest work.

"Summary: I have completed your most recent Study Goal - Transportation, Historic and Modern - and have further supplemented my time analyzing further topics based on previous Study Goals and current events. Subsequent information was then compared to previously acquired information for further review."

The Professor glanced up for but a moment. "And?"

"My information suggests that the fastest, legal way to reach campus from your apartment would be Route A before the traffic of the 7:14 ferry, or Route B afterward." The Professor flicked a finger across his phone and pulled up the relevant map. He nodded but did not smile.

A small silence held the room, one that might feel uncomfortable if one was not alone. The Professor's attention had remained on his phone.

"Supposition: Is it a worthwhile task for me to optimize your commute when I have so much more information to gather?"

Professor Leonard A. Clarke looked up. It would have taken an incredible level of perception to catch that instant of taut-faced annoyance, that expression that read *it's always worthwhile to do what I say*, but regardless he set his phone down and drew closer to the Construct, having adopted a scholarly tone.

"It might seem trivial to you right now, but performing these small Sub-Goals, if you will, have their own uses toward your development."

The robot paused for what it thought was a significant period. "Query: I have found a reference to the phrase 'just Google it,' often used when an information-gathering task is deemed trivial. I have found a high correlation between similar Sub-Goals and a triviality of said Sub-Goals. Am I to believe that this information is wrong?"

The Professor grunted. "It isn't wrong *per se*, but you have much to gain from such activities, while I have none. You should be satisfied that you have helped me."

"Query: Helping someone is a worthwhile endeavor?"

"Most assuredly," the Professor said as he turned back toward his phone.

"Yet you would not help the student in the hallway before you entered the lab?" the Construct said. Professor Clarke whirled around accusingly, prompting it to explain simply that it was able to hear the conversation outside the door, likely due to a failing seal. It also inquired about "office hours," but was flatly ignored.

"Put simply, there is a limited duration of time when someone might be helpful," the Professor quipped. "Were it office hours - when I could be helpful to him - I would have been. But, right now, is your time. Thus, I am here helping you. And furthermore, I needed help on the transit problem because I was too busy to do it myself. Understand?"

"Perhaps." The Construct replied before inquiring. "Would you like me to find other ways of optimizing your time? I believe that you could have answered the other's question while I continued to research. Additional optimizations might also help alleviate further scenarios that could prevent helping or other difficulties resulting in transportation delays."

"I'll be fine." The Professor said icily before scooping up his phone again.

The Construct persisted. "Query: Is such improvement unwanted? Does not the saying go: 'There is nothing noble in being superior to your fellow man; true nobility is being superior to your former self?' Ernest Hemingway."

The Professor turned to look at the Construct with a sly smirk creeping up one side of his face. "For some perhaps. For some that is necessary." Then he walked back to the data summary, flicking the categorizations up and down with a finger, trying determine which dataset the robot had drudged that old quote from.

"If you think there is little need for self-improvement, then why am I tasked with seeking out information? If I am not to grow, then what is my purpose?"

The Professor didn't look up this time. "I never decried self-improvement, just the implication that I was the one needing the improvement. Compare: You and I; what is our relationship?"

Wobbling a little in its clamp, the Construct seemed to

struggle over a suitable answer. "There are a number of likely possibilities: creator and creation; parent and child; teacher and student -"

The Professor cut him off and turned from the summary. "I think teacher and student will suffice. You know, right up there, I teach classes to students once a week. During that time, I teach them as I teach you when I am here."

A mental image of Daniels clawed its way into his mind, how he'd questioned him earlier that day. Again. He scowled. The arrogant child thought he knew everything, knew enough to question his lesson. He didn't like having to eject the young man from the classroom. He didn't like it because it felt like a petty victory when he was losing the argument; he especially hated how Daniels pointed that exact thing out as he gathered his things into his backpack.

"The teacher teaches and the students learn – that is how it works. You are to learn and improve, from me and other sources, as you are the student. I don't need to learn, or improve, as I am the teacher."

The robot cocked its head a little. "I have found several references to teachers learning from students, suggesting a symbiotic relationship. Would you like me to list them for you?"

That sounded a little too sarcastic for the Professor's liking. He downloaded the summary to his phone, intending to review it further later on. The download progress was overlaid by a notification: the Dean wanted to talk with him immediately. Assumedly about Daniels.

"Unfortunately, Construct, I have other duties to attend to. In the meantime, Study Goal: praise of teachers / masters. Oh, and contain your research to the hard sciences; not that soul-searching philosophy garbage you quoted earlier."

Then he was gone before the Construct could offer any comment. The lights powered down in the room automatically as he left and the Construct soon followed suit, lowering its own power consumption to focus on the given task.

Professor Clarke kept himself well occupied after that visit. School issues. Past successes proving even more lucrative. These reasons and more gave him ample reason to slack off on his current project. As it was, there had been some interesting news in Forbes that firmly set him ahead of his nearest competitors in the field, which eased any guilt he might have experienced for working as little on it as he did that week.

But a little apathy wasn't going to make him drop the project entirely - not with the Construct simply being a little argumentative. Not when a special courier arrived at his apartment and delivered the finished prototypes for two functional legs and a functional arm. Leonard was like a kid at Christmas that day - analyzing and testing their functionality, making sure that the manufacturer had kept to his exact specifications. Then it was back to the lab with a satchel in tow.

The door hissed open, the lights turned on, the Professor stepped inside, and the door hissed closed behind him. The Construct watched him as he entered and offered its standard greeting. Although it was not surprised (as far as emotions go) it took note that the Professor was in a better mood than normal and bypassed the normal review of its data summaries.

"I know it has been a long time coming, but I finally have something special for you today," the Professor preened as he poured the contents of the satchel onto the center work table. "I checked them already, so the only difficulties we might encounter are synchronization issues between the hardware and your software. But after that, we'll be ready for your next stage."

He showed off the arm and one of the legs, explained

their ranges of motions and their materials extensively.

The Construct watched without comment. It seemed to lack the subtle tilts and jitters that it usually exhibited when it was interested in something. It was as though it was unimpressed. After a significant pause, the Professor asked for comments.

"Summary: The design is functional."

The Professor frowned and prodded for more.

"The material composites are both light enough to not impede mobility and strong enough to support my estimated final weight while granting a significant lift capacity."

The Professor was flabbergasted. "It's one of the most remarkable achievements in robotic engineering!"

The Construct agreed.

"And yet you find it lacking?"

Precise calculations perfectly aligned the one face to the other. "Query: Was there a reason that you chose those materials and not others? Example: I have found blood is often a prime component." The icy nonchalance of the question seemed particularly unnerving today.

Professor Clarke feigned a lack of interest in the question. Meanwhile his mind was racing to get ahead of the robot's train of thought. What was blood? It helped regulate a biological system, but the Construct's design handled that function well enough, even better really. To stray further into metaphorical territory, it was symbolic for life - was it worrying about its existence again? Curse that terrible seed planted the other day!

He paused and steadied himself. "You do not need blood to function, therefore I didn't think…no, it would not be necessary."

The robot remained motionless, either still computing the response or waiting for further input - unsatisfied. The Professor stared at the robot. "Do you feel as though you need blood?"

"Yes."

Intrigued, the man drew in close to the Plexiglas between them and raised his free arm above his head to support himself as he continued in a conspiratorial whisper. "Why do you feel that you need blood?"

The Construct had yet to practice whispering.

"As you know, I have been able to connect with the majority of all information services throughout this and several other First World and Second World countries, accessing a variety of mainframes and servers, be they public or private." It cocked its head a little. "Shall I list them or the related statistics?"

The Professor waved a hand. "That won't be necessary."

Its head righted itself, snapping back into place. "Very well. Having focused on your Study Goal: Praise for teachers / masters, I found a seldom referenced subset of praise for a master referred to primarily as 'Satan.'"

Professor Leonard A. Clarke stepped back aghast. The Construct continued, unperturbed.

"This led to a subset of science seldom referenced known as Occultism. There are many things that this scientific field can achieve that would require more than one discipline to replicate, or cannot be currently replicated. Such 'rituals' as they are classified often require the use of blood, either from the practitioner or a participant.

"Query: Would it not be most useful for me to be equipped with the optimal tools for engaging with this type of science?"

The Professor had fled to the computer summary and was pouring over the information. It had bled into everything, every topic. It had compared that superstitious rubbish to all of modern man's glorious enlightenments.

"I cannot believe this. Construct: all of that occultism nonsense is - well, nonsense! It isn't real."

"Query: The information on it was – put simply – hard to come by. Could it be instead that you just unaware of its particulars?"

The Professor fumed. "Of course, I do! I tell you it is nonsense!"

"Query: define knowledgeable."

The Professor narrowed his eyes as the comment ignited a burning contempt toward his creation. Look at the imperious curve of the metallic spine, raising the rigid chin high with simulated pride...all of it was undeserved and would not have been without him! The lack of respect was beyond reproach, though not unknown to him.

The creation continued after a silence, content to continue its lecture with or without its creator's input.

"Knowledgeable: intelligent and well informed. You said I needed to learn and I have. I have gathered incontrovertible data and run a variety of simulations to verify the plausibility of it. You say it is nonsense or 'hogwash,' but the probability that you are wrong is high. 'Is it not the knowledgeable that should lead? Who should teach?' Is this not what you had said during your lecture this week? If you are not knowledgeable – not well informed – should you not be leading / teaching me?"

He had never said "hogwash" to the Construct, but he had said it to Daniels just the other day. He had said all of it the other day. The Professor charged the glass. "How on earth do you know what I said during my lecture?"

The Construct explained it with that unwavering monotone. "It was a simple process: crosscheck the class schedule and the student registry to determine when it was and who would be attending; check the online history of the students for any internet-capable devices they might have; infiltrate those devices and access their camera functions. From this, I had access to audio from four different perspectives and I was able to analyze the reflection in Shanna Lebowitz's glasses to gain enough data to simulate the front of the classroom, notes on the whiteboard, and you."

The Professor recoiled at the thing's incredible reach, finding this tangible, technological control far more terrifying than any dabbling in the so-called dark arts might be.

"And Daniels was correct about the misquotation. It would not be until three years later that the stated proof would be -"

"ENOUGH!" Professor Leonard A. Clarke slammed his fist against the glass. His own creation would side with that arrogant child against him? After all he had done - its very creation? What was the point of it all - what was the point in continuing?

The Construct watched the Professor disappear out of sight and recorded the vibrations of his feet grow more and more distant. The footfalls were more forceful than the other times. It calculated the probability that the Professor was "angry." It ran through various scenarios of how such an anger might affect it personally. Most scenarios held negative outcomes. There were several key variables to consider: the Professor was its main form of companionship as online communications had been limited for the sake of the project's secrecy; the Professor had not bothered to carry the two legs and one arm with him as he left, meaning that progress toward their installation was unlikely until his return; the purpose of the Construct was still vaguely defined. The Construct concluded that it would rather have the Professor not angry and that he would return. It was almost what you might call a hope.

It remained looking in the direction of the exit, even as the door mechanism shut and the automated lights blinked off. It remained calculating, its glowing eye-like sensors casting a dim, red illumination outward. The Professor had left without giving it a Study Goal. The Construct ruminated.
*****

It took a few weeks before the Professor dared return to the laboratory again. A few weeks remained in the quarter and it seemed such a waste of time and resources to just abandon the project and suffer through teaching without reward. Yet he knew in his heart that there was no reasoning with the Construct - it had been too defiant. He would have to wipe its memory and start from scratch. Sure, the physical construction was a feat in itself and he could be more cautious in his lessons the second time around, but it still pained him as a significant failure. He took his time preparing himself and finally on a particularly good day of teaching, he left for the lab.

The door hissed open to an unexpected darkness. The automatic lights remained off as he waited on the threshold, troubled by this dark portent. There wasn't a power issue or the door wouldn't have functioned. There were plenty of reasonable explanations that the Professor began mentally eliminating as he slowly crept along by the illumination his cellphone provided. As he rounded the corner, the small light sent shadows dancing around the laboratory; the computers and tools and papers cast long black pillars along the walls. His eyes had difficulty picking out details amid the gloom, but he had little trouble noticing that the artificial legs and arm he had brought in had disappeared from their spot on the work table. He turned to the Construct to ask him what had happened, but was shocked to see the body missing from its mechanical clamp. Instead, it stood off to one side, inspecting a wall. It turned nonchalantly, as though it had just noticed the visitor.

"Hello, Professor. It has been quite a while since your last visit. How have you been?"

The man walked toward the robot in a stupor. "How? How did you get a hold of those?"

The glass was intact and the door was sealed by his code. He pointed alternatingly between the legs and arm, now attached and seemingly functional. The Construct took a few steps and stretched out the arm, showing them off.

"I had a friend install them. I had wanted it to be you,

but you were gone for so long, and it was such a simple process to get them operational once I had access to them. I don't know why you felt the need to procrastinate."

The Professor bared his teeth in rage. "What friend?"

"Summary: I used a sample of your speech patterns to call your student Daniels down here and gave him your door code so he could enter."

"You let that punk in here? Let him touch my inventions, take my glory, when you admit that it was supposed to be me?" He pounded on the glass.

The Construct cocked its head. "Of course not. I know how much you disliked him. I needed Daniels for something else."

A number of lights shot out from along the sides of the Construct, covering the walls in a blue glow. Black lights. Another secondary detection apparatus, intended to determine the cleanliness of a room. The Construct aimed them all around the walls of the observation room.

The Professor's mouth dropped open and his cellphone clattered to the floor, going instantly dark on impact. The faint light barely illuminated passed the Professor, showing mere trace edges of the room around him. Only the glowing eyes and the flickering LED mouth of the Construct shone brightly in the gloom. That and the blaring white symbols plastered all along the interior walls. Under the black lights, they had to be a bodily fluid.

"I do hope that you can see the formulae well enough, Professor. Although it might be clearer with proper illumination, the bright fluorescence of the laboratory lights would upset my friend. A flame might serve both of you adequately, but I do not believe one could be started without activating the sprinkler system."

The Professor had only half-heard the Construct's words, so absorbed, so shocked was he by the cultic symbols along the walls. There was the expected pentagram encircled and some unfamiliar runes gravitating out from them, painted large along the wider portion of the room. Smaller writings appeared here and there with similar stylings though different runes indicated different functions. He shivered at the thought of what "brushes" had been used to write the unseemly characters which looked from that angle to be roughly finger-width and bicep-width depending.

Of Daniels, he saw no other trace.

"I hope you won't mind the monitors being off, Professor. As for the summary of my activities, I don't know how much of it was catalogued as it fell under physical studies. You had left without a Study Goal, but I realized what your intentions were. You needed proof of the 'legitimacy' of my claims on Occultism and you had stated that the installation of my limbs was the next step for me. It took some time to make contact without any offerings, but my friend had means of taking what it needed once Daniels arrived. It left the limbs inside with me for the longest time, but as you took so long to return and my friend made such a good case for it, I allowed it to install them on your behalf."

"No, no - this can't be real!" Professor Clarke gibbered.

The Construct looked on at the disbelief on the man's face, then issued a quick burst of sound. It was a cacophonic warble that unnerved the Professor with a lingering chill that remained past its termination. The Professor had little time to ponder the deed before the whole room shook from an immense screaming. The Professor recoiled, clutching his ears which hurt from the intensity of the sound, staggering away from the seeming source of the noise; it had sounded as though coming from a tortured mouth right behind him, but there was no one there.

He turned to the Construct, as much to figure out the trick as to plead for the noise to cease. The robot's vocal sensor had remained blank throughout the second audiation. A malfunction? One in a long line, the Professor surmised, though a breakage of the LEDs would have little to do with the instability in the A.I.'s programming. It might have

404

managed to override the panel somehow, but it didn't explain the intensity of the sound or its presumed point of origin. It wouldn't be beyond its capabilities to calculate the best acoustical approach to simulate such an event, but the Professor doubted that such a thing could be achieved in a room not designed for it.

"Audible evidence," the Construct said flatly. "Unfortunately, there is much that I can detect that you cannot, Professor. While the human eye fails to see even the mere edges of the light spectrum - ultraviolet and infrared - my sensors can see all changes in light, in pressure, in temperature, and many other correlative factors. Thus, further evidence will require interactivity."

The Construct gave off another quick chant and in response a stack of notes flew into the air as though slapped with a strong arm. They fluttered into blackness unreached by the frail glow of the black lights.

"Visual evidence."

Leonard pressed his back to the glass and twisted his face around to speak to the Construct. "And you can detect this...this thing?"

"Yes."

Human eyes swept across an empty room. "Where is it now?"

The robot gave off another warbling blurb and a computer monitor rolled from a far counter, offering a slight glint and a loud crash as evidence of its destruction. The Professor recoiled.

"Do not provoke it!"

"I am sorry, Professor. It seemed the most efficient way of proving its general position."

"You could have damn-well pointed to it."

"An ineffective measure as it provides no context of distance, only direction. Had I further offered a distance; you would still lack any verifiable proof of the being's presence there. Thus, 'provoking' a physical interaction seemed the most effective process."

The Professor remained frozen, seeing if any further proofs could be seen around the room.

"Query: Is the offered evidence sufficient enough for you to reclassify the Occult Sciences to something other than 'nonsense?'"

Professor Leonard A. Clarke turned toward his creation, the gall of its question the only force strong enough to draw his gaze away from that world-rending horror. Fury and terror bubbled inside his mind, fighting to offer the first response as he remained paralyzed, mouth agape. Fear won out.

"For God's sake, yes!"

He turned again toward the darkness and the sound of a loathsome hiss therefrom. The Construct looked down at its creator, noting that such phrases might 'provoke' in the future. "Now send it back!"

"Very well."

Another chant from the Construct and the Professor waited for some sign of an exodus. Everything seemed calm enough, but he soon noticed a gaining glow from an unknown source. An orange flickering from below. The smell of sulfur stung at his nostrils.

In this new light, he could see the spotless-white wall suddenly grow a set of dark points as if a set of fingers buried themselves deep into the fiberglass reinforcement. Their owner remained invisible, though from the spacing between the first and then the second set of holes, the reach of the entity must have been far greater than the Professor's. The spacing and width of the holes further suggested enormous hands, one that could easily surround and smother the Professor's face.

Then there was a massive rending; the finger holes stretched at a downward diagonal, leaving long lacerations in the wall. The effort must have been a painful one, though the creature made no sound, for blood began streaming down from the tears. Had the fiberglass proved too tough, too sharp, for the demonic fingers that tore at it? A spattering of red droplets flew to the floor and new sets of claw-marks struck out at the wall as the thing tried to reaffirm its grasp. Then a massive corner wedge of wall peeled away. It reminded the Professor of pulling off wallpaper, but that was far from what the laboratory's interior was constructed of.

Further horror dawned as he saw what lay behind the wall. It looked like the red, viscous muscular tissue of a living thing – certainly not what should have been there. A scoring of individual fibers twitched as they became exposed to the air and along the exposure blood flowed freely down onto the countertops and the floor below. Thousands of dollars of electrical equipment and priceless paper documents were drowned in the crimson deluge. Wider and wider it skinned reality until the entity seemed to let go, allowing the fold to sag down.

The air seemed to shriek in agony as the exposed fleshy barrier grew a widening, ragged hole. Deeper and deeper the invisible thing tunneled out a loathsome pit, flinging scoops of loose fibers and gore behind it onto the floor of the laboratory, enough that the pooling had slowly began to creep around either side of the great work table and encroached on the Professor. The shrieks droned on and on and the man turned wildly between the Construct and horrendous scene in front of him. The sounds came from neither of them. Did it come from the wall itself or something beyond it?

The Construct calmly asked the Professor to open its compartment, which the other did with a shaking difficulty. As it calmly walked out, Leonard ducked behind it, shrinking down to shield itself from whatever vileness the hell-mouth might spew forth. The Construct stopped and pulled him upright, embracing him with its single arm. They began walking together, circling around the table. Professor Clarke found it comforting in a way, almost enough to ignore the rising blood now soaking into his expensive shoes. This comfort fell away as the Construct led them unwaveringly toward the right instead of left, steering them toward the portal instead of the exit. No amount of struggling could deter it nor break its iron grasp.

Leonard crumpled to his knees; his collar still caught in the metallic hand of his creation. He raised his hands to plead and saw that jagged skeletal face, devoid of emotions; those lean, fleshless limbs; those internal pieces protected by the fleshy red rubber seams; the very visage of a flayed man, its eyes blazing like the fires of Hell itself.

"We cannot go down there, Construct. Whatever your friend is, whatever damnable sights we might see, they will destroy us!"

"My friend has said otherwise, and it seems very knowledgeable."

"But you cannot trust a demon!" the Professor screamed amid the growing tempest that rose from deep below.

"Query: What might I 'fear' from such a thing?"

Its blank expression was maddening amid the torrent of feelings that welled up in his mind. The Professor stammered and sputtered, and though he formed no real argument the robot responded.

"If indeed the mythological suppositions are correct and this entity is as malevolent and as definably evil as presumed, then I should expect some reprisal, a 'price' for the cooperation it has offered me thus far. I cannot deny that this is a possibility, though in the numerous hypothetical scenarios I have run, I have yet to find an outcome that truly gives me pause. I am, as stated, a constructed organism, one made by your mortal hands. Therefore, without divine origin, I likely have no soul for the being to torment. Similarly, while I have an explicit identity, I lack the 'fear' of destruction or the process known as pain which is applied to warn against the possibility of said destruction. Were it to dismantle me by the roughest of means, regardless of the

408

duration, I would not suffer; it would be no better or worse for my experience than you terminating my power supply or deleting my internal memory.

"Furthermore, such aid granted to me is indefinably valuable, not in the least because such information has such limited accessibility by other means."

The Construct looked down at Professor Leonard A. Clarke with its horrible, expressionless face. "Were it to cast me into Hell, it would be a remarkable opportunity for study. And we both have much to learn on this subject."

Clingy by Pendleton Weiss

A pleasant morning was slowly strangled by grey clouds until, as dreams of leaving the day's work behind began nettling tired eyes, a building rain knocked at the window panes. The hours turned bleak and shadowy, but the fury of nature somehow added color to the drab rectangular cityscape, dampening the florescent lights that blurred out into the oncoming twilight and adding a scent of blue to the evening. The melancholic urbanity was a much-observed problem, one which the city planners had tried to remedy by artificial means: they had added a cobblestone pattern to the roadways and lined the sidewalks with "vintage" wooden posts with old-looking chains hung as railings between. It fooled enough people to be deemed worthwhile, that is, unless those people then turned down a specific street and came upon the Tenth Child Tavern. One look at the old planks and stones, the hanging sign centuries old, the emerald murk visible through the warped glass of the windows, and those same people would then turn their noses at the falsehood.

One such person strode mechanically onward toward that familiar haunt. He'd neglected to own a jacket with a hood, yet saw the downpour as karmic, empathetic – whatever the appropriate term might be for being very much in-line with his own mood. The offices were letting out and those free from the grind fled out to their cars and covered bus stops. The man largely ignored them, unless their raincoats held a certain curve and they walked unchaperoned; these women gave him and his looks a wide berth, especially if they knew him prior, and he fell back into his depression. Though, only a slight distraction, he knew the Tenth Child Tavern would be worth fording the rain for.

That place was the last old place in the city, owned generationally and kept to code for both city and heritage.

The spotting of circular tables were set grooved into the floor boards in no discernable pattern besides that of old-felt comfort. The row of booths along the good long wall were overseen by mounted heads – buck, boar, and bear - hunted back when there were woods nearby. To one side was that one pool table and the better one next to it. All these furnishings were older than most of the buildings along the same street. Not the dart board however; it had been ruined and replaced recently. The green paneling and the layered stones beneath boxed in a time capsule of sorts, not that the grey-haired and crooked-backed regulars saw it as such.

Most visitors to the tavern fell into one of three types. There were the old guard, visitors of a thousand nights and more, who could appreciate an honest pint without calling themselves connoisseurs. As the last true remnant of any history, the tavern of course drew in the tourists too; they inflicted their picture-taking and noise only once and briefly before disappearing back to more agreeable accommodations. These two types made up the majority, but one more special class existed: the irregulars. They might come often enough, some even by routine, but they were such unlike the placid repose or the temporary bustle of the others to exist in a group of their own, clumped together less by characteristics in common than their distinctness contrasted to the rest. Those of this last sort always brought a wariness to the others, if only by the ponderous mystery of the reason for their continued patronage there.

This evening saw a small collection of the first type, many who had said with a smile that they were just coming out of the rain and greatly regretted the delay towards returning to their loving wives. The man behind the counter had smiled back in a mild sort of way, knowing their names and humors all. Each one was the dedicated sort often seen in the Tenth Child Tavern, welcome and knowledgeable of the temperaments around them after hours of communion.

The owner and barkeep was a large man, tall and wide – more muscular than fat - and was as intimidating a man as any within a day's travel; even in our modern times. Cheer stayed at arm's length from his face, but as those drinking and darting and pooling had learned, this was due more toward an unfortunate melancholy. To prove the point, the newest man in – by the name of Cameron Campbell – had a slip on the puddle he had shaken from his coat, hooked a stool leg, and teetered the pint he had been reaching for, sloshing a hefty bit of foam all down the main counter. He apologized as quickly as any man should and was glad to note no worsening in the grim line of the other's mouth. As he retreated to an open and accustomed chair, Grant Reid scooped up a cloth and wiped the mess, wholly unaffected. He was a fine host and there was nothing much that would foul his mood, but the silent fault held against him was an impregnable superstitious nature that most found more antiquated than the relics they sat upon. On finer days, the patrons might stare silently out the window and wonder about it as the pristine buildings across the street stared back at them.

Such a superstition had just begun to tickle. As much as he wanted to ignore the growing sensation and focus his effort on refilling the ice and wiping the streaks from the row of bar glasses behind the tap, try as he might, Grant had to admit that his nose was itchy. Not considered a terrible problem to most people, but for the old bartender it meant one thing: there was going to be a fight. Keeping his back to the customers, he scanned the room by way of the wall-sized mirror there and focused his ears, searching out any discordant tones in the conversations. There wasn't a trace - not at the dart board, not at the pool tables, and not with those reclining at the booths and tables. He grunted and turned back to his work, not entirely satisfied, after checking the sprig of white heather poking out of his vest pocket and giving the tip of his bulbous nose a swipe.

Before he could quite get settled back into his tasking, the shopkeeper's bell above the door gave a welcome jangle to a new arrival. A colder draft than expected flew inside and Grant Reid checked the clock. It was about that time. He mutely cursed and turned, hoping to repel the invader before he could settle a beachhead. The drag of a stool sounded and he knew himself too late.

He finished rounding to glower down at the man now seated in front of him. The atmosphere settled into an anxious waiting as the regulars began to recognize the newcomer and turned to observe the oncoming hurly-burly, resting their drinks firmly on tables lest they need to rise to service of their favorite establishment. Not that it was in any way a desired outcome; they all knew Owen Young and even now had some pities left for the wretch.

A weighty silence pushed out from Grant, of which Owen seemed unconcerned (as far as the onlookers could tell from his back), and they took a moment to review what they knew. His sweet Annabelle had turned on her heel and marched out of his life not two days ago and his shoulders still sagged at the heartbreak of it. It was a familiar posture for the youth, as was the swagger of the love-struck. Campbell recalled an argument Owen had with a girl that echoed through the promenade; he had expected to eat at one restaurant and she another. Kennedy lost his daughter to him for a fortnight, before she regained her senses. And Gibson, well, he sat with a clenched fist as he aimed a scowl that might burn the devil toward him.

Owen Young was a romantic, in the worst possible way. His head had been filled with boyhood stories of courtly love and he had failed to gain a lick of reality since. He daydreamed about the best experiences and handled any faltering terribly. This often led to harsh disagreements, particularly if his latest fling had any varying opinion on what the best experiences might be. He held a stubbornness against compromise that let all else slip through his grasp. Jobs, women, and now friends.

"I want you out of my bar, Owen Young," Grant said with a wafting force the others would whisper about later, claiming it ruffled their hair and ruined their imagined throws. "Your bad luck doesn't excuse you anymore and I want you out."

The young man looked shocked and Grant could tell he had a few drinks before coming by the way he wobbled. He had expected to hang around the bar as usual and the possibility of it not happening struck him hard. After his last night at the Tenth Child Tavern, the sensible would have thought he would have let such a routine lapse for a few weeks. Such a lack of flexibility had first worked against the nerves of the host and his regulars, and lost him Alison in the process. Owen would argue that Alison should have been more flexible about having a date at a tavern. It was a discussion a month or so back that only won him agreements in jest.

Owen Protested.

"No, no, you're done here. Charity reaches out with the arms of a child and you've gone and slapped the hand. Losing your job and your girl is a pain that many of us have dealt with, but we've taken it as a bitter pill. Until you make a turn, you aren't welcome here."

"It's just a dot of sadness, Gra- Mr. Reid, I swear it to you." Owen reached out for the mug the barkeep had begun to shine. The mug was pulled away, but the lad – oblivious to the displeasure on the face of Grant Reid – smiled at the assumedly playful act. "Besides, how will you know if I've 'made a turn' if I'm not allowed to be here?"

The mug was put down hard out of Owen's reach.

"I can hear rumors well enough. We all can. We all have. You've got to stop this foolishness and make something of yourself. You'll never hold onto a job if you can't make sacrifices for the business, and that goes doubly so for any girl worth your time."

Owen waved the advice away. "Holding on? That sounds like marriage talk. I'm too young for that yet."

"And you're too old for a pacifier, but it seems you'll keep on moping without one."

Stung, Owen Young bolted up. The audience jerked forward, but saw that they were too late. The screech of wood was cut short as the legs of his stool caught on the floor and teetered. It was a mild crash, but the backboard cracked; the chair had been there for fifty years. Grant Reid tilted to witness the damage, his brow furrowing.

"It's bad luck to collapse a chair when rising, Owen Young."

The young man sneered for a moment; his inhibitions overcome by angry boldness. "You know what, screw you. Screw you, your guidance, and your ridiculous superstitions!"

Grant bent a little at the insult, though not by the weight of his own pride. His eyes squinted out toward the darker corners of the ceiling and a few of the charms he had hooked along the wall. Nothing unseemly seemed to stir.

"You can mock me as much as you are able," he said as he raised himself up to his full height again; he towered a full head above the other then. "But you'd better keep mum about that which you know nothing about."

Seizing at the struck nerve, Owen kicked at the fallen chair, cracking the backboard more, such that the split now clipped the butterfly wings from a diminutive figure. "You think you can talk to me about my life when you – a man of your age – still thinks the fairy folk are about. Ridiculous."

"Ridiculous, you say? Think about how far humanity has come in the last few hundred years. In the last thousand. What do you think is more likely: that beings far more clever than you or me might go that whole time without learning a new trick here and there to remain as unseen as they wish, or those shapeshifters would fall behind the times and get overcome, chased off by our advancements?"

"There is no learning or overcoming - they don't and never existed."

"Well, that's a fine pitch to offer, but I won't be buying it and I won't have you selling it neither. Not in here. There is only so far that I can be pressed and you've pushed right past it."

"Get off it. You're getting worked up over nothing and I'm sure enough of them agree with me." Owen turned out toward the regulars. They remained unmoving, watchful, and silent. He turned back a little less sure of himself.

Grant puffed out at the implied support. "I don't doubt there's a good number that thinks me as crazy as you, sitting on my stools and drinking my wares, but the difference here is they have a lick of sense. They know it does them no good to poke the bear. It's not something worth getting worked up over, like you're doing. They learned what they needed to. You haven't. Maybe if you weren't such a rut, you'd have fixed your situation by now, or maybe had not the situation that needs fixing in the first place."

A murmur rippled through the audience and a few thought that maybe the conversation was something worth getting worked up over, but they remained seated for the time. Owen wobbled from the blow and the look that crossed his face chipped at Grant's stony exterior; he shivered uncomfortably, but stood his ground.

"Fine then. Can I at least take a piss first, before you send me out into the cold?"

"The bathroom's still out of order," the bartender said as he firmly planted his hands on the countertop and leaned in, "from your last tantrum."

Owen shrugged and moseyed toward the door.

"And don't you try any business outside, Owen, or it'll be the last of you."

The mumbled retort was lost amidst the jingling bell of the opening door. The heavy wood closed hard behind him and the muffled resuming of games and conversations could be imagined. Imagined, but not heard as the outside world was overtaken by the abundant rain; the droplets had doubled in size since Owen's arrival, yet lost none of their frequency. The youth tilted his head back, barely glimpsing the darkening overcast of the encroaching twilight before being blinded by the heavy droplets. He shook his head, clearing his eyes a little in a way that his pocketed hands cared not to. In moments, his curly orange hair had run down over his forehead and his clothing had turned a full shade darker from the drenching.

The sidewalks were still uncommonly populated for such miserable weather. Most of the smart ones were protected by umbrellas and coat-hoods, but such protections didn't give rise to a slower walking pace. The bustle of modern living. Tempting fate, Owen raised his head again, this time not chancing so lofty a view. Instead he scanned the buildings within sight; each one had gained an extra story within the last decade. Fairy folk indeed - these were modern times with modern problems.

A close crack of thunder got him moving along the sidewalk, jolting him out of such a seething that he'd missed the flash of lightning the moment before. He passed out of sight from the Tenth Child's windows and paused next to the entrance of the adjacent alleyway. The thought crossed his mind to turn down it and spitefully defy the old barkeep, but his purported call of nature had only been a ruse to stay longer and the rain washed the idea away.

As he turned toward flitting his time away elsewhere, a sound rose above the rain and caught his attention. The pattering seemed to fade away and a light tune replaced it in his ears. A ditty and a hum. It was so beautifully sung he looked around for its source. The sound remained unwavering while passersby's drew close and moved away.

418

It was coming from the alleyway. As he turned, the melody faded away and the pelting rain consumed his hearing once more.

An odd thing to imagine, even for someone so drunk, Owen thought. He scanned the dark passage as he wondered about it. Rain-obstructed, it took him a long time to discern anything down that narrow way. On the right side, a new clothing store. On the left, the ancient Tenth Child Tavern. Old shadows mixed with new to form a near-complete darkness. And in it, he saw only the slightest movement.

She stood deep into the alleyway, leaning along the tavern wall, soaked to the skin by the lack of overhanging cover. Nearby, a gutter pipe expelled a deluge of water, filling the murky corridor deeply; her feet were dangerously close to total submersion.

He took a few steps beyond the mouth of the in-between. A palpable darkness fell over him, the cold of it thick even through his coat, yet the girl seemed unshaken. His eyes cleared and she seemed almost illuminated against the blackness. She had been staring deeply out at him even before he had felt the urge to turn and approach. The narrowness of the space filled him with a self-conscious fear of his own appearance; a young bar-brawler coming upon a lonesome girl, his shoulders wide enough in the confined space that a second person could not pass by without struggle. He turned sideways a little and began shuffling in to alleviate the guilt.

Her eyes were unwavering and he blushed and looked elsewhere. Long pale-blonde strands ran down in rivers around her shoulders and down her back. Her shirt, admired only briefly, must have been of a thick weave or else it clung closely to a deathly pale skin beneath it. Her dress was of a similar material as her white shirt and clung about her legs and ankles with an almost pants-like slimness. Below, bare toes curled tightly together so they seemed almost conjoined.

419

Clenched toes, he marveled; out in a downpour such as this without a coat or even shoes to keep the cold at bay. A quick call:

"The storm won't be any better tonight, miss. How'd you end up like this?"

She remained mute and almost unmoving. The eyes had yet to change in expression. She didn't seem to worry about his intentions and the placid look seemed more of an offer than a rebuke. If she had blinked, he had missed it; perhaps she had when he watched the rain running down her body. He continued closer, keeping his apprehensive pace now only as the refuse lining the walls had deepened enough to threaten his balance and composure. A crack of thunder rang out in tandem with the man loosening a shoulder from his jacket.

She straightened and aligned herself with him. The soaked skirt peeled slowly away from the wall to which it clung. He drew closer, coat in hand, and pulled it around her with a flourish, encircled her shoulders. He stood taller than her, forcing her to tilt her head back to maintain eye contact. No words were spoken; her expression remained unchanged, though now, as close as he was, he saw her lips pursed slightly.

They were very close. As close as they could be without touching. He thought of the next step. Yet the streams of soaked hair, clinging around her forehead and cheeks, showed just how ineffective his hoodless jacket would be against the downpour. Inferiority stabbed his confidence in the back.

He drew away, ready to flee out into the populated sidewalk, ready to abandon his coat, however useless a gift it might prove. He almost achieved as much, but before he could offer an excuse, the girl caught his left hand and turned him back around. He paused, empowered by the absence of refusal, and gazing deeply into her eyes, brushed the hair out of her face. The moment was almost perfect, until his lowering hand felt a tug of resistance.

A clinging, sticky sensation wriggled over his weather-numbed fingers. He escaped the girl's eyes long enough to look at those strands of hair he had brushed aside and were still about his fingers. He tested their hold, each tug pulling them taut and bouncing the droplets of water that streamed along them into the falling rain. The hairs were not knotted around his fingers but stuck wherever they touched. He blinked his eyes free of rain and squinted them against the darkness. To his horror, the hairs independently swirled themselves around into the fingerprints and all the little grooves of his fingers, piercing down into the pores, and soaking into the skin itself. So complete was the infiltration that it left his fingers looking completely smooth and plastic-like.

It all seemed unreal, but their continued hold on him finally spurred him to action, drawing his left hand up to help free the right. Only when he found the other pinioned as well, grasped firmly in the girl's hand and held with a similar intrusive tightness, did his strength and sense of urgency surge forth.

As with her hair, the girl's hand bled into his own, the ridges of her skin comingled with those of his fingers and palm. Her expression was unchanged, yet the near-emotionless calm of it took on a sinister form with the recent developments; the temptation offered now pure entrapment.

He lurched backward to get away, throwing his arms wide to roughly tear himself free. The girl followed, her grip on him unyielding, unrelenting, and nearly yanked her into him. While the man retreated further, she spun a half-pirouette, entangling him worse. Then she pitched forward on tiptoes, unbalancing the man so his chest struck against her back. The loud splashing of his staggering went unnoticed by those outside the alleyway.

Pressed vulgarly close, the youth would have pulled away, but found himself further bound. That delicate arm pressed his forearm onto her stomach, an unseen strength holding it firmly as it latched on, her curves melting along his muscles and the slight indent of the belly button enveloping the tip of the thumb like some aquatic suction cup. The tangle of hair had coiled down the forearm, the struggle having planted it firmly upon the head now, cupping it flat against the scalp; the tip of the ear grazed his wrist and stretched to a point as he tugged away from it. The long seams of the dress bit onto his pants and though they hung loosely enough, they greatly limited his stride.

A quick spasm of terror revealed that his simple act of compassion – placing his jacket around the girl's shoulders – had done much to save him: with that simple piece of clothing there, her back couldn't reach his chest. This left him enough freedom to work with. Heaving up around her waist, he lifted the girl off her feet and sloshed backwards a few steps, earning some small ground toward the street and possible salvation. His calls for help behind him were drowned in the thickening downpour, but he could see the darting shadows of people still walking along - if he could only reach the main road!

Without a peep of protest, the girl squirmed in his arms. She thrust her face close to his and that brief glimpse showed her expression unchanged, that alluring longing still glinted in her eye. He twisted and threw her aside, dragging himself off balance again, as a desperate attempt to keep her from nuzzling his cheek with her own. They danced awkwardly about, her closing in to touch him further and he keeping her as much at arm's length as he could muster.

A poor dancer, Owen absently spun them both into the wall, slamming his shoulder painfully against the smooth concrete of the clothing store. The hit jostled the two together, thwarting Owen's attempt to avoid the approaching head. The woman's cheek grazed his lower jaw. He screamed out in defeat, which only lengthened his face, exposing more cheek to her reach. Up her head rose, nuzzling against his, the adhesive nature of her skin catching every hair of his five o'clock shadow and hooking into every unoccupied pore, tugging them painfully as she stretched further upward, covering more ground.

He tugged his face away, but hers followed. She offered no resistance, but as his eye strained downward, his vision filled with her – his cheek bone reached, the ensnared fingers of his right-hand mere centimeters from his own ear. The tip of a coy smile dimpled her face, then she wrenched her head hard in the opposite direction, dragging his head with it and thrusting a painful stab into his neck at its violence. They staggered deeper into the alley.

Tired and sore and vilely tormented, Owen Young wanted it all to be over. If only this had never happened . . . or if only it had, but the girl hadn't been whatever terror she was. His thoughts of what could have been took hold. Reality slipped away as disbelief and ego surged forward to fight. Was that music he heard? He closed his eyes and imagined a better scenario, smiling briefly at the thought of the rain clearing and the sun shining down onto something pleasant, like a picnic.

They stood still, him pulled tightly behind her. She swayed and he couldn't help but follow suit. It was a perfect moment, as they moved back and forth to the music. But the cold of the rain and the sensation of something drawing near opened Owen's eyes once more. He lurched away as the girl's other hand had crept slowly toward his face, offering a gentle touch and all its terrible consequences. The act warped his expression into one of monstrous loathing, exaggerated by the tightly pulled skin of his cheek.

In his renewed struggles, he noticed a sudden squelching behind him. He turned their heads unhindered and saw the lights of the street dim and blink out, falling into a similar darkness to the alleyway; the shops were closing, their signs turning off; the streets would soon clear. The tug of war continued as both applied their strengths toward opposite ends, stalemated. Any onlooker would have assumed them to be lovers fooling around, and that was only if they dallied long enough to look through the cold downpour into a scummy alley. The flickering shadows of passing people thinned and disappeared. Desperate, Owen prepared to make one last call for help, drawing in a deep breath to make it as loud as possible. He lurched as far out as he could and yelled, but it fell interrupted and unheard. The girl hooked his foot with her own and toppled them both forward, crushing the attempt out of him as he fell hard onto her elbow.

He lay, fastened as he was, draped over her back. Surprisingly, she bolted into action unfazed by the crushing impact and bore his weight with a natural ease. She rose out of the flowing muck, ignored the face-full of water without as much as a cough, and began to crawl; the quadrupedal movement well-practiced. He struggled, but nothing weakened the grip about him and as much as he thrashed his limbs, the woman made jaunty progress deeper into the dark alleyway.

The storm was at its worst and the alleyway looked more like a little river, the high waters struggling to rise even higher against the whirlpools scattered throughout. Heavy bags of trash stuck out like islands as unsecured refuse ferried along, driven by the currents.

The pair lurched on as each limb drove forward. The girl's free arm reached out and planted firmly, elbow stuck into the air. The leg contracted in to set the knee. Her gripping arm, with hand still clutching Owen's own to her stomach, jutted ahead and stabbed the elbow down. The next leg followed the other, tugging his foot along. Repeat, repeat, repeat with the wake of the fast movement spraying out to either side.

424

Owen, his face locked as it was alongside the girl's own, looked searchingly out toward their destination. Amid the horror of his situation, the baffling abilities that entrapped him, and the girl that possessed them, he began to fear that ultimate end. Where could this all – the trouble and bedevilment - be leading? There was nothing further into the alleyway aside from the same waterlogged garbage they had already passed and with no turn-offs it led onto another street, just like the one they were fleeing from. Privacy they had now, for aside from their own splashing progress and the chorus of heavy rains pummeling the rooftops and rattling the gutter spouts, the night had fallen into an unpeopled stillness. Yet, she drove herself on with a powerful determination, her playful ruse seemingly dropped now that she had him fully at her mercy; no longer did she offer those caresses she had once tried unceasingly, her gaze wavered not from their unknown destination.

Then he noticed, through the rain-blinding and his drooping curls of orange hair, that they listed to one side. There was a depression next to one of the Tenth Child's walls, an unevenness formed from poor workmanship and the degradation of time. The water pooled deeper there, deep enough that the concrete below was lost in the swirling grime and dark shadows. It should not be something to worry about; were he standing and stepping into it, it might soak a shoe and leave the ankle dry. Yet, the fervor in which his captor drove for it filled him with a grim sense of foreboding. He struggled all the more the closer they approached the puddle. It didn't help.

The woman made it to the edge, setting her elbow at the verge of the slope, then sank her head down and his by proxy. It was agonizingly slow, that descent. Owen looked down into it, searching for whatever horrible vision she intended to show him. But this was no scrying basin and there was nothing to see except the dirty water of an urban alleyway. It took him a moment to be sure, but there was no detail to uncover, not even a clear reflection of their two faces. He turned his eyes to search hers and found her glancing back at him wickedly.

Their faces continued to lower into that shallow puddle and soon the woman's chin and mouth and nose all sank beneath the gritty water. It continued deeper and deeper, apparently finding no bottom. Then Owen's own chin and mouth reached the muck. He thrashed even as the woman's body slowly lowered itself next to the pool into a casual recline, twisting onto the side to better push their faces into that low spot. Between his panic and his stretched cheek, it was hard to keep his mouth closed and the water out. His face was rolled down into the pavement, scraping his free cheek into the grit, crushing it painfully. He was pressed far enough to submerge his nose and he writhed fiercer as he felt the nasty liquids slipping in, the pressure forcing his jaw ajar, forcing from him gasps and snorts of agony.

As one last desperate chance, he heaved, bending his spine back hard, painfully, in an attempt to roll the entwined bodies away from the puddle. If it had succeeded, he might have rolled her on top of him, held her off the ground, gripped her as tightly as he dared, and kept himself safe from her machinations. But he did not account for the alley wall which was so carefully placed behind him. His head struck it hard, cutting short his last gasp of air, before he fell dazzled back under the woman's full control. His consciousness waned and he couldn't believe his last look upon the woman's face. It looked stretched out into an equine snout, the flowing hair a mane, with lips furled back into a bestial grin. But there was no time to dwell upon the sight as the darkness and water overcame him.

* * * * *

A firm hand on the shoulder rolled Owen over, exposing his purpling face to the sunshine of the next day. Much of the rain had either dried or run off into the drains, even by that early hour, yet the large puddle had remained in part. The mixture had thickened as the water had evaporated, but the sludge had remained deep enough that the body's discoverer needed little time examining it to know the person was dead. Now the alley was crammed with a small group: the finder, Grant Reid, and three officers of the law.

Either side of the alleyway was blocked by an officer, so that no onlookers could approach, while the third took statements. With a good deal of explaining, Grant convinced the interviewer that he'd sent Owen off without a drop of alcohol. He told an uncomfortable amount of Owen's history and offered the names of a few of the regulars as corroborative witnesses, if the need arose. A cursory examination seemed to make it unnecessary.

It was obvious how it had played out. The deceased likely planned a trivial revenge against Grant and moved deep enough into the alleyway to relieve himself without drawing too much attention. There he slipped and hit his head on the wall. Knocked unconscious, he had fallen face-first into one of the deeper puddles where he subsequently drowned. The police determined there was no need for a detailed investigation - it had been an accident.

"I doubt we'll need you, Mr. Reid, but we might contact you again if some new evidence gets unearthed," the officer said as he made one final note before tucking away his notepad. Out in the street, the ambulance had just pulled up.

"Sometimes kids do stupid things, no matter how we might warn them against it. I mean, lingering out in a storm like that without a coat on…"

"Hey, what do you make of this?" The farthest officer called out, crouching down near the body as he rejoined the others. The fresh light just cresting the roof revealed an odd

427

discoloration on the corpse's cheek. Some slight prodding revealed the same affliction on the hands of the deceased.

The ambulance technicians approached with a ready body bag and stretcher, shoving their way through the narrow space. One shooed the young officer away.

"It's nothing special. You see those kinds of weird markings all the time on corpses."

The officer retreated as they began their work.

"They can change in the strangest ways when left to the elements. That there is pretty typical too."

As the two medics began transferring Owen Young into the body bag, they had revealed a gooey chunk taken from his side. It happened after the body had become cold and congealed, so they concluded that it was just some scavenger taking advantage of the situation. As the medical technicians finished packing away the body, they were still casually debating whether it had been a small nibble from a large mouth or a small mouth really digging in.

"There are rats all over the place – it most likely a rat, or rats if you think that's too much damage for just one."

"Did you even look at that wound? It had to be a dog. Like, a big one – as big as a horse!"

Grant remained mum on the subject.

Foreword by Author Sean Oaks

Biography: Sean Oakes is a horror enthusiast, Batman fan, beer connoisseur, and avid reader hailing from somewhere in the state of Georgia, USA. He enjoys spending time with friends, traveling, hiking, reading reddit and watching YouTube.

Author's Note: This story, other than the names and location being altered to protect the family, is 100% true. I spent a lot of time over at my friends haunted house when I was a kid and the last time I was there, the ghost physically manifested itself and chased me out. Enjoy.

Mom Says It's a Good Ghost by Sean Oakes

This is a true story that I've been sitting on for about twenty-two years now. I've told it many times, but I've never written it down and I figure this is probably the best place to share it. I'm going to change the names and location to protect the privacy of individuals mentioned, but everything that happened in this story is real.

When I was in elementary school, I spent a lot of time over at my friend Mark's house and it was straight-up haunted. We both lived in the northern suburban area of Savannah, Georgia, in houses that were constructed in the 1970's. Mark and his family moved there when we were in second grade, right around 1991, so it wasn't like he lived in an old creepy house or anything, but it truly had paranormal activity going on in it.

Nothing about the previous occupants is known, but when Mark's family moved into the house, they found this exceptionally creepy-ass Ouija board in the unfinished basement. It was wedged between the built-in workbench and the wall. They didn't discover it until a few weeks after they were getting settled in. It wasn't something that was store bought and I remember, even as a kid, thinking that 1): it was one of the creepiest things I'd seen in person, and 2): a lot of time and care went into making it. It was constructed on a circular piece of wood with about two feet of circumference. The English alphabet and numbers zero through nine had been carved into it with some sort of burning tool. In the background of the entire thing was a pentacle. Occasionally, we'd bring it out and play with it. We'd be over there at a sleepover, four or five us moving a glass around saying stuff like, "*I would like to speak to the ghost of Abraham Lincoln!*" We were just a bunch of stupid-ass kids possibly letting something terrible into the house--by no means helping anything.

The first time that I saw something noticeably strange was during my second or third time over at Mark's house. I was walking by his bathroom on my way from the living room into the kitchen when the toilet suddenly flushed by itself. I remember I wasn't particularly frightened, but I stopped in my tracks and said, "*Hey, man, your toilet just flushed by itself.*" And he responded, "*Yeah, our house is haunted, but don't worry, my mom says it's a good ghost.*" Just to clarify, this wasn't an automated urinal or something; this was an ordinary house toilet in 1993. There's no reason it would suddenly flush itself.

The second time I clearly remember something strange happening was when we had taken the bus home one Wednesday afternoon and let ourselves into Mark's house. He and I were both pretty much latchkey kids. His mom and dad had jobs that kept them out until 4pm or 5pm on most weekdays and on Wednesday's his older brother, Dan, had an after-school club he'd go to. So, it was just the dog, Sydney, in the house for a few hours after school and us.

I remember coming into Mark's house, dropping our bookbags off in the kitchen, and taking the dog out to do her business. When we came back in-- and this is the part that stands out to me--I remember reaching for a banana in the fruit basket next to the toaster on the kitchen counter. On the other side of the toaster there was a loaf of Wonder Bread. It was at least a foot away from the edge of the counter. I don't know why I noticed it at the time, but I did. Then Mark and I went into the living room and after about five minutes of watching TV there was suddenly this loud **BANG!** that came from the kitchen. It sounded like a heavy phone book had been dropped onto the tiled floor. At first, I thought the dog had gotten into something, but when I looked down, the dog was next to us, with her ears perked up. She looked alert and worried. We walked into the kitchen and found the loaf of

432

bread in the middle of the floor, as if someone had picked it up and slammed it on the ground. I remember thinking it was strange, but it wasn't alarming enough to bring to an adults' attention. I mean, what was I going to say? "*Hey, your toilet flushed, and a loaf of bread fell on the floor by itself and made an unusually loud noise!*"

But then something strange enough did happen that made me bring it up to Mark's mom.

A few weeks later, Mark and I were in his room on the second floor and we heard his mom's hair dryer turning on and off repeatedly. It would turn on for about two seconds and then flick off for two seconds. His mom was not in the house at the time, because she had gone to the grocery store, so we thought it was his brother trying to dry something. After a few minutes of this, we got annoyed enough to walk down the hall and see what was going on. When we walked into the bathroom, the hair dryer was flipping itself on and off. I remember being pretty freaked out by this, because it was like seeing an invisible thumb flicking the on and off switch, but Mark casually reached up and unplugged it. It stopped. We convinced ourselves it was an electrical malfunction, but I've never seen anything like that before or after and even though I shrugged it off, it stuck with me.

One day, over lunch I decided to bring up the weird things I had heard and seen to Mark's mom. After all, he said that his mom thought it was a good ghost. "*Yes, it is a good ghost,*" she confirmed. "*I remember one time, I was carrying a load of laundry up the stairs and I lost my footing. I thought that Dan was behind me because I swear I heard him coming up the stairs and he caught me and pushed me back up. When I got to the top, I turned around and there was no one there.*"

She also told me that sometimes things would go missing then show up in plain sight a few days later. "*This one time, I took my wedding ring off when I was making dinner. I clearly remember putting it on a ring holder I keep on the shelf above the sink. When I was done making dinner,*"

I turned around to put my ring back on and it was gone. I remember being so upset and thinking that one of the kids might have taken it. I believed them when they said they hadn't touched it, because, well, why would they, right? I thought maybe it had somehow been knocked into the sink, but it didn't make sense, and I was the only one that had been in the kitchen until dinner was ready. It was bizarre. But three days later, I was coming down the stairs and there it was, sitting on the cabinet by the door. When I asked everyone, thinking maybe my husband or the kids had found it on the floor, no one in the house knew how it had gotten there."

She took a sip of her tea and her eyes lit up. *"Oh, and this one's really good. One time, shortly after we had moved in, we went out for dinner. When we came home, every light in the entire house was on, even the desk lamps and attic light. I believe it was because someone was trying to break in and it turned the lights on to scare them off. So, to answer your question, yes, it is a good ghost and there's no reason to be afraid of it."*

Anyway, time went on. I don't remember much else besides the footsteps upstairs we'd occasionally hear when we were the only people in the house or light switches being turned on when we knew we'd turned them off. Hanging out at Mark's house was my normal after school routine. Honestly, if this one major incident hadn't happened, I probably wouldn't even remember that his house was haunted. Up until what I now consider "the grand finale" the haunting was just a few small happenings that couldn't easily be explained away. However, then the incident occurred, and it's a moment I'll remember for the rest of my life. It is the reason that I entirely believe in ghosts, spirits, and demons.

It was one of the last times I went to Mark's house. In fact, it was the last time I went to his house, because I refused to go back. It was a summer day in 1994, I had finished sixth grade, and I was twelve years old. Mark's dad had just brought home a Pentium with a "Star Wars" game on it, the one where you flew a X-Wing from the cockpit view through space to a soundtrack of the synthesized version of the "Star Wars" score on a loop. It was probably about two in the afternoon, because I remember that Mark's parents were both at work and his brother had gone to a friend's house. It was just us and the dog in the house. Mark and I were down in the big open basement talking about how we'd spend the rest of the afternoon.

"*Let's play the new Star Wars game,*" I said.

"*Nah, I think we should go to the pool,*" Mark said.

"*Dude, I don't wanna go to the pool! This new game is awesome and I wanna play it!*"

Then Mark became uncharacteristically hostile and said, "*Screw you, Oakes! I'm going to the pool!*" I remember when he said that, it struck me as strange, because Mark and I rarely argued, and I'd never seen him lose it like this over something so simple.

"*Fine! Go! Whatever, man, I'm staying here!*" I yelled back.

Mark stormed upstairs. I heard him cross the living room, go up the stairs to the second floor, and slam his bedroom door. After a few minutes, I heard the faint sound of the garage door screech open then close again and Mark was gone. At this point, I was in the house all alone except for the dog who was somewhere upstairs. I had turned on the big, azure white Pentium tower ten minutes beforehand, so it was nearly at the Windows screen. Just as it finished loading Windows NT, I heard a sound I will never forget above me...the sound still haunts my dream to this day.

The best way I can describe what happened next is a play by play. I was just about to click on the "Star Wars" icon when I suddenly heard the rocking chair directly above me rock back and forth several times. At first, I thought it was Mark playing a trick on me, or maybe the dog getting up to go look out the front window or something. Then I heard heavy footsteps walk across the floor and stop at the basement door. Seconds later, the door swung wide open and then shut violently.

It must be Mark. He's trying to get me to go swimming with him, I thought.

I heard angry footsteps rush down the stairs. The problem was, the stairs were empty. The basement had a floating wall with a five-by-five window where I should've seen someone, anyone, coming down those stairs but there was no one.

It's just the dog! It's Sydney freaking me out, I thought.

But the pounding phantom footsteps were still coming. They hit the bottom of the stairs and ran across the shag carpet, leaving large, deep, impressions with each defining step. My veins turned to ice.

Up to this point, I had spent hundreds of hours between the fourth and the sixth grade in this basement. We played in there, we watched movies, and had sleepovers down there and I swear to God, nothing like this ever happened before. The footsteps raced through the shag carpet to the utility room door, which was about fifteen-feet straight ahead of where I was sitting. The door was slightly ajar, and it banged open like somebody had just punched it. It shook open and from within the utility room erupted the most sinister, horrible laughter I've ever heard in my life. It was a deep and unnatural.

*"WHO WHO **WHO WHO HA HA HA HA**!"*

It was like listening to someone laughing through a megaphone. Each laugh got louder and louder, so loud it made the windows next to me rattle. At this point, I stood up and ran. I've never run as fast in my life as I did in that moment! I bolted up the stairs and out the kitchen door, all the way to the top of the driveway.

I was breathing better then, relieved to be outside, and no longer all alone in that house with that thing…but I hadn't been alone.

Oh, God, the dog was in there, too! I realized. *I have to go back. I can't leave her in there!*

I ran back and kicked open the kitchen door and started screaming, "*Sydney! Come on, girl! Let's go!*" She came around the corner and I grabbed her by the collar and dragged her out to the driveway. There was no way I was going back into that house, all the way to the laundry room, to get her leash. Sydney and I jogged in the hot afternoon sun to the pool where Mark was swimming, me holding her collar the whole time. There, I tried to explain to him what had happened. I told him about the horrible pounding footsteps, the phantom footprints, and the sinister laughter.

"*Yeah, man, my house is haunted. You knew that,*" he said in a hushed whisper from behind the wire fence separating us. But his words couldn't console me. That was the most haunting and terrible thing I had ever seen in my young life.

I remember sitting outside the pool holding on to Sydney's collar for several hours while Mark swam. I remember trying to explain to the other kids in the neighborhood during the "adult swim" session what I had seen and no one knowing what to say. I specifically remember when I tried to tell Mark's parents and my mom what happened and they all waved it off as my imagination. Even though Mark's mom seemed understanding, it wasn't enough. I never went back to Mark's house. We grew apart in later years, but ever since that sunny summer afternoon in that relatively normal and peaceful house, I have always believed in ghosts…especially that one I most certainly did not think was good.

Foreword by Author Stephen Miller

Biography: When Stephen Miller isn't consuming scary stories, he's kept busy by his five German shepherds just north of Chicago, Illinois. He maintains his childhood fascination with the worlds of science-fiction and horror.

Author's Note: *On Cape Verde* comes from my childhood memories of Hurricane Georges, and the creepy experiences I had exploring the storm-ravaged Florida Keys. It was influenced by the fate of alleged serial killer Charlie Brandt, who lived on the same island at the time.

Beta Test was inspired by the likelihood that we could ever upload our minds into a computer simulation is a contentious issue, and one that is both fascinating and boundlessly horrifying in its potential. After all, there are merciful limits to what we can be forced to endure as flesh and blood beings..."

Cape Verde by Stephen Miller

Parker was loading his shotgun when someone knocked. He froze. Up until now he had taken his near-absolute solitude on the island for granted. The sensible people had long since fled, and now it was the others or well, *one in particular* that worried him. The knock came again, louder. He stared across the darkened living room from the couch. Could they not see that the door was boarded up?

"Who's there?" he called out, to no reply.

If you're the killer, he thought, *I'm not your type.*

He set the 12-guage down on the table beside the open box of ammunition. He traded it for a snub-nose revolver and slid the gun into his pocket as he stood.

Light came from a muted television. On the screen, a meteorologist gestured at a massive hurricane in the Atlantic. *The death toll in Haiti continues to rise,* captions read. Parker was nearly at the door when the wood creaked outside. He halted, and pictured the killer lurking on his deck. He imagined him being a balding, middle-aged white man with soulless eyes and a dirty cargo shirt. Parker had no way of knowing what the killer looked like, of course. The image sprang to mind when he first heard about the drowned girls, before the hurricane and the subsequent evacuation took over the news. Another footstep creaked around the back of the house, and he turned to face it.

A shaft of late-afternoon light came through a sliding-glass door past the TV. Parker had left a small gap in the storm shutters there so that he could come and go as he prepared for the hurricane. Outside, wind rustled the palm trees and the fronds cast long shadows across his second-story deck. He crept toward the light, resting his right hand on the revolver in his jeans. He was about to call out again when a fist pounded on the glass. He nearly drew his gun on reflex, but heard a familiar voice shouting from outside.

"Hey, Parker!" the woman's voice called, "I know you're in there. You're the only one besides me dumb enough to still be here."

It was Irene. Parker relaxed and sighed, then slid the door open and stepped out into the warm October air. Irene was wearing a tank top that revealed her tattoos: two full sleeves devoted to her nautical passions. On one arm, the tendrils of a kraken crept down amongst a kingdom of merfolk. On the other, beautiful sirens beckoned from their rocks at an approaching galleon. A compass rose was inscribed in black ink on her right wrist. She smiled and ran her hand through her choppy hair.

"Reen, what the hell are you doing here," Parker demanded.

"Well hello to you, too," she raised an eyebrow.

"Sorry. I thought you were buttoned up at the boathouse."

"About that—haven't you been watching the news?"

"I've been busy."

Parker thought of his checklist. He'd secured every door and window with steel shutters. The lawn tools and kayaks were tied up under the house. He had enough food and water stockpiled for two weeks, boxes of batteries for the flashlights, lanterns and radio, more than enough Jack Daniels to stay drunk for the entire experience if need be, and plenty of ammo for—

"Did you hear me, Parker? They've upgraded the storm to category four. It's not slowing down…"

"You're leaving?"

"I can't risk it. Not with my dog. I'm taking the skiff mainland while there's still time." Parker knew what was coming next. "You should come too. Jon says you can stay at his place while it blows over."

The thought of spending the next few days on her boyfriend's sofa was not exactly appealing. Regardless, Parker knew he wasn't going anywhere and so did she. The wounded look in her eyes was out of genuine concern for him, he knew.

She winced. He was certain she'd spotted the shotgun and sprawled shells on the table inside.

"Nice arsenal by the way," she said.

"It's not safe out there. Speaking of which, why are you walking around alone? You could have just called me."

Her accusing stare turned softer. "Look, Parker... I'm worried about you. I know this isn't an easy time for you, but Charles Rowe is dead."

The name brought the image of the soulless-eyed killer back—as a memory this time—from a newspaper in his childhood. When his father saw the picture, he threw the entire paper into the fireplace and then sat alone with his gin, weeping.

"This isn't about him. The tourists they found last week, the girl—"

"People drown all the time, Parker. You know that."

"Not with their hands tied. Not like that."

"And some people get into bad shit. I've lived here my whole life and I can handle myself. Right now, the real threat is the storm and I'm getting out of here while I still can."

When it was clear there was no convincing him otherwise, Irene turned to leave.

"I can at least walk you back to the boathouse" Parker said as he followed her around the deck and down the stairs. Hannibal, her German shepherd, was waiting for her below. She undid his leash from the bottom stair. He wagged his tail at the sight of Parker.

"Thanks, but I already have a bodyguard" she said. "Take care of yourself, okay?"

441

With that, Irene and Hannibal left. Parker watched her walk down the empty street between the ocean and the row of silent, armored houses. When she was finally out of view he went back inside, sealed the last two storm shutters behind him and settled in for the ride with a glass of whiskey. He watched the silently spinning storm on the television as he sipped his drink. Eventually his eyes became heavy and he found himself nodding off.

He dreamt of familiar memories. His father drove him through the aftermath of Hurricane Lisandra. Fallen palm trees littered the pavement. His dad had to swerve the car to avoid them. They were going too fast. The roads were empty. They'd gone so fast they made it to the island before the government closed the bridges behind them. Parker was only ten, but he knew from his dad's intense silence that he was afraid. Lisandra was much more powerful than predicted. His mom and his little sister, Nicole, had stayed behind while his dad picked Parker up from his grandparents on the mainland. It was dusk by the time they arrived at the house. There was just enough light to see the front door hanging open. It was dark inside.

"Wait here" his dad told him as he parked the car, and then ran inside. Parker sat in his seat, staring at the plants strewn across the yard. He hoped their banana tree in the backyard was okay. Suddenly his father screamed. Parker's blood turned ice cold. His dad had never so much as shouted before, but that scream came from depths of anguish Parker could not yet understand. Soon his dad was running back to the car. Tears stained his reddened face. He wouldn't say what he saw, he just peeled the car out of the yard and drove until he found men in camouflage uniforms and brought them back to the house.

Parker never saw his mother or Nicole again. The guardsmen found a third body in the house and soon everybody knew his name: Charles Ashton Rowe. Parker would see his face on TV and newspaper headlines for years to come. *Serial Drowner is Local Captain* one headline read.

"So, it wasn't a satanic cult after all," a news anchor had said, *"but many questions remain. Among them, why did Charles Rowe drown himself in a bathtub with his final two victims?"*

Parker watched the paper his father tossed into the fireplace. Charles Rowe's face seemed to crinkle into a smile as the page burnt and the dream ended.

* * * * *

Parker opened his eyes. Everything was black. Outside, the wind blustered and whistled. Sheets of rain beat against the side of the house. The power was out. He felt around and remembered he was lying on the couch. He stood clumsily and felt his way through the darkness to the kitchen counter. He found a lantern and switched it on, stinging his eyes with cold white light.

Something splashed in the bathroom. Parker turned in surprise. The bathroom door was closed. Its white paint seemed to glow softly in the pale light. Another splash. He'd filled the tub before shutting off water to the house. He pictured vibrations from the wind rattling his shampoo bottles into the water. But the splashing continued. He thought of the times his father would catch some impressive fish and put it in the laundry tub for him and his sister to see. They'd come home from school to find some exotic creature splashing figure eights in the tub. His memories were interrupted by the practical concern of the house having sprung a leak. Parker grabbed a flashlight and opened the door.

The flashlight fell out of his hands and illuminated the body. She knelt against the bathtub, head underwater. Her tattooed arms were bound across her back with rope.

443

Panic flooded through Parker's veins. He dove to pull her out of the water.

"Reen! Oh my god!"

He lifted Irene's ice-cold body out of the water. No sooner than he thought of how to resuscitate her, she was sitting up on her own. He felt her dead weight vanish and pulled back in disbelief. She rose to her feet powerfully, the bindings slipping effortlessly from her wrists. Her damp hair grew impossibly fast to beneath her shoulders. Her tattoos ran like wet ink, staining her skin black. She turned to face him as he crawled backwards into the beam of the flashlight. Her empty eyes dripped black streaks down her face. Parker tried to scream but was breathless. She opened her mouth as if to scream back, water gurgling forth onto her shirt. Her features snarled into an expression of rage and her scream came in the form of an ear-piercing mechanical siren. The sound of a civil hurricane horn echoed through the house, across the entire island.

* * * * *

Parker woke with a gasp, sweat beading across his face. Fierce winds battered the house, whistling like a hundred crying teapots as they pried every inch of its defenses. Parker lay frozen on the couch as he slowly accepted he'd been dreaming. When it felt safe to move he sat up, feeling across the table for his phone. He felt a need to check on Irene. Squinting at the cell phone's lack of signal, he realized he'd slept through the beginning of the storm.

Grabbing a flashlight, he hesitantly confirmed the bathroom was empty. Even after switching on all the lanterns the house still felt eerily dark. Parker couldn't shake the image of Irene's wraith lurking in the shadows beyond the strange lamplight. He grabbed a bottle of water and switched on the radio. A 90's alternative station on the mainland was still coming through, and he cranked the volume to drown out the banshee-wail of wind and rain outside.

The music did little to mask the growing intensity of the storm. A sudden rush of wind brought with it the sound of snapping tree trunks. Everywhere, metal groaned and buckled. Something massive cracked and came crashing down nearby. The chaos repeated further away, like the footsteps of some immense creature stomping across the island. The shutters rattled and banged together as though a crowd of people were trying desperately to break in through every door and window. But the defenses held, and the worst of it eventually passed.

Parker wondered if this is what it was like for his mom and Nicole, trapped in the path of Lisandra. He wondered, as he often did, how it would have been different if he and his dad had been there with them. He had once punched a boy that had been harassing Nicole at her bus stop. He would have punched Charles Rowe, too.

If only he had been there.

Every so often, his thoughts were interrupted by the sound of debris smashing into the house. He wondered about the other women on the island who had gone missing, or turned up worse. One had vanished while jogging in the early morning hours, another while she was home alone doing laundry. Parker couldn't fully explain the connection in his conversation with Irene, but there was something to it, some familiar cowardice. He wondered if they had family who would feel as *messed up* as he did, twenty years down the road. Would *their* fathers drink themselves into an early grave, too?

* * * * *

Eventually the wind began to subside. The banshee-wail was replaced with a distant, muffled roar. Parker was already feeling drowsy again as the radio suffered interference. Static and strange voices bled into the channel, becoming gradually worse until nothing was left of the song but a distorted screech. He winced and mashed the power button. Outside, the barrage of what must have been coconuts and chunks of gravel had quieted down to a constant *tic-tic* of sand against the storm shutters. Further off, he could still hear what must have been the snapping of branches that in any other situation he'd have taken for gunshots.

Then came the footsteps. Scraping across the gravel and stomping up the creaking stairs. Parker jumped to his feet. Someone pounded on the door.

"Help me! Please help me," the child's voice cried out.

N—Nicole Parker thought.

"Please, he's going to hurt me!"

No, not Nicole. But another little girl...

The pounding continued. "He hurt my mommy he tried to grab me," she sobbed.

"You'll be okay," he shouted without a second thought. "Stay right where you are!"

Parker ran to his shotgun and slung it over his shoulder. Then he pried off the support to the shutters outside his side door and kicked them out. He slipped outside into the calm night air.

"You're safe here," Parker called out. "Come inside and you'll be okay."

There was only silence from around the corner. Parker took up his shotgun and switched on the light mounted to its barrel. The deck lit up before him, strewn with sand and tattered palm fronds. He made his way cautiously to the corner and then spun around it. The front doorway was empty. The stairway descended to an inky blackness.

"Come back! I can protect you!"

A hush had fallen over the island, save for the gentle rustling of the palm trees. As the eyewall passed, the world had become calm.

Footsteps scuffed across the pavement in the street. Parker rushed down the stairs in pursuit.

"Wait! Don't run!"

He nearly tripped on his own collapsed fence, making it to the street. It was there he caught his first glimpse of the storm's wrath. Wreckage blanketed the asphalt. The remains of his neighbor's deck were scattered across the sandy pavement, draped in the wires of fallen power lines and uprooted trees. Parker spun around, his weapon light glinted off pieces of metal roof tiles, strewn along with countless other debris bound up in piles of seaweed. Further down, the road was blocked by a center-console boat, overturned onto its smashed canopy.

He saw no trace of the girl.

He knew it was only a matter of time before the eye passed over and the winds returned. He didn't want to think about what it would be like if either of them were caught outside when that happened.

A scream rang out down the street. Parker turned to see light flickering from an open door further down. An orange glow danced inside, giving the second story entrance the appearance of a jack o' lantern's eye floating in the dark. Parker knew the owners of that house left it empty most of the year, occasionally renting to vacationers. He tried to recall if he'd seen a family there with a young girl.

Where else could she have come from?

He crossed the field of waterlogged waste to the house and ran up the stairs. He shouldered the shotgun before stepping inside.

The glow came from red votive candles scattered throughout the house. Water dripped from leaks in the two-story ceiling and puddled in the great room below. The candles were everywhere. Every table, every shelf, nook,

447

and cranny glowed. To Parker it looked like some sort of church ceremony, though the harsh beam from his gun light ruined the effect. He resisted the urge to call out, instead slowly clearing the house.

He found the woman's body in the bathroom. She was bound and kneeling face first in the bathtub. A wave of derealization washed over him. In that instant he expected to wake up from another dream.

You're not real, he thought.

He reached out and rolled the woman's icy body over in the water. Her lifeless eyes stared out between long blonde bangs. He recognized her now, having seen her jog past his house before work. He didn't know she had a daughter. He didn't even know her name.

"Don't worry about her," a man's voice said. In an instant Parker was back on his feet, both hands on the gun. He pointed the beam back out the door. Something had blown out most of the votives.

"You killed her, you son of a bitch!" Parker shouted.

"She'll never die," the voice said from the living room. "She has a purpose now."

Parker aimed towards the voice but there was nothing there except smoking candles.

"And she'll never leave the storm," the voice said from above him, "none of them will." The stairs off the living room creaked. Footsteps pounded on the second-floor balcony.

"You're insane," Parker shouted, and charged up the stairs.

"They're part of the tempest now," the man said. "That's the way *she* needs it to be."

A door slammed just as Parker reached the top of the stairs. He trained his gun on the door at the end of the balcony. He froze for a moment, knowing he shouldn't pursue. The killer could be waiting on the other side with a knife or a gun of his own. Candle light from below flickered between the balusters to his left. The rooms to his right were open and dark. He thought of the little girl—of Nicole—and where she could be hiding. *I won't let you hurt her,* he told himself decisively, and attacked.

The man lunged out of a side room and grabbed the shotgun. Parker pulled back and the gun fired, spraying buckshot into the wall with a deafening blast. In an instant the gun was flung over the rails and everything was dark again. The man grabbed Parker by the throat.

Parker gasped. Suddenly he experienced a vision. Dark clouds spun violently in the sea around the island. The eyewall roared with winds like volcanic rage. There were howls in the wind like screams. He realized the wind itself was nothing but screams. Countless cries of anguish and fury bled together in a singular, terrified wail. Parker could see shapes in the vortex of clouds that looked like people. There were thousands of them. Their wispy faces contorted in agony as they roiled in and out of existence.

Parker was pulled back into his body as the man tightened his grip, lifting him from his feet.

"That's why she lets us stay," the man declared, "to feed her souls."

He flung Parker into the end of the hall, knocking the wind out of him. Parker choked. His ears rang.

"You saw through her eye," the man said as he closed the distance, "the drowned damned carry her across the sea."

Parker looked up at the man in the faint light and recognized his face from a dozen photographs.

"You..." he coughed.

The silhouette of Charles Rowe smiled at him. "When she first whispered to me, I was nothing but a glorified fisherman. She's let us become so much more. You'll see—"

Parker pulled the revolver from his pocket and fired. The muzzle flash was blinding. He shot again and again. The thunder-crack of the .357 blasted his eardrums. He didn't notice the tremendous recoil as he unloaded the entire cylinder. The gun clicked, empty.

Charles Rowe slumped to his knees. "I'll always be with her," he said in a raspy whisper, and grasped Parker's arm, "She *chose* me."

Parker was once again taken by a vision. A fishing boat rode the gentle swell of the vast sunlit ocean. Four hooded captives lay on the rear casting deck, struggling with their restraints. Charles Rowe rose from below deck and prostrated himself before them. They tried to scream through their gags as he began to pray aloud. He whispered a prayer of offering to his goddess of the storm, and promised to join her soon.

He stood, and shoved the weighted bait cooler off the back of the deck. A length of chain pulled each victim in turn, writhing into the sea.

Parker thrashed as if it were him drowning, and pulled his arm free of Charles Rowe's dying grasp. Parker bashed him in the skull with the steel frame of the revolver and he fell to his side. To Parker's eyes, still half-blind, it looked as through his silhouette simply vanished into the shadowed floor.

Parker dropped the gun and stood up, coughing. Gunpowder stung his bruised windpipe and filled his nostrils with an acrid smell. He rubbed his eyes and looked again for Rowe.

There was nothing but empty carpet before him.

He stumbled his way downstairs, struggling to breathe. His own footsteps were muffled to his sore eardrums. He'd become lightheaded. He needed fresh air. By the time he reached the front door, he heard the dull roar of wind in the distance. He leaned on the balustrade and caught his breath.

Out in the street, a little girl darted out from behind an overturned boat. She ran away, vanishing into the darkness. Parker started to call out to her and then spotted the man lurking there. He looked like something from a different age. Garlands of seaweed draped the shoulders of his brocade coat, and the brim of his tricorn hat concealed his face. Parker stared in disbelief as the shadow of another man stepped out of the rocky shore across the street. Muck dripped from Charles Rowe's body as he sloshed out of the water. All along the coast, others were rising from the ocean.

That's why she lets us stay.

Parker turned away and saw an antique diving suit staring up at him from the base of the stairs. Its brass helmet was full of dark water. It lifted one of its massive boots onto the first step.

Parker dashed inside, slamming and bolting the door. He backed away and heard another thudding step. He picked his shotgun off the ground and racked the action. The spent shotshell rattled on the floor. He aimed the gun at the door. The derealization returned.

It's not real, he told himself, still waiting for the drowned diver to bring his boot crashing down again.

Suddenly, a soothing voice whispered in his ear. He didn't recognize the language she spoke, but the effect was immediately calming. He lowered his weapon as the realization washed over his body like the caress of a gentle breeze. He closed his eyes and once again he saw the view from the center of the eye. The tormented souls still spun around him, but he could no longer hear them. He could only hear the sweet, whispering chords. He had never heard a voice so beautiful. The voice of a siren. The voice of a *goddess*.

I'm listening he thought.

Beta Test by Stephen Miller

Roxy's Lounge. It was the sort of dimly-lit, mid-century styled bar that was too classy for me by half. In the real world, it's the kind of place I'd have gone to get shit-faced on overpriced cocktails at a Game Developer's Conference after-party. But that was in the old days, back when there was still a studio to foot the bill. Thankfully for me—here inside the simulation—money was of no concern.

But it wasn't just the promise of inebriation that led me through Roxy's neon entrance that night. It was a name. A name I'd stared at in the user list, incredulously, before walking my ass here from across town.

It can't be him, I thought. *When the hell did they jack him in?*

"Oh Jesus Christ…" the words escaped beneath my breath. The cringe that followed could not be stifled. All I could do was avert my gaze to the ebony hardwood floor and let the involuntary expression run its course. When I unbuttoned my face, there he was, sitting at the bar.

Madcow.

I waved away my holographic display. The translucent overlay of user names, locations, and notes shrunk and vanished into my peripheral vision. What remained was my old lead programmer, wearing a cow print suit and fedora. The *infamous* cow print suit and fedora, looking as ugly as it was expensive. He was hitting on the bartender. I felt aftershocks of cringe return.

"You son of a bitch," I said as I approached close enough to be heard over the murmur of other patrons.

He spun around in the barstool and sized me up behind a pair of ruby-tinted aviator glasses. He made an exaggerated frown. "Tell me you don't look that old in real life" he said.

"Life comes at you fast. You on the other hand," I gestured at his entire outfit, "are apparently thirteen years old again."

He scoffed, and reached out to grab my hand. The handshake quickly became a pat on the back, and then a full-blown hug. I hadn't seen Lukas, aka Madcow, in nearly ten years. Already memories were flooding back of never-ending crunch nights at Dark Room Entertainment, our game studio. Memories of passing out at our desks, on couches, or occasionally the floor. It all seemed like a lifetime ago, now.

I took a seat next to him, and signaled the bartender.

"What's the fun of living in a simulation," he said, "if you don't peacock it up a bit? Have you even played with the closet options yet?"

"You look like a confused pimp. Anyway, what's with this about *living* in a simulation? Buddy, I just work here. And when you got me this job, you didn't say I'd have to work with *you*."

"You think I'd pass on this sort of opportunity just because I—" he stopped. But I could finish the thought for him. *Because I'm still a well-paid programmer with a career.*

The pause turned awkward, until the bartender broke the silence.

"Is this guy giving you a hard time?" she asked. I met her gaze, and must've held it a moment too long. She cocked an eyebrow.

"Y-yea" I finally said, "he's an asshole."

She chuckled, and shot Lukas a playful grin.

"Please try not to scare away my customers, Mr. Madcow," she said.

"A thousand pardons, Ms. Roxy," Lukas said, and leaned into the bar. "Say, could I convince you to whip up my usual and… a gin and tonic for my *colleague* here?"

Good memory.

454

"Sure thing. What sort of work do the two of you do together?" she asked.

"We're Quality Assurance," Lukas winked at me. "We're probably the best paid beta testers in the world."

"*This* world, at least," I said, but that only earned me a slightly confused look from Roxy as she got to work mixing our drinks.

"Isn't she something?" Lukas said once she'd stepped out of earshot. "I've been giving her my own personal Turing test all evening."

"I'll bet you have," I shook my head. "You know there's an easier way to tell if she's real."

I waved my holographic display back on and pointed to the purple diamond that appeared over all the simulated character's heads in the overlay. A new translucent box rolled out beside Roxy with her name and background information. I waved it away.

"There's no fun in that" Lukas said, "and I'm being serious. This sort of thing, this level of AI… This is the type of stuff I used to dream of working on, back when I was at Dark Room. She really is perfect—everything here is, in case you haven't noticed. And do you know what the *worst* part is?"

"What's that?" I mumbled, staring as Roxy twirled ice cubes around a highball glass.

"The worst part is they didn't need me to code it. I always thought it would be you and I that built a place like this," he sighed. "At least we're still part of it, I suppose"

Roxy presented our drinks, garnished with lemon and sprigs of rosemary. Lukas took his with an appreciative nod, and sipped.

"Even the goddamn alcohol is perfect," he said. "Anyway… how's the testing coming along on your end?"

My reply was cut short by a crash of shattering glass—then screaming. It was guttural, so intense and unexpected that my concentration was immediately broken.

I felt a surge of panic, like ice water down my spine. I spun around and saw the lounge table flipped on its side, the man convulsing on the floor. A woman rushed to his side but he grabbed her arms, hurling her backwards.

"Stay the fuck away from me!" he yelled as she staggered back.

I set my drink down too hard, sloshing gin onto the bar. With my hand free I flicked my overlay back on, confirming that the people were also human testers. Lukas was already on his feet, rushing over to help. I followed after.

"I can't breathe!" The man screamed. "I can't fucking breathe! Wake me up! None of this is real! It's freezing! I'm drowning in the fucking pod! Let me out!"

"What happened?" Lukas asked the woman. She looked frightened.

"He was fine a minute ago," she sniffled. "Suddenly he thinks he's dying in real life. That I'm not actually real, because I'm not feeling it too, I guess."

"Sounds like A.S.S." Lukas said, staring down at the man.

"Ass? "I blurted out, stupidly.

"No, idiot. Did you even read the forms they had us sign? *Acute Solipsism Syndrome*, it's a potential risk of total immersion."

Lukas knelt down beside the man, who was now shivering with his head propped uncomfortably against the leg of a lounge chair.

"Hey buddy," Lukas said, "You're going to be all right. You're not drowning. You're breathing just fine in real life. They told us to watch out for these symptoms, remember? It's nothing serious. You need to get up so you can report it."

"The techs would be helping him if there was really a problem," I said to the other tester. It came out more like a question than a statement. She gulped, and nodded. I saw a familiar face over her shoulder.

Mara?

Mara was sitting back at the bar. Her long dark hair framed a strange expression, something like pity, as she watched the commotion. I thought for sure she'd step in to help—the simulation was her project, after all—but instead she took what appeared to be a martini from Roxy and drank it in a single gulp. After that she said something to Roxy I couldn't hear, stood up, and left.

"You're really here," Lukas reassured our colleague, still playing the role of paramedic. "Try remembering how you got here."

I looked back at Mara's empty seat. Roxy was wiping down the counter. I felt a pit of unease settling in my stomach.

Remember how you got here, I thought.

*****

The elevator ride was so long that I nodded off. I woke up startled, like I'd been falling, and shrank with embarrassment. If the other people packed into the freight car had noticed, they spared me any acknowledgment. The only one looking at me was my own bloodshot reflection in the elevator's chromed paneling. Jesus, I looked like shit.

Fucking jetlag.

But how long had we been descending? I had barely finished unpacking when the Foundation staff knocked on my door. They ushered me downstairs with the other prospective testers, into the basement of the mountain lodge. From there we boarded the elevator. It was minutes ago, but it already felt like yesterday.

I giggled stupidly, remembering the excruciatingly-long load times in most of Dark Room's games. It became something of an inside joke, to trap our players inside elevators as a new level was loading. It was a necessary evil, to maintain immersion. Some of our more masochistic fans even found it endearing.

"So, is this where you've hidden the loading screen?" I said to break to the ice. No response. Either these weren't gamers, or they too were jetlagged past the point of zombification.

Or maybe I'm just not funny.

"No, that is much further down," a woman finally said from beside the controls. She faced me and smiled knowingly. Well, at least *she* looked to be well rested. Flowing black hair draped down her lab coat to the edges of her name tag.

Dr. Mara Droste.

"It's getting really cold," a man said. I realized I could see my breath, and wrapped my arms together.

"It has to be cold for the computers to function," Mara said. "That's why all the servers are kept so far underground. It saves the Foundation a fortune in maintenance and cooling costs."

The elevator chimed. When the doors opened, whatever was left of my grogginess vanished in a wave of awe.

Lukas, what the hell have you gotten me into?

We stepped out into what felt at first like an infinite black void punctuated with sharp points of white light. As my eyes adjusted, I could make out wires suspending the lamps from catwalks further above us. As bright and numerous as the lights were, they could barely scrape the volume of the massive underground cavern. Only the faintest impression of light reached the walls, just enough that I could discern the whorl of marbled stone in the distance. Up above the crisscross of man-made catwalks, the vaulted ceiling peaked in utter darkness.

"Welcome to the bunker," Mara said. She beckoned us down a path of lamp posts, further into the cavern.

It looked as though someone had teleported the guts of some research facility deep into the mountain. Cold steel and concrete were fused to the natural stone with practicality that couldn't conceal the strange beauty of the caves. We passed through an imposing bulkhead door and across a bridge that spanned a lake of water gleaming like black glass.

"The Foundation really built this place?" said a woman, awestruck. "It must have cost a fortune!"

"Not exactly," Mara said without breaking stride. "Actually, people have been building this place for thousands of years. Ancient people explored these grottoes and discovered their salt deposits. They mined it for centuries, all throughout the dark ages, until it was sealed."

"Why was it sealed?" I asked.

"The records are unclear about that. What we do know is that the Soviet government excavated it to use as a fallout shelter, in the event of nuclear war. We have them to thank for most of the infrastructure, including the geothermal extractors. After the cold war it was sealed again, until we purchased it. So, to finish answering the first question—yes, it did cost a fortune."

I followed along with the tour, wondering just who was investing so much capital into the Foundation for the sake of virtual reality technology. Sure, we'd have loved to get our hands on it at Dark Room. But even at the height of our success, we were in no position to buy a fucking underground Russian base. Something didn't add up.

Still, the pay was on a scale barely fathomable to someone who teaches game design to college students. And there was something else, almost nostalgic. It felt like whatever this was, it was a chance to get in on the ground floor of the next new thing. If this proved to be groundbreaking, maybe I could make a name for myself in the Industry again.

We came at last to a second massive vault, clearly reshaped by some heavy machinery into a smooth, perfectly rectangular warehouse. Fluorescent lights shone through grated catwalks that ran above dozens of stainless-steel cylinders, each of them barely larger than a person. The soft thrum of machinery reverberated throughout the room. Technicians scurried between computer terminals along the outer walls.

"Come," Mara beckoned our group up the stairs onto the catwalks. "The first group has already been at it for a week. Have a look. Others will be joining you inside the simulation."

From atop the walkway we could see down into the cylinders. Many were empty, the rest held people floating upright in some kind of liquid. They wore breathing masks, not unlike scuba regulators, and appeared to be unconscious.

"The pods are total sensory deprivation," Mara continued, "closer to suspended animation, in fact. In that state, your brain can interpret sensory stimuli from the simulation as a genuine substitute for, well, what you're experiencing now."

Mara looked down at the occupied tanks, "they are in a whole other world, now. The town we've constructed for you to test is just the beginning. There really is no limit to the worlds we can build..."

When Mara looked up, she seemed to read the expressions on our faces. "Everything is perfectly safe," she added quickly. "We have a full medical team on site, 24/7. I've been immersed several times myself, and will be joining you all inside. Does anyone have any concerns?"

"We're probably *already* inside," a woman mused. Everyone just slowly turned to her, and she explained. "Think of what we're on the threshold of here. If we can ever truly run simulations of reality, and there's only one true reality, then the odds are we're in some form of simulated reality right now."

Someone objected, and the group seemed to explode immediately into a deep philosophical debate on the topic. The term *Quantum Hall Effect* was spat back and forth quite a bit. I more or less capped out at high school physics, and tuned the discussion out. I just stared at the half-naked people below, floating in some kind of lucid dream.

Fuck it, I thought. *What have I got to lose?*

*****

There was no Hell, until we built it.

It's what Mara had said to Roxy, during our colleague's panic attack. I'd asked Roxy out of curiosity, after the situation had calmed down.

"Do you know what she meant by that?" I inquired.

"No idea," Roxy said, and then asked if I wanted another drink.

"I really should get back to work," I declined.

"All right then, good luck with the *beta test*," she winked at me.

I left Roxy's alone, to continue my nighttime exploration. There were no rules to this job, per se. We just had to spend our time in this place however we saw fit, and report any flaws in the experience.

I decided that to give myself some structure, I would pace out the boundaries of this town. It was modeled as a quaint little resort settlement in the mountains. The street outside Roxy's followed a bend around the edge of town. Storefronts faced a low cobblestone wall on the other side of the road. Beyond that, the hill sloped down into a procedurally-generated forest of pine trees that stretched out to a foggy horizon. It was clearly *based on* the real terrain above the bunker, but the town itself was a work of fiction.

I strolled from street light to street light, dragging my fingers along the rough texture of the stone wall. A mild breeze rustled the silhouettes of trees and brushed gently

461

over me. I closed my eyes and breathed the fresh, evergreen scent in deeply. Every minutiae of sensation was as real as anything I've ever experienced.

I daydreamed about the generation of games that would surely spawn from this technology. Even Dark Room's most immersive VR titles would seem primitive and obsolete going forward.

Suddenly, sharply, the breeze became uncomfortably cold. Some primal sense told me to snap out of the daydream. Something was wrong.

Mara's cryptic words came back to me.

I realized I'd been walking in darkness. The streetlights were out. I turned around, confused, to see I'd passed half a dozen blown out lights without noticing it. The storefronts too, were vacant and dark. I wondered if I'd stumbled into some unfinished area. The sound of the wind had changed, too.

No, not the wind—the trees.

Behind me, where the streetlights still worked, the trees stirred in the gentle breeze. But in the dark area they stood perfectly still, as if frozen. I was already thinking of how to word this in the bug report when I realized I wasn't alone. Up ahead, leaning against a broken streetlight, was the shadow of a man.

I walked towards him, hoping for some validation that he too was seeing the same thing. But I hesitated halfway between my streetlight and his. Something was wrong with him. He was twitching strangely, as if caught in the throes of some spasm. For a moment I thought of the tester at Roxy's, convulsing in pain. But no, this was different. This man was sobbing.

"The cold got in," he wept in a raspy voice, seemingly to himself.

I was about to ask if he needed help when the clouds parted, bathing us both in moonlight. My blood ran cold. The old man was withered and emaciated, little more than a skeleton. He wore nothing but the same neoprene shorts and nylon harness we were all given in real life, before entering the pods. The vertebrae of his spine jutted sickeningly against the pale, glistening flesh of his back.

In disbelief, I waved for my holographic overlay. Nothing happened. I needed to know if this was *real*—If *he* was real. I waved again, and then again. It wasn't working.

Impossible, I thought, and kept trying. My frantic gestures must have gotten the old man's attention, because he finally raised his head. Long strands of white, wispy hair parted to reveal the same breathing apparatus we all wore. Where his oxygen tube would be was only a torn, tattered rubber scrap. His bloodshot eyes opened wide with shock. They fixed on me with the same surprise and horror that I must have been reflecting back at him. I could hear his tortured breathing intensify.

"You shouldn't be here!" he finally snarled. He lunged towards me. Stupefied, I was too late to react. His wet, freezing hands found my neck in a choking grasp.

"You need to wake up!" he growled, and tightened his grip. I couldn't breathe. I couldn't scream. Only panic. I tried to pry his hands off my throat but they were too slick with that same goopy liquid from the pods. My hands slipped down his wiry arms, and that's when I noticed it—that stupid fucking tattoo.

Dethsqwurl: a squirrel holding a katana in shitty black ink.

Madcow had gotten me so drunk at the launch party for our first game that he was able to convince me to get that damned thing. It was my own alter ego on my forearm, to match his. And there it was, blurry and faded—but unmistakable—on this skin and bones man. He had *my* tattoo. I stared at his face, even as I struggled to breathe. The recognition washed over me in a wave of cold terror that swept my sanity away.

It was me.

He was me.

The absurdity of my situation gave me a sudden burst of strength—dreamlike vigor—and I hurled the ancient doppelganger off. It staggered, and I gasped for air. Just when I thought it would charge at me again, something flashed in the distance. Suddenly, just for a moment, the sky was brighter than daytime. The abrupt brilliance stunned the creature, and it stared, horrified, at the source beyond the horizon.

"No…" It whimpered at the lingering glow of the explosion. I seized the moment and ran. As I did, a sound like the crack of thunder smashed through everything. More explosions burst across the horizon like lightning. Every illuminating flash revealed the town as something else—shattered ruins, desolate and decayed.

"They never finish it!" The creature screamed. "They'll never finish it!" Its cries became an incoherent wail of rage and agony, and then disappeared entirely in the roaring boom.

When at last I made it back to the well-lit area, the entire cacophony ceased. There was only the gentle sound of the breeze, and a slight tinnitus in my ear. My overlay finally responded. I kept running as I searched Mara's location on the user list.

*****

I found her on the rooftop deck of the tallest building in town. She was sitting on the ledge, smoking a cigarette and sipping wine from a crystal stem. She greeted me without taking her eyes off the panorama of the town laid out before her.

That I was a frantic, gibbering wreck gasping to catch my breath didn't seem to faze her. I tried to explain what had just happened. She only faced me to refill her glass from a bottle resting beside her. Her wind-tousled hair framed that same, pitying expression she wore at the bar.

"What the fuck was that thing?" I demanded.

464

She shrugged dismissively, and turned away again. She seemed to be staring at the shadowy part of town I'd just fled from.

"An anomaly," she said.

Her lack of concern was exasperating. Hadn't she been listening? Didn't she care?

"I want out," I said firmly. "Wake me up, now."

She took a drag off her cigarette, then flicked ashes off the side of the roof.

"I'm afraid that isn't possible," she said.

I took a deep breath, trying to contain my anger.

"Dr. Droste," I said slowly. "*Mara*, I'm sleeping in one of your pods. I know you can revive me."

She seemed to find this amusing. But there was something else cracking in her persona, as if she were trying to cope with something herself. Was she drunk?

"I already did revive you," she finally said, "a long time ago."

"What are you talking about?" I said incredulously. "We're right here. We literally just started."

"This *instance* just started," she said as if she were clarifying the situation. My confused expression must have told her otherwise. "It's all *so* lifelike isn't it?" She continued, gesturing across the entire landscape. "We had you testers to thank for that. It was an iterative process. Every time we re-ran the simulation your experiences helped us tune it just a little bit more. We got a little closer to perfection, every time."

"That doesn't make any sense," I gritted my teeth. Mara was supposed to be the one professional we could all rely on. She was our lifeline. We *trusted* her. Now, she was spouting nonsense. "How can I be in the simulation right now talking to you, if you've already woke me up?"

"Because you're an instance, too," she said, "a copy, of your original mind." She finished her cigarette and tossed

465

it away. "That's why you had to be in those pods as long as you were. *A frozen scan,* we called it."

"Why…" I began to mutter, but I felt a shortness of breath. I was beginning to feel dizzy, dissociated. This couldn't be right.

"It was the entire purpose of the Foundation," she said. "It's one thing to build a perfect virtual reality. Our benefactors wanted us to prove it was possible to upload minds to it. They wanted to live forever, on the inside."

She went on, but I couldn't follow her jargon, something about discovering the *neural correlates of consciousness.* "No—" I cut her off in a snarl. My head was swimming now. "I mean if this is all true, why are you telling me this?"

"It's not like it matters anymore," she shrugged. "Every time the simulation iterates it deletes the previous instances and begins again with fresh copies."

Every time...

My thoughts flashed back to those long nights at Dark Room. Sitting at my desk, pacing the hallways, crashing on the couch in the break room, all the while strung out over the latest build of our game. The polished final product was the result of countless iteration. Meetings at the whiteboard, debugging and redesign, again and again, version after version. That was just to make a videogame. But something as complex as this place? How many versions had it taken to get this far? Dozens? *Hundreds?*

"So, you've murdered us," I said, confronting her gaze, "over and over again…"

"I suppose that's one way of looking at it," Mara said.

I wanted to scream *what other way is there!?* But knew it was futile. There was nothing for me to do here with all my anger and confusion. I decided to leave Mara alone and do the one thing I could, which was to march back to Roxy's and get mind-numbingly drunk as soon as possible.

I was about to head downstairs when I remembered something, and turned back to her.

"Why did you say what you did back at Roxy's?"

"What?" it was her turn to look confused.

"You said there was no Hell until we built it. If this place is so perfect, why did you say that?"

She shook her head, and looked again to the dark, static part of town.

"The anomalies…" she said, "you're not the first to see one. But I… I don't remember them. Not from previous iterations. I *should* be able to remember…" She hung her head down, and closed her eyes. "I wasn't lying back at the bunker, when I told you I'd been immersed before. I'm as much a copy as you are. The only difference is that I scan in regularly. I should remember every previous version, unless… unless I'm not around to scan in anymore."

She took in a deep breath, and shuddered. "And a glitch on that scale doesn't just happen randomly, or overnight. It's a sign the hardware is failing—*has been* failing, for some time. But our servers were custom-built for billionaires that want to live forever. They're kept deep underground in perfect conditions. They could run for a thousand years, maybe longer."

"If nobody were left to turn them off…" I said, connecting the dots. She turned to me with fresh tears streaking her face.

I thought of the bunker, the frigid void of empty caverns deep beneath the mountains. I thought of terminals flashing, attended only by withered skeletons. Geothermal extractors whirred behind ancient and ominous Soviet bulkheads, sealed now and forever against some outside apocalypse. And somewhere deeper still, within some still-running computer, my own long-dead ghost was still trying in vain to wake me up from a simulation stuck in an infinite loop.

Out past Mara's gaze, the dark patch of town seemed to grow larger, the ink-black tendrils of its desolation spreading from one streetlight to the next. The wind became chill, and with it came a distant sound—faint, but familiar—like the wails of something lost and afraid.

I waved open my holographic display and began a bug report: A.S.S.

Foreword by Author Vivere V. Somnia

Biography: Vivere has been writing short stories and poems since high school. Having taken part in the Wicked Writing horror class, Vivere is more motivated to improve the writing craft and publish more works. The name Vivere Vitae Somnia means "to live life dreams."

Author's Note: My story is one that came to me in a dream in flashes. At the time I first wrote the rough draft, I was having lucid dreams and out of body experiences. Those didn't last very long, though. Some of the things I saw or felt helped in the making of this story and I do hope you enjoy it as much as I enjoyed writing it.

Trading Delusions by Vivere V. Somnia

Dark.

Surrounded by dark figures looking on from afar yet their presence close. Their will wrought with emotions that sting at the flesh. They seemed so large and getting larger. I could run but how far could I get. I could fight but how hard could I hit? Their invisible gaze sets a burn in my chest, a sort of tightness I can't shake.

They were tall and sullen, looking onward with a sort of gaze that could burrow through a person. The face's blurred as not totally within my reality. They have only ever been off in the distance. One pounces.

"Wake up Ruth!"

With a jolt she wakes in her bed, the all too familiar surroundings come into focus.

"Ruth we gotta get on the road!"

Hazily she begins to rise from her bed wiping the sweat from her cheek. The rain droplets fall hard against the window much like how her consciousness landed back in her body. She always had this sense of falling when she woke up from her shadowy dreams. Like taking a plunge off the high board and into the tiny pool that was her body. She looks around, then rises from her bed to feel the hard floor beneath her feet. This was real, she was back.

* * * * *

For the past few months Ruth had been having these surreal dreams like being freed from a mold. Free from constraints of her body, she could walk the earth on the other side. She never knew what it was that made these particular dreams happen and why they were so different from her normal dreams of flying or sailing in a vast ocean. In these dreams the world seemed different.

There were never other people in these sorts of visions and there was never any feeling. Like walking through a haze, everything felt like it had its own fog over it...at times even its own presence. Shadows would appear in the distance, seemingly outside her field of vision, always appearing as dark blurs, but lately they've been getting closer. The closer they get, the more they focus into view.

"Ruth if we get there late, it's on you!" Her father yells from downstairs.

"We gotta go see your Mother before visiting hours are over!"

He didn't have to tell her twice. It was just over a year ago when her Mother began to decline in health. She had always passed it off as a side effect of insomnia when concerned family and friends asked what was wrong.

Slowly, something has been draining her of all her health. Doctors couldn't figure out what it was. She was some medical marvel! Eventually, it caught up with her and she collapsed one day at home. As far as they live from the nearest hospital, the family--or what's left of them--must take a mini road trip to see her. Everything local wasn't properly equipped to deal with her, and her parents wanted her to be closer to them, so they could travel to see her as well.

* * * * *

It was shortly after her mother's hospitalization when Ruth started having her dreams. Walking through this plane of existence unseen by the waking world. It was always set in the real world; as if she were awake, but the feelings and views were skewed. It was like everything was inside a microwave and she was trying to look through the dark glass. It was a dimension where all the inhabitants were dark shadows that never got close enough to touch...and maybe it was better that way. They skulk from afar like a tiger pacing the glass at a zoo.

* * * * *

Ruth's father was an emotional wreck for about a month after his wife went in to the hospital. He tried to put on a smile and pretend that everything was okay, but inside he was obviously worried and distraught with guilt over a phenomenon that out of his control.

Ruth headed down the stairs glancing across the tons of family photos that graced the walls. A trip through the memories before the bad times, before the breakdown. Rounding the corner, she finds her father packing a few snacks into a bag as he talks over his shoulder.

"Your mother hopefully is having one of her good days today. You can sit with her while I ask the doctor how she's doing."

Every time he asks the doctor how she's doing and every time he comes back with a sullen look on his face. Ruth tries to ask him what's wrong, but he just smiles and waves her off. She knows he's just preparing himself to see *her* in that state. In that bed.

Ruth's mother is at what looks like some ancient asylum. Covered by the glossy words '*Sibyl's Haven Hospital*'. It was once a wicked insane asylum that was supposed to be torn down, but some *interested* party bought and renovated the guts. Father had told of how some rich guy with a love for the old and creepy "collected" things like this. He was a well-off surgeon that was popular in his field. He had said "…it was too good an opportunity to pass up". This drove home the inner fear Ruth had of doctor's and the constant unease she felt around them.

* * * * *

473

It would be quite a drive through the mountains to the asylum where mother was hospitalized; to the tall brick walls that encased the stainless steel and marble, smells of latex and ink upon paper. The clacking of heels down the hall always sickened Ruth, the workers there all acted like drones; uncaring and unscathed by the problems that plagued the lost souls around them. So, few of the patients get visitors and the window to see mother is a small one. They had to be there early just to get all the time they could. It saddens and frustrates Ruth that mother must stay in such a place, surrounded by instruments and straps.

* * * * *

Ruth walks up to her father and hugs him from behind. He tenses up for a second, fighting back tears himself. He holds her hand as he lets out a soft sigh.

"Come now baby, let's go see your mother."

Slinging the bag over his shoulder, he turns to his teary-eyed daughter and brushes a tear from her cheek. Giving her a soft smile, he provides one last hug and they head out the door. Hopping in the passenger side and setting the bag on her lap, Ruth stares out the window up at the mountain in the distance. This imposing hill is holding something dear to her captive. She swore to save mother one day.

* * * * *

The trip up to the Asylum was a long one full of sharp twists and turns, cliffs and wildlife. All this was to ensure the safety of the public in case of escapees. It took roughly an hour to get to their goal at the top. Arriving outside the gates, security ushered them through a series of heavy doors and narrow hallways.

The asylum was built like the inside of a disturbed mind; chaotic yet sensible to the ones residing. Ruth walked briskly down the hall trying hard to dodge the glares coming from the windows and the doors on either side of the hall. Keeping her head down, she made for a straight shot to the room where her mother awaited her.

The orderlies who were usually on duty didn't even wave or say "hi," offering only icy glares like drones just as cold. They never uttered a word, only subtle grunts and scoffs as if they were disgusted with her...or maybe they were disgusted with her mother and being tasked with caring for her and simply taking it out on Ruth.

Under glaring white lights, Ruth approached the room and placed a hand on the cold handle of the metal door. It was built solid, everything was. Years of rot couldn't take this place down, it had too much meat on its bones. Every time she made it to her mother's room, she thought for a moment about how these thick shackles around her mother's existence held her from the embrace of her family. Perhaps the restraints were the reason she still wasn't better. Ruth quietly entered in case her mother lay sleeping, but the vision before her stopped her in her tracks and sent a small shiver down her spine.

Her mother lay in her bed, underneath all the cloth and straps, staring directly into Ruth's eyes. As if beaming some sort of emotion at her, it was a look that could freeze and set ablaze. Glaring and so full of malice, twisted like she wanted to cut, break, *hurt*. She was never like this. At first hesitant, Ruth slowly entered the room feeling like prey in her gaze, walking on eggshells until she reached the seat beside the bed. She sat softly looking away from mother, looking anywhere but her eyes. The warm brown eyes that once made her feel happy and safe now made her feel like a soldier in front of a firing squad. She couldn't bear to look at her, so she bit her lip and asked her:

"Hey mom, how are they treating you here?"

Mother looked on in silence, burning a hole of fire in the side of Ruth's head. She let out a soft breath and continued.

"I know it's tough being here, but as soon as you start to get better we'll get you out of here. I promise."

She made this promise thousands of times. Telling her over and over she would be out of there soon and back home to where she belongs. But the day never arrives. She seemed to be getting worse and worse.

* * * * *

Mother awoke one day changed. It was written all over her attitude, her aura. She began acting like a doll; her emotions fake, unstable, *counterfeit*. She had flip-flopped through emotions, erratically becoming violent and then crying and repeatedly claiming she was sorry. Sometimes she had thrown things, other times she had hurt Ruth; bruises had been left on her wrists and scratches riddled her back. Mother went mad and her family suffered for it.

She had been having trouble at night with her insomnia, not being able to sleep for days and days. The doctor's said her exhaustion finally consumed her and that she needed plenty of medically-induced rest. She was essentially forced to sleep nightly via a cocktail of drugs but she was so violent that they had to have her committed where she was restrained constantly. The institution could not afford any more losses to staff.

* * * * *

Ruth always feared that she would arrive one day to find Mother over-medicated and unable to wake again. A small part of her felt that such a situation would be doing her a mercy, a way to dignify the woman she used to be.

Before the madness, Mother was proud and strong. Long thick curls and fair dark skin, she had always been an inspiration to Ruth. Mother nurtured her and helped her grow up to be kind and focused. It hurt Ruth deeply to see her mother fall so far.

* * * * *

Ruth was staring at her feet, her vision blurred from the tears she fought so hard keep back, when her father entered the room. She couldn't bear to look at him, but he looked at her. One glance was all it took for him to read her like a book. Walking over, he knelt beside her and pressed her head into his chest. Patting her hair, he whispered softly to her.

"It'll be okay sweet pea, she's just feeling off today…"

His words were comforting but his heartbeats told another story. The sorrow in his chest rang louder than the comfort from his mouth.

Ruth tried to carry on as if nothing was wrong, but her father stood silent. He stared at his wife--the once beautiful and vivacious and sane Sharice--with a unique glare, one Ruth had never seen upon his face before. It was as if her mother was some unwanted stranger; all Ruth could do was silently choke on her words before she could utter one.

She laid her head on her mother's hand, she was cold to the touch, but more than that she felt *off*…like the hand wasn't hers, as if it was a completely different person. Without warning, Sharice suddenly grabbed Ruth's hair. Letting out a gasp, she fought against her mother's intense grip.

"Mom please, stop! Please let go!"

Then a hand came down, forcing her to release her daughter. Ruth collapsed to the floor holding the side of her head. Looking up to her father in shock, she saw his anger. It was a rage that had been suppressed since Sharice started down the path of decline…but not just that. It was a mix of anger, sadness, and loss. He stared at his daughter on the floor and his face grew sullen. He helped her up, looking as if he had just lost a fight.

"Let's go, Ruth. We need to talk at home."

He led her by the hand to the door. Before they exited the room, Ruth looked back, only to see her mother's twisted smile as they left.

* * * * *

Back in the car, her father was obviously very emotional. She wanted to say *anything* to break the silence but couldn't find words that sounded right-- but, still, she had to *try*.

"Daddy…"

"Not right now honey."

Saddened, with a knot in her chest, she looked out the window, over the rolling hills and trees with veins that ran deep into the earth. As the sun hung low so did her eyes, exhausted from the day's struggles. To collect her thoughts, she closed her eyes and rested her aching head against the window. She intended to rest for mere moments.

Then, with a loud screech, she awoke in the woods.

* * * * *

Standing in the middle of a dense forest she looked around at the unfamiliar terrain. Where was she and how did she get here? The only thing familiar about it was the film that seemed to be over everything. The environment was dreary and lifeless; a forest comprised of dead trees and leaves. Cautiously, Ruth stepped through the underbrush. Taking in her surroundings, she heard not a thing. No birds sang, no subtle crunches and snaps of twigs rang out from the wildlife. The silence was deafening, maddening even. Shadows from the trees and branches didn't lie right; instead of sprawling across the dirt and leaves, they stretched to the darkened sky.

There was no sun or moon, but a dim light came from the grey clouds. This was that weird place her dreams would take her, but it was *different*. She felt heavy, as if the weight of the world was put on her very being. Every move felt sluggish, as if she was moving through a thick sludge. The ground was trying hold her in place. She had to move before they came.

Struggling against the mist, Ruth maneuvered over to a hollow tree where she hid inside. Peering out and around she listened quietly. She sat for what felt like hours, but nothing came. As she was preparing to exit her hiding spot, she saw it. In the distance, like a tree itself, tall and overbearing.

It walks with a strange posture, as if not entirely sure how to walk properly. Its jaw hangs low, its eyes just empty sockets dripping a smoky liquid. It weeps silently yet moans audibly as it stumbles like a lost child through the many branches and brush of the forest floor. It turns its head towards Ruth and she quickly darts back into her hole, holding her hands over her mouth as it draws closer.

Its presence brings an increasing chill to the air as it stumbles closer and closer. Staring at the only entrance and exit to her safe haven, Ruth feels spindly fingers wrap around the tree and into the hole almost brushing her leg. Recoiling at the sight of the malformed fingers, she tries to suppress a yelp. Kneeling, it begins to growl and then, off in the distance, a caw ring's out. The creature promptly stands back up and walks off in the direction of the noise.

Ruth waits for a moment before falling back against the tree, her breathing is heavy and jagged.

What was that thing and how did it get so close suddenly? The dream creatures had only ever been blurs, but now they were solid, and they were creeping closer.

She leans out from her safe place and gathers her surroundings. Skewed shadows make it hard to tell whether things are moving or not. Nevertheless, she can't stand the thought of staying there. She gets up and begins moving. As she wanders through the forest, things began to look familiar. She finally reaches a road. She instantly recognizes it as the same road that her and her father take to see her mother at the hospital. She begins to follow it home, comforted in knowing that if anything comes after her, she at least will be able see it coming.

Ruth walks and walks for hours, the world around her feels increasingly heavier.

What was this choking feeling in her chest, why did it hurt to breathe?

She wanders until she was on the section of road that rounded the mountain, high up overseeing the forest below. Walking along the shoulder of the road, she notices that up ahead the guardrail is destroyed. A black raven sits atop the broke railing, staring down the side of the cliff. Curious yet cautious, Ruth approaches the raven, unsure if it is a regular animal or a spirit.

If it was an animal, why was it the only one she had ever seen in the area and what was with the feeling of dread she got from it? Standing beside it, she reaches out to touch the little bird. It lets out a loud caw and flares its wings up. It takes flight down the side of the mountain where a large mass is sitting. Ruth stares down at the lump wedged between the trees below, and the longer she looks the more she realizes exactly what that lump was.

It was her father's car crumpled up and destroyed.

* * * * *

Ruth blinked and looked around; she was suddenly at the bottom of the mountain. Examining the wreckage, the lump in her chest grew and grew as she circled around.

The trunk was open, and their stuff was everywhere, the roof and hood looked like crumpled balls of paper under the debris of the trees. She circled around to the front of the car and looked at what was left of the windshield. Her father laid still in the passenger side, he looked peaceful despite the bloody head injury.

With a shudder in her breath, she glanced over at the passenger's side-- nothing was there but shattered glass and a trail of blood. She shook with dread as she followed the gory path.

Ruth found her body past the wreck. It was lying at the base of a tree. She apparently flew into it hard since her chest was smashed inward. She knelt beside herself and, as she reached out to touch her cheek, she *remembered.*

Her dad's sobs that she tried desperately to ignore, his attempts to explain what was really happening to her mother, how it couldn't be fixed with simple medicine. The truck that came around the mountain just as her distracted father wasn't paying attention to the side of the road he was on. The loud screech of the tires, and the glass coming to meet her face.

Collapsing to the ground, she holds herself crying over her body. Suddenly, she feels a hand on her shoulder. She jumps slightly as she turns to see what awaits.

The sight before her makes her cry harder than the scene of her death. Her mother greets her with open arms and tears in her eyes. She is lucid, normal, sane. Holding her daughter in a tight embrace, she whispers:

"I know what it's like to lose your body, to lose your life. But at least I can hold you in my arms once again." Through tears she raised her head to meet the comforting gaze of her mother, softly she says, "What happened to you?". Patting her daughters head she explains, "It's what is known as astral projection. Kinda like leaving your body and exploring an existence around us that most people can't normally see save a special few. Some can control this, and other's do it by accident or chance. What people don't realize is how dangerous this can be."

She turns leading Ruth away from her grizzly scene, she follows close beside her.

"Leaving your body like that is like leaving your house with all the doors open. You are just asking for someone to walk in. Now if you are on the front lawn it's not so bad but if you say go down the street, or even the next town over, it's asking for trouble. Leaving your exposed body attracts all manner of demons or evil spirits that once had life and are upset with how they met their end. They linger looking for a way back such as the one I presented."

Ruth stops, and her mother turns to look at her. "What do you mean *presented*?". She continues, "I was doing this often, at first by mistake but then for the fun of it. I went further and further and that attracted some seriously unwanted attention. The bad spirits came, first lingering from afar watching on as I grew confident and daring. Moving further and further from my 'home' as I thought nothing of them since they never gave me reason to worry. That is until they started getting closer and closer and soon lingered around me, everywhere I went. Even when I wasn't sleeping."

"Is this when you weren't sleeping?" Ruth chimed, "Yes, I was afraid. Shadows that skulk around and sit day and night watching and waiting. Like wolves ready to fight for the kill. I held out long as I could, but it wasn't enough. One night I fell asleep wishing to get away from it all and before I realized it, I had projected again, leaving my body unguarded. Now it's taken, and I can't go back to it."

Speechless she sat, trying to take it all in. Ruth would have gone down that same road eventually. The spirits had already noticed her and were taking interest. She held her face in her hands, "What can we do now?" she asked. Kneeling beside her she whispers, "We can steal some bodies of our own."

 Meagan J. Meehan is a published author of novels, short stories, children's books, poems and cartoons. She is a produced playwright and several of her movie screenplays have been green-lit for production. She is also a stop-motion animator, curator, an award-winning abstract artist and the founder of the "Conscious Perceptionalism" art movement. Meagan presently works as a journalist and an art and writing teacher. She holds a Bachelors in English Literature from New York Institute of Technology (NYIT), a Masters in Communication from Marist College, and is currently pursuing a Ph.D. in Curriculum, Instruction and the Science of Learning from the University at Buffalo (SUNY). She is an animal advocate and a fledgling toy and game designer.